About the Authors

Ann McIntosh was born in the tropics, lived in the frozen north for a number of years, and now resides in sunny central Florida with her husband. She's a proud mama to three grown children, loves tea, crafting, animals (except reptiles!), bacon, and the ocean. She believes in the power of romance to heal, inspire, and provide hope in our complex world.

Fiona Lowe is a *RITA*® and R*BY award-winning, author. Whether her contemporary books are set in outback Australia or in the USA, they feature small towns with big hearts and warm and likeable characters that make you fall in love. Sign up for her newsletter at bit.ly/1FmSvHN and all social media links are at fionalowe.com

Margaret Barker has always enjoyed writing, but it wasn't until she'd pursued several careers that she became a full-time writer. Since 1983 she has written over fifty Medical Romance books, some set in exotic locations reflecting her love of travel, others set in the UK – many of them in Yorkshire where she was born. When Margaret is travelling, she prefers to soak up the atmosphere and let creative ideas swirl around inside her head before she returns home to write her next story.

The Surgeon Collection

The Surgeon's Affair

ANN McINTOSH

FIONA LOWE

MARGARET BARKER

MILLS & BOON

First Published in Great Britain 2023
by Mills & Boon, an imprint of HarperCollins*Publishers* Ltd,
1 London Bridge Street, London, SE1 9GF

www.harpercollins.co.uk

HarperCollins*Publishers*
Macken House, 39/40 Mayor Street Upper,
Dublin 1, D01 C9W8, Ireland

The Surgeon's Affair © 2023 Harlequin Enterprises ULC.

The Surgeon's One Night to Forever © 2018 Ann McIntosh
Forbidden to the Playboy Surgeon © 2017 Harlequin Enterprises ULC.
Summer With A French Surgeon © 2012 Margaret Barker

Special thanks and acknowledgement are given to Fiona Lowe for her contribution to the *Paddington Children's Hospital* series

ISBN: 978-0-263-31953-8

THE SURGEON'S ONE NIGHT TO FOREVER

ANN McINTOSH

To Michael.

Your love and belief give me wings.

CHAPTER ONE

A FRESH START. That was how Dr. Cort Smith thought of his position at Hepplewhite General.

A new beginning, far away from Denver, the snide remarks and pitying glances he'd gotten after being dumped by his fiancée just weeks before the wedding.

It was the type of move he now wished had been possible right after his honorable discharge from the army five years previously, but it hadn't been. He'd had a promise to fulfill, and now, having done so, was free to go on with his life.

The New York City job couldn't have come at a better time.

When he'd applied for the trauma surgeon position at Hepplewhite General, the board members who'd interviewed him had explained the hospital was undergoing a period of expansion and regeneration. There had been a sizable, anonymous donation, which, coming at exactly the right time, had allowed them to purchase land where an old warehouse had stood and begin construction to increase their capacity by twenty percent.

As the surrounding neighborhood was also undergoing some regentrification, they'd been able to raise additional funds to revamp the emergency room and surgical floor. Hepplewhite had always been rated a level two trauma center but the plan was for it to be ungraded to a level one, once all the improvements were finished. Cort didn't mind that things were in flux. Serving in the Army Medical Corps had made him pretty much immune to chaos and, since he'd wanted to move from Denver as soon as possible, taking the job had been a no-brainer.

Walking alongside Chief of Surgery Dr. Gregory Hammond, Cort tried to take in everything the older man said, although he knew, from experience, it was only with time that he'd remember it all.

"There have been, in the past, some…friction between the ER staff and the surgeons, but we're working assiduously to iron everything out before the expansion of the hospital is complete. Once we're upgraded to a level one trauma center, we must have things running smoothly."

"Of course."

No doubt he'd find out soon enough what types of friction Dr. Hammond referred to. Yet, in Cort's experience, there were always disputes between ER and Trauma, no matter how smoothly the hospital was run. That was just a product of human nature, and the instinctive need most doctors had to be in control.

They'd toured the surgical floor, and Cort was aware of the stares and murmurs of the staff as Dr. Hammond and he passed by, the searching glances of those he was introduced to. Not unusual, or unexpected, since everyone would want to check out the new surgeon, but he'd started to feel a bit like a specimen in a bottle. Something strange, like a teratoma, or a two-headed fetal pig—seldom seen and therefore gawk-worthy.

It didn't really bother him, though. He'd gone through too much in his life to be annoyed or made uncomfortable by others' curiosity.

Downstairs now, Dr. Hammond was showing him the construction zone, explaining what the various rooms still being built would be and how the new configuration would work.

"The expansion should be completed in about four to six months, and we'll be hiring new staff to fill the newly created positions in Trauma. There will be a slowdown in our emergency intake, so all the departments can be set up, and, as the board of directors indicated, you'll be assigned some general surgery cases to keep you busy."

Dr. Hammond turned down another corridor lined with heavy plastic sheets to contain the dust, beyond which a construction crew was working. There was a flurry of sound as an air hammer started up, and then the cacophony was overlaid by shouts.

"Hey, stop—stop—stop—*stop*!" followed by a string of curses so foul they would have made a sailor blush.

Dr. Hammond's face took on the pained expression of a man not used to such salty language, and he picked up the pace, heading for the exit at the end of the corridor. Once on the other side of the door, the noise reduced to almost nothing, he jerked a thumb over his shoulder.

"Sorry about that. Huh, construction workers."

His disgusted tone made Cort's hackles rise, but he didn't have time to say anything as just then the other man's cell phone rang. Taking it out, Dr. Hammond glanced at the screen and was already moving away as he said, "Excuse me a moment, Smith. It's my assistant."

Cort sighed. His annoyance faded, to be replaced by amusement at the memory of the older man's expression, but with it came familiar pain.

Brody had cursed like that all the time, even when he hadn't been on a job site.

"My goodness, Brody. Not in front of the kids," his wife, Jenna, would say after a particularly colorful outburst.

Hearing it had sometimes felt like going back in time to the foster home where Cort and Brody had met as teenagers. Except back then the admonition would usually come with a backhand slap from one of their foster parents too. Brody and Cort had always agreed that the place wasn't the worst either of them had been in, but they had both been glad to age out of the system and leave it behind.

They'd stayed close, even when life had taken them in different directions, Cort to the army and Brody into construction. The only reason Cort had returned to Denver when he'd been on leave, rather than travel the world the way he'd always wanted to, had been to see Brody and Jenna. He'd stood as godfather for their son, had luckily been on leave and in the hospital waiting room when their daughter had been born. They'd been the closest thing to family he had.

Brody's death had sent him reeling and, coming just before Cort had been due to reenlist, had seemed like a sign. How could he not have known his best friend had been in so much pain? He'd known, of course, about Brody's original, job-related injury, but not that his best friend had descended into a full-blown opiate addiction. Jenna said she hadn't known either, but that didn't make it any easier to deal with. Cort felt as though he *should* have known, despite being so far away.

He'd always promised Brody to look after Jenna and the kids should anything happen, but leaving the army hadn't been easy since it had been his life for so long. But there really hadn't been an option, and he'd headed back to Denver when his tour was over and his contract had expired.

Now, in hindsight, he realized he'd been drifting along ever since.

Even getting engaged to Mimi had been done almost unthinkingly. She was Jenna's cousin, and she and Cort had gotten close during the dark days following Brody's death. It had felt good to be a part of Jenna's wider family, and when Mimi had hinted it was time to get married,

Cort had agreed without thinking too deeply about what that entailed.

Three weeks before the wedding she'd called it off, saying she just didn't think it would work out. That she'd realized she didn't love him enough to be his wife, and she'd already found someone else.

After months of soul-searching, Cort knew he'd been unfair to Mimi. In a way, she'd been a crutch, holding him up after Brody's death. An imperfect replacement for the companionship he'd lost.

Despite the embarrassment and hurt, he'd known she'd been right not to go through with it.

Brody had always been the one who'd longed for a family, for roots, while Cort had wanted to see as much of the world as possible. Perhaps the difference stemmed from the fact Brody had lived with his mother until the age of seven, and knew what it was like to be a part of a real family. Cort had never had that, and knew he wasn't cut out to be a part of a family, didn't even know how to be.

Apparently he wasn't even fit to be a family member by proxy either since, soon after, Jenna too had cut him loose.

"Me and the kids, we'll be fine," she said, while they sat on her back step. "Mimi is a flake for waiting so long to break things off, and I know you're just hanging around here because of us. Brody always said you wanted to see the world. Go. Do it."

The sadness had weighed so heavily in his chest he'd been unable to even look at her. How many evenings like this had he and Brody sat in this same spot, beers in hand, talking? The twilight sky had gleamed between the branches, and a cool wind, harbinger of fall, had rustled the leaves, making them whisper and sigh. Her words had felt like another rejection, in no way softened by the squeeze of her fingers on his shoulder.

It was then he'd accepted that nothing good in life lasted.

He was better off not getting attached, because to do so just brought heartache.

But this was a new day, full of potential and future adventure, and he wasn't going to let the past encroach on it. Shrugging off his dark thoughts, Cort wandered along the corridor, away from the chief surgeon and the construction zone.

At the end of the corridor was a T-junction, with a bustling nurses' station on his right and, as first one person and then the next turned to look at him, he once more became the cynosure of all eyes. Making eye contact with a few people, he nodded and smiled, until a noise to his left caught his attention, and he turned to look.

A woman stood at an exit door, holding a travel cup and tucking a cell phone under her chin. Something about her carriage, her profile made Cort's heart stumble over itself. And, as she turned slightly to swipe her access card to open the door, for the second time in less than five minutes his world tilted on its axis.

It can't be.

Yet, as she used her hip to push open the door and slip outside, he knew he wasn't imagining things.

It definitely was the woman he'd met in Mexico, who'd given him the most sublime night of pleasure he'd ever had, and had then run out on him without a word.

Without even giving him her name.

Worse, he'd confided in her about being dumped just before his wedding. No doubt, with the way hospital grapevines worked, that tidbit of news would be on everyone's lips by the following day.

A sour sensation filled his stomach, and all the anticipation regarding his new job leached away in an instant. It didn't matter that he didn't plan on staying at Hepplewhite very long. He'd only signed a one-year contract and, although the board had made it clear they hoped he'd renew at the end of that time, the plan was to move on to somewhere else. Have another adventure.

Right now, though, this felt less like an adventure and more like a mistake.

So much for a fresh start.

Cell phone held to her ear with one shoulder, Dr. Liz Prudhomme stepped out into the quiet of the staff parking lot and let the door swing shut behind her. Although there had been a midwinter thaw of sorts along the east coast, it was still cold, but after the dry heat of the hospital the damp chill felt good against her face. Grabbing the phone before it slipped, she found an alcove out of the wind and took a sip of her rapidly cooling coffee.

She normally didn't make personal calls while on duty, but her mother had just flown in from Milan the day before and this was the first opportunity Liz had had to speak to her. With the time difference between New York and California, it was perfect. Her mother would have just finished breakfast.

"The dress is delightful. Giovanna picked a strapless mermaid gown, made completely of Guipure lace. It's elegant and suits her so well. Although the designer isn't one I would have chosen, I have to admit it is beautiful."

In Liz's opinion, her future sister-in-law could wear a gunny sack and still look gorgeous. After all, Giovanna modeled for some of the world's best designers and probably wore a size negative three. Pulling off a dress like the one her mother was describing wouldn't be difficult for her at all.

Even if she wanted to, that wouldn't be the case for Liz. When it came to height and bone structure, she'd inherited her father's mostly Anglo-Saxon genes, rather than her mother's mix of Latin and Asian. She had a farm-girl sturdiness that once upon a time had been the bane of her existence. Now she was proud of her strength, and confident in her womanhood.

Most of the time.

Unless she let old insecurities rise up and blindside her.

But it wasn't jealousy making Liz feel out of sorts as she listened to her mother breathlessly give her all the details of the dress and their subsequent orgy of shopping. It was the usual feeling of inadequacy, knowing her ex-beauty-queen mother would have loved to have a daughter like Giovanna, rather than the one she had. Someone as passionate about fashion and decorating as Lorelei Prud-homme was herself. A daughter who could follow in her footsteps and excel at being a member of high society, not single-mindedly focused on her medical career.

Better to be useful than decorative.

Funny how often, at times like these, Nanny Hardy's voice popped into her head, reminding her of what was important. The nanny had left when Liz was eight, but her legacy was lasting.

"I don't know why they chose New York for the wedding." Lorelei sighed the special sigh that usually turned all members of her family to mush, and had them falling over themselves to give her whatever she wanted. She'd learned, however, that it didn't work on the strong-willed Giovanna. "It would have been so much nicer here in San Francisco."

Liz stifled a prickle of annoyance at hearing the same complaint for the hundredth time but just replied, "It's where Giovanna and Robbie wanted to have it."

"I know." There was no missing the pique in her mother's delicate tones. "But it's so inconvenient for us, really."

So said the woman who flew to Milan to look at a wedding dress, and help her future daughter-in-law shop for a trousseau! Liz shook her head silently, amusement making the corners of her lips quirk. Her anxiety, which always made itself known whenever she spoke to her mother, abated slightly. Taking another sip of her coffee, she swallowed her instinctive, somewhat snarky reply along with the strong brew.

"However, I'm sure it will be lovely. Giovanna has exquisite taste. Are you bringing anyone to the wedding?"

Caught off guard by the quick change of subject, although that was her mother's usual style of conversation, Liz said the first thing that came to mind. "Highly unlikely."

As her mother sighed again, Liz got that familiar sense of being not quite enough of a woman to suit.

Despite it being eight years since Liz had had a serious romantic relationship, her mother never stopped hoping, asking leading questions whenever the opportunity arose. Although she'd never say so to her mother, there was no way Liz was going down that painful road again. Lessons learned the first time around didn't have to be repeated, and Andrew had certainly taught her to keep her heart closed.

"Your father sends his love."

The muscles in Liz's neck and shoulders tightened so suddenly, so painfully she almost gasped aloud. Instead, she pressed her lips together for an instant and clenched her fingers around the cup. When she replied, it was years of practice that allowed her to keep her tone level.

"Tell him I said hello."

It was the best that she could do right now. The wounds were still too fresh, her sense of betrayal still too painful for anything more.

"Eliza…"

But that was all her mother said, and the silence stretched between them, filled with the ghosts of past mistakes and family secrets too long hidden. Liz wasn't surprised by her mother's inability to articulate whatever it was she wanted to say. Heart-to-hearts and speaking about emotional subjects weren't "done" in their family.

Things might be a damned sight better if they were but, after all these years, they wouldn't know where to start.

She was gripping the phone so hard her fingers were beginning to ache, mirroring the pain in her suddenly roiling stomach. She didn't have time for this. Not right now. Probably never.

"I have to get back inside, Mother. I'm still on duty. I'm glad you enjoyed your trip."

"Thank you, dear." Her mother spoke softly, almost wistfully, and Liz wondered if she, like her daughter, wished things could go back to the way they used to be. "We'll talk again soon."

Disconnecting the call, Liz thrust the phone into the pocket of her coat and turned her face up toward the murky sky, taking a deep breath, trying to relax.

It was actually funny, in a twisted type of way. She'd always been an outsider in the family, set apart. While she loved her parents, she'd often felt emotionally distant from them, while Robbie, three years her junior, had been the affectionate one, the glue holding the family together. The fact that he was adopted hadn't mattered. She'd been too young when he'd arrived to care, and had loved him, unconditionally, ever since.

Perhaps it was the thought of settling down with Giovanna and starting a family of his own that had prompted Robbie to ask for information about his biological parents. Whatever the reason, neither he nor Liz had been prepared for the answer, delivered one summer's evening last year while the family had spent a couple of days together at the beach house.

Robbie was Brant Prudhomme's biological son, conceived when Brant had had an affair not long after Liz's birth.

"We went through a bad patch," Lorelei had said, her

still-beautiful face pale, her eyes damp. "But, in the end, we decided to make it work. And when Brant told me Robbie's mother was dying…"

"Your mother is a wonderful woman," Brant had interjected, in the tone Liz had known from experience meant the conversation was all but over. "I don't think either of you would argue that point."

Too stunned to say anything, or ask questions, Liz had watched her father walk out of the room, his back stiff and straight. Lorelei had looked suddenly more fragile but, as usual, it had been Robbie who'd gone to her, hugged her, and reassured her everything would be fine.

Liz hadn't shared his optimism. From that moment, her world had felt off kilter, and she doubted it would ever be completely put back to rights again. Knowing that her father, who Liz would have sworn was a good husband, had betrayed her mother's trust like that had devastated her.

What little faith she'd had in men had practically been destroyed.

Since that day, anger had lain like a rock in her chest. Why the situation affected her this way was something she was loath to look at too closely. All she knew was she couldn't deal with being around or speaking to her father yet. Maybe the anger would fade over time and she'd relent, but not yet. Sometimes that anger spilled over to her mother too, but Lorelei, for all her bustle and chattiness, had somehow always struck Liz as being in need of protection. Being careful not to let her know the extent of the rage her daughter felt was important.

Suddenly realizing her face tingled from the cold, Liz took one last deep breath and twisted her head from side to side, trying to work out the stiffness in her muscles. It was time to get back to work, to lose herself in the job she loved more than anything else in the world, at the hospital that held a special place in her heart.

Liz's great-grandfather had been one of the founding fathers of Hepplewhite General, which eventually had been named after him. When she'd completed her residency and applied there she hadn't revealed her connection to the hospital, which had made winning the position that much more satisfying.

She was sure that somewhere, in the afterlife, her great-aunts had chuckled.

Her Great-Aunt Honoria had wanted to study medicine, but her father had refused to allow it. And when Liz's father had expressed reservations about his daughter going into what he'd described as "a grueling, heartbreaking profession" Honoria and her sister, Eliza, had paid for her schooling.

"Do what you want in life," Aunt Honoria had said. "Be useful, and don't allow your father, or any man, to dictate to you. Eliza and I wish we'd had the courage to do that ourselves."

The advice had been sound, and in line with what her nursemaid, Nanny Hardy, had taught her as a child. Heeding their collective guidance had led to her success, while the one time she'd not followed it had led to disaster and heartbreak.

No, she loved her work and Hepplewhite, with its associations with the past, and had made it the main focus of her life. Never had she been more grateful for how busy the ER kept her than now.

There was nothing like a full workload to keep the chaotic thoughts at bay. This winter had seen a particularly active flu season, still in full swing, and with the waves of snowstorms hitting New York City had come an uptick of heart attacks, slip-and-fall injuries and the like. The hospital staff wasn't immune to the flu either, and there were a few out sick, which increased everyone's workload.

As she swiped her badge to open the door, Liz's stomach rumbled. She'd been heading for the cafeteria a couple hours ago when a commotion in the ER waiting area had caught her attention. Four clearly frightened young men had been at the intake desk, supporting a fifth who'd appeared to be unconscious and bleeding from a facial wound. They had all been talking at once.

"He fell—"

"Momma's gonna kill us—"

"He won't wake up—"

Lunch forgotten, Liz had grabbed a nearby gurney and hit the electronic door opener, not waiting for an orderly. Even from a distance she had been able to see the youngster had needed immediate treatment.

As it turned out, the teens had cut school and somehow found their way past the protective fencing surrounding the hospital's ongoing construction project. Once there, her patient decided to use the equipment and building rubble to practice his parkour skills. Probably not the best of ideas, given the slick of ice that still covered some surfaces. It had cost him a broken jaw, a concussion and the kind of laceration that, without plastic surgery, would leave a disfiguring scar.

By the time she'd examined him, made sure he was stable and sent for the oral and plastic surgeons, she'd only had another two and a half hours before her twelve-hour shift would be finished. Rather than bother with a break, and cognizant of the full waiting room, she'd only taken enough time to call her mother.

Striding down the corridor toward the ER, Liz put her family drama, and its attendant pain, aside. There was no place for it here in the hospital, where all her attention had to be on her patients' well-being.

That was what was truly important.

On the way home she'd stop at her favorite diner and treat herself to an everything omelet with home fries. Just the thought made her mouth water and her stomach rumble again.

CHAPTER TWO

AFTER TAKING OFF her coat and making her way back to the ER, Liz noticed a certain buzz in the air that hadn't been there before she'd gone outside. Before she could ask one of the other doctors what was going on, she was called away to deal with a patient brought in by ambulance.

Paramedics had received a report of a man acting irrationally and, on arrival, had found Mr. Josiah Collins combative and uncooperative, with a severe laceration on his arm. Although they also said he'd calmed down quickly, and there'd been no problems with him since, there was something about the man's watchful quiescence and refusal to give much information that had Liz on high alert.

She ordered blood tests, and stitched the laceration. Then, signaling to one of the nurses to join her, she stepped out and walked a few paces along the corridor leading to the ER nurses' station.

"Put a rush on those samples. I need those results, stat, so I can know whether he's on something or is just having a psychotic break. And have one of the security personnel keep an eye on him, please."

"Yes Dr. Prudhomme."

The nurse immediately started off, but paused as Liz said, "And, Stella? Nice job on that thoracotomy patient earlier. I appreciate it."

With a smile and a nod of acknowledgement, Stella went on her way, and Liz walked toward the nurses' station.

There was no need for her to elaborate. Stella knew to what she was referring. The patient had been awake, alert and in extreme pain. Taking advantage of the brief thaw, he'd been working on a roof and slipped, the fall causing chest trauma and fractures to both arms and one leg. Already distressed, he'd grown more distraught as a massive hemothorax had caused blood to fill his chest cavity, compressing his lungs and making breathing increasingly difficult.

Inserting a chest tube was a great deal easier to do when the patient was unconscious and Liz had been prepared to have a difficult time of it until Stella, with impeccable timing, had distracted the patient, held his attention and kept him calm through the painful procedure. Stella's intuition and ability to connect quickly and effectively with the patient deserved acknowledgement.

Liz was more than aware of her own shortcomings in the human interaction arena. Her lack of affectionate gestures, her cool contemplation of, and reaction to, life had been pointed out repeatedly, and not as positive traits. She wasn't into giving constant praise for every little thing. They all had their jobs to do, from the ER doctors and trauma surgeons to the orderlies. She didn't expect congratulations for every correct diagnosis she made or course of treatment she set in motion, and neither should anyone else for doing their job.

However, she also knew her reputation was one of a hard-assed, unsmiling witch. It was true, and she had no complaints on that score. However, just because she didn't make nice with everyone, it didn't mean she didn't care about the people she worked with.

It was just simpler not to care *too* much, not build friendships and relationships that could, potentially, interfere with her job. She already had close friends from her university days. Although they were now scattered across the globe, Liz really didn't see any need to make new ones.

She was heading to the nurses' station to get a jump on her charting when she was interrupted by a nurse informing her that her young parkour patient's mother had arrived, and was in the waiting room.

Her stomach rumbled again, reminding her she'd been on duty for eleven and a half hours and hadn't ingested anything more than a couple of energy bars and half a cup of coffee. It was just one of those days.

Micah Johnston's mother was by turns livid at her son and scared about his prognosis, and it took some time to calm her down. As soon as she'd escorted the lady to her son's cubicle to speak to the surgeons, Liz strode purposefully once more toward the nearest nurses' station.

She really had to get her charting done ASAP, so maybe, just maybe, she could leave the hospital on time and stop her stomach from devouring itself.

"Ah, there she is. Liz, a moment please."

Damn it!

She turned toward Gregory Hammond's voice, biting back a growl of annoyance at being waylaid once more. Luckily she'd assumed a politely questioning expression because, as she looked at the man walking next to the chief of surgery, her face, along with the rest of her body, froze.

There was no mistaking his carriage, the set of his head, the clear-cut features of the man she'd had a glorious one-night stand with in Mexico. To suddenly see him again, when she'd thought she never would, made her head feel light and her legs weak.

How could she not recognize him? First off, he was tall. Tall enough that she, five-ten in her stockinged feet, had to look up at him, a rarity indeed, and he carried himself with easy assurance, his back militarily straight, his strides long and strong.

Second, although she wouldn't classify him as handsome, there was something compelling about his face. It was wide, with a prominent nose and deep-set, hooded eyes. A firm chin and mouth rounded out the picture. From a distance she'd been attracted, but it was seeing him up close that had cemented her interest. His eyes were spectacular. Dark amber in the center, shading to brown around the edge of the iris, they were serious and hinted at the kind of intelligence Liz always found appealing.

Heat rushed from her toes to the top of her head as her gaze was captured and transfixed by those unforgettable eyes, partially masked behind lowered lids. They gleamed, and she wasn't sure what the glint in them was. Anger? Annoyance? Amusement?

Her heart went into overdrive, a mixture of irritation and mortification rushing through her in an instant.

Then all the years of training drummed into her by her mother and tutors arose to come to her rescue. Inner heat was replaced by cold tension, but she refused to allow it to show. Straightening her back and lifting her chin, she tore her gaze away from his companion and gratefully turned her attention to Gregory Hammond.

"Liz, I want you to meet our newest trauma surgeon, Dr. Cort Smith. Dr. Smith, this is Dr. Liz Prudhomme, one of our fine ER practitioners."

Politeness dictated she look at Dr. Smith again, but it took considerable effort to make herself do it. Her brain was racing as fast as her heart, wondering if he was about to say they'd already met; if somehow he would make it clear their involvement had been of the intimate kind.

There were plenty of men who wouldn't be able to resist doing so, just to up their reputations as ladies' men.

But Cort Smith just stuck out his hand and said, politely, "How do you do, Dr. Prudhomme?"

Just the sound of that deep voice, so familiar and arousing, made her wish she were a hundred miles away. How could he be so cool, while she wanted to run for the hills? It was tempting to focus on his Adam's apple or chin, rather than meet those compelling eyes again, but that would be the coward's way out, so she met his gaze with what she hoped was a calm one of her own.

"Very well, thank you," she replied, as she took his hand. A *zing* of electricity rushed up her arm, and she tugged her hand away as swiftly as she could without being rude.

The corners of Cort Smith's mouth twitched, making Liz want to smack him.

"Dr. Smith starts his first full day tomorrow," Gregory said. He seemed oblivious to the tension swirling between herself and Cort, which Liz swore was so thick she could taste it. "I hope you'll take whatever time is necessary to point him in the right direction while he gets settled."

She'd point him right out the door, if she had her way! But Liz only nodded, and decided the politic answer was best. "Of course."

Thankfully, before the voluble Gregory could get chatting again, Stella interrupted.

"Dr. Prudhomme, I have the lab reports on Mr. Collins."

"Thank you." Her relief was almost strong enough to make her smile, but not quite. With a quick, "If you gentlemen will excuse me," she hightailed it away as fast as she could without actually running.

Why did it feel as though the universe had decided her previously nice, orderly existence was too good to be true, and was throwing her curveballs left, right and center?

Cort watched Liz Prudhomme walk away, amazed at how unruffled she'd been by a meeting he'd found hard to face with aplomb. Besides a reddening of the tips of her ears when she'd turned and seen him, there had been no other discernible reaction to show she'd even recognized him.

After he'd caught sight of her at the door earlier, he'd tried to convince himself it wasn't really the woman he'd spent the night with in Mexico. For the last seven months he'd been so hung up on the memory of that encounter he'd dreamt about her almost constantly, and had thought, erroneously, he'd glimpsed her in crowds at least a hundred times.

And she looked different, with her brown hair pulled back into a simple ponytail instead of in a sleek bob to below her chin. The streak of aqua she'd had framing one side of her face was gone too, but they were definitely the same strong features he'd committed to memory. Those mesmerizing, mossy-green eyes, almond-shaped and thick-lashed, had the same steady, controlled gaze that had attracted him before.

She wouldn't be classified as beautiful by most people's standards. Tall, solidly built, with strong shoulders and wide hips, she was anything but model skinny. From a distance, she would seem the perfect fit for the girl next door, or the sidekick in a romantic movie. But once a person saw her up close, Cort knew they couldn't see her in either role.

Her face was too strong, with high cheekbones, lips a trifle thinner than were fashionable, and a chin that hinted at a stubborn, willful nature. Here was a woman unused and unwilling to bend and, although he admired strength of character, he'd always been attracted to a softer type. Until the night they'd slept together, and she'd proved strength when yielded for desire brought more pleasure than he'd ever imagined.

Yet even if he'd still been unsure whether it was her or not, once he heard her speak there could be no question. Despite its careful control, her voice was still rich and decadent, like Cherries Jubilee without the brandy burnt off, and hearing it had made goose bumps race along his spine. Realizing it absolutely was her had filled him with a mixture of disbelief, horror and unwanted excitement. Life would be a lot simpler if she'd stayed just a memory and attendant fantasy, not a flesh-and-blood person he had to work with.

And always remember how she'd run out on him that night without a word.

"Liz is a fine practitioner. One of our best diagnosticians," Gregory was saying. "And although some of the staff seem to find her rather standoffish, we've never had any complaints from patients about either her standard of care or bedside manner."

Standoffish? He could only hope she would be standoffish with him too. Against his will and best intentions, already the memory of having her, flushed and damp with pleasure in his bed was threatening to push everything else out of his head.

"And I have to warn you she will not stand for any nonsense when it comes to proper protocol." Gregory started walking again, and Cort fell in beside him. "Not that she should, you understand, but she's particularly unforgiving when it comes to our surgeons overstepping their boundaries."

Ah, so she was at least one of the sources of the "friction" Dr. Hammond had spoken of earlier. He was searching for the correct way to ask for more information when a howling cry arose from down the hall. It was followed swiftly by a metallic crash and a shout. Instinct had Cort running toward the noise, following Liz as she disappeared, also at a run, around a corner.

She was closer to the commotion, but he had the advantage of longer legs, so he was only two steps behind her when she dashed into one of the cubicles.

Everything seemed to slow down, allowing him to take in the large man thrashing about on the bed, a security guard struggling to restrain him. Liz sprang forward just as the patient's arm swung back, and Cort bit back a curse, knowing he was too far away to stop her from getting hit...

Liz twisted away from the flailing fist, the move so graceful and efficient Cort could hardly believe it, then she grabbed the patient's wrist.

The man went rigid, all the fight going out of him, as though Liz's touch sucked it away. The guard quickly secured one wrist with a restraint cuff while Liz secured the other, and Cort got to work putting ankle belts in place, assisted by a nurse who'd come in behind him.

"I know you're frightened." Patient secured, Liz leaned over him, spoke to him with what Cort recognized from their time together in Mexico as habitual directness. There wasn't a hint of stress in her voice, and Cort, whose system still hummed with adrenaline, mentally shook his head at her cool. "But we're going to help you."

Cort backed out of the room as Liz started giving orders to the nurses. He wasn't even supposed to be there, and he wondered if he'd already earned a strike with her, given her strictness on protocol.

Dr. Hammond was down the hall, speaking into his phone again, so Cort waited outside the patient's cubicle for Liz to come out. Might as well take whatever she had to say on the chin and apologize if necessary, rather than let it fester or have her formally complain.

When she stepped out of the room she paused, allowing the nurses to pass them before she spoke.

"It wasn't necessary for you to jump in like that. We have exceptionally well-trained staff here, and rushing to the rescue every time there's a hint of excitement isn't within your purview."

He shrugged, and stuck his hands in the pockets of his

lab coat, annoyed once more at how unconcerned she was about seeing him again. He felt as though there was an egg-beater running amok in his stomach. "It was instinct. The sound of a fight and a kidney dish hitting the floor will always bring me running." She'd warned him off clearly: the patient inside that room had nothing to do with him. So, just to needle her, he asked, "Do you have a diagnosis?"

The look she gave him was level, but he was sure there was a flash of annoyance behind her veiled glance. Which was why he was surprised when, after a moment, she actually replied.

"Just got the labs back. There are trace amounts of clozapine in his system. I think he stopped taking his medication and is having a schizophrenic episode. The psych team is on its way down." Her gaze dared him to express an opinion, and he figured it was time to change the subject, even before she added, with a touch of ice in her tone, "Nothing more either of us can do right now."

If he hadn't figured it out before, now he knew for sure. Dr. Liz Prudhomme was as tough as rebar and cooler than a mountain spring. Yet under that realization was the still clear image of her in Mexico, vulnerable to his every touch. It took every ounce of willpower to lock the memory away again. He had to deal with her simply as a new colleague, a potentially difficult one at that, in the place he'd chosen to start over. Whatever had happened between them in the honeymoon suite in Mexico had no bearing on the here and now. Yet he felt he owed it to himself, and to her, to clear the air.

"Listen." Cort lowered his voice. "I wasn't sure you'd want anyone to know we'd met before. I was trying to be discreet."

"That's fine." The steady gaze didn't waver, but the ice in her voice was solid now. "I keep my private life private, so I... I actually appreciate it."

That little hesitation tugged at his chest, although he wasn't sure why. Perhaps it had something to do with its incongruity, given her air of total confidence. Without thought, he said, "Well, I'd rather the staff here didn't know I'd been dumped right before my wedding too, so being discreet is pretty easy for me."

She didn't reply, except with a lift of her eyebrows and a sideways tilt of her head, which he interpreted as a dismissive gesture, before she turned to walk away. He should leave it at that, yet the urge to keep hearing that Cherries Jubilee voice was hard to ignore, no matter how aggravating she was.

She was already a few strides down the hall when he called after her, "What was that wrist lock you used? Aikido?"

That brought her up short, and those telling eyebrows rose again as she paused and looked back at him. "Hapkido. You're a martial artist?"

"Used to be, full on, until I got accepted into med school. Kept involved while I was in the army too." He held out his hands and flexed his fingers. "But I've stopped sparring, since I don't want to break anything, although that didn't end my fascination."

For a moment she didn't reply, seemed to be staring at his hands, then she looked back up at him. "Huh. Wimp."

Wow, she didn't pull any punches, did she? But he couldn't help the smile tugging at his lips. "Want to test that hypothesis sometime?"

Liz just shook her head, but the corner of her mouth twitched. "I'd kick your butt."

"No doubt," he replied, making no attempt to stop her this time when she moved away. "I've no doubt at all."

And it occurred to him, as he watched that delectable

body disappear around the corner, she could do a great deal more than just kick his butt physically.

If he was stupid enough to let her.

CHAPTER THREE

"I SHOT HIM," the patient moaned, her voice distorted not just by the oxygen mask but also her severe facial injuries. "I shot him."

It was all she'd said since she'd been brought in, over and over again, no matter what Liz asked her. She'd barely reacted to any of the procedures they'd done to try to stabilize her condition, despite the additional pain they must have caused her.

"Kaitlin, where hurts the most?"

"I shot him. I shot him."

"Any word from Trauma?" Liz asked the room at large.

"I'm here."

Cort Smith dumped a bloody surgical gown into the bin by the door, and paused to drag on a fresh one. "What do we have?"

Even as focused as she was on her patient, Liz's heart did a little dip when she heard his voice.

I'll get used to having him around.

That was what Liz had been telling herself repeatedly since the day Cort strode back into her life but, a month on, she still had a visceral reaction every time she saw him. Having to work with him presented another layer to her problem, since she found herself sometimes having to fight to concentrate.

The movements of his hands, the calm, soothing quality of his deep voice when he spoke to patients, did things to her insides. They brought to mind the way he'd touched her so masterfully as he'd murmured in her ear that night so long ago, telling her to come.

It was extremely annoying and she once more resolved to ignore it. The badly beaten and stabbed woman in front of her deserved all her concentration.

"Twenty-four-year-old Kaitlin Hayle, facial trauma and multiple penetrating wounds to thorax and abdomen, both anterior and posterior. Limited lung sounds on the right when brought in; chest tube inserted."

As she continued to bring him up to speed, she chafed at the delay having to do so caused. It was information she'd already transmitted to Dr. Yuen, and she was surprised that Cort had attended. Normally the doctor she'd spoken to initially would be the one to come down. Something had caused the change in procedure, and therefore the delay, and she wasn't happy about it.

One thing Liz could readily admit to with Dr. Smith, though, was how thorough he was.

"Hey, Kaitlin," he said, in that deep, calm voice, while checking her pupils. "My name is Dr. Smith. I'm going to be examining you, okay?"

"I shot him."

Cort continued his methodical examination, working his way down to the two penetrating wounds on Kaitlin's thorax.

"They look to be at least two inches deep," Liz said, as he started palpating the area around the first wound. "And that one seems to angle downward."

Having examined both the anterior wounds, he merely said, "Roll her," so he could examine the posterior one.

Once he was through, he moved back to the head of the table and leaned over the patient. "Kaitlin, I'm going to have to operate. You have internal injuries that have to be repaired. We'll take good care of you, okay?"

Kaitlin's gaze flickered to Cort's face, and stayed there for a moment. Then, surprisingly, she said, "Okay. Okay."

"Good girl," he replied, giving her shoulder a quick squeeze.

The shock must be wearing off, thanks to the drip, Liz thought a little sourly. How else to explain his ability to get through to their patient when she hadn't been able to at all?

With a little jerk of his head, Cort beckoned Liz to the far side of the room, out of Kaitlin's earshot.

"I want her to have a CT scan before I go in. She seems stable enough to take the time, and I'll have a better idea of what I'm facing before I open her up."

"I'll call up to Radiology right now," Liz replied. "And I'll go up with her."

"Thanks." He gave her a half smile. "I'll keep an eye on her vitals while you're gone."

As she turned away to go to the phone, Liz was annoyed with herself all over again.

Why was it his smiles, even half ones, made her want to smile back? She wasn't the smiling type at all, and yet something about him made her almost wish she were.

She'd been careful to keep him firmly at arm's length and act with the utmost professionalism toward him, determined to eventually exorcise the hyperawareness she experienced around him. It was aggravating in the extreme that the rest of the Hepplewhite staff seemed equally determined to keep Cort in the center of the gossip mill, and she could hardly move without hearing someone say his name.

Just that morning, when she'd been in the line at the cafeteria, there had been a couple of nurses in front of her talking about him, as though there was nothing else of any interest to chat about.

"He's been here for a while, what have you been able to find out about him?"

Liz knew who Marcie was talking about even before Trisha answered.

"Nothing but what I was able to find in the Cramer General website archives. Served in the army and got his training through it. Honorably discharged about five years ago and went straight to Cramer."

"That's it? Do we even know if he's married or not?"

Trisha shook her head, disgruntlement clear in her tone when she replied, "He's real nice, but a clam when it comes to talking about himself."

"Even with you, Miss Southern Charm?" Marcie snickered. "I'm surprised you don't have him spilling his guts over some sweet potato pie and a mint julep."

"Ha-ha-ha," Trisha replied, as she elbowed her friend and they both laughed.

Liz too was surprised that Trisha hadn't had any luck. The nurse was petite, almost elfin, with the most beautiful dark mocha complexion and the face of an angel. Plus, she had the kind of voice Liz remembered, as a teen, wishing she had. It was as sweet and light as fresh whipped cream, not low and raspy, like its owner subsisted on a diet of rusty nails and rye whiskey. Mind you, a voice like Trisha's would sound pretty stupid coming from her, who was almost a foot taller and nowhere near petite.

As she relayed Cort's request to Radiology, she resolved once more do something about how often she thought about him, dreamed about being with him in Mexico. She was loath to admit it, even to herself, but he'd turned her inside out that night, given her an experience she'd never had before.

Maybe because of her forthright nature, men seemed to assume she'd be demanding in bed and, since it was the best way to get the satisfaction she deserved, she usually was. However, Cort Smith had taken masterful control of her body, coaxing her to new erotic heights and making her have to reevaluate what it was she truly desired. When she'd snuck out of his room in the early hours of the morning, it hadn't just been because she'd had a flight to catch. She'd been awash in pleasure so intense as to be frightening.

There was no secret enjoyment in the fact she knew more about the sexy doctor than anyone else at the hospital. Intimate facts that still made her skin heat and her libido go through the roof. Instead, the knowledge she possessed just made working with him harder. Trying to view him just as a colleague was difficult in the extreme, but she was determined to do just that.

Hopefully, the more she had to interact with him, the more likely the annoying attraction she still felt would wither away.

"There." Cort pointed to where the CT images of Kaitlin's body were on the screen. "Definite laceration to the liver. And…" He was aware of Liz leaning closer, her attention focused on the movement of his finger, and for a split second lost his train of thought.

"Is that fluid around the stomach?" she asked.

"And air," he replied, pulling himself together. He was about to operate to try to save a young woman's life. There was no time for loss of concentration, no matter the source. What he was seeing on the CT scan indicated the internal injuries were probably quite extensive.

And they were. What he had estimated would be an hour-long operation stretched to two and a half hours, as he discovered Kaitlin's diaphragm and stomach, as well as her liver, had been damaged. As he cauterized and stitched, he reflected on how lucky the young woman had been.

He wasn't really surprised to come out of surgery and

see Liz waiting to hear the outcome. Yet as he took a few moments to take off his surgical gear and wash up, his awareness of her just on the other side of the doors was disconcerting.

Settling in at Hepplewhite, in New York City itself, had been difficult enough, but every time he came into contact with Dr. Liz Prudhomme it intensified his sense of disorientation. Which was funny, in a weird rather than amusing sort of way, since it was something she'd said to him in Mexico that had prompted his move from Colorado.

Although they'd just met, he'd found himself telling her about being jilted only weeks before the wedding. What she'd said to him had lingered in his mind.

Sometimes, when life seems to be screwed up, you need to take a chance on the change that's been forced on you, you know? Figure out what it would take to make the crappy stuff into an asset, or a benefit. Maybe you've had a lucky escape, being dumped. I don't know, but now's the time for you to make a new, better plan. That's what I do when life tries to mess with me, anyway.

On reflection, her advice had made perfect sense. Wasn't he the poster child for overcoming? For taking whatever effluvium life flung at him and making something worthwhile out of it? In comparison to all he'd been through, being jilted was, in the final analysis, insignificant. It was nothing when weighed against being abandoned as a baby, surviving the foster-care system, or losing his best friend. It was even small potatoes when compared to the depression that had blanketed him following Brody's death. What it had done, though, was underscore how much he'd been drifting along through life.

The job at Cramer had been a sound choice, given his desire to be close to Jenna and the kids, and, although demanding, strangely easy after being deployed. He'd done well but after Mimi's defection had decided to reactivate his childhood wish to travel the world, get to know new places intimately, before moving on to the next. And where better to start than in New York City?

It had seemed a perfect plan, until he'd found himself working with Liz Prudhomme and had realized he'd not just made a change but turned his entire life upside down.

He couldn't make her out.

While he'd never heard her be rude, there was a distance between her and the world, a wall created of solemn, clear-eyed looks and cool professionalism. Although being the epitome of calm whenever they worked together, occasionally she'd glance at him, and all the arousal he tried to suppress rushed through him anew. For him, the spirit of the woman he'd had in his bed hovered in the back of his mind continually. A ghostly fantasy, flushed and excited, her body bowing and twisting with ecstasy yearned for and then achieved.

He'd give anything to be rid of those memories and the fantasies they inspired, but not even seeing her in her usual milieu, which was anything but sexy, helped.

If anything, it made her more fascinating. Every time he met those clear green eyes, or saw her striding purposefully through the hospital, it enticed him further.

Apparently, along with all his other issues, he was a masochist too. If that weren't the case, surely it would be easy to push aside the attraction he still felt? And it wasn't just the sexual appeal either. Something about that self-containment of hers interested him. Maybe in it he saw an echo of his own distance from others, and couldn't help wondering where hers sprang from.

Whatever the reasons, it made dealing with her a constant strain, and now he wished she'd simply called up to the surgical floor to find out how the operation had gone, rather than waiting around. With a sigh of resignation he pushed through the doors into the corridor beyond.

She was in street clothes, a pair of jeans that fit her curves perfectly and a coral sweater that somehow made her skin glow. A handbag, the size of a small suitcase, was on her shoulder, and she carried her winter jacket over one arm. Apparently she was about to go home.

"How did it go?" she asked, with habitual directness.

"Pretty well," he replied, before giving her a more detailed account of the injuries he'd found and repaired. "I think she'll make a full recovery."

Liz glanced down the hall, toward the waiting area. "The police are waiting to speak to her. Apparently, she did shoot her boyfriend. I didn't realize he'd been brought in too, not long before she was."

Cort nodded. "Initially I was treating him, and then Dr. Hammond told Dr. Yuen to take over and sent me down to attend on Kaitlin."

Dr. Yuen was young, newly licensed and not as experienced as Cort with the types of multiple injuries Kaitlin had experienced. The younger doctor had seemed nonplussed to have been pulled away from such an interesting case, but what the chief of surgery decreed went.

Liz's face tightened for an instant, then smoothed out again. "Well, the boyfriend survived, and is telling the cops she shot him, and he was just defending himself when he beat and stabbed her. It'll be interesting to see how it all pans out."

"I'll let you know if I hear anything," he said. "It'll probably take a while for the cops to figure it out."

Liz nodded, turning on her heel. "Thanks. I'm on my way out, so I'll see you."

"See you," he replied to her retreating back, leaving him watching the enticing sway of her hips for a few moments before he caught himself and went to talk to the police.

CHAPTER FOUR

CORT WAS JUST doing his job, Liz thought sourly a week later, but that didn't stop her wishing he was doing it somewhere else. No matter his intent, his presence sure didn't improve productivity in the ER department.

She was sitting at a computer, doing some research, when Cort came down to speak to one of the other physicians about a case. It was slower in the department. While the emergency room was being revamped and expanded, there was less traffic, with more serious cases being routed to other hospitals in the area. Cort had been asked to take on more general surgery cases until things picked up again, and had apparently agreed without demurring. Right now he was consulting with Dr. Durham and a steady stream of nurses was coming by, each one lingering for what Liz considered to be an unconscionable time within gawking range.

He was a menace!

And why was he hanging about so long too? Surely he had rounds to do up on the surgical floor?

Yet all the gossip she'd heard about him so far was still of the glowing variety, not even counting the comments about his looks. The nurses loved him, had no complaints about either the way he handled his patients or how he dealt with staff, and they were usually the first to grumble and moan about the surgeons. Her own co-workers in the

ER department also seemed happy with how he interacted with them. Even Durham, the crankiest of them all, was right at this very minute grinning like a demented fool at Cort Smith.

Mind you, it was fairly rare to find a surgeon who was content to take a wait-and-see approach when the patient might, in the end, still need an op. From the conversation going on between Durham and Smith, that was exactly the situation they were discussing. Keeping her gaze on the screen in front of her didn't stop her from listening in.

"I'll be going off shift in about twenty minutes," Cort said. "But if Mrs. McClacken's obstruction doesn't sort itself out, I've briefed Dr. Morrison, and he's prepared to do the operation."

Durham snorted, his version of a laugh. "She'll be disappointed you're not operating."

Liz wanted to snort too, but not with laughter. She was too exhausted to find it funny, and blamed her sleepless nights squarely on Cort Smith. It was all too ridiculous, like working with a blasted rock star, having him around. Everyone wanted a piece of him. Not her, though, she reminded herself stoutly, despite the memories that had her tossing and turning at night, equal parts aroused and furious. It made having to see him every day a torment.

Worse, his easygoing manner and smiling demeanor reminded her of Andrew. Charming, lovable Andrew, who'd had everyone falling over themselves to please him, even Liz. But what he'd wanted from her had been so much more than she'd been able to give. He'd complained she wasn't affectionate enough, and the memory of being told she was too cold and controlled for him still stung all these years later.

It wasn't that she hadn't loved him. She had, so much so that she had been tempted, when he'd asked, to give up her studies and travel with him in Europe. Yet, in the end,

Andrew had broken her heart and gone off on his own, preferring adventure to a life with her, and leaving her to pick up the pieces of her life the best way she could. There had been a corner of her heart still hoping he would come back, say he'd been wrong and she was all he'd ever need, but it hadn't happened. Would never happen as, before they'd been able to mend the rift, he'd been killed in a motorcycle accident in Germany.

Durham had gone but now one of the nurses was asking Cort something, gazing up at him as though she'd just discovered religion and it was the Church of Smith. It was the same way women of all ages had stared at Andrew, and the similarity made Liz's stomach clench.

Forcing her gaze back down to the monitor, she tried to push aside the painful thoughts, but one thing remained clear. Staying away from Cort Smith as much as possible was the very best thing she could do, for her sanity, if nothing else.

"Excuse me, Dr. Prudhomme."

Liz looked up on hearing her name, but didn't recognize the young man standing beside her. "Yes?"

"Mrs. Lister, in HR, asked me to let you know that there are some changes being made to the credential verification process. She noticed it's been over nine months since your trip to Mexico and, since you tend to go on a medical mission trip once a year, she wanted you to be aware of the changes."

In her peripheral vision, she noticed Cort's head turn, as though he were looking at her, and she knew the mention of Mexico had attracted his attention. Her toes curled in her sneakers, heat bloomed in her belly, and it took all her concentration not to glance his way. Just the mention of her trip threatened to overwhelm her with all the memories she was trying so hard to suppress.

"Oh, thanks." She kept her voice level and her focus on

the man in front of her. "Could you tell Mrs. Lister I don't have a trip planned right now, but ask her to email me the new protocol so I have it on hand?"

"Sure, Dr. Prudhomme."

As he walked away, she turned her attention back to the website on myasthenia gravis. Committing to memory the information she wanted, she signed out of the system, but before she could get up, her cell phone pinged with an incoming text message, and she took it out to look.

Robbie, reminding her about her promise to attend a fundraising luncheon in his place the following day, since he was in London with Giovanna.

It made her annoyance peak.

When her great-aunts had left the majority of their wealth in a philanthropic fund and had named Liz as the trustee, she'd balked at the responsibility. Yet she owed them a debt and had known she couldn't refuse. Not only had they funded her schooling without hesitation, they'd also been a refuge for her, stalwart in their support of her ambitions when her parents had tried to talk her out of pursuing a medical career.

As a compromise, Robbie had agreed to sit on the board and become the face of the trust, which had made sense, since his financial contacts and experience would be invaluable. Not to mention how much more easily he mixed and mingled in the high social circles her family frequented.

But he was all caught up in the preparations for his wedding and, not unreasonably, wanted to spend as much time as possible with Giovanna. London Fashion Week was about to start, and he'd promised to be there while his fiancée modeled for a new, haute couture designer. Liz didn't blame him, but having to dress up and press the flesh while talking about nonprofits, investments and the like wasn't anywhere near the top of her favorite things list.

More like at the bottom.

Shoving her phone into her pocket, she tried not to look, but found her gaze drawn straight back to Cort. He was still listening to the nurse, but his attention was on Liz, and she couldn't help wondering if he, like her, had been drawn back into thoughts of their night together.

Dragging her gaze away from his, she got up. There were patients waiting for her, and putting some distance between her and Cort would be a very good thing just then. Liz pushed in her chair and had only taken a couple of steps when a nurse called out.

"Incoming baby, found in a dumpster. Hypothermic, unresponsive. Cops aren't waiting for the ambulance. They're bringing it in themselves."

Immediately Liz was moving, training taking over. With a glance at the board, she barked, "Room two. Sanjay, heat lamp and thermal blankets. Marion, warm saline and an oxygen hood. Jessica, call up to Pediatrics and have them on standby."

Then, as she set off at a run for the ambulance bay, she realized Cort was ahead of her, rushing to meet the incoming police car as though he were wearing a cape and only he could save the patient.

Oh, hell, no.

This was the kind of usurpation that shouldn't be allowed. There was absolutely no reason for him to be involved, and she didn't care if it was an instinctive reaction to hearing it was a child coming in. He couldn't be allowed to overreach his purview. Not on her watch.

He was sprinting toward the intake door and, with a burst of speed, she caught up to him just as he was going through it. The cold slapped her face, hard, stealing her breath for a moment, but then, with the sound of sirens screaming closer, she came up beside him. As she pulled on a pair of gloves, she said in her firmest voice, "Dr. Smith, you're not—"

Cort Smith turned and glanced down at her, and whatever she was planning to say next caught in her suddenly bone-dry throat.

There was an expression on his face she'd never seen before, and yet instinctively recognized. The blank stare spoke of hyper-focus, the tightness of mouth and jaw heralded not an unwillingness to yield but an inability. Curling her fingers into fists so tight she could feel her short nails through her gloves, she realized the futility of trying to block him from treating the child.

He turned away as the police car fishtailed on the thin slick of snow at the entrance to the bay, dismissing her, and Liz took a calming breath.

Later. She'd take him to task later.

The police car's front passenger door flew open even before the vehicle came to a complete stop, and a burly officer swung out. He looked to be hugging himself, holding his winter jacket closed as the wind caught the edge of the emergency blanket hanging down from below the edge of the coat, making it crackle and shimmer in the harsh lights.

Cort didn't try to take the child out of its warm cocoon but rushed the officer into the hospital.

"Room two," Liz called out, a step behind them.

"Homeless guy said he heard a noise from inside the dumpster, fished the baby out while someone called us." Even though he was running, the officer's voice was steady, factual. "Took us three minutes to get to the scene from the time the call came in. I thought I felt a pulse when we first got there, but there's been no movement or sound since. I think it's a newborn, but I'm not sure."

Cort swung through the door, guiding the officer, and Liz made no attempt to take the child, knowing Cort would do it, compelled as he was by some unknown force to take the lead. Instead, she moved quickly to the far side of the examination table, looking for the position of the heat lamp, making sure everything she needed was in place.

Cort unwrapped the child from the emergency blanket and the smelly fleece one beneath. The baby was tiny, smaller than she'd expected, and Liz pushed aside the stab of grief and fear she felt on seeing the fragile, exposed skin red from hypothermia. As the nurse lifted the baby to whisk away the blankets, Liz cut away the footie pajamas and then pulled off the diaper, revealing the gender.

A little girl.

Gauging the heat from the lamp, she pulled it slightly closer, warming the air around the table a bit more.

With a glance at her watch, she called out, "Someone call for a neonate team to attend, stat." In a quieter voice she continued, "Umbilical stump still attached, inexpertly tied off and cut. I estimate her to be about two days old."

Immediately on placing the baby on the table, Cort had fit his stethoscope into his ears and, as soon as practicable, put it to the tiny chest. Even with that in place, he also pressed fingers into the space between the head and shoulder for good measure, hoping for even the faintest pulse.

One of the nurses fit the oxygen hood over the infant's head, another stood by with electrodes, which Liz took from her and applied. Cort had to shift the chest piece of his scope to allow her to put the second one in place but, even as they were connected, and the agonizing sound of the flatline filled the room, he didn't move from his watch. Liz checked the time.

Thirty seconds.

She knew they had to wait at least a minute before declaring the baby to be without a heartbeat, but the urge to begin CPR was almost overwhelming.

Steady. Steady.

"Forty-five seconds," she said, her voice and the drone

of the cardiac monitor the only sounds audible. For a moment it felt as though no one moved, as if even her own breathing had stopped in sympathy. All were caught in the gray area between despair and hope, anticipation of what would come next filling the emergency room with swiftly ratcheting tension.

Then the monitor beeped, just as Cort said, "We have a heartbeat," and they were all in motion again.

"IV," Liz said, putting out her hand. It was difficult to find a vein but she got the needle in place just as the neonate team arrived. Cort stepped back to give them room, stood there as Liz brought them up to speed and they transferred the tiny figure to the rolling incubator in preparation for taking her to the NICU.

With a final flurry they were gone, and Liz exhaled, slowly pulling off her gloves. Cort turned and left the room, and she hurried to catch up to him, cursing under her breath. Just outside the door the police officers stood, one on either side of the door, as if on guard.

"Doc, what's—?"

But Cort, who'd never shown himself to be anything other than courteous and considerate, strode past the cop who was trying to speak to him, as though unaware of the officer's existence. It was left to Liz to stop, and she bit back a surge of annoyance as Cort disappeared down the corridor.

The look on the officer's face stirred her pity, made her think that because of Cort's behavior he expected to hear the worst.

"Officer..."

"Wachowski," he supplied.

"Officer Wachowski, the baby is still alive, though in critical condition, but I'm personally hopeful she'll survive."

He turned away, but not before she saw his face crumple and she knew it was relief making this huge, grizzled officer lose control and cry.

With a hand on his shoulder, she leaned closer, so only he could hear, and said, "You saved that baby's life today. Anything we could do would be useless if it weren't for you. Never forget that, okay?"

He nodded, gulped once, and his voice was rough and barely audible as he said, "Thanks, Doc."

"It's a girl, Wach," she heard the other officer say, as she took off down the corridor, chased by the sound of back-slapping and relieved laughter. "We need to get some cigars."

Although she searched for him, there was no sign of Cort so, still fuming, Liz went back to work. No doubt he'd avoided her and then gone home, his shift over for the day.

Three hours later, when her shift too came to a close, Liz changed into her street clothes and, unable to resist, made her way up to the sixth-floor neonatal unit.

She'd always been superstitious about certain things, including checking on patients after they'd left the ER and been admitted. More than once another doctor or a nurse had said, "Why didn't you just call for an update, instead of coming all this way?" but that didn't feel right. If she wanted to know how a patient was doing she either checked the system, knowing it might not be up to date, or physically went to check on them. Having not been able to get the tiny baby off her mind, she definitely had to go up and look in on her.

And there, in the NICU, was Cort.

Liz came to a halt, watching through the glass as, the infant held securely in the crook of his arm, he used his foot to move the rocking chair back and forth. Completely focused on the little girl, he was looking down into her face, and the infant seemed to be just as focused on him, her eyes open, unwavering.

His lips moved and, although she couldn't hear him, Liz knew he said, "I've got you, sweetheart. I've got you."

Taking a shaky breath, feeling exposed, stripped bare, Liz backed away, not wanting him to see her; afraid of what was written on her face.

Afraid of the shocking desire rushing through her veins to go in there and hold them both.

CHAPTER FIVE

"JUST CHECKING IN with you." Robbie's voice, annoyingly cheerful, boomed through the phone into her ear. Liz could hear a babble of conversation and peals of laughter behind him. It was early afternoon in London, but it sounded as though a party was already in full swing. "You remember the luncheon, right?"

"Yes. I'm on my way there now."

Not quite accurate, since she'd mislaid her invitation and was actually on her way to the hospital, hoping it was in her locker. While looking for things in her handbag, she had a tendency to pull out whatever was in her way, leaving them where they lay. She'd searched her entire house without finding it, and was trying to convince herself it must be in her work locker. If it wasn't, she was in trouble, since the organizer had specifically said the invitations were necessary for admission.

"Well, have a good time."

Laughter was clear in Robbie's voice. The brat knew how much she hated these types of events.

"Yeah. Sure."

He snickered, then said, "While we're on the subject of favors, I have another one to ask."

"Really? This isn't enough for you?" she teased. "You

want to impose on me further, after making me have to spend the morning at the hairdresser and get dressed up?"

"Oh, you're not wearing your scrubs? I'm shocked!"

The over-the-top horror of her brother's comment made her give a snort of laughter.

"That's right, go ahead and make fun of me, even though you want something. See how far that gets you."

When Robbie replied, he'd grown serious. "I want you to be my best woman."

"Your what?"

"Um, best girl? I don't know what to call it. Female best man? Damn it, I want you to stand up with me at my wedding."

Shocked, she said the first thing that came to mind. "But…what about Simon? Didn't you already ask him to be your best man?"

"We've known each other so long he knows how I feel about you, and he won't mind. Besides, he's already stressing about being in charge of the rings. You know how he is."

She did indeed, since Robbie and Simon had been friends from grade school. "He is a little scatterbrained," she remarked, grimacing at saying so when on her way to try to find her lost invitation.

Misplaced, not lost. Just misplaced.

"And," her brother said quickly, as though sensing he was winning, "I'm a groomsman short, so it would be perfect."

She wasn't surprised to hear that, really. Although Robbie knew lots of people, and had the kind of personality that attracted others to him, when it came to true friends he was highly selective. Liz and he were very different in many ways, but identical in that one.

"Robbie, I don't think—"

Robbie interrupted to say, "Giovanna has already picked out a dress for you to wear and everything."

Liz suppressed a groan. Her mother had sent pictures of not only the wedding dress but the bridesmaids' dress too. They were beautiful. Artistically sublime.

And she would look like hell in one, with far too many curves to do justice to a dress like that.

She was scrambling to figure out the best way to get out of it without hurting her beloved brother's feelings when there was a muffled conversation on the other end of the phone, and then Giovanna came on the line.

"Liz, you must do this. It would mean the world to us. I understood when you said you didn't want to be a bridesmaid, really I did, but this is Robbie asking, not me."

"Giovanna—"

"Liz, we *love* you. It wouldn't be the same if you're not involved."

There was the sensation of being run over by a steamroller, and Liz chuckled, knowing her mother had definitely met her match in her future daughter-in-law.

"I could just wear a morning suit, I guess. To match the men."

"Are you *nuts*?" The outrage was almost palpable. "Not on my watch. Never. But there's a designer in New York who does menswear-inspired formal gowns, and I know I can get her to kit you out. I'll send you a link to her website. When she's done with you, you'll outshine me, with your glorious figure and perfect shoulders."

Liz snorted. "Yeah, sure, Giovanna."

"Trust me, okay? It'll be perfect."

"All right, all right. I see I have one more person in my life I'm not going to be able to say no to. I'll do it. For you. And Robbie."

"Yes!"

Luckily she liked Giovanna too much to be put out by that triumphant crow.

The town car was pulling into the hospital parking lot so she said, "I've got to run. Love to you both, and keep Robbie out of trouble, okay?"

After hanging up, she directed the driver to the staff entrance and, once he'd pulled up, she didn't wait for him to come around and open her door but jumped out.

"I shouldn't be long," she leaned in to say as she pulled her badge out of her handbag. "If they come by and tell you to move, just drive around and meet me back here, please."

Thank goodness the maintenance people had been out and the path to the door had been shoveled and salted. Winter was behaving like a petulant child who was overtired and fighting sleep. Every time she thought it might be dozing off, it awoke again and had a snow-and-ice tantrum.

Cursing the high-heeled boots she was wearing, Liz held her coat closed and made her way as briskly as possible into the building, then set out at a trot for the changing area. She barreled through the door just in time to be treated to the sight of Cort Smith pulling off a bloodstained scrub top.

It brought her to a screeching halt.

There was the long, strong back she remembered all too well, muscles flexing and rippling the way they had under her grasping, greedy hands. His scrubs bottom hung low on his hips and clung to his perfectly shaped backside. As she stood, frozen in place, watching him, he stretched and yawned, then twisted his head from side to side, as though working out muscle kinks.

She had a few kinks she wouldn't mind having him work out, she thought through the lust fogging her brain.

He reached into his locker for a clean shirt, thankfully still turned away so he wouldn't see her gawping. She tried to get her feet to move, even as her gaze devoured the sheer gorgeousness of him.

The door clicked shut behind her and he looked over his shoulder. For one long moment, which seemed set to stretch into infinity, their gazes locked, and an electric current filled the room, making all the hair on her body rise in a prickling wave.

Mortified to be caught staring, as aroused as all get-out, she sprang into action, aware of her racing heart and the incredible heat rampaging through her body. Willfully keeping her face averted from him, she made it to her locker without falling, although her legs were trembling.

"Hey," he said from behind her. "I thought you were off today."

"I am." Her voice sounded strained, even to her, so she swallowed before she continued. "Just stopped by to try and find an invitation I've mislaid."

"You look…spiffy."

She snorted as she got the locker open and stared at the mess of papers and detritus on the shelf, frustrated at herself for letting it get so bad. "Spiffy? Who on earth uses a word like spiffy? Besides geriatrics and a few nerdy history buffs."

"I do," he said. "Are you calling me old? Because I sucked at history in school."

Her heart was still beating too fast, but the banter, so unexpectedly easy, helped to calm her overexcited system. "If the shoe fits…"

"Really?" Outrage and disgruntlement battled for supremacy in his tone. "It's a perfectly viable word. Perfectly politically correct. Better than saying something inappropriate to your coworker."

"Inappropriate? Like what?" she asked, glancing at him for an instant over her shoulder. His hair was adorably rumpled from pulling the shirt on over his head, and her fingers tingled with the urge to smooth it, or mess it up even more.

"Like saying she looks delicious enough to eat."

And there went her heart rate again.

Unable to come up with a suitable reply, she desperately shuffled through the teetering stack of bills, notes and other detritus. Where the heck was the darn invitation? He was standing close enough that the subtle scent of him, warm and delicious, wafted over her, all but making her mouth water.

"Where you off to anyway, looking so *spiffy*?"

Normally she wouldn't answer such an intrusive question, but she was still flustered and the words just popped out.

"A luncheon for donors and trustees of philanthropic trusts to meet and network with each other. There's a trust my family administers, and normally my brother would have gone but he's in London with his fiancée for Fashion Week, so it's all on me this time."

"Okay…" It was said slowly, almost hesitantly. "Sounds good."

"Boring as hell," she replied, trying to get back onto the brisk, no-nonsense footing she was used to. "All investment potential, capital growth, and talking about 'beneficial partnerships,' none of which interest me in the slightest. To be honest, I'd rather be lancing a boil than facing this do."

He chuckled, and it seeped into her bones, made her fingers suddenly clumsy, so she pulled too hard on the stack of papers she was riffling through, causing a mini-avalanche. "Dammit."

"So the medical mission to Mexico the HR guy mentioned was arranged by this family trust of yours?"

He sounded merely curious, but the mention of Mexico brought a fresh wave of heat washing through her.

She'd tried so hard not to think about what had happened on that trip, hoping the after-effects would fade, but now had to admit to herself they hadn't, and probably wouldn't.

Perhaps talking about it with Cort would help take the edge off her obsession with it.

And him.

Taking a steadying breath, she turned to face him.

"No. Mexico is outside the trust's purview. It was set up to help organizations here in New York City, where my grand-aunts lived. Do you remember the group of women I was with in Mexico?"

He nodded, a little smile coming and going across those beautifully shaped lips.

"Vaguely."

"We've all been friends from when we were teenagers and don't get that much of a chance to see each other. About six years ago we decided we'd take trips together but make them useful, not just fun. So we take turns picking a place, usually somewhere that has some meaning to us, and the first part of the trip is spent working with locals to do whatever will be of the most help to them. Then we spend the last few days at a resort, relaxing and enjoying ourselves."

His eyebrows quirked upward slightly, and he asked, "You're all doctors?"

Liz chuckled. She couldn't help it, thinking of her friend Jojo, who fainted if she got a paper cut. "No. I'm the only one, so I helped out at the local pediatric clinic while the others did some building repairs and teaching."

"Ah, a pediatric clinic. Does that explain the aqua hair?"

She'd forgotten about the colorful extensions she'd gotten on a whim for the trip, thinking it would be something fun for the kids. It felt strange to think he'd already gotten to know her so well he was able to figure that out.

"It was an icebreaker," she admitted.

His eyelids drooped, concealing whatever thoughts might be given away in his gaze.

"I liked it," he said.

A simple statement, but for some reason it packed a punch. Perhaps it was his expression, which took her right back to that gloriously decadent night they'd shared, or the way his voice dropped low. Whatever the reason, memories bombarded her—of his fingers fisted in her hair, his lips ravaging her throat, the ecstasy building and building until, at his growled demand, she'd imploded.

Insides thrumming with rising want, Liz knew she'd been right not to want to talk about Mexico with him, but it was too late. The remnants of the night swirled between them, creating a sultry current, as warm and humid as the air on the Mayan Riviera. She knew Cort felt it too. He'd gone still, his face tightening to a mask of naked yearning.

Liz shivered, trapped by his desire, and her own. In Mexico, in his arms, she'd felt more a woman than ever before in her life. And now, seeing him once more focused completely, intently on her, the same sensation flowered into being again.

The urge to take the steps necessary to embrace him, pull his head down and kiss him, was so strong Liz wasn't sure how she resisted.

Then, just as suddenly as the expression of desire had appeared on his face, it was gone.

Shaken, Liz tore her gaze away, turning back to her locker. Her hands were trembling, her insides churned with need. She had to get out of there. Now.

Where on earth is that damned invitation?

Cort took a deep breath, but it did nothing to quell his libido. And it definitely needed to be quelled. Liz Prudhomme attracted him in a primal way but, even if he weren't determined to stay away from entanglements of any kind, she'd already run out on him once. No doubt she'd do it again, should he give her a chance. Besides he knew, without a doubt, she was way out of his league socially.

She spoke about philanthropic trusts and London Fashion Week as though they were everyday things that everyday people like him would know all about. Even the way she looked today screamed wealth of the highest order.

In complete contrast to her usual ponytail or simple bob, her hair was upswept in an intricate yet subtly sexy style. And even he, who knew absolutely nothing about designer clothing, could tell there was something special about the long, luxurious-looking coat and knee-high boots she was wearing. The coat fit perfectly over her curves and swung with casual elegance as she moved. Beneath it he glimpsed a teal dress that again, to his eye, looked to have been made just for her.

Liz was all class, and nothing but trouble, and he was kicking himself for wanting her so badly.

She'd gone back to searching her locker, and it felt like a subtle dismissal, yet not even that dulled his desire, or made him leave, the way he knew he should.

What had happened in Mexico hung between them. He couldn't help thinking they would never have a truly easy working relationship until they had talked it out. Clearly the attraction between them hadn't abated, and he wasn't sure what that would mean. All he knew was that he was compelled to let her know where he stood, no matter where it eventually led.

"I know you don't want to talk about Mexico."

"You're right," she replied briskly, as another little cascade of papers fell from her locker. "So let's not."

"Too late," he retorted, and saw her shoulders stiffen slightly. "Listen, we're both adults, and it's best we deal with what happened between us. It was an amazing night. One I'll never forget. I was angry, and lonely, and you helped me forget the pain and embarrassment, even if just for one night. But, although I'm still extremely attracted to you, I'm not going to try to get back into your bed, because…"

Why not?

He took a breath, considering what he needed to say next. Liz's fingers stilled, her hunt paused as she waited for him to continue. His brain scrambled for the reasons, knowing they were many, trying to move past the attraction and get to the reality.

"Not only do we work together, but I don't want to lead you on. I've come to realize I'm not cut out for long-term relationships. Couldn't offer you anything more than the chance to keep scratching the itch, the way we did in Mexico."

She looked at him over her shoulder, eyebrows raised, her gaze searching his. "But you were about to get married. I'd think that would have been a long-term relationship, don't you?"

He nodded. "Sure, but I realized having the wedding called off was a good thing. There were…extenuating circumstances that caused me to sort of drift into a situation I really shouldn't have."

"How does one drift into an engagement?" she asked, not derisively but obviously curious.

His first urge was to deflect the question, but something about the way she looked at him drew the words from his lips.

"Mimi, my ex, was there for me during a bad time in my life, and gave me the support I needed. It was only after she ended our relationship that I realized we'd mistaken our friendship for something more than it was."

Her eyes narrowed slightly, but her gaze was level as she said, "When we met, you were pretty upset about the break-up. How can you be so casual about it now?"

Cort sighed. He must sound like the kind of guy who shrugged things off when he didn't get what he wanted, and somehow the thought of her pegging him like that was abhorrent.

"I've had some time to think it through, to realize that, while her rejection hurt like hell, we really wouldn't have been happy together. I have itchy feet, Liz. Being in the army alleviated some of that, even though the coveted posting to Hawaii never materialized."

That made the corners of her lips twitch, but when she didn't say anything he continued. "I stayed in Denver too long, and now I'm determined not to settle in any one place for any length of time again. I've never spent any time in New York, and there's a lot to explore, but once my contract is up next year, I'll more than likely move on."

Liz seemed to be considering what he'd said, her gaze searching his face. He'd come to realize she was a thinker, one of those people who liked to mull things over and rarely acted impulsively. It was obvious in how she handled patients and their families, as well as the people she worked with, although in an emergency she was absolutely decisive.

So it came as no surprise when she just made a noncommittal sound in the back of her throat before diving back into her locker.

Taking that as a clear dismissal, he was about to leave then remembered there was something more he wanted to tell her.

"On a totally different subject, I thought you'd want to know. The police cleared Kaitlin of wrongdoing. From the forensic evidence, she shot her boyfriend in self-defense."

"Good to know," she replied, emerging triumphantly with an embossed card in her hand. When she bent to pick up the bits of paper that had spilled out onto the floor, he stooped to help her and was surprised by the obvious anger in her expression.

"You're angry that it was self-defense?"

"What? No! Why would you ask such a question?"

"Oh, maybe the way your brows are scrunched together, the slight snarl on your lips."

Cort thought that would, at least, merit a snort or the Liz Prudhomme version of a smile, which consisted of a twitch of the lips, but her frown just deepened.

"He beat and stabbed her, almost to death, and all she was worried about was that she'd shot him to save herself. Even when I went to ICU to see her, she was asking about him. I don't get it. I really don't."

Getting up, she shoved the papers back into her locker and slammed the door. Cort shook his head. He didn't get it either, but he'd seen it too many times not to know the answer. "She'd say she loves him."

Liz snorted then, but not with anything close to amusement, as she picked up her handbag and headed for the door. "Makes no sense to me. Never has. Never will. That's not love. That's some kind of terminal disease that weakens the brain."

Yanking the door open, she turned back and said, "Wait, that sounds like an accurate definition, doesn't it? At least, from everything *I've* seen."

Then she was gone, leaving Cort stunned at the emotion in her voice, which had turned the decadent tones into something rougher. Raw.

It was not the kind of response he expected from the no-nonsense Dr. Liz Prudhomme.

CHAPTER SIX

Dr. Hammond's secretary looked up as Cort opened the door and, without pausing in her telephone conversation, jerked her head toward the inner office. Taking the gesture from the stern, gray-haired lady as an indication he should continue straight through, Cort thanked her with a wave. He knocked on Gregory's door and, when the chief of surgery called out, entered the sunny, cluttered office.

"There you are." The smile on Gregory's face had the tension in Cort's shoulders easing fractionally. "And right on time too. Come. Sit."

Making his way to the stiffly stuffed chair across the desk from his boss, Cort did as bade, still unsure about the reason for the summons. There was no way to get comfortable in the visitor's seat, probably by design, but he forced himself not to search for one. Instead, he simply propped one ankle up on the opposite knee and resigned himself to the ache he'd no doubt develop in his back if the interview went on too long.

He also figured it best to cut right to the chase.

"Is there a problem, Gregory?"

"No, not at all." The older man leaned back, linking his fingers behind his neck, the picture of ease. "I thought, since you've been with us for a little over a month now, it was time to check in with you and see how you're getting along."

That was surprising. Cort had been almost completely sure Liz had complained about his takeover of the infant emergency case, had been prepared to apologize and reassure everyone it would never happen again. Even though that really wasn't a promise he could truthfully make.

"Everything is fine so far." There really was nothing he could complain about to Gregory. All his issues with being at the hospital revolved around one strong, sexy doctor, who was never far from his thoughts.

"Glad to hear it." Gregory rocked back and forth. "I know things are a bit slower than you're used to in the trauma department, but the board has said the construction should be finished in another few months. Things will definitely pick up soon thereafter."

"I'm sure they will," he agreed.

"And how are things otherwise? Did you get your house in Denver sold, and have you found something appropriate here?"

"Finally got an offer on the house last week, and hopefully it'll close in thirty days," Cort replied, giving the older man a rueful smile. "But as for here? To be honest, I haven't really been looking very hard."

He didn't feel the need to house-hunt. He'd only bought the house in Denver because he and Mimi had been getting married and it had seemed appropriate. His New York apartment, while small, was perfectly suitable for the year. Of course, he wasn't planning to say that to Dr. Hammond, who no doubt hoped Cort would be a permanent member of his surgical team.

Gregory shook his head, and sat forward with a thump of feet hitting the floor. "No, no, Cort. If you want to stay anywhere within the vicinity of the hospital, with the gentrification now is the time to buy. Even if you eventually leave Hepplewhite General, and I hope that won't be for many years, by then the property should have appreciated nicely." The telephone on his desk buzzed, and Gregory put his hand on it but didn't pick it up right away. "Well, unless there's anything you want to discuss…"

Cort levered himself from the chair. "No, thank you, Gregory."

"Excellent." Gregory smiled, but he was already looking at his phone, and Cort strode to the door and let himself out, just as he heard the other man say, "Yes, Brenda?"

Brenda, the secretary, was speaking in a discreetly low tone into the phone when Cort walked through her office and didn't look up from her computer screen, so missed his goodbye wave.

That annoyed him a little. No matter what your position in life, there was no need to be ill-mannered. No doubt, as Gregory's secretary, she had to be firm with some of the doctors, perhaps even patients too, but there were ways to do that without being rude.

Like the way Liz handled things, straight up but never impolite.

He mentally kicked himself for thinking about her again, yet she continually invaded his consciousness like a superbug, impervious to every course of treatment he came up with to oust her.

As he'd told her the day before, there were at least two really good reasons for them not to be together again, but unfortunately neither stopped him wanting her. The way she'd run out on him in Mexico still stung too, especially now he'd gotten to know her day-to-day persona better. Had that night never happened, he'd have sworn Liz Prudhomme wasn't the kind of woman who'd sneak away without saying a word or even leaving a note. She was too no-nonsense and polite, too straightforward. The anomaly of what he thought of her and the reality of that night should be a warning and have tempered the longing, but hadn't.

There was something about her that called to him and that draw of hers was a source of constant distraction and annoyance.

He forewent the elevator, opting for the stairs, hoping to work off some of his frustration.

Avoiding entanglements was the right thing to do, he reminded himself as he pounded down the stairs. Getting too involved with people just caused pain, and he was tired of being hurt.

So many good reasons to avoid Liz and squelch the attraction still dogging him. In time to the slap of his feet on the steps, he listed them in his head one more time, hoping they'd finally take root in his stubborn brain.

She was a colleague, and he had to work with her almost every day.

He had a life plan all worked out, which didn't include sticking around in New York City for very long. There were new places to discover, new worlds to explore, and he who travelled fastest travelled alone.

Best of all, he already had proof she was the kind of woman who had no compunction about leaving a person high and dry, without explanation.

Like his parents had, when they'd abandoned him as a baby.

Like Brody had, without giving Cort a chance to help him through his pain.

Pushing open the door to the on-call room, he was glad to see there was no one there. Letting out a relieved sigh, he moved to the coffee station and poured himself a cup. Thankfully the meeting with Gregory hadn't taken as long as he'd thought it would, so he had time to gather his thoughts before his shift started.

He'd been sure there would have been a complaint regarding his conduct when Baby Jane, as the unidentified infant was being called, had come in. Even now, the memory of hearing the nurse call out about the baby being found in a dumpster raised goose bumps down his spine.

It was like being present at his own finding, the instinct to help another foundling so strong it had completely blocked all thoughts of protocol.

Why hadn't Liz complained? He'd been certain that she would.

The woman was a mass of contradictions.

Some of the nurses called her "Dr. Grim," yet it was said with a certain amused fondness that told him they actually liked her. Many of the doctors grumbled about her stoic demeanor, but not one touted her as being anything but a superb practitioner. Everyone knew she was a stickler for protocol, and it was clear Cort had overstepped his bounds by a mile. Not reporting him to Hammond was totally out of character for her.

And he didn't like it that he was beginning to know her so well.

Getting to understand her on a personal level wouldn't help him at all. Easier to get past his attraction if he could keep his interest in her purely professional. He had no interest in getting close to Liz Prudhomme in any way other than they already had been.

Carnally, erotically, sexually.

He drew in a sharp breath at the memory of her arching beneath his caresses, shuddering with release. Trying to push aside the images just made them somehow sharper, and it was as though he could feel her legs around his waist again, the slick pulses of her body gripping his, the swift, sweet ache of her biting his shoulder as she'd come.

Taking a too-hot gulp of coffee, he cursed. Yet he welcomed the burn of tongue and throat. It forced some modicum of control, allowing him the opportunity to settle his breathing and will away the unwanted erection pushing at the front of his scrubs.

That was in the past, never to happen again, he forcefully reminded himself. The sooner he took that fully on board, and stopped obsessing over one night in Mexico, the better it would be for his peace of mind.

The door behind him opened and he turned, a polite expression firmly in place, to see who it was.

And, just like that, he had to marshal his willpower all over again as he stared into Liz's gleaming green eyes.

He would have greeted her, but something about her expression kept him frozen in watchful silence. She was leaning on the door, as though to stop anyone else from entering, both palms pressed against the wood, fingers slightly curled, and something about the position of her hands stirred that ever-present desire again.

The silence seemed to stretch on forever as she looked around the room before she quietly said, "I want you to know, I'm not interested in a relationship."

Surprise was too mild a word for what he felt, and a harsh bark of laughter came from his throat. Her eyebrows dipped together as he replied, "I told you, I'm not either."

"But I want you, physically. If you're interested, can you deal with that? Sex without any kind of commitment?"

His heart was pounding, and his impulse was to agree quickly, before she changed her mind, but he turned what she said over in his mind first, strangely prudent in the face of what looked like her impulsiveness.

"I can do that," he said slowly, inwardly cursing himself for what he was going to say next. Knowing it would probably make her change her mind. "But you should know, I actually *like* you. What happens if we become friends?"

She tilted her head slightly, as though this was an eventuality she hadn't considered, her gaze searching his intently. Whatever she saw there seemed to satisfy her because she nodded and asked, "Do you know where the old isolation ward is?"

"Yes." Gregory Hammond had shown it to him on the first day, while they'd toured the construction zone. Cort was pretty sure he remembered how to get to it.

"Meet me there in five minutes."

Then, without another word, she spun on her heel and pulled open the door.

It wasn't until the door closed completely that Cort could exhale, and there definitely was nothing he could do about the need tearing through his system.

Slapping his coffee cup down onto the table, he glanced at his watch.

He was sure it would be the longest five minutes of his life.

If Liz knew one thing about herself it was that she tried to face things head on and didn't back away from the truth, even if she was the only one who knew what that truth was. That facet of her personality made her come to accept the fact she had to do something about Dr. Cort Smith, something to exorcise the hold he had on her imagination and libido.

He'd taken over her mind in a way she'd never experienced before, filling her with yearnings she didn't know how to control.

It was, she told herself, simply that he'd given her the most memorable night of sex she'd ever had, and then, to add insult to injury, had touched her emotionally too. Seeing him so tenderly holding the baby in the NICU had been like having the wall around the feelings she so fiercely guarded severely dented.

On the one hand, she hated him for it. On the other, it made her want him ten times, a hundred times more than she already did. The conversation in the changing room had just cemented the longing that had shimmered beneath her skin from the first night they'd met.

Striding down the corridor past the heavy plastic sheeting, from beyond which came the noise of the construction workers, she once more reassured herself she was taking the right course in dealing with Cort.

He had taken her to new heights with his dominant style in bed, giving her more pleasure than she'd even suspected was possible. A shiver worked its way along her spine and heat blossomed low in her belly as she remembered it once again. That pleasure that had lingered in her system, rather like a bad case of the flu or Lyme disease, she thought rather sourly. She needed an antidote, and perhaps familiarity would provide it.

After all, their encounter in Mexico had happened before he'd known her, before he'd seen her at work or worked alongside her.

Now he'd had a chance to see her the way others had and did. To her family, and to Andrew, she was a tough, cool, unemotional woman, used to taking charge, unwilling to relinquish her control.

Would he still feel comfortable taking command of her body the way he had before?

She doubted it. And if he didn't, she was quite sure she'd lose interest in him very, very quickly.

And if he did, then at least she'd have the chance at the physical satisfaction she craved.

His stated aversion to a relationship made it all the better. Unlike Andrew, Cort at least was honest about that, and about his wanderlust. She could go into this knowing there wouldn't be complications. That she wouldn't be blindsided by unreasonable expectations or a sudden abandonment when those expectations weren't met.

Reaching the end of the corridor and leaving the main construction zone behind, she turned down another hallway, then made a quick left into the isolation ward. It had been packed with some of the equipment they'd had to store during the expansion, so that on entering the room she was presented with what looked a bit like a maze. And, as she stood a couple of steps from the door, she was suddenly assailed with something akin to fear. It held her where she was, her back toward the door, heart pounding, lust like quicksilver in her veins. Her legs trembled as the need in her core spread outwards and her nipples ached in anticipation.

Not fear, she reassured herself. Desire, and the overwhelming need to know whether Cort would assuage it or be found lacking this time around.

She wasn't sure which she'd prefer...

The quiet click of the door opening had her scrambling for enough control to turn and face him, but she didn't get a chance to pull herself together before his deep voice reached her.

"Are we here to talk, or something else?" He was close behind her. The heat pouring off his body made gooseflesh pop up all along her back and arms, and had her breath catching in her throat. "I'm taking nothing for granted when it comes to you, Liz, so tell me why I'm here."

"I want you." The words flowed far too easily from her lips, but it was the truth, and she was big on the truth, even if she didn't feel ready to face him just yet. "Right now."

"Good." It was a growl, and he surrounded her with his strong, solid arms, the hardness of his erection pressing between her buttocks. "I wasn't sure I'd be able to restrain myself if you wanted a discussion."

She would have replied, except he nipped her nape, the sharp scrape of his teeth along the sensitive skin making her breath hitch and her mind stumble over its thoughts.

"Over here," he said, the harshness of his voice striking sparks over her skin, ratcheting up the tension in her core. He curved his arms tighter around her waist and half guided, half carried her between two fabric-shrouded machines into the dim space beyond. She caught a quick glance of more machinery, some gurneys, other unidentifiable shapes, before he turned her within his arms and kissed her.

Her bones went liquid. The rush of lust engendered just by the touch of his lips on hers, the tangle of their tongues was almost too much to bear. A moan rose in her throat and she couldn't curtail it. The sound, needy and rushed, was one she couldn't recall ever hearing herself make before. When she felt the cool of a wall against her back, she arched into Cort, her need all she was aware of.

Strong hands tugged her scrub top up, and she raised her arms, eager for it to be gone, to get flesh-to-flesh with Cort. They broke the kiss to be able to get it off, but when Liz turned her face, searching for his lips, and wound her arms around his neck again, Cort didn't respond the way she expected. Instead of kissing her again, he dropped her top and grasped her wrists, lifting them above her head and holding them there with one hand.

"You've made me crazy." His free hand slid down her arm to skim the side of her breast through the remainder of her clothing. Just that indirect touch made her tremble, yearn. "You owe me."

"For what?" She had to force the words out past the desperation clogging her throat.

The sound he made was possibly supposed to have been a chuckle, but it came out as a snarl. "For every swing of your hips as you walked down the corridors. For every word you've spoken to me since I got here. For every look from those beautiful eyes." He let his voice trail away, his dark gaze holding hers effortlessly in the gloom as his fingers found her nipple, pinched, and proved he remembered exactly what turned her on. "I want payment."

"With what?"

She tried to make her voice defiant, amused, but there was no mistaking the slight tremor in the words. Cort smiled, a predatory, knowing grin she could see even in the low light. When he leaned in and put his lips close to her ear, Liz already knew she was in trouble before he whispered, "Your pleasure. And mine."

When had he lifted the camisole she wore under her scrubs? And how had he got her bra undone with one hand? Then the questions were driven from her mind by the sensation of his mouth on her breasts, the promise made by his pushing her scrub bottoms and panties down to her knees.

Desperation rose in her, she was already so close to the edge. The urge to widen her stance, give him full access, made her shift her legs, restlessly trying to work her pants down farther. He said, "Stay still."

With arms still upraised, although he'd let them go, Liz froze, shivering at the command in his tone, at the way her desire flared even higher. It was like Mexico all over again, when he'd held her in thrall, taken her compliance and turned it into ecstasy. As he kissed and nipped and sucked his way down her body, it felt as if time slowed, warped, and it took forever for him to reach where she wanted him; where she needed him to touch. When she finally felt the heat of his breath between her thighs, she again wanted to open for him, but his injunction to remain still held her where she was.

"Don't hold back," he said, the words vibrating into her flesh, making her bite her lip to stop from begging, her breathing so erratic she felt light-headed. "Come for me, Liz. Come hard."

And when he pressed his mouth against her, it took only the lightest touch for her to explode.

"Good girl," he groaned against her still-quivering flesh. "And one more…"

CHAPTER SEVEN

LIZ MADE A quick dash into the ladies' room, which was thankfully empty.

Her legs were trembling, her body humming with endorphins. As she washed her hands and splashed cold water on her face, she tried to put aside all thought of what had just transpired. According to the page she'd just got, there were casualties coming in from a multivehicle accident so she needed to be prepared, not shaky and discombobulated.

She'd think about the fact Cort Smith had once more rocked her world later. Much later.

After all, it was just sex.

Fabulous sex.

But just sex.

Nothing worth disrupting her life over.

If nothing else, she had her answer. Getting him out of her system would probably be more difficult than she had anticipated. Yet they had an agreement. No entanglements, no repercussions from their pleasure. No bleeding over from the personal into the professional. And she would swiftly put an end to this new arrangement if he made the mistake of changing the way he behaved toward her on the hospital floor.

She'd been brutally honest about not being interested in a relationship, and he'd said the same. Hopefully she really could trust him to stand by their agreement to not get in any way attached. It wasn't that she thought herself irresistible or anything like that, just that men hardly ever said what they meant or stood by their agreements. She'd be on guard for any change in his behavior, and that was the best she could do. She was still sure that propositioning him again had been the right idea, even though something niggled at the back of her mind, trying to sow doubt.

Perhaps it was how much his personality reminded her of Andrew. The charm that had people falling over themselves to please him, and had them gravitating into his sphere. She'd fallen for that once and refused to fall for it again. Men like him would suck you dry, demanding you change to suit them better, and then, when you were willing to do anything to keep them, left you anyway. At least Cort had been up front in saying he wouldn't be around for very long, and Liz had no intention of allowing herself to get emotionally involved in any way.

What he'd said about them becoming friends didn't deserve a lot of consideration. She'd never made friends easily and guarded her friendships fiercely. Her friends could be counted on the fingers of one hand and were people who accepted her as she was, without expectation that she'd change to suit them or the situation. Who understood that to ask her opinion was to get an honest answer, even if she knew it wasn't what they wanted to hear. Perhaps her only male friend was Robbie, and did he even count as he was her brother too?

There was a lot to think about now that she'd taken this irrevocable step, but she'd never been the type to dwell, or have regrets, or constantly rehash every decision she made, and she wasn't going to start now.

Giving herself a last long look in the mirror, hoping no one would notice how puffy her lips were, she strode out of the restroom, heading for the ER.

* * *

By the time the first casualties got to the hospital, Liz and the rest of the staff were braced for the controlled chaos to come. A tour bus, on its way out of the city, had struck a couple of cars and gone off the road. The more severely injured patients were being sent to Roosevelt, the nearest level one center, with the rest of the injured being distributed between Hepplewhite and another level two facility.

She just had time to notice Cort putting on a disposable gown before the first ambulances pulled up. For an instant their gazes locked, and a shiver raced down her spine. Then the doors flew open and the gurneys started coming in, and she had no time to think about anything but her patients.

And it was only at the end of the long, grueling day she realized there'd been no awkwardness. They'd worked together as smoothly as they had since he'd arrived, treating a couple of patients together without even an untoward glance or comment from him. And, although her heart still did that silly dip when she heard his voice, she was pleased to realize the anxiety and desire that had kept her on edge seemed to have waned.

It seemed as though her plan to mitigate her reaction to him might just be working after all.

Cort couldn't find an ounce of regret about his tryst with Liz, although part of him was kicking himself for letting it happen.

There had been no postmortem between them. No questioning whether it had been right or wrong, good or not as good as either of them remembered. Her beeper had gone off and, with calm deliberation, she'd righted her clothes and given him one of her clear-eyed looks.

"I have to run," she said. A ghost of a smile had the corners of her lips twitching momentarily upward. "Although that will be difficult, since I can hardly feel my legs."

Then, just like that, she was gone, leaving him wondering exactly what the backlash of what had just occurred would be.

It was stupid to have given in to his desire for her, he knew. Complicating a working relationship with sex wasn't smart, and never ended well.

And sex was all it was, or could be.

Yet, despite his worries, Liz Prudhomme treated him exactly the same way she had before.

Although it went against his better judgment to have a sexual affair at work, it also made sense to keep it casual, and taking it outside the hospital felt like taking it a step further than either of them wanted.

So, after that first time in the isolation ward, they found other places to be together whenever they could. Liz, Cort came to find out, was completely open when it came to where, when and how he pleasured her and took pleasure in her body. And he became diabolically inventive in finding places and ways to please her. It shocked him a bit. He'd never considered himself the type to have an affair with a workmate, but he couldn't seem to stay away from Liz.

Every encounter just made him want her more, although he was as determined as she'd said she was to keep it purely physical. Occasionally they had the same day off, with the ER and surgical team having different schedules, but there was never a suggestion, from either of them, that they take it outside the hospital.

There was no future for them, so it seemed ridiculous to intertwine their lives more than they already were.

Because of their schedules they were usually able to grab only a half hour or so together, just enough for him to make her crazy with lust and then send them both flying. He sometimes wondered if it was wrong to continue what he knew was a dead-end affair. Yet since Liz didn't seem to mind and, in fact, never indicated any wish for anything more, he let it ride. It felt too good to stop.

No, not good. Amazing.

Something about the way she surrendered to him, gave in to his demands, found obvious satisfaction in what they did together, was surprising, but he loved every minute of it.

So they met wherever they could be assured of a few minutes of privacy. In storage closets, the isolation ward, the construction zone on the weekend when the workers weren't around. Even, on one memorable occasion, in the rest area off the on-call room, when neither of them could bear to wait.

He'd sat on the narrow cot and pulled her to straddle his thighs, and the similarity to the first time they'd been together in Mexico had seemed to echo between them, heightening both their arousals. He'd known she'd been ready but had wanted it to last so, instead of telling her to let go and find her release, he'd told her to wait, kept her on the knife-edge for several long, deep strokes, before commanding her to come. His own orgasm had been so powerful it had been almost painful. Just thinking about it made his head want to explode all over again. Liz had that kind of effect on him every time they were together.

They might have gone on that way forever or, at least, a lot longer, if they hadn't almost got caught in flagrante delicto about a month after they'd started having their trysts around the hospital.

It had been in the old isolation ward, with him behind Liz, buried deep in the sweet, wet heat of her body. The arch of her back and trembling of her legs, the way she'd rhythmically clenched around him as he'd thrust had told him she was close. He'd pinched her nipples the way he knew she loved, hard enough to take her almost over into orgasm, when the door opened and the lights came on, almost blinding him.

Cort froze, of course, suddenly furious with himself, and her. They were deep in the maze of equipment and beds, but he still glanced over his shoulder, hoping they weren't visible from the doorway. Not that that would help them should the people entering the room start walking around.

"Over the next couple of days, we'll start pulling out the equipment that needs to be installed." He recognized the voice of Jennifer Marshalec, the administrator in charge of the expansion, who sounded as though she was coming farther into the room. "I want to take a look around now to see exactly what we have here. The inventory lists I found really don't seem complete to me."

There was a deep murmur in response, and Cort felt a burst of adrenaline fire through his veins. His brain was swirling with five hundred different thoughts. Should they take the chance of being heard and try to re-dress, or stay still? Was there another way out of the room, or somewhere to hide until Jennifer and whoever she was with were gone?

I'm too old to play hide-and-seek...

"Okay, we'll start—" A phone rang. "Excuse me a moment. Hello? Yes. Oh, for goodness' sake, I'm not at my desk..." Jennifer sighed extravagantly. "Okay, give me five minutes. I'll call you back. Ramone, I'll come back down in a little while and we can continue."

"Sure, Ms. Marshalec." Ramone sounded bored. "I'll be in the construction office when you're ready."

Cort heard the tip-tap of Jennifer's heels and the clump of Ramone's boots as they headed for the exit. The light went out, the noises from outside flared and then were once more cut off by the closing of the door.

Neither of them moved right away, but Liz was trembling, her entire body quaking...

With laughter?

"Oh, really?" Cort growled into her ear. "That wasn't funny. Not…at…all."

With each of the last words he stroked into her, long and deep, and, to his shock, realized the fear of discovery had only stoked the flames of his desire. It seemed to have had the same effect on Liz. She pushed back to meet his every thrust until, still shaking with what was apparently laughter, he felt the quickening of her movements and she came apart on his command, just as always.

Afterward, Cort didn't said anything. In fact, he didn't speak to her, other than in a purely professional way, for a couple of days. There was a lot to think about and, still angry at the risks they'd taken, he didn't want to go off half-cocked.

Realistically, he enjoyed what they had very much, but he wasn't willing to risk his career to keep it up. If she wanted them to keep sleeping together, they'd have to take it outside the hospital. That was, after all his ruminating, the final analysis. Whether she agreed or not was up to her, and he'd abide by her decision.

He rather hoped she was willing to go on seeing him since he was reluctant to see it end.

When he finally brought up the subject, he had no choice, in his own mind, but to give her an ultimatum.

"We can't keep taking chances at the hospital, Liz." He said it dispassionately and when she looked away, instead of meeting his gaze in her usual forthright manner, his chest tightened. It was just as well, really. He didn't want her to guess how much he hoped she'd agree. "I don't want to jeopardize either of our jobs anymore. I think we were a little crazy to be doing this to begin with."

"I understand." Her voice was steady, almost but not quite uninterested.

The tone made his jaw clench, but he decided to ignore it. "So, hereafter, if you want to see me, we're going to have to meet outside work." She shot him a quick glance, her intent, seeking gaze scouring his face. "You can come to my place if you'd like."

For a long moment she didn't say anything, just looked at him, her head to one side. When she finally spoke, he realized he'd been holding his breath the entire time.

"I realize we can't continue the way we've been going, but I still don't want a relationship." She lifted one hand, as though to take back the words, and then let it drop. "Not that what we have isn't a *kind* of relationship, but you know what I mean."

"I'm not asking you for anything you don't want to give, and I think it's safe to say things were going along the way we'd agreed." He kept his voice as matter-of-fact as hers had been, although it took some effort. "I'm just saying I, honestly, don't really want it to stop. I just won't keep it up here. That's all."

She nodded, glanced away again, as though considering what he'd said. It was her way, giving everything deep thought before responding, but knowing that didn't stop his heart from racing or sweat from building along his spine.

It's just sex, he reminded himself. *Don't make it more important than it is.* But knowing that didn't reduce his stress level.

Finally she nodded again, looked at him with a bland, noncommittal expression. "Okay. We can try it, see how it goes."

Why was he so relieved? Cort took a prescription insert out of his pocket and found a spot to write on. The effort needed to concentrate on what he was doing was a welcome excuse not to keep looking at her, so hopefully she wouldn't see how much it meant that she was at least considering it. When he held the sheet out to her, and she took it, the relief morphed to elation.

"This is my cell number and address. We'll work out the timing when we get a chance."

"Okay," she said, taking the paper from his hand, a hint of some emotion he didn't recognize breaking through her level tone.

Was she annoyed? Fed up? He couldn't tell, but was left with the distinct impression that hearing from her was out of the question. Which was why he was frankly shocked when he got a text from her just as he was preparing to leave the hospital at the end of his shift that same day.

Will you be at home later?

Cort stood, staring at his phone, wondering if it was a figment of his imagination brought on by his driving need for her.

"Everything okay?" Reggie Morrison asked.

"Hmm?" Cort looked over at the other surgeon, who was also getting ready to go home. "I'm sorry. What?"

Reggie slammed his locker door shut. "I asked if everything was okay." He lifted his chin toward the phone still clutched in Cort's hand. "You're glaring at that phone as though you want to strangle it."

"Oh, yeah. Everything's fine." Cort managed a smile and stuck the phone into his pocket. "Just an unexpected message."

"You still meeting us at the Red Rover Inn later?" Having plopped onto the bench, Reggie was putting on his street shoes. "Last I heard we were aiming for seven."

"No." There was no way he would put off Liz just to have drinks with the guys. "I don't think I can make it. Give the others my apologies, would you?"

"Sure." Reggie got up and stretched. "Maybe next time?"

"Definitely." Cort pretended to be engrossed with something in his locker, desperate for a little privacy. He had a message to answer. "Have a good time."

"Will do." Reggie lifted a hand in farewell. "Bye."

"Bye."

Cort whipped his phone back out even before the locker-room door closed.

CHAPTER EIGHT

OKAY, SO SHE was weak.

Pathetic even.

When Cort had issued his ultimatum she'd walked away, already having decided to tell him to go to hell. Instead, here she was on her way to his place.

Liz switched the bag of Chinese takeout from one hand to the other so she could wipe the sweat off her palms on the legs of her jeans.

It's not a date. More like...um...a tryst. Yeah. A tryst.

Yet thinking that didn't make her feel any less nervous. It had been a very, very long time since she'd gone out of her way to be with a man, other than just for sex. Cort may have said he wanted to continue what had, to that point, been strictly a sexual relationship, but going to his place bearing food from her favorite Chinese restaurant smacked of it becoming something more.

And it was that *more* she'd been assiduously avoiding.

She couldn't help thinking of how Andrew had charmed her into doing whatever he'd wanted, no matter what her instincts had been saying. The resentment she felt now seemed an echo of those times, and she cursed herself for a fool. She should have told him to go to hell.

"Too late now," she muttered to herself, stepping out of the elevator onto the floor where Cort's apartment was.

Taking a deep breath, reminding herself she didn't have to stay, or come back if it didn't go the way she wanted, she marched up to his door and rang the bell. It felt as though it took forever for Cort to answer. By the time he did, she'd tried to convince herself to leave one more time, then talked herself out of it again by remembering just how incredible he made her feel.

It's just for sex...

When she heard the sound of the door being unlocked, she stiffened and held her breath.

"Hi." Cort stood there, smiling, and despite her anxiety, or maybe because of it, Liz's heart fluttered. He pulled the door open wider and stepped back, gesturing her inside with a sweep of his hand. "Come on in."

Not sure whether to be annoyed or relieved that he hadn't done something trite like kiss or hug her, Liz took him up on the invitation. Once inside, she pushed back the hood of her jacket and thrust the bag of food toward him. "I got Chinese. Wasn't sure what you'd like, so a got a bunch of different dishes."

Good grief. She was babbling, and forced her lips shut to stop it. The visceral response she experienced whenever she saw Cort was magnified by being in his home, making her brain race and her heart thump.

"I'm sure it'll be fine." Still smiling, he closed the door. "You can hang your coat in the closet there."

Cort disappeared around a corner, into the kitchen, she suspected as she unwound her scarf and opened the door he'd indicated. Unlike her own hall closet, which often looked as though a bomb had gone off in it, his was incredibly neat. She shrugged out of her winter coat and then hung it, together with her scarf, on a free hanger. Then she perched on the bench near the door and took off her boots. With a deep breath, she got up and went after Cort.

He was, indeed, in his galley kitchen, which was separated from a living/dining room by an island, on which he was unpacking the food. He glanced at her and smiled without pausing in what he was doing.

"Have a seat. What'll you have to drink?"

"Just water, thanks." Ignoring his suggestion to sit, she prowled around the room, taking it all in.

The rest of the apartment was as neat as the hall closet but had an unfinished, hardly lived-in feel. Yes, there was a sectional and an easy chair that toned with it, and a small bar-height dining table surrounded by four chairs. Sure, there was a coffee table and an end table, and a large-screen TV, but there was also a lack of decorative touches. No pictures or mementos on the console beneath the TV, no paintings on the walls. Not to mention the pile of boxes in the corner. Not that any of it was her business anyway...

"Not settled in yet?"

She could have bitten off her own tongue for giving in to her urge for small talk. That wasn't why she was here.

"No." He was clattering stuff around in the kitchen, doing who knew what. "It didn't seem to make sense to unpack, only to have to pack it all up again in a year. Actually, any box that I don't open between now and then I'll probably just throw away."

"Hmm." Restless, not knowing what to do with herself, she moved closer to the boxes. Although handwritten, the labels all looked exactly alike and were aligned on the boxes in precisely the same way. He'd been in the military, she remembered, so maybe that type of precision and his neatness were holdovers from his training. Not a bad trait for a surgeon to possess. "'C. M. Smith,'" she read aloud. Cort wasn't really a name, was it? It must be short for something. "What's your full name anyway?"

Maybe it was the sudden silence, or the fact he didn't answer right away, but whatever it was had Liz turning to look at him. When he glanced up at her, his face was non-committal, and the expression had her antennae quivering.

"Cortland Main Smith."

"*Maine*, as in the state?" She drew closer to the island as he turned his back to her and opened a drawer.

"Nope, just *M-A-I-N*."

"Cortland Main." Liz sat on one of the bar stools, all her focus on the man setting chopsticks on the counter in front of her. "Interesting names. Are they traditional to your family?"

"No."

The curtness of his reply took her by surprise, but she only said, "I'm not judging, believe me. My full name is Eliza Honoria." That got the expected response of raised eyebrows and a barely controlled upward twitch of his lips. "My parents had the bright idea of naming me after two of my father's old aunts who never married, hoping they would leave him something in their wills."

He was trying manfully not to laugh, but she was sure she still read tension in the set of his shoulders. "Did it work?"

The old bitterness-tinged amusement rose in her. "Nope. At least, not the way my parents wanted it to. My great-aunts were the ones who left the trust I told you about, the one I had to go to that damned luncheon for. But don't change the subject. How did your parents come up with your names?"

"They didn't." Both hands on the counter, he held her gaze. There again was that noncommittal expression, but his eyes were too carefully shielded. "Child protection agents gave me that name after I was found in a cardboard box at the corner of Cortland Road and Main Street."

Cort waited for Liz's reaction, his skin clammy, his heart pounding. There were few people who knew his story and how she reacted would determine where they went from here. He didn't need pity, or to be looked down on because of his rootless existence.

Liz's eyes widened, but he should have known she wouldn't react like anyone else.

"Oh, that explains it," she said, her gaze clear, penetrating. He must have shown some sign of his surprise at her matter-of-fact comment because she added, "Your reaction to Baby Jane coming in. Were you hypothermic too, when they found you?"

"A bit." He watched as she almost unconsciously picked up the chopsticks in front of her and dipped into one of the containers of food. As she popped a piece of Schezuan chicken between her lips, he found himself continuing, "It was early spring, still cold."

"Hmm." She finished chewing, swallowed, and then said, "Any other problems?"

He took a moment to slide a plate toward her, then rounded the island. Her pragmatic approach to his story caused the tension that had built in his muscles to dissipate with each step. For perhaps the first time, the story seemed to belong to the past, and could be discussed with a certain amount of detachment.

"A broken arm," he replied to her question, as he sat on the stool next to hers and reached for the fried rice. "And they discovered I had nonstructural scoliosis."

Following his lead, she started piling food onto her plate. "Cause?"

"Inflammation. It was successfully treated."

For a while they concentrated on eating, but Cort could almost hear the wheels turning in her head. Liz Prud-homme wasn't the type to let a conversation like this just drop. Not if she was really interested.

So it wasn't a surprise when she finally asked, "Were you adopted?"

"Nope." That also didn't sting so much anymore, although when he'd been a teenager it had. "I ended up aging out of the foster-care system."

She nodded. "Nowadays there would be all kinds of posts on social media, people lining up to adopt you. Back then, not so much." The glance she sent him had warmth rushing down his spine, although he didn't know why. "You made it through the system, though, and all the way to success. That takes guts and determination."

He couldn't hold her gaze, pleasure at her praise making him turn away. Looking down at his plate and wrestling with a particularly slippery tangle of noodles was a welcome distraction. Getting them into his mouth and chewing also put off the need to reply until the unexpected rush of emotion subsided. "I had help."

"Really?" When he looked at her out of the corner of his eye, Liz was no longer watching him but helping herself to more food. "That's unusual in the foster-care system, or so I've heard."

"Yes, well, some of my foster families were good people." Not all, but he didn't want to go there. "But it was a couple of teachers who really got me on the right track at the right time." When she made an interested sound in the back of her throat, he continued. "I had a football coach who kept at me until I joined the school's officer trainer program, and a science teacher who saw something in me I didn't see in myself. She suggested I consider medicine." Even now, the memory made him laugh. "Imagine a scruffy, angry teenager in dirty, too-small clothes being told he should aspire to be a doctor. I told her she was nuts, but she persisted and the two things, the training program and her insistence, came together in the end."

When he least expected it, she sent him another of those clear-eyed looks. "Somewhere along the line your own determination had to come into play. No matter what anyone else says to a person, if they're not committed to a goal they won't make it." She mimed doffing a hat. "Kudos to you."

What could he say to that? Desperation had been his initial driver, but he doubted she'd understand the life he'd lived, so he just sketched her a bow and saw her lips quirk with her version of a smile.

"The army played a huge role too."

"You sound almost nostalgic about the service. Why'd you leave?"

Memories, like noxious smoke, suddenly filled his head, and had to be forced away. Keeping his gaze on his plate, he said, "It was time." Knowing how abrupt it sounded, he forced a smile and asked, "What about you? How did you end up in medicine?"

She shrugged, pushing away her plate, but there was an infinitesimal tightening of the skin around her mouth before she replied, "I knew from when I was a child what I wanted to do."

"And no one was talking you out of it, huh?"

He said it as a joke, but the way she nodded told him there was a lot more to the story. "Hell, no." When she met his gaze, her eyes were gleaming with the laughter she hardly ever allowed to escape. "Many tried, none succeeded."

Desire stabbed through him, shocking in its swiftness and intensity. It was the twinkle in her eyes, her candid acknowledgement of her strength of will, and, he admitted to himself, the easy way she'd heard and taken in his story. No drama, or false sympathy. It all just made him want her with the same ferocity he'd felt when knowing they only had a few minutes to be together in the hospital. And now remembering they had all night heightened his arousal. His need.

It must have shown on his face, because her eyes got slumberous, her lips softened, and a hint of color touched her cheeks and the tips of her ears. It made him want to tease her, much as he had the night they'd spent together in Mexico. That night had seemed to stretch to infinity, redolent with soft gasps and hot kisses, the intimate stroke of hands and lips across skin, the rise of unstoppable passion.

Getting up, he held out his hand to her.

"Come, let's go sit on the couch, maybe watch a movie."

Those eloquent eyebrows twitched, and her eyelids drooped farther. "Sure," she said, and took his hand with no hint of hesitation.

His heart leapt at that calm acceptance.

Tugging her to her feet, he let go of her hand to unbutton her sweater. "Make sure you watch the movie carefully, no matter what happens," he said. "There will be a test later."

"Ha-ha-ha," was her reply, but there was a breathy quality to her voice that told him she knew exactly what kind of distraction he planned. "And what kind of reward will I get if I get all the answers right?"

Leaning in close as he slid the sweater off her body, he whispered into her ear, and got his own reward when a pleasure-drenched little sound broke from her throat.

"I'll pay really close attention." It was an amusement-laden croak. "I want my prize."

"Good." He started on the button of her jeans, excitement firing across his flesh as he anticipated making her climax over and over again. "I want you to have it."

Want you to have it all.

CHAPTER NINE

SHE WANTED TO STAY.

Liz lay still beside Cort, trying to convince herself to get up and go home.

Staying the night had never been part of the deal.

It smacked of that *more* she'd promised herself to avoid at all costs.

Yet his bed was comfortable and, so far, there was no snoring to disturb the quiet of his apartment. Coming from outside, the hum of traffic, muted by gently falling snow, was also having a soporific effect.

She forced her eyes open to stare at the window, which was covered by light sheers, while she catalogued the pleasant aches caused by Cort's incredible lovemaking.

Sex. It was wonderful, but just sex.

A shiver crept up her arms, making her nipples bead. Whatever she called it, it was fantastic. Something about looking into those eyes, dark with passion, intent on her, elevated the experience from purely physical to something she didn't want to think about, much less name. Just the thought of it brought a sheen of anxious sweat to her forehead.

So, instead, she thought about what he'd told her about his beginnings, and how he'd ended up a surgeon. Knowing where he'd come from to become the man he was filled her with admiration. And that didn't even include whatever it was that had caused him to leave the service. There was a story there, one he'd shied away from telling, which probably meant it was really bad.

She doubted she would have survived, much less thrived the way he had.

The man in question rolled over onto his side to face her. Immediately her body quickened, tingles racing through her belly to settle between her thighs.

He made her so greedy.

So when he reached for her, pulled her close, she didn't resist, even though her head was telling her to. And when he kissed her, his hand slicking across her skin again to find a spot she hadn't even known was an erogenous zone until he'd shown her it was, she melted, gave in once more.

Later, floating down from the high he'd taken her on, she again thought about leaving, convinced herself she'd do it in a couple of minutes.

"There's something I have to say."

Liz braced herself, ready to get up and go if he made some fatuous comment about the sex, or spouted some romantic nonsense. So she made her tone cool as she asked, "What?"

"I'm starving."

That was so unexpected it startled a chuckle from her throat before she could stop it. Then her stomach rumbled, as though in agreement, and he laughed too.

Liz replied, "I guess I am too. What do you feel like having?"

She was thinking about the leftover Chinese in the kitchen, but Cort had other ideas.

"Arepas," he said promptly, following it with a little hum, as though already tasting them. "I haven't had a really good pulled pork *arepa* sandwich since I got here."

Now, that was something she could help with. Her love

of food was well known among her intimates, and one of her favorites was Hispanic food in all its various incarnations.

"Colombian or Venezuelan?" Already she was running through a list of her favorite spots, trying to figure out which was closest.

"Mmm, Colombian for preference, although both are delicious."

Liz bounced out of bed to start looking for her scattered clothes. "Great, because there's a place about ten blocks from here that sells the most amazing Colombian food you've ever tasted outside Bogotá."

"Isn't it kind of late?"

Liz glanced at her watch, and then gave him a wrinkled brow look. He was still lying in bed, his arms crossed behind his head, as relaxed as anything.

And so delicious her insides melted a little.

Having that broad chest on display in front of her almost made her give up her planned excursion and hop back into bed, but once set on a course it usually took a stick of dynamite to divert her.

Hands planted on her hips, she asked, "Are you kidding? This is New York City. Whatever you want to eat, whenever you want to eat it, you can find a place, and I know most of them. You coming with me or what?"

"All right, all right. Don't get bent out of shape," he grumbled, as he swung his legs out of bed, making her mouth water.

And not for the promised food.

He strolled over to his chest of drawers, looking back at her over his shoulder. "I was enjoying the sight of you running around looking for your clothes."

"Ha-ha," she replied, heading for the bathroom and not mentioning how much she had enjoyed the view of him emerging from under the covers like some mythic god rising from the sea.

The night was cold. The earlier fluffy snow had morphed into small, stinging bits of ice, and Liz and Cort spent much of the journey to the restaurant talking about the never-ending winter and wondering if spring would ever arrive. They agreed the flu outbreak seemed to have slowed, but if the weather continued to be cold, it could pick up again.

The small restaurant, La Tortuga Roja, was down a short alley off a main road, and not visible from the sidewalk. While the outside seemed grubby, the inside was clean and simply decorated, and it was full.

Cort looked around with obvious surprise.

"I guess I wasn't the only person craving *arepas*," he remarked.

"Apparently not," she replied, leading the way to the only available booth.

After the waitress had brought menus and taken their drink orders, Cort asked, "How do you know about this place?"

"I like food." There was the familiar nagging shame she'd been fighting her entire life, but she just lifted her chin and continued, "I always try to find the best restaurants I can for the different types of food I like, usually by asking someone who comes from the country or region where it's native."

"That makes sense." He was looking at the menu, a little line between his brows. "I love food too, although I'll be the first to tell you I can be picky."

"I'd have thought the army would have cured you of that."

He glanced up, a smile lighting his face. "Not even the foster-care system cured me of being picky."

He spoke so easily about what had to have been a difficult and perhaps frightening childhood. That, along with the knowledge their relationship had a predetermined shelf life, caused Liz to open up in a way she normally wouldn't.

"I had a love-hate relationship with food when I was young, now it's just a love affair."

Cort's gaze sharpened. "Love-hate? As in an eating disorder?"

It felt good to talk about it. She never did, but he somehow made it easy to reply. "Looking back on it now, as a medical practitioner, I don't think I was there yet. I was, however, doing unhealthy things, trying to achieve unrealistic goals and make other people happy."

Her mother had never overtly said anything, but there had been others not so kind. *Are you sure you want another piece? Oh, you've put on so much weight.* She'd compared her chunky, preteen self to the girls in her class and to her waif-thin mother, and had felt inadequate.

"How old were you?"

Liz closed her menu, having decided what she wanted to eat. "It was between the ages of about ten and fourteen. I take after my father's side of the family, who are all big, raw-boned people. My mother, on the other hand, had a tiny Japanese grandmother, and the rest of her family isn't much bigger. I know she must still look at me and wonder how she produced such a huge human."

She could say it with amusement now, but when she'd been the fat kid at school, taunted by the other girls, picked on by the boys, it had been anything but funny. Not even the knowledge that she was smart and capable and had wanted to be a doctor had made her not long to fit in. Or taken away the need to see admiration in her mother's eyes. Just being a straight A student hadn't seemed enough.

"What changed?"

"Now, that's a story in itself."

Just then the waitress brought their drinks and, since

they'd both decided what they wanted, took their orders. As soon as she walked away, Cort said, "So, what happened?"

Liz let a little smile pull at her lips. His enthusiastic interest was pretty cute.

"My mother started talking about my debutante ball."

His brow wrinkled slightly. "Not sure I know what that is."

"Lucky you. It's just a big formal dance where very rich people put their daughters on parade. At least, that's how I see it. My mom, however, was far more excited. She didn't know what was happening to me in school, how the same girls I was going to have to go to the ball with despised me, and I despised them. Just the thought of having to wear a ballgown made me want to break out in hives."

Cort's eyebrows lifted. "Come on, it couldn't have been that bad."

"At the time it felt like they were opening the gates of hell and telling me to step in. Truthfully, I was so scared of having everyone compare me to the other girls, seeing how much bigger I was than them, how different I looked."

Or being compared to her mother, who'd won beauty contests and been voted "Most Popular" in school. By every measure, except scholastically, Liz had seen herself as a failure.

"Now I realize I was frightened, but back then I convinced myself I was taking a stand for feminism and equality. I told my parents I didn't want to go to a ball, I wanted to be a doctor, and doctors didn't need to be debs."

Cort was actually leaning forward, his elbows on the table, his intent gaze fixed on her face. "How did that go down?"

She chuckled. "Like a lead balloon. They tried to reason with me, but I was terrified and determined and wouldn't give in. The one good thing to come out of it was that they sent me to boarding school in England the next school year."

"Why'd they do that?" Cort sounded both perplexed and a little angry. "What did they hope to achieve?"

"Not sure. I never asked, but being there, meeting new people just as I started to grow into my body, made all the difference in my confidence. For the first time in my life I knew no one was comparing me to my mother, or expecting me to be anyone other than I was. The friends I made then are still my best ones, because they accepted me exactly as I was."

Of course, her transformation hadn't happened overnight, and it had taken Andrew to completely cure her of the urge to try to change to please others. He'd reiterated all the bad things she'd felt her parents thought about her, and she'd realized that if she didn't accept herself the way she was, she'd never be happy in her skin.

A shadow crossed Cort's face, the corners of his mouth dipping down for an instant, before he said, "Yeah, having friends is important, especially at that age."

Another story she itched to hear, yet something in his eyes made her hesitate to ask. Instead, as the waitress approached with a groaning tray, she said, "Oh, good, here comes our food."

And thereafter the conversation turned to other, less personal things, while her curiosity simmered in the back of her mind. Cort Smith was turning out to be far more interesting than she could ever have imagined, even outside the bedroom.

Cort had a hard time believing he was sitting across from a totally relaxed Liz Prudhomme at ten o'clock on a Friday night, eating an *arepa* stuffed with *lechona*. As he took a bite of his sandwich, the delicious pork filling practically melting in his mouth, he watched Liz help herself to a sampling of the various dishes on the table—*arroz con coco*, *carne asado* and *tostones*, as well as *arepas* to go with it all.

He contemplated what she'd revealed about her childhood, having a difficult time picturing her as an outcast in any setting. Now, as an adult, her confidence seemed unassailable but clearly it hadn't always been that way.

Knowing she came from a wealthy family, if he'd thought about her childhood at all he'd have guessed she'd always been surrounded by admiring friends who'd wanted to be just like her. Probably a letter athlete and class president as well, like the star of a teen movie of the week.

Just went to show you really couldn't judge what a person's life had been just from outward appearances.

Hearing that little bit of personal information made him hungry for more. From the moment they'd met in Mexico, Liz had proven herself adept at getting him to talk about his life without revealing much about hers. Despite how easily she was divulging information now, he figured he'd have to be careful not to have her clam up on him again. He knew, without a doubt, she wouldn't hesitate to cut him off at the knees if she thought he was overstepping his bounds.

Swallowing the bite he'd been chewing on, he said, "If this food is any indication of your standards, you're going to have to give me a list of places to eat at."

"It's really good, isn't it?" She pointed to the beef. "Have some."

Snagging a piece, as directed, he asked, "So, have you lived in New York all your life?"

The look she gave him was one of amusement. "Do I sound like a New Yorker? No, I'm from the San Francisco Bay area. That's where my parents still live."

"How come you didn't go back there after your residency?" If he had a family, real roots in a community, that would probably be what he'd do.

Liz shrugged one shoulder, and for a moment he thought she wasn't going to answer, then she replied, "It's complicated."

She took another bite of food and chewed, leaving him to wonder if that was all the answer he was going to get. After she swallowed, then took a sip of her iced tea, she said, "Truthfully, I spent a lot more happy times here in New York than I did back home. Those two aunts I was named for asked for me to come to spend part of summer with them when I got into my teens, and my parents insisted I go. At first, it felt like another punishment, but those two old ladies were amazing and I looked forward to those weeks every year. I fell in love with New York and now there's nowhere I'd rather be."

He wanted to dig deeper, feeling there was more to it than just that, but before he could formulate his next question, she continued.

"What do you think of New York? What have you seen and done since you got here?"

Deflected again, and yet he couldn't really blame her. Theirs wasn't the type of relationship that inspired confidences. They weren't looking to get to know each other too deeply, just enjoy the attraction.

"I like it, so far. Took some time to get used to the pace of the city, and the noise, but I'm enjoying exploring. Did some touristy things, like the Empire State Building, and Liberty and Ellis Island, but besides that I've just been nosing around a bit."

"If you're only going to be in New York for a fairly short time, you need to cram as much in as possible." She raised one eyebrow. "What are you into, besides martial arts and traveling?"

Her question made him have to think. For the last five years he'd been struggling to get back into civilian life without his best friend to do things with. It suddenly struck him how much he'd deferred to Mimi's wants when it had come to what they'd done together.

"I like live music, but not at big venues. I used to play a lot of pool, and miss it. Just checking out different neighborhoods, seeing how other people live and have fun, that's how I usually try to get to know a city."

With her wealthy background that probably sounded boring and pedestrian to Liz, but he wasn't going to present himself as anything other than what he was. He was a simple man, with pretty simple tastes and interests. Racking his brain, he continued with his list of things he liked to do.

"Usually when I travel I go to natural history museums, and rent a motorbike to look at the countryside. I'm looking forward to exploring outside the city on my bike when the weather gets nice."

It was as though a curtain came down, and the relaxed, almost smiling Liz disappeared in an instant. She looked down and pushed her plate aside.

"Well, you won't lack for things to do and see here. If you need any suggestions, let me know."

As was often the case, he was left wondering what had cause her abrupt change of mood. Was it because she'd suddenly realized just how incredibly boring he was?

When she glanced at her watch, he knew the evening, which he'd been enjoying so much, was coming to an end. He didn't want it to. Instead, he wanted to ask her to come back home with him, spend the night. Seeing her so laid back and obviously enjoying her food had made him hungry for her again. Just one look at her closed-off expression and veiled eyes told him it would be useless to ask.

But there was one thing he had to say before they parted ways. Catching the waitress's eye, he motioned for the bill, then said to Liz, "I definitely want suggestions, so make me a list of must-sees. Better yet, show me around yourself. You love the city, so I have no doubt you know all the best places, and the best times to go to them."

That earned him one of her sharp, solemn glances.

"I'll think about it," she said, turning to pull her coat off the back of the chair.

And he was smart enough to leave it at that.

CHAPTER TEN

LIZ LEFT CORT standing on the sidewalk outside the restaurant and jumped into a cab to head home. All the fun and enjoyment she'd felt in his company had drained away at the mention of the motorcycle, and she had to wonder why her taste in men was so predictable. The more time she spent with Cort, the more he reminded her of Andrew, as if one man hooked on adventure and the need for speed wasn't enough.

At least they didn't look alike, at all. Andrew had been blond and sleek, with a swimmer's physique, while Cort was more the epitome of tall, dark and handsome. A solid man, built for holding a woman in such a way that she felt safe. Protected.

Not that she needed protection. She was more than capable of protecting herself, thank you very much! Yet when Cort held her the very center of her feminine core was touched, and she felt beautiful.

But the mention of the motorbike had made her blood run cold.

When she'd first started going out with Andrew, she had ridden on the back of his bike all the time. Although he'd had a car, it had been his favorite way of getting around and Liz, not having had much experience with motorcycles, hadn't minded until after the late fall night when they'd crashed. Luckily for her all she'd sustained had been some painful road rash and a slight concussion. Andrew had broken his arm. Had it been her with the broken ulna and radius, she'd have had to miss a key part of her practical anatomy course, and that had been a nonstarter for her.

"Come on, Liz," Andrew had wheedled. "It's like riding a horse. You have to get right back on. It'll be fine. The odds of having another accident are astronomical."

Much as she'd wanted to demand he show her those statistics, she hadn't bothered. It wouldn't have changed her mind. The thought of how close she'd come to losing a year of schooling had been like a shock of cold water to her system, not to mention how close they'd come to real disaster.

Andrew had slowed considerably just prior to going around the corner and having the back tire slide out from under them. Usually he'd ridden like a madman, going at phenomenal speeds. If he'd been running true to form, she had no doubt they'd both be dead.

It had been the end of her riding pillion on his bike.

And perhaps the beginning of the end of their relationship.

Sometimes she tried to tell herself that she'd just matured faster than he had, but she knew in her heart it wasn't true. Andrew probably wouldn't have changed and, while perhaps it made her a hypocrite to be mad at him for wanting her to change, she'd hoped *he* would. She'd had her life mapped out, at least roughly, and she'd longed for his approval of her plans. Instead, he'd wanted her to put her dream of being a doctor on hold, had treated it as though it hadn't been important.

"You can always go back to it," he'd said, as he'd laid maps of Europe, already marked with routes he planned to take, out on her kitchen table. "We're young, and this is the time to travel and see the world, not when we're too old to enjoy it."

She'd been tempted. Oh, yes, she had. When faced with the choice of losing him or going with him, she'd hesitated. Each had tried to convince the other their way was the best, Andrew arguing for her to take a year or two off, Liz arguing for him to wait until she was through with her studies.

Eventually it hadn't mattered. While she'd been looking into what it would mean to put her school career on hiatus, Andrew had decided he didn't want her to go.

"We've had some good times, Liz, but you're not spontaneous enough for me. Sometimes I wonder if you really have feelings for me at all because, if you do, you don't show it. I think it will be better if I make the trip on my own."

It hadn't been fair, at all, what he'd been saying. She'd tried to be more like him, dropping everything to go out even when she'd known she shouldn't, staying out later than she should, even occasionally missing a class because Andrew had wanted to ride down to the sea or go to a concert. The difference was she'd wanted to succeed and had known she couldn't do well if she constantly did those things. So sometimes she'd tell him no, and it had never gone over well, but she'd stuck to her guns. Just as she had with not riding the motorcycle anymore.

Better to be useful than decorative.

Don't allow your father, or any man, to dictate to you.

Leaning her head back in the taxi, Liz brooded on those words. She still believed in what Nanny Hardy and her great-aunts had said, and honestly felt if it hadn't been for their wise words, she'd have thrown it all over for Andrew.

And probably would have died with him during an early snowfall in Germany, when he'd destroyed his bike on a lonely road, too far away for help to get to him in time.

Her love for Andrew had made her so weak, it was frightening. The irony that his change of heart had been the only thing that had stopped her from throwing everything away she'd fought for hadn't been lost on her, but hadn't made it hurt any less.

For a moment, before she got herself under control, her eyes stung with the tears she'd steadfastly refused to allow to fall for all these years.

Stupid for it all to be coming back to the surface after all this time, interfering with what should be a good time with a man she already knew was transient in her life, and therefore safe. Better to put it out of her mind, once and for all, and just enjoy the amazing sex and Cort's company, which was surprisingly easy, and casual enough to not make her want to run.

He wanted to see New York, and had been right when he'd said she could show it to him in a way most other people couldn't.

She could see no harm in that and, if she was being scrupulously honest with herself, she wanted to enjoy him for as long as he stuck around, especially now she was pretty sure he wouldn't make something out of it that wasn't there.

Pulling out her tablet, she started typing in a list of places she'd take him, and things he should do, at least once, while he was there.

It should be fun.

Right?

Standing outside the Colombian restaurant and watching Liz's taxi drive away, Cort was sure it was the last time they would go anywhere together. Her change of attitude after asking him what he liked made him sure he wasn't interesting enough for her, and not worth bothering about.

It turned out he was wrong.

She actually approached him the following day with a list of things to do, and a plan for how and when they'd do them.

Liz Prudhomme was nothing if not organized.

Well, except for her locker.

Looking down at her tablet, where he could see an extensive list, she said, "There are some things we'll leave for when the weather gets better, like the New York Botanical Garden, Coney Island and Governors Island, but there are so many other things to do, you won't be bored." And now, as they walked along a sidewalk in the East Village, he had to admit she was right. He'd been anything but bored. They'd become workout buddies when he'd complained about the gym near his house not being open twenty-four hours a day, and she kept him on his toes when they went at the same time. She'd taken him through the Arms and Armor Department at the Metropolitan Museum, to a play Off-Off-Broadway and a musical on Broadway. In between there had been a variety of food, a martial arts tournament, and a number of nights at clubs listening to blues, country, and indie performers.

The breadth of Liz's interests and knowledge was amazing.

Cort looked back at the venue they'd just left, where people still trickled out into the night.

"What did you say that was we just watched again?"

"A poetry slam," she replied, giving him an amused glance. "I'm guessing it's your first?"

That made him chuckle. She knew it was, if only from the way he'd sat there with his mouth hanging open. It had been one of the most wonderful things he'd seen.

"Some of those poets were like listening to the blues being spoken, rather than sung."

She stopped in the middle of the sidewalk and stared at him in such a strange way he felt self-conscious.

"I guess that didn't make any sense," he said quickly, but she interrupted him with an uplifted hand.

"On the contrary, that's the best description I've heard

in a long time. I'd never have guessed you had the soul of an aesthete."

The back of his neck got warm, although he wasn't sure whether it was with embarrassment or pleasure. All he knew was that he had to laugh it off somehow.

"Ah, so you thought I was just a Philistine, huh?"

The corners of her lips twitched, her mouth softening into her version of a smile. When she started walking again, he fell into step beside her once more. "Actually, the Philistines were highly cultured. It's one of those pieces of misinformation that gets passed down because the victors always get to write the history."

They walked for a while more, discussing the poetry slam and their favorite performers, until they came to a well-lit pool hall. Cort turned to her, raising his eyebrows.

"Pool?"

She shrugged. "You said you liked to play, so I figured you could teach me. Neither of us work early tomorrow, so we can stay out a little longer."

"Sure," he said, surprised she'd even remembered he'd said it.

For a Wednesday night there were quite a few people in the club, which also had an arcade and dartboards.

"Now, if you want to give me a fighting chance of winning, we could play darts," Liz said.

"Next time," Cort said, pulling out money to feed into the pool table. "It feels good to find something you're not an expert at."

Liz snorted, watching as he racked up the balls. When he was finished and selected a couple of cues, he started his instructions, telling her the basics and then showing her the break. A solid ball went into a pocket, and he stopped to explain that, since he'd sunk that one, it was up to him to sink all the other solids, before sinking the eight ball.

"So when do I play?"

"If I miss a shot, you're up."

She sighed, as though they'd been there for an hour rather than ten minutes. Realizing she was getting bored, he intentionally missed the next shot.

"Your turn," he said. "You need to sink the striped balls."

Liz gave the table a skeptical glance. "In any particular order?"

"Nope," he replied.

"Okay," she said. "This'll be a short turn, so get ready to play again."

She awkwardly tried to set up for a shot, holding the cue short and too far away from her body.

"Hang on," he said. "Will you let me help you?"

"I suppose," she huffed.

Chuckling at how much she obviously despised being at a disadvantage, he moved to stand behind her, putting his hand between her shoulder blades and gently pushing her lower.

"Bend over further."

"As the bishop said to the actress," she muttered.

"What?"

"Never mind. I'll explain later."

She always came out with little sayings he'd never heard before, mostly, he figured, because of the difference in their experiences and upbringings. He didn't mind, though, since she was broadening his horizons and giving him a whole new way of looking at things.

Instead of asking anything more, he leaned over, snuggling up to her bottom. It took all his concentration to help her position her arms, since being that close to her was so arousing.

His fascination with and attraction to her certainly hadn't waned. If anything, getting to know her better had made their continued intimate relationship even hotter, wilder.

And when she wiggled a little, shifting position, he almost groaned aloud.

Ignoring the erection pushing at the front of his jeans, he said, "Okay, aim for that red-striped ball there. Try to hit it a little to the left of center, so it goes into the side pocket."

"Easy for you to say."

He backed away, watching as she made a couple of practice feints. At least the hand she had on the felt looked to be in a good position. Most new players had a hard time with that...

Crack.

"All right! You sank it. See, that wasn't so hard, was it?"

The look she gave him made him smile, a smile that slowly faded to be replaced with a wide-eyed stare as she ran the table.

"Why you little..."

She shrugged, her eyes twinkling, a grin stretching her luscious lips.

"I'm sorry, I couldn't resist. My brother taught me to play years ago, and then wouldn't play with me anymore because I kept beating him."

Cort burst out laughing, going over to put some more money in the table so they could play another game, trying to ignore how fast his heart was beating at the sight of her smile.

"Well, let's see how you do this time around."

He was actually still laughing when they left the pool hall an hour and a half later. He'd won two games, she'd won three, and they'd trash-talked each other the entire time. Even Liz had laughed out loud a couple of times.

Outside, the early-spring air was cool, but the sky was clear, an almost full moon hanging like a milky lamp above their heads. Cort had been around her long enough to know Liz didn't go for public displays of affection, didn't even like holding hands, and it didn't bother him. Not when he woke up every morning when she'd slept over at his place to find her draped over him, providing more coverage than his comforter.

But sometimes he needed her to know what she did to him, whether they were out in public or not.

As they came abreast of a closed shop, he swept her into a hug, and backed her into the darkness afforded by the recessed doorway. Her only reaction was a little gasp, and then he felt her melt against him.

"You make me crazy," he whispered into her ear, and was rewarded by her shiver. "I want you, right now."

She pressed against him, swiveled her hips in the way she knew made him go nuts. The attraction between them was always simmering just below the surface, waiting to explode into passion at a look, a touch, a whisper.

"I'll call for a taxi," she said, but neither of them made a move to disengage.

"In a minute," he said, looking over his shoulder at the almost deserted street. "I just want to…"

And he kissed her until she was making little noises in the back of her throat, and until he knew if they didn't get out of there soon, they might be arrested for indecent exposure.

"Are there any hotels nearby?" He growled it against her neck, pinched her nipple in the way she loved, rocking his leg up into the junction of her thighs.

Liz gasped, shuddered, and said, "A decent one, about two blocks west."

Forcing himself to let her go, he backed out of the doorway, the ache in his groin excruciating. Every time they were together was like the first time for him. Liz could turn him on by simply being.

"That'll work," he said, taking a deep breath. "Race you."

CHAPTER ELEVEN

MAY HAD FINALLY brought the full promise of spring, with balmy weather and, most of the time, not enough rain to make it difficult to enjoy. Today, though, wasn't one of those days, as a front moved through the northeast, bringing thunderstorms and the occasional bout of hail.

The hospital renovations were getting closer to completion, and they were on no-intake for emergency and surgical patients as the technicians were moving equipment into the newly arranged departments. Without the usual flood of patients, staff and visitors, those floors of the hospital had a ghost-town feel to them. Even Radiology was on a skeleton crew, with only one room open for use.

Liz was bored, taking the quiet time between non-emergency patients to catch up on paperwork and do some research she'd been putting off. She felt a little guilty at her secret glee when a young baseball player, whose attempt to slide into third had ended with a broken collarbone, came in for treatment. It really was a slow day when applying a figure eight bandage was as exciting as it got.

On her way back to the nurses' station, she saw Cort turn a corner ahead of her and come her way. Despite seeing him almost every day, her heart still did that little leap whenever he came into view, and the sight of his smiling face lifted her mood, no matter how testy she was feeling.

It really was a good thing he wouldn't be sticking around for too long. Already she'd been forced to acknowledge how easy it had been to get used to, and enjoy, his company.

Thank goodness there was no chance of falling for him. She was smarter and stronger than that.

He paused next to her and casually asked, "Gym later?"

She was working early the next morning, so they didn't have anything else planned. She replied, "I was hoping it would be nice today so we could go for a run in Central Park, but the gym will have to do."

Cort stepped aside as a technician came by, wheeling an EKG monitor in front of him, the bulky machine taking up most of the hallway. The movement brought Cort closer to Liz, and her body reacted to the proximity, the now familiar sensation of arousal making her tingle, on the verge of shivering.

"Sounds good," he said. "I'm here for another hour and, for a change, there shouldn't be anything stopping me from leaving on time. So, say, six?"

For once they were actually on the same schedule, so it worked. "See you outside at six."

"Great." Cort gave her one of his knee-weakening grins, before heading off toward the elevators, leaving her standing there staring at his broad back as he walked away.

Tearing her gaze away from him, she looked blankly down at the clipboard in her hand, realizing that for the last couple of months they'd been more together than apart.

Yes, it really was a great thing that he was planning to move on in a few months. He would be so easy to get attached to.

Sometimes she thought, to be on the safe side, she should call a halt to whatever it was they had going on between them, yet just the thought of putting a stop to it made a sour spot grow in her stomach. Cort was easy to be around; fun to be with. Plus, he made her toes curl and her eyes cross in bed. She should just keep on enjoying it for as long as she could. On top of everything else, he still treated her as though she was a friend, never pushing for more or complaining if she turned down the opportunity for them to do something together. Giving her the space she needed to live her life.

It might sometimes feel like it was slipping out of control, but it was also perfect. Why mess with that?

Stuffing the clipboard under her arm, she rubbed her suddenly damp palms down the legs of her scrubs.

Yet she felt so conflicted. Wouldn't it be better to end the friendship now, rather than wait for the inevitable messy break-up to happen?

"Dr. Prudhomme?"

Startled out of her reverie, Liz pushed all the muddled, confusing thoughts from her mind. She'd think about Cort Smith, and how much space he was taking up in her head and life, later.

"Yes?" The intake nurse was holding the phone to her chest and looked frazzled, which was surprising on such a quiet day. "What is it?"

"I have a call from an ambulance a block away from here. They're taking a vehicle accident victim, male, twenty-five, with suspected brain injury, chest and abdominal trauma to Roosevelt, but there's been a water main break and they're stuck. The patient's crashing."

It couldn't happen at a worse time, with the hospital in such disarray, but Liz didn't hesitate.

"Tell them to bring him here, and get me a trauma team, stat."

"But, Doctor, I was told—"

"I don't care what you were told." Her veins were like ice now, her focus solely on saving the patient. "Tell them I'm waiting for them in the bay, and page the trauma team. Then get a medivac helicopter dispatched. As soon as we stabilize him, we're going to have to fly him to Roosevelt." She was already moving, heading to the entrance, the nurse's raised voice just a buzz of background noise.

There was one emergency room kept undisturbed for walk-ins and, although they'd all been told in no uncertain terms they weren't to take any trauma patients, Liz didn't care. They were the only chance the young man had to survive, and she'd do everything she could to save him. Yet her stress levels went through the roof. This wasn't business as usual, not by a long shot, and she was aware of the risk she was taking with the patient's life.

Perhaps with her career at the hospital she truly loved.

She was shouting orders as she ran, and grabbed a surgical gown from a handy stack. Cold sweat beaded her skin under her scrubs, and she barely noticed the driving drizzle that hit her face when she crashed through the bay doors. A nurse came up behind her, reached out to tie the gown in place as Liz dragged on a pair of gloves.

Everything became a nightmarish blur as the ambulance seemed to take forever to enter the bay. They all rushed forward, Liz leading the charge, to open the doors to get at the patient. The gurney's wheels dropped to the ground with a clang, the sound reverberating in her chest, as she got her first look at the young man lying there, so perilously still.

Her gut clenched and for a sickening instant the edges of her vision grew dark.

Wheat-blond hair, a little too long, matted with blood. A hawkish nose prominent in the narrow, too-pale face. The motorcycle leathers, black with splashes of decorative blue.

Andrew.

Then reality returned, although her stomach continued to churn.

It wasn't Andrew, who, had he lived, would be in his midthirties now. It was just a young, desperately hurt young man who happened to look remarkably, almost horrifyingly, like him.

Even so, it took everything she had to gather her control, to take firm hold of her senses and the gurney as they ran back into the hospital, the paramedic in charge spewing information she somehow heard and absorbed over the clamor of her heartbeat. OS rate, BP, the horrifying list of known injuries, which made a hole of despair open in her stomach. Even if they had been functioning at full capacity, just from the severity of his wounds his chances of survival were slim.

Into the emergency room, Liz giving the count to hoist him onto the stretcher, beginning her examination even as the nurses were cutting his blood-soaked motorcycle leathers away, inserting the IVs and then administering Ringer's at her command.

Steady. Steady. Focus.

Put everything else aside and focus.

But even as she admonished herself, her gaze went back to the young man's face, and her heart contracted with pain.

"Should we remove the neck brace, Doctor?"

"No," Liz replied, swallowing against the sick taste rising at the back of her throat, doing everything she could to sound normal. "He's going to be flown to Roosevelt. Keep it on."

It made completing her examination more difficult, but taking it off and putting it back on would only increase the risk of exacerbating any potential neck injury.

His breathing was ragged, shallow, his oxygen saturation so low it was at near critical levels.

"I'm going to intubate."

She stuck out her hand and closed her fingers around the laryngoscope when the nurse slapped it into her palm. Moving to the head of the stretcher, she tilted his head back. When she opened his mouth and inserted the laryngoscope, her heart sank even further. Bloody mucus obscured her view.

"Suction."

How calm her voice sounded, in contrast to the desperate chant in her head. *Hang on. Hang on. Hang on. We can save you if you just hang on.*

There. Now she could see a clear path down the trachea. "Eight-point-five millimeter," she said, sticking out her hand for the endotracheal tube. The brief spurt of relief she felt when the patient was properly intubated and she resumed her examination didn't last long.

Depressed skull fracture. Pupils responsive but sluggish. Broken ribs and suspected sternal fracture. Muffled heart sounds. Bruising forming on his abdomen. Severely broken femur.

And that was just for a start. Just what she could see in this first examination.

"Blood pressure dropping, Doctor. Eighty over sixty."

"I suspect cardiac tamponade. Portable ultrasound."

She'd been distantly aware of Dr. Yuen, who'd come in and had been doing his own examination of the patient, but she'd been too focused on her own to even look up. Now, hearing his words, she moved to the left side of the exam table in order to see the ultrasound screen. The surgeon squirted gel on the patient's chest, then started running the wand over the area. Liz watched, seeing the heart beating frantically, trying to keep working although surrounded by blood.

"Pericardiocentesis kit."

Liz gave the order, but Dr. Yuen said, "I've got it, Dr. Prudhomme."

"Yes, Dr. Yuen." But she stayed in place, ready to assist should he need it.

Another nurse came in, and said, "The 'copter should be here in ten minutes."

Dr. Yuen froze for a moment, his hands poised over the patient, whether from the nurse's words or from some reluctance to do the procedure, Liz didn't know.

"Dr. Yuen, either you insert that tube, stat, or I will."

The fierceness in her tone drew the younger man's gaze for an instant, his eyes wide behind the splatter mask, and then he turned back to the patient.

Cort stood against the wall, staying out of everyone's way, observing the team working to stabilize the young accident victim. There was really so little going on otherwise that when the call had come for a trauma team, he'd come down, even though he'd known Dr. Yuen would probably beat him to it.

Now tension tightened the back of his neck as he watched the young surgeon perform the pericardiocentesis.

There was something wrong with Liz, with her reactions, the way she was moving. He'd had ample experience of working with her, so it was easy to recognize the difference between her usual way of behaving and what he was seeing.

She looked pale to him, and her movements were choppy, although he could discern no lowering in the standard of care she was providing for the patient. But it was the way she was hovering over Dr. Yuen, almost crowding the young surgeon and snapping at him to do the procedure that was most surprising.

Then she turned to one of the nurses and said, "Make sure Roosevelt has a neurosurgeon on standby when the helicopter lands."

"I've got it under control, Dr. Prudhomme." Dr. Yuen's voice held a hint of steel. "Nurse Hayes, watch that line."

As the team worked in tandem to stabilize the young man, Cort kept his gaze on Liz, becoming more convinced there was something going on with her.

"Helicopter is here," someone called out.

Liz checked to make sure the endotracheal tube and IV lines were properly secured for transport while Dr. Yuen checked the pressure cuff surrounding the young man's leg.

With one more check of the young man's vitals, Yuen said, "He's as stable as he's going to get. Let's get him on the transport board."

The team checked and rechecked the lines and tubes, clearing any in jeopardy of being displaced by the move, and then, on Yuen's count of three, transferred the patient onto the board. Once he was strapped down, covered to keep him warm, and everything had been checked once more, they were moving, heading for the roof.

Cort hung back, but instead of following them to the nearest elevators, he ran to the bank on the other side of the ER. By the time he got to the roof observation area it was to see the patient being transferred over to the flight crew, Dr. Yuen going along to monitor the young man en route.

The rest of the trauma and ER team members turned and came back inside, chatting amongst themselves, but Liz stood watching as the patient was loaded. And she still didn't move when the helicopter took off, the rotors kicking up a cloud of dust and swirling rain, or after the aircraft disappeared into the New York skyline.

There was a slump to her shoulders and her fingers were fisted so tightly that even from a distance Cort could see her knuckles were white.

She looked so defeated Cort's chest ached just looking at her. Knowing her, she probably wanted to be alone, but he couldn't just walk away and leave her without trying to find out what was going on.

Even if she rejected his interference, and him.

CHAPTER TWELVE

IT WASN'T UNTIL he got out to the helipad and next to her that he realized she was crying, tears streaming down her face, her body shaking with stifled sobs.

"Liz—"

"Go away, Cort."

She said it fiercely, but there was no mistaking the pain in her voice, the hitch between the words. Part of him wanted to honor her request, turn away from the hurt of being shut out that way, but somehow, now he was standing beside her, that wasn't an option.

"I can't. Not when you're like this. Talk to me, Liz. Let me help if I can."

He was confused, unsure of what was upsetting her so much. From what he'd seen, the young patient's prognosis was poor. There had been signs of abnormal posturing, which often indicated a less-than-happy outcome. Yet this was something all ER doctors and trauma surgeons faced. As much as they wanted to, they couldn't save everyone and Liz's reaction to this patient was more intense than any he'd seen her display before.

"I don't need help."

"Everyone needs help at one time or another, even if it's just a shoulder to lean on or an ear to listen."

Still she hesitated, taking deep breaths, obviously trying to stem her tears.

"Please, let me help in whatever way I can."

"There's nothing you can do," she finally said, swiping her sleeve across her face. "It's just ghosts."

"Ghosts? What kind of ghosts?"

She exhaled hard, through her mouth, and shook her head. "Once, a long time ago, I knew...someone. He died in a motorcycle accident in Germany. I've been thinking about him a lot recently, and when I saw that patient..."

"He reminded you of your friend."

Liz nodded; just a sharp dip of her chin. "He even looked like Andrew. It...threw me."

The knowledge came to him in a flash, made a sour taste tickle the back of his throat. "You loved him."

"Yes."

It was a stark admission, almost resentful, and Cort remembered her indictment of love, her definition of it as a terminal disease that weakened the brain. His stomach churned as he realized Liz was still in love with this man Andrew.

Yet he had to put his muddled feelings aside, concentrate on doing whatever he could to ease Liz's distress.

But what could he say? What could anyone say to alleviate her pain?

"I'm so sorry, Liz."

She bit her lower lip then let it go on a hard exhalation. And, as if the rush of air somehow released the words, said, "He always rode too fast, took too many chances. But it was a long time ago. I should be over it by now."

Now he finally understood why, during their time in the Colombian restaurant, she'd withdrawn when he'd mentioned his motorcycle. There was no doubt bikes and riding held nothing but bad memories for her. Time didn't heal all wounds, he knew that from hard experience, so he gently touched her shoulder, needing her to know she wasn't alone.

"It's not something you can get over, I guess. You just learn to live with it."

She turned to him so suddenly he wasn't expecting it, but when she gripped the front of his shirt with both hands and buried her face in his neck, he pulled her in tighter, embracing her.

Wanting to shelter her from the pain.

She was trembling, her agony a physical thing.

"We'd argued," she whispered, almost too low to hear. "He wanted to see the world. I wanted to finish med school. I was supposed to go with him, was on the verge of saying yes, but he decided he wanted to go alone. Didn't want me to go with him."

"Why?"

"He wanted to tour Europe on his bike, but we'd had an accident the year before, and I wouldn't ride with him anymore. We were so mean to each other, Cort, saying cruel things. Then he left. I was a little relieved because then I didn't have to put my studies on hold, but I always thought there would be time to make it up. There wasn't. That was the last time I saw him."

Cort was at a loss as to what to say. To him, it sounded as though her Andrew had been a selfish man who hadn't deserved Liz's love, but he certainly couldn't say that. He wasn't sure if he should push for more information either, afraid Liz would clam up on him, but he had to say *something*.

"Was he a doctor too?"

Liz sniffled, the sound heartbreaking Cort tightened his hold on her, pressed her close, wishing there was more he could do.

"Yes. He was a year ahead of me, but medicine wasn't

a calling for him, more of an expectation, since his father was a doctor and hoped Andrew would take over his practice one day. Andrew was smart, but just scraped through. He wasn't dedicated, you know?"

No doubt that had been another bone of contention between them, Cort thought. Liz wasn't the kind to do anything half-heartedly. She would have been determined to be at the top of her class.

She sighed. "I know it's wrong to second-guess everything, but it's hard not to think about what might have been if the choices we'd made had been different."

That he could understand but, at the same time, she had to stop beating herself up over someone else's decisions.

"That's true, but if you'd gone with him, you might not have survived the accident either."

Just saying the words made his heart contract, filled the pit of his stomach with an icy ball.

"Or I might have convinced him not to be on the road when a snowstorm had been forecast. Or…"

"Or what?" he asked, hearing deepening pain in her tone. "Or what, Liz?"

"Or I might have been able to keep him alive until they got him to hospital."

There. Now he knew the crux of her agony. Recognized it far more clearly than she could ever imagine.

"Survivor's guilt, doctor edition," he said quietly. "I completely understand."

"Do you?" she asked, lifting her head to search his face.

"Oh, yes."

"Tell me."

He never spoke about Brody with anyone except with Jenna, and had never, ever mentioned his feelings of guilt to Brody's wife. But this was different. Liz needed to know she wasn't the only one who had those kinds of feelings.

"My best friend died almost six years ago from a prescription drug overdose. He worked construction and I knew he'd hurt his back a couple years before, but it didn't even occur to me he might be hooked on painkillers. Despite the fact he'd hidden it even from his wife, I can't get over the guilt of thinking I should have known, should have been able to help him."

"Were you already back home then?"

"No, I was still posted overseas."

"So, if he didn't want anyone to know, why do you think you could have helped him?"

The pain around his heart intensified. He didn't want to talk about it anymore, but she'd opened up to him and deep down inside he wanted her to understand how hurtful it had been.

Still was.

"I learned early not to get attached to anyone, Liz. When you get passed from one foster home to another, you get a clear understanding of how impermanent everything in life really is. But Brody... Brody was different. We were fourteen when we met, and we were like brothers almost right away. We aged out together, and I wanted him to join the army with me, but he wasn't interested. Yet, although we took different paths in life, we were still family, always in touch. He was the only person I trusted completely, the only person I had a real bond with. Of course I blame myself for not considering what the pain medication might do to him."

She'd been holding onto his shirt the entire time, but now she wrapped her arms around his waist and hugged him as tightly as he'd been hugging her.

"You can't keep blaming yourself, Cort. There was nothing you could do."

He leaned back, and used the side of his hand to lift her chin, so they were eye to eye.

"I'll stop, if you will."

* * *

As she looked into Cort's dark, pain-filled gaze, Liz's heart skipped one beat, then another, before it began to race. The emotions battering her were as overwhelming as they were unexpected, making her eyes sting with tears all over again. Yet she couldn't put name to them. They were alien, unrecognizable. She should be frightened by them but she wasn't.

Being held so tightly in his arms had muted her sorrow to melancholy, and it felt right to agree to let her guilt over Andrew go, although she knew doing so wouldn't be easy. She'd carried it too long, let it become ingrained over the years. But if saying she was willing to let it go would ease the pain Cort carried…

"I'll stop," she whispered, searching his face, feeling a weight lift from her chest when his lips quirked upward. "Will you?"

"I know I have to. It hurts too much to keep thinking that way." He took a deep breath, sighing on the exhalation. "And Brody wouldn't like knowing I'm twisting myself up in knots over him. He was too down to earth for that."

Before she could reply, there was the distant clatter of helicopter blades, bringing Liz suddenly back to reality. She blinked, almost surprised to realize they were still on the roof. It felt as though she'd fallen through the rabbit hole and landed in a new, unexplored country.

She stepped back, breaking their embrace, glancing around. They were alone in the dusk beneath the still overcast sky, the noise of the city muted. Her heart felt light and yet beat with deep, steady ferocity.

All she wanted was to be back in his arms, to hear his voice in her ear, sink into the warmth of his strong embrace. A little voice in the back of her head whispered she was over-emotional, needed to gather her self-containment around her once more, so as to stave off the danger.

But she didn't listen.

"I want to hear more about him," she heard herself say, as if from a distance. "Come home with me."

For all the time they'd spent together, she'd never invited him to her home, needing that last little bit of distance, a sanctuary. Now there was nowhere she'd rather be, and no one she'd rather be there with.

Cort's gaze scoured her face for what seemed an eternity until he said, "I'd like that."

After changing into their street clothing, they caught a cab to her townhome, and she led him up the steps to her door. Suddenly clumsy, she fumbled her keys, almost dropping them, before fitting the correct one into the lock.

They stepped inside into the darkened hall, lit only by a small nightlight she kept burning for those times she came in late.

As she reached for the light switch, his hand caught hers and he pulled her back into his arms.

No words now, just the hot, hard pressure of his lips on hers, the almost frantic embrace. Hands finding fastenings, sweeping over flesh, holding on, pulling closer.

For a moment it was like being swept back in time to Mexico, when the power of their attraction had been purely carnal, and there had been no barriers between them.

No need to hide, to protect herself against him, since she'd been sure she'd never see him again.

The first night he had taken her with such concentrated passion she'd been forced to run the next morning, unwilling, perhaps even unable to face him in the morning light.

Now, though, she knew him, had every reason in the world to pull up the drawbridge and secure her emotions in the stone castle of her heart.

But it was impossible to do that tonight.

Her resistance had melted away as he'd held her on the roof, as though trying to shelter her from pain. Everyone always assumed she was capable of handling anything and everything life threw at her. It had been that way all her life, with her family, Andrew, even her friends. They assumed the cool, tough façade she wore went right down to her soul, so rarely did anyone ask if she was okay, if she needed them, their strength or understanding.

Cort hadn't just asked, he'd given it freely, and turned her heart upside down at the same time.

Now she knew she'd never be able to close him out completely again and, instead of being terrified, she was elated. A strange new power seemed to flow through her blood and bones and sinews.

She wanted Cort, more than she'd ever wanted him before.

"Liz," he growled, as she pushed his shirt off over his head. "Which way?"

Without a word, she led him into her living room, turning on a lamp as she went.

"Sit." She pointed to the couch.

Cort sank down onto it as ordered, and held out one hand.

"Join me."

"Shush," she said, standing in front of him, imbued with the need to make him as crazy as he always made her. "In a minute."

He'd always taken the lead in their lovemaking, and she'd enjoyed every moment of it, but tonight felt different. Cort had cracked her emotions open like a clamshell, and she wanted to pour them out all over him. That wasn't part of their bargain, though, so the physical fulfillment of that need would have to suffice.

She undressed slowly, revealing her body to him, watching as his eyes darkened to gleaming black. As she took off each article of clothing she remembered how he'd touched her, making her feel beautiful with the purposeful movement of his fingers, the sweep of his palm, the forcefulness of his embrace. His strength matched and complemented her own, so she never felt overpowered, simply feminine as he urged her to new heights of desire and ecstasy.

As the last article of clothing fell, she trembled, almost unbearably aroused by the expression of need tightening his face, the way his eyes burned as they moved with delicious intent across her body.

He held out his hands to her, but she shook her head, taking a step forward to kneel between his thighs. She was surprised to realize her fingers were steady as she reached for the button on his waistband.

"Wait," she said. "Let me…"

The rasp of his zipper going down was loud in the room, where the only other sounds were their breathing. He shifted to help her pull his pants and underwear down and off, and then he settled against the back of the couch once more.

"Now?" he asked, his voice little more than a growl.

"Almost," she replied, as she put his clothing aside.

He obviously wasn't prepared for the swipe of her tongue along the length of his erection, if the hiss of his breath was any indication. The sound of Cort groaning her name pushed her own desire even higher, but she didn't relent in the attention she lavished on him. Beneath her fingers his powerful thigh muscles tensed, coiling tight, yet the hand he placed on her head was gentle, not insistent.

"Liz." The rasp of his voice was like music to her ears. "Babe, please."

She'd taken him to the edge, and now she eased him down tenderly, letting him catch his breath for a moment. Lifting her head, she found him looking down at her, his eyes barely open, his face flushed and damp.

With a little moan of surrender she rose to straddle him, taking him deep, shuddering at the way he filled her completely. Body. Mind. Soul.

It was sublime, with a bitter-sweet edge that made it even more precious and arousing.

Rising and falling, slowly rocking, she took them both back to the edge, then her movements becoming frantic, demanding.

"Wait," he gasped.

But she didn't listen. She knew he'd reached the end of his control, and reveled in the knowing.

Then he slipped his hand between their bodies, and touched her in just the right way.

And they flew.

CHAPTER THIRTEEN

CORT SAT AT the table, watching Liz as she moved with her usual calm efficiency around the kitchen, putting together a snack for them to share. Music played in the background, and she hummed along. Neither of them seemed inclined to speak, and that suited Cort fine just then.

Something had changed between them. He felt it, like embers in the air, stinging his skin, making it hard to breathe. Liz didn't seem affected, her demeanor unaltered.

So the change must be in him.

Memories of their lovemaking filled his head like smoke. Although satiated, his body stirred anew thinking about the way she'd made love to him, taking control, making him lose his. In a strange way he felt it as another form of her surrender, the power of it entering his bones, pushing him across an emotional line from which there was no return.

Goose bumps rose on his arms and along his spine, and he forced those thoughts away, unwilling, unable to face them just then.

Theirs was not a traditional relationship. The boundaries had been firmly established. Neither of them was looking for any kind of commitment, and he would be moving on in a few short months. He hoped that when he did, the friendship they'd developed would endure. Perhaps there'd be visits, as he passed through New York on his way some-where else, birthday and Christmas cards, telephone con-versations in between. That was the best-case scenario, in his mind, so why did thinking that way make him feel melancholy, as though the end was about to come tonight?

To distract himself, Cort looked around the huge kitchen, his gaze settling on a photograph on the mantelpiece above the fireplace. It was of a young, blond man, smiling into the camera as though he were the master of all that lay be-fore him. Was that the man who had broken Liz's heart, who'd left her unwilling to trust, to believe in love again?

"That's my brother, Robbie." There was no mistaking the fondness in her voice. "He was about twenty-one when that was taken. He was always such a party animal, it still seems surreal to think about him getting married."

She'd talked about the upcoming wedding, and he'd heard the ambivalence in her voice, but hadn't pried. Be-fore today she'd been so private, hoarding personal infor-mation like a dragon with its gold, so her family situation was still a mystery to him.

Now somehow it seemed okay to ask, "Do you like his fiancée?"

"I do. She's been good for him. You'd think, with him being in finance and Giovanna a fashion model, he'd be the more grounded, but it's the opposite way around."

Turning from the chopping block, where she was cut-ting cheese into squares, she gave him one of her pene-trating looks.

"Did I ever tell you that Robbie was adopted?"

Surprised and intrigued, he replied, "No, you didn't."

"I was about five and he was two when he came to live with us and, to me, it was as though he belonged as much as, if not more than, I did. I can safely say he's my best friend, and was from that first day we met."

Cort was glad she'd turned back to her chore, not looking at his face. Hearing her say how much she loved her brother caused him a totally unreasonable flash of jealousy, which he was sure showed in his expression before he got it under control.

It must be the stress of the day, making him react that way.

"Here's the thing," she continued. "A few years ago Robbie meets Giovanna, and he falls like a rock. He chases her all over the world, wherever she's modeling, until she agrees to marry him. Then he goes to my parents and finally asks about his birth parents."

"He hadn't before?"

She shook her head.

"You'd have to know Robbie, and my parents, to understand why it took that long. My parents don't talk about feelings, about emotion, or any part of the past that isn't perfectly respectable. It's ill bred, *common*."

The emphasis she put on the word actually made him smile. She'd sounded like an old schoolteacher.

"And Robbie…well…he's the complete opposite of me, really. He's friendly, charming, outgoing, smiles all the time. He doesn't like to rock the boat, wants everyone to be happy."

The knife in her hand stilled for a moment then she shrugged lightly.

"I think he just figured if they'd wanted to tell him, they would have. Anyway, he finally asks about his parents, and it turns out he's actually my father's child. The product of an affair Dad had not long after my mother had me."

He hadn't seen that one coming, and felt his eyebrows go up.

She gave him a sideways look over her shoulder. "Right? So, you see, I'm still a little…upset with my father. What kind of man has an affair when his wife just had a baby?"

Cort was still trying to process what she'd told him.

"And your mom knew your brother was actually your father's child?"

"Yes. Isn't that insane? I wish I could understand how it all came about. It's really eaten at me since I heard, and I haven't really spoken to my father since."

"I know you said your parents don't talk about things, but can't you ask them?"

Her sigh almost broke his heart.

"I know it won't make a difference. My mom looked so frightened when she talked about it, and Dad just walked away. They haven't even told Robbie the full story, only that when his birth mother got sick and was dying, my mom agreed to take him in. Honestly, she's treated him as though he were her own, without any reservations. They're actually closer than my mom and I are."

That gave him pause, as he worked it all through in his head.

Why was she so angry at her father for something that had happened so long ago? It hadn't destroyed her family. In fact, she'd ended up with a sibling she obviously adored. Remembering how upset Liz had been with the young stabbing victim who was still worried about the man who'd almost killed her, he had to ask.

"You're not angry with your mother?"

Laying down the knife, she busied herself with arranging everything on a platter.

"I always thought of my mom as being delicate, you know? I couldn't be the daughter she wanted, so I try not to hurt her any more than I have to, and my being angry with her would hurt her horribly."

When he was young he'd longed for a family, believing it would be like in the TV shows. Of course, as he'd grown older he'd realized relationships weren't as simple as portrayed in the media, but the complexity of Liz's family made his head swim a little.

One thing was obvious, though. Liz somehow saw herself as a disappointment to her mother, which seemed crazy to Cort. What mother wouldn't love to have a beautiful, successful woman like Liz as their child? He also wondered if Liz saw her mother's actions in forgiving her husband and accepting his child into her family as a weakness. It made sense, considering Liz's overall view of love.

"I think," he said slowly, "your mother is probably a lot stronger than you give her credit for. I mean, she has to be, to have forgiven your father and treated your brother the way she has. Why not ask her, let her explain what happened? At least then you can maybe put it behind you."

Still with her back to him, Liz muttered, "It wouldn't be an easy conversation to have."

"I'm sure it won't be, especially since you say talking things through isn't your family's way, but it might be the best thing. For you, at any rate."

Which was all he really cared about anyway.

Finally she turned and walked over to the table, carrying the platter, her noncommittal expression one he knew well.

"Let's eat," was all she said.

Everything had changed, but Liz was determined not to let Cort see. As usual busying herself, being useful, allowed her to avoid revealing her emotional state, which was frankly chaotic.

The entire day had taken its toll on her, but she didn't regret any of it, just didn't want to think too deeply about what was happening to her feelings for Cort right now.

Better to do that when she was alone.

In the meantime, talking about Robbie and her family helped to take the edge off. Cort had a way of cutting through to the heart of things, she mused as they munched their way through the platter of cold cuts, antipasto, vegetables, cheeses and crusty bread.

While she'd been concentrating on being angry with her father, it was just a way to avoid acknowledging it was her mother she really needed to speak to.

It all just seemed so complicated, and she sometimes found herself wishing Robbie had never asked about his origins. Yet she could completely understand his need to know, and felt selfish whenever she had those thoughts.

"Have you ever tried to find your parents?"

She saw Cort stiffen, and then his shoulders relaxed fractionally, and he shook his head.

"No, I haven't."

"Never wanted to?"

"When we were younger, Brody and I used to talk about it, trying to decide whether to do it or not. In his case, he'd lived with his mother until she died, when he was eight. His father was never in the picture, and he figured it was probably for the best. Who knew what he'd dig up, trying to find out? In my case, I couldn't see the upside to finding the people who tossed me out with the trash, you know?"

As nonchalant as he tried to sound, she heard the residual pain in his voice. Who could blame him? She'd guess it was something he'd had to reconcile himself to, even if it had been the most hurtful thing anyone could do.

"I understand, but you're stronger than I am. My curiosity would have gotten the best of me."

"In one respect I gave in to my curiosity. I got my DNA tested, for medical purposes, a couple years ago. Well, that and because I was tired of people asking me what my ancestry was." He smiled slightly. "People would ask me if I'm Hispanic, Brazilian, Native American, Italian. Hell, when I was in the army there was a Filipino guy who could have been my brother. And, before you ask, no, he actually *wasn't* my brother. I checked."

Filipino, Italian, Native American, Hispanic. Yes, she could see him fitting into any of those groups.

"So, what was the result?"

"I'm almost exactly one half Native American and one half European, mostly Irish."

"Exactly half?" That was strange.

"Yep, pretty much."

She turned over all she knew about DNA testing in her head. "It's a shame it can't pinpoint a tribe, isn't it?"

Cort shrugged, but she read tension in the set of his shoulders. "Not really. It's not that important."

"Hmm. I asked Robbie what had prompted him to want to find out about his birth parents, and he just said, "Everybody wants to know where they come from so they can figure out where to go." Pretty profound, for my knuckle-head brother, but it made sense to me."

Cort swallowed the last of his bread smeared with Brie before he replied.

"Everybody needs something different in life, I guess."

Like she needed the stability of Hepplewhite and New York City, and he need the adventure of traveling around.

"True," she replied, trying to ignore the ache in her chest at that admission.

"So, are you going to talk to your mom about what happened?"

"Maybe after the wedding. Everything is too crazy right now." She was prevaricating, and even she realized it.

Cort gave her a sympathetic smile. "You'd probably enjoy the wedding more if you got past it, though. Nothing like unspoken tension to ruin a happy occasion."

He was right, of course, but she knew she wouldn't.

"There's too much going on, getting ready for the wedding. Mom's already in a tailspin. Throwing that at her right now would be downright unkind."

She ruminated on her own cowardice for a moment, but then an idea hit her, and made her heart race.

For too long she'd run from emotions, feelings, happiness. Lied to herself that she didn't need anyone. Today had, if nothing else, shown how good it could be to have someone to lean on, even if just for a little while.

Until Cort left New York, or decided to end their affair, he was hers, and she didn't want to deny herself the pleasure of being with him. While others made her doubt herself, something about him made her feel stronger than she ever had before. She would take advantage of that for as long as she could.

"What?" Cort asked, the corners of his lips lifting.

"You know what would make my mother very, very happy? If you came to the wedding with me."

"What?" he asked again, this time with a tone of such horror it actually made her snicker.

"She's asked me a million times if I'm bringing anyone, and it would be a huge favor to me if you'd come."

"But—"

"Cort, listen. We both know you'll be gone on to your next adventure in a few months, and this thing between us will be over, but my mom doesn't know that. It'll make her happy to think I'm in a relationship, you'll have a great time, and it might even pave the way to my having that difficult conversation with her."

The last part she threw in for effect, knowing nothing would make that talk any easier, but also cognizant of Cort's belief in the importance of it. Manipulative? Maybe a little. But having Cort around would make the wedding more bearable.

She really was dreading it.

"First off, isn't it dishonest to let your mother think our relationship is more than it really is? And, secondly, I'm pretty sure I wouldn't fit in with your family and their friends."

"Yes, and no," she answered succinctly. "It is sort of dishonest, but you have no idea how much pressure I feel every time she asks me about my relationship status. It would get her off my back, at least for a little while, and genuinely make her happy. I don't see the problem with that, as long as we're on the same page.

"As for you not fitting in, besides the fact that Robbie and Giovanna have a wide variety of friends, and my family, both sides of it, are a mess, you're a handsome, charming doctor with a sterling reputation. Believe me, you'll fit in better than I will."

The look he gave her made her feel twitchy. It was the kind of expression that said, louder than words, that he saw through her argument to the heart of the matter once more.

And her instincts were proven correct when he said, "You really aren't sure of your place in your family, are you?"

How could she explain it to him when it was something she'd grappled with all her life? But she felt as though she owed it to him to at least try.

"I know they love me," she said slowly, "but I've really never felt as if I fit in. They're charming and sociable and, in their own way, affectionate. I've always felt a little distant, never knew how to get along in the world they traverse so easily, and always knew I wasn't able to meet my parents' expectations. So I set my own, and decided to live my own life, and that just widened the gap."

Without warning, he reached across the table and took her hand, rubbing his thumb over her knuckles, the smile on his face both gentle and conspiratorial.

"Can I say, from my perspective, it's a life well lived? I'm so glad we met, because you've opened up my horizons in the best of ways. I think you're amazing, and shame on your parents if they don't too."

Warmth flared up into her face. Dear goodness, when was the last time she'd blushed? Maybe fourth grade? It made her want to duck her head, but Cort held her gaze with his effortlessly. Best to capitalize on the moment, if she could.

"So you'll come with me?"

His lips quirked, and although he shook his head he also said, "Yes."

CHAPTER FOURTEEN

BEFORE LIZ COULD even touch him, the patient jerked away.

"Whaddaya doing? Haven't yah poked me enough?"

As his alcohol-soaked breath blew across her face, Liz tried not to inhale too much of it. While he'd been given thiamine and glucose intravenously, and had been in the ER for a while, he was still intoxicated enough for some symptoms to potentially be masked. Frequent examinations were necessary to make sure nothing had been missed, although she suspected the old saw about drunks and children being protected was true of this patient. His injuries were minor, considering he'd been struck by a car.

"Mr. Kendrick, I have to keep checking you to make sure you don't have internal injuries."

"But I'm fine."

As if to prove it he tried to roll, perhaps to sit up, but was stopped by both Liz and the attending nurse holding him down.

"I'm afraid that isn't true. You were hit by a car. At the very least you have a broken nose and I suspect a fractured ankle."

"Jush get thish thing off me and let me go home. I tell you, I'm fine."

Liz and the nurse, Marta, then found themselves in a bit of a wrestling match with the inebriated patient over the cervical collar. Although Liz hadn't detected any neck or back injuries, she wasn't taking any chances and had ordered a C-spine X-ray, which hadn't been done yet. Just as Mr. Kendrick gave up, apparently deciding instead to treat them to a mangled, off-key rendition of a song Liz was sure she'd never heard before, the door opened and Cort walked in.

For a moment even Mr. Kendrick went still, and Liz's knees went ridiculously weak on seeing him, her entire body thrumming to life.

She refused to think about how attached she was getting to Cort. How he'd invaded every facet of her life. A part of her wanted to just enjoy it all, but the realist in her kept reminding her that he wasn't going to stick around so she should start rebuilding her defenses.

That was proving extremely difficult.

Which was why she made sure to keep her work persona intact with him.

But it didn't help that just seeing him filled her with warmth and still made her sometimes forget what she was doing.

Like just now.

Gathering herself, she asked, "Can I help you?"

The words came out sharper than she'd planned, but Cort didn't seem fazed.

"I was called down to examine an accident victim. I could have sworn this was the room they told me to come to."

"Oh, no." There was clear annoyance in Marta's voice. "We have a trainee on the desk today, and she's been messing things up terribly. I know I told her Dr. Nolan Smith, the orthopedic surgeon. I'll go and rectify the situation, Dr. Prudhomme."

She made a beeline for the door, and Liz replied, "Thank you, Marta."

"Doc. Doc!" Mr. Kendrick lifted a hand and waved it at Cort. "Can you get these women off me, please? I just wanna go home and they won't let me."

Cort stepped closer to the bed, into a position where Mr. Kendrick could see him clearly, thankfully on the opposite side from Liz. She'd had to attend Giovanna's bridal shower, which had been a two-day spa retreat in the Hamptons. While she'd enjoyed the change of scenery and the pampering, the downside had been two nights away from Cort, and she was feeling the lack. The last thing she needed right now was to be too close to him. She might forget herself and touch him.

Her fingers tingled at the thought.

"Well, if they won't let you, it's because they have good reason. Why don't you just relax and let Dr. Prudhomme fix you up?"

"There's nothing to fix. I feel great."

Cort shook his head. "Listen, Dr. Prudhomme is one of the best. Let her take care of you, and you'll be out of here as soon as possible."

Mr. Kendrick replied with a belch, then mumbled under his breath. Cort shot Liz a knowing half smile, then said, "Sorry for the intrusion. I'll be on my way."

Before she realized what he was about to do, Mr. Kendrick grabbed Liz's wrist, saying, "My face hurts. And my leg."

The drip was finally doing its job, sobering him up enough for the pain to break through. "I'm sure they do, Mr. Kendrick. As I told you, you have a broken nose and an ankle injury. Does anywhere else hurt?"

"No. No," he mumbled, closing his eyes. "I don't think so."

But something bothered her about the bruising she'd noticed as they'd cut away his clothing. Still, she hesitated. If she let Cort leave and then called for a surgeon, someone else might respond and she wouldn't have to deal with working with him right now.

Realizing what she was doing, she gave herself a mental kick in the butt. Endangering a patient because her hormones were in disarray? Ridiculous.

"Excuse me, Dr. Smith," she called out, just as Cort got to the door. "A moment, please?"

As it turned out, Mr. Kendrick had a splenic rupture requiring surgery.

After Cort left to go and scrub in, while Liz was signing off on her part of Mr. Kendrick's care, she was still brooding about her almost compulsive need to be around Cort, which led her to think about the days just past.

The spa retreat hadn't been all fun for her. Giovanna, caught up in what Liz thought of as "bride fever," had turned her attention to Liz.

"We need to find you a good man," she'd declared to the entire group at dinner. "I don't understand why no one has snapped you up yet."

Thankfully, Giovanna hadn't mentioned Liz was bringing a plus one to the wedding. Probably because Liz had explained Cort was just a friend from work, invited to get Lorelei off her back about her constantly single state. Giovanna had bought the story without question.

Liz's cousin, Moira, had giggled and interjected, "I'm not sure the man exists who could deal with Liz. He'd either have to be a saint or a doormat."

"What do you mean by that?" Giovanna asked, obviously annoyed and narrowing her eyes at the other woman.

But Moira just shrugged. "Liz is stubborn, and cranky. Not to mention obsessed with her job. What man's going to put up with that long term? He'd have to either deal with constant arguing or give in all the time."

"She's none of those things!"

Liz loved the way Giovanna had jumped to her defense, but she was forced to admit, "I am dedicated to my job. And stubborn too." She drew the line at admitting to "cranky," although all her life she'd had people constantly telling her to smile, and getting annoyed when she refused. If that made her cranky, so be it.

"And you're difficult," Moira pointed out, obviously enjoying herself. "Everyone says so."

Unable to resist, Liz gave her cousin a bland look, and rebutted, "People only say that when I won't give in to them, and they know I'm right. Who has time to pander to anyone's ego like that?"

"*If* you were married, or even seriously involved with someone, you'd *have* to, just for a peaceful life," said another woman.

That started a debate about the fragility of the male ego, and the lengths women sometimes had to go to in order to get their own way. Sitting back and listening to it, Liz knew herself incapable of sustaining a relationship if that was what it took. Yet she didn't feel superior, or disdainful toward the other women, just pensive and a little sad, as it seemed to solidify all the thoughts she'd had about herself.

She also couldn't help wondering if this type of mindset was what had led her mother to forgive her husband and take in his love child to raise as her own. Yet wouldn't there be some of the thinly veiled resentment the women she was listening to confessed to feeling and acting out in myriad little ways? Lorelei Prudhomme had never exhibited that, as far as Liz could see. And if she'd done so to her husband, would that bond, that united front they always exhibited as a couple, truly exist?

The more she wondered about it, the more confused she got. Cort had said she'd need to get to the bottom of it before she could get past it, and he was probably right. But the more time that passed, the more it seemed she was the only one who wanted to know, and the harder it became to bring up. While she was direct and no-nonsense with everyone else in her life, somehow it was almost impossible to be that way with her parents.

Old habits ran too deep.

Now, as the nurses were wheeling Mr. Kendrick up to the surgical floor, Liz's phone vibrated, and her heart missed a beat when she realized it was Cort texting.

You busy tonight?

No.

Thankfully, Robbie's friend Simon had taken on the stag party organization, and since it was being held at an exclusive, men's only club, Liz not only didn't have to go but was actively *not* invited.

Meet me at my apartment after work? Got my uniform back from the cleaners. You need to tell me if it still fits.

Sure.

Looking at her laconic reply and comparing it with the eagerness she actually felt at the thought of being with Cort that evening made her snort. Just the thought of him in his uniform made her mouth water.

He'd be lucky if he got a word out before she jumped all over him. As much as she hated to admit it, even to herself, she'd missed him that much.

The city had been struck by a rare mid-June heatwave, catching many people by surprise. Apparently including the maintenance people at Cort's apartment building, which he realized when he got home that evening to find the air-conditioners weren't working.

Letting himself into the apartment, he found Liz lying on the couch with a couple of fans blowing directly on her. All she was wearing were her panties and a thin cotton camisole, sweat making them stick to her luscious curves, revealing more than they concealed.

"Why didn't you call and tell me what was going on here?" he asked, closing the door behind him, wanting only to go over there and make her even sweatier. "We could have met at your place instead."

"I don't mind," she replied, stretching one leg out and pointing her toes at him. The motion was erotic, electrifying his blood, making him instantly hard. "I like the heat. Makes a nice change from the winter and cold, damp spring. Hopefully it'll go away before the wedding, though, or I'll be a sweltering mess."

He dropped his backpack and toed off his shoes, his eyes never leaving her. They knew each other well enough now to know the signals. Liz wasn't in the mood to talk and, truth be told, neither was Cort.

It had only been a couple of days that she'd been gone, two nights when he'd tossed and turned and woken up in the morning, disappointed not to have her draped across his chest. The sense of danger rising inside him ever since that day on the hospital roof had grown almost too insistent for him to ignore, but once more he pushed it aside. There was no way he could ignore his visceral attraction to her as he watched her eyelids slide almost closed, saw her lick her lips in anticipation.

He unbuttoned his shirt. Once it was off, he made short work of the rest of his clothes. Liz shifted on the couch, her fingers curling into her palms.

She was waiting for him to take control, and the sense of power her quiescence gave him sent a streak of fire through his blood. He could never get enough of that feeling. Never get enough of her.

The thought made his heart miss a beat, but it didn't make his hunger for her abate, his ravenous desire, his heart-deep want.

Later he'd deal with the fallout, plan his exit strategy, before it became impossible to contemplate. Before he made a fool of himself and opened the way to the heartbreak he knew this glorious woman would cause.

Right now, though, all he could see, all he could think about was her.

CHAPTER FIFTEEN

THE DAY OF the wedding dawned bright and warm, the heat-wave thankfully having dissipated. Cort took a last look at himself in the mirror before leaving the house, making sure his mess uniform was pristine.

It felt strange to have it on again after all this time. He'd contemplated renting a suit for the wedding but had decided not to. He wasn't going to go to Liz's brother's wedding as anyone or anything other than himself. While being an army medical officer no longer defined him, it was still better than pretending he was the kind of man who had a morning suit hanging in his closet, no doubt perfectly pressed by his valet.

Did men even have valets anymore? And if they did, did those valets press their suits?

Those were the kinds of questions Liz, and most of the people he was about to meet, would have answers to, whereas Cort had no clue.

Weird, the types of things that went through his mind when he was on edge. And he definitely was on edge. He'd go so far as to say nervous, which wasn't a sensation he enjoyed in the slightest. Neither he nor Liz had been at their best the last few days. Cort had tried to put it down to the fact the hospital had problems with some of the new equipment and staff, making normal activities more difficult than usual. And, of course, there was the upcoming wedding, which necessitated her running up and down and them spending less time together.

But he knew there was more to it than that, at least on his part. He couldn't shake the feeling this wedding was going to prove the beginning of the end for his intimate relationship with Liz. He didn't believe in precognition or anything like that, but had felt something building between them, like the precursor to lightning. Or a harbinger of a turning point, and he had no reason to believe it would be a positive one. Cort did believe in following his instincts, and those instincts were telling him to brace for whatever was coming.

Better yet, get out in front of it, which was what he'd been trying to do. He always felt better with a plan B in his back pocket.

Cort just didn't want to think about telling Liz his plans. Not that she'd care one way or the other. But he cared. Thinking about saying goodbye to her made him feel slightly nauseous.

Not the time to think about it, he told himself, checking his appearance one last time then brushing at a barely visible speck of dust on his service cap. Getting through the day was going to be stressful enough.

Right on time, the car service called to say the town car was downstairs, and Cort let himself out of the apartment.

"Don't worry about it," Liz had said yesterday, before heading off to the hotel where all the wedding party was staying. "I told Giovanna and Robbie you were just a friend I invited to keep Mom off my back and neither Mom nor Dad are the kind to question you about our relationship. Although Mom will make a fuss over you, wanting to make a good impression, in case you stick around."

She'd said the last part with a small chuckle, acknowledging the fact they both knew that wasn't going to happen.

Neither telling himself he, in turn, didn't need to make a good impression, nor reminding himself he'd faced far more dangerous missions, helped. Whatever the relationship really was between Liz and her family, the last thing Cort wanted was to do anything to make it worse. And he couldn't see an upside to her fooling her parents about her relationship status. If it came out later, wouldn't they be hurt by the subterfuge?

However it all fell out, he'd decided to make the most of the time they had together, if Liz would let him. Sometime, in the not-too-distant future, it would all be over and he wanted as many memories of her as he could make.

About a block and a half before they got to the church, they hit a traffic jam. Ahead Cort could see barricades across the road, and was about to ask the driver if there was a problem when she said, "It'll take a little while to get to the church, sir, but we're in good time. You won't be late."

To his surprise, he realized not only was the road barricaded so the wedding guests could be dropped off at the entrance to the church but there were photographers and videographers outside.

"The paparazzi are out in full force," the driver remarked cheerfully while they waited their turn to get to the head of the line, as though that were the most normal thing in the world. "Everyone wants to see Giovanna Alberghetti's wedding dress."

Cort hadn't even known who Giovanna was until Liz had mentioned her brother was marrying the woman. He'd come into the situation already feeling completely out of his depth, and it wasn't getting any better.

Thankfully, none of the photographers were interested in him when he got out of car. It was a relief to walk up the steps of the cathedral without any of the excitement he'd witnessed after the car ahead had disgorged its passengers, who, according to his driver, were a couple of fashion models and their sports star husbands.

In the narthex he joined the line of people snaking into the church, and when Cort gave his name to an usher at the door the young man smiled.

"Oh, yes, Major Smith. This way, please."

They proceeded up the main aisle, Cort expecting to be slotted into one of the back pews, but once they passed the halfway mark and kept going, his stomach dropped down into his socks. Aware of people turning to look at him, no doubt wondering who this nobody was, he kept his eyes straight ahead and pretended to be on military parade.

"Here we are, Major."

The usher stood back and gestured Cort into the second row on the right of the aisle.

A pew even he knew was usually reserved for family.

There were already a few elderly couples seated at the opposite end of the row, and one of the gentlemen gave Cort a very obvious once-over before nodding at him then turning to face forward again.

Gathering himself, not wanting to make a scene, Cort said, "Thank you," and stepped into the pew.

He was quite sure there'd been a mistake, and dreaded the embarrassment of someone coming to move him farther back in the church. In the meantime, however, all he could do was pretend it was all fine.

There wasn't much space left in the pew, so he moved down as far as he could go without crowding the lady he was next to, and sat down, balancing his cover on his knees.

It was tempting to simply stare straight ahead, but a glance to his right found the lady next to him smiling his way, so he returned the gesture. That was all she needed.

Leaning toward him, she whispered, "Who are you, young man?"

"Dr. Cort Smith, ma'am," he replied just as softly.

"I'm Melisande Prudhomme, the groom's great-aunt. Are you Eliza's young man? I heard she had someone accompanying her today, but wasn't sure I believed it."

In for a penny, in for a pound.

"Yes, ma'am, I am accompanying Liz."

Her face brightened. "I'm so glad to see her with someone, and someone of substance too. Are you stationed nearby, or are you two having one of those long-distance relationships?" She waggled a finger at him. "Those hardly ever work, you know."

"I'm retired from the military, ma'am. Liz and I work together."

"Oh, that's better, then. And you should call me Aunt Millie, like Eliza does."

The gentleman seated beside Melisande leaned forward and said, "Stop interrogating the major, Millie." Then he stuck out his hand toward Cort. "Cecil Prudhomme. This busybody's husband."

Cort suppressed a grin, as he shook the proffered hand. "Dr. Cort Smith. It's a pleasure to meet you, sir."

"I'd introduce you to the rest of the folks in the pew, but it might cause a bit of a commotion. My sister, Bunny, is as deaf as a post and given to bellowing rather than speaking. Whispering is far beyond her capabilities at this point. You'll meet them all at the reception."

"Bunny's also a little gaga," Aunt Millie whispered, a mischievous twinkle in her eye. "If she asks you what you did in the war, just be warned she'll be talking about World War Two."

"Millie. Behave," Cecil Prudhomme said, but there was undeniable amusement in his voice.

"Thank you for the head's up, ma'am," Cort replied, unable to suppress a little chuckle.

The organ, which had been playing classical music quietly in the background, suddenly took on a more sonorous tone, and a ripple of excitement ran through the congregation.

A door to the right of the altar opened and a man Cort recognized as Liz's brother Robbie stepped through, followed closely by Liz.

But this was a Liz Cort had never seen before.

Sophisticated.

Movie-star glamorous.

Gloriously encased in a dress that, although it mimicked her brother's suit in coloring, showcased her beauty in such a way that Cort was left wondering who would bother to look at the bride.

Creamy shoulders rose from a low-cut neckline, framed by a wide, dark gray collar. The buff-colored bodice somehow wrapped and emphasized Liz's perfect, curvy body, while the same gray came around to cinch her waist and fall away almost like the tails of the men's morning suits. Beneath was revealed a straight skirt, seemingly of the same fabric as her brother's trousers.

She was so beautiful he couldn't take his eyes off her and his heart skipped a beat as heat gathered at the base of his spine.

Liz scanned the front rows, and her gaze settled on him. She didn't smile, but the corners of her lips twitched and she sent him a little wink, before walking to her place at her brother's side.

"Oh, how lovely Eliza looks," Aunt Millie sighed, while giving Cort a surprisingly hearty poke in the side. "If that dress doesn't give you naughty ideas, young man, I'll be sadly disappointed in you."

"Oh, it does, ma'am," he whispered back.

At the same time her husband said, "Millie!"

The wedding service went off without a hitch. Even Giovanna was on time, for what was probably the first time ever, Robbie whispered to Liz with a chuckle. Testament, Liz thought, to her now sister-in-law's delight in marrying the man she'd so assiduously fended off for almost a year.

Of course, after the ceremony the wedding party and immediate family had to have pictures taken, and by the time they got close to the end of the photo shoot Liz was impatient.

She was worried about Cort. How he was managing by himself at the prereception gathering. Mind you, he'd been sitting next to her Aunt Millie in the church, and if there was anyone who'd be inclined to take him under their wing, it was her.

She really shouldn't have been concerned. As the wedding party made their entrance into the beautifully decorated ballroom where the wedding brunch was being held, she spotted Cort standing to one side, sandwiched between Aunt Millie and Aunt Bunny.

"Good grief," she muttered, earning a laughing look from Robbie as he followed her gaze and saw the trio.

"Your poor guy," Robbie said.

"He's not—"

"Your guy," her brother finished for her. "So you've said ad nauseam."

Liz sent him a glower, which just made him laugh. It was a continuation of sorts of their conversation in the church.

"That guy of yours looks like he's contemplating how to get that dress off you." Robbie smirked, apparently unbearably pleased with himself and wanting to spread the love around. "And don't bother to tell me you're just friends. I know you too well, you know."

She hadn't even realized she'd gone back to staring at Cort, so handsome in his dress blues, until her brother's comment hit home.

"Buzz off," she'd replied out of the corner of her mouth,

as their mother appeared at the end of the aisle on the arm of an usher, their father walking behind them.

Watching her parents coming toward them, beaming with pride, caused a flood of emotion so intense it was as though a hand closed around her heart. Instinctively she looked again at Cort, seeking reassurance, and when he smiled at her she was suddenly able to breathe again.

"Will you at least talk to Dad today?" Robbie had asked. "Rather than pretend to?"

That question still echoed in her head hours later, and she still hadn't formulated an answer. Her father and her had drifted around each other like planets whose orbits never really crossed, although Liz thought she'd seen a hint of melancholy in Brant's gaze when she'd caught him looking at her.

What she needed to say to her father, to ask him, wasn't an appropriate subject for such a happy day, was it? Even as she justified her continued silence, she knew herself to be a coward.

It was really her mother she needed to break the silence. To, in a strange way, give Liz permission to forgive her father. In her heart, Liz already knew how sorry Brant was, but the anger she felt on her mother's behalf kept her holding him at arm's length.

Giovanna had planned a simple yet elegant brunch for after the ceremony, but the real party wasn't until the evening. In between she and Robbie would have some more pictures taken and then supposedly rest up for the festivities to come. The ravenous way her brother looked at his gorgeous bride made Liz think he had something other than resting on his mind for those hours in between.

"You look amazing," Cort said softly, for her ears only, as he held out her chair for her. Thankfully Giovanna had dispensed with a more formal seating plan and they were sitting together. "That dress wraps you up like the perfect present."

She gave him a bland look as he waited for the other ladies to be seated, standing beside her with his hand on the back of her chair, his fingers just brushing the exposed skin of her shoulder.

"You like gifts, don't you?" she asked, earning herself a heavy-lidded look that turned her insides liquid with desire.

"So, who are you?" Moira asked, giving Cort a flirtatious look as she slid into her chair, despite her husband being right there.

Straight-faced, Liz answered. "Oh, this is Saint Cort Smith. Cort, my cousin Moira."

Moira turned pink and, after a hasty greeting, quickly turned to speak to Giovanna's cousin, who was seated next to her. The men had taken their seats, and Cort leaned over to ask, "When was I elevated to sainthood, and by whom?"

Liz shrugged, smoothing the napkin on her lap, regretting the impulse that had caused her to say what she had. But honesty won out, as it always did with her.

"Moira said the only men who would be able to put up with me were either saints or doormats. You're definitely not a doormat, so..."

Cort laughed softly. "Your cousin doesn't really know you that well, does she? If she saw how all the men in the hospital follow you longingly with their eyes wherever you go, she'd realize how silly she sounds."

Then he leaned in even closer so he was speaking right into her ear. "And my thoughts toward you right now aren't very saintly at all."

It made gooseflesh break out all up and down her arms.

And she knew Robbie wasn't the only Prudhomme who was going to be naughty between brunch and dinner.

CHAPTER SIXTEEN

IF THE BRUNCH was the epitome of elegance and refinement, the party that evening would best be compared to a rave. Giovanna had rented one of the hottest night clubs in Manhattan, complete with DJ, and invited a crowd of people who hadn't been at the actual wedding ceremony. Some of the older members of family and elderly friends forwent the evening festivities, but for those who attended there was a private upstairs lounge with a bar and comfortable chairs. There they could look down on the dance floor through the large windows or step out onto the balcony, which had a nice view of Central Park.

That was where Cort and Liz ended up, since neither of them were inclined to join the gyrating mass of bodies on the dance floor or have to scream to hear each other speak.

"Are you having a good time?" Liz asked Cort, as they stood on the balcony, sharing a drink and getting a breath of warm night air.

He smiled in response, casually looping his arm over her shoulder.

"You've asked me that at least a hundred times today. Yes, I've had a good time."

She couldn't help worrying. Her family could be heavy weather to those not used to them, her father's side filled with eccentrics sprinkled with snobs, her mother's with snobs sprinkled with eccentrics. And everyone knew the only difference between eccentricity and insanity was how much money the person had. No doubt Cort had been exposed to a lot more than just what she'd witnessed herself, since she'd been busy with wedding duties.

"Even with Aunt Bunny asking you if you were at the Battle of the Bulge? Or Francesca acting as though being a surgeon in a hospital, rather than in private practice, was akin to working as a pool boy?"

He laughed then, his arm tightening around her in a comforting hug.

"Your aunts were a delight, and it's not the first time my career path has been questioned, believe me."

Curious, she twisted slightly to look at him. "Really? How so?"

"Oh, my ex, the one who dumped me right before our wedding, seemed to think it would be more appropriate for me to be a plastic surgeon. I think she was hoping for free cosmetic work down the line."

Horrified, she actually gasped. "What? Did she understand the training you went through to be a trauma surgeon? The dedication it took to get to where you are, and how good you are at your job?" She huffed, disgusted. "How silly can people be?"

"I don't let it bother me. I've come a long way, and although I sometimes have to remind myself of that, the bottom line is life is good."

The door behind them opened and Robbie said, "There you are."

It was only when she turned, a smile already in place, that she realized her brother wasn't alone. Their parents stepped onto the balcony behind him and, on seeing Liz and Cort, seemed to hesitate for an instant.

Robbie grinned, one of his cheeky, inviting grins, and said, "I was hoping to get the chance to talk to you one on one, Dr. Smith. My father isn't the kind to ask what your intentions are toward Liz, but I don't have the same scruples."

"Robbie!"

Both Liz and her father said it at the same time, in the same warning tone, the similarity so marked they all just stood there for a beat.

And then Robbie said quietly, "Ah, nature wins out every time, doesn't it? You two are so alike, sometimes it's frightening."

Cort's arm had dropped away from her shoulders when they'd turned to greet the others, and Liz shivered, missing the comforting warmth. As though sensing her need for reassurance, Cort reached out and touched her wrist, his fingers rubbing back and forth a couple of times.

"I came prepared for an interrogation," Cort said, smiling. "And after spending time with your Aunt Millie, I'm confident I can stand up to anything."

"Ah, sir, I think you'll find she merely softened you up for me," Robbie replied with another grin and a sweep of his arm toward an unoccupied group of chairs at the end of the balcony. "After you."

With another light touch to Liz's wrist Cort strode off with Robbie, and she watched them go, trepidation keeping her gaze fixed on their retreating backs so she didn't have to look at her parents.

"Go with them, Brant," Lorelei said to her husband. "Make sure Robbie doesn't do anything to make Dr. Smith uncomfortable."

"Yes, darling," Brant replied, before bending to kiss her cheek.

Then he strode off, leaving Liz alone with her mother.

Lorelei smiled at Liz. "It all went well, don't you think?"

"Yes, Mom. It did."

Just moments before she'd thought this the perfect time to ask her mother about the past. Now she was kicking herself for her cowardice. Her mother's contented smile was well earned, and Liz was loath to see it disappear.

Then her mother said, "This is the first opportunity I've had to tell you how proud I was of you today."

Liz dredged up a little smile of her own. "It's amazing what a designer dress can do."

Lorelei's perfectly shaped brows rose. "Eliza, the woman makes the dress outstanding, not the other way around. I know I've told you that before."

"Yes, Mother," she said dutifully, having indeed heard it many times over the years.

Her mother huffed. "You're beautiful, Eliza. I think you're old enough now to know it for yourself and not dismiss me when I say it, the way you used to when you were a child."

The sharp retort was so surprising Liz only just stopped herself from gaping at her mother.

"What? When did I do that?"

"All the time. You'd quote that odious Nanny Hardy at me. 'Better to be useful than decorative.'" Lorelei made a sound as close to a rude one as Liz had ever heard from her. "And, of course, it's important to be a useful member of society. You becoming a doctor was the proudest moment of my life, because you worked so hard for it. But the way she went about it gave you a complex about your appearance, and that was unforgivable in my book. How I despised that woman."

"If you hated her so much, why did you keep her on?"

All the fire seemed to go out of Lorelei, and she turned to look out over the park. Although her back was ramrod straight, she seemed to droop.

Liz suppressed the sigh rising in her throat. "Mom, it's been a long day. Do you want to sit down?"

Lorelei shook her head. "I'm fine, Eliza. Why do all of

you treat me as though I'm made of glass? I'm far stronger than any of you seem to think."

The echo of Cort's words gave Liz the courage she hadn't thought she'd ever be able to find. For so many months she'd avoided asking the questions she needed to ask to move through it, afraid of what she'd hear. Now she was ready, if her mother was willing.

"Mom, will you tell what happened all those years ago with you and Dad and Robbie? I really need to know."

Liz saw her mother's lips tighten, and then she nodded.

Turning so they were face to face, she said, "After you were born, I suffered from postpartum depression. Worse, I learned that, because of an infection, I would never have any more children. The only way I knew how to deal with it was to stay busy, take on more charity work, keep moving and be out all the time."

She lifted her chin, not defiantly but as though taking ownership of something she hadn't been able to at the time.

"I was drinking too much, wouldn't even discuss what I was going through with your father, who tried to get me to go to therapy. It was as though I was outside myself, watching my life disintegrate around me, and could do nothing about it."

She fell silent for a moment, reached for Liz's hands. Gripping her mother's fingers, Liz waited, her heart heavy with sadness for all Lorelei had been through.

"We were young, Eliza, your father and I. I was barely nineteen when you were born, your father not even twenty-one. It's not really surprising we couldn't handle what was happening. I knew he was having an affair, even through the fog in my head, but I didn't care. I didn't care about anything."

"Oh, Mom."

"One night I came home, and I just couldn't do it anymore. I took a handful of sleeping pills with a glass of vodka and lay down, ready to get it all over with."

Without conscious thought, Liz stepped forward and hugged her, holding on as hard as she could, horrified by the knowledge she'd almost had to grow up without her mother.

Having her had never seemed that big a deal before, but now it did.

"Dad found me in time, and I was admitted to a treatment center." She pulled back, out of Liz's embrace, so she was once more looking into her daughter's eyes. "This is the important part, Eliza. We forgave each other, and made a promise to be honest, to stick together and never shut each other out again. Our love was strong enough to weather the storm of all that had happened. Made us strong enough to come out on the other side."

"But what about Robbie?"

"Brant broke off the relationship with his mother, and she left the firm without telling him she was pregnant." Lorelei shook her head. "I don't think she would have ever told Brant about Robbie if she hadn't got sick and been given a short time to live. I'll be honest, I was angry at first, but then I realized he was just a little baby who was about to lose his mother. I had enough love to give to both of you. How could I refuse to take him in? But..."

Something in her expression made Liz's stomach clench, brought a wave of defensiveness she couldn't seem to subdue.

"But what, Mom?"

Lorelei's eyes gleamed with tears. "But by then we'd realized you were the one affected most by what had happened."

"Me? How?"

"While we were running around, actively trying to ruin our marriage and life together, who was looking after *you*?

For the first four years of your life we weren't there for you, weren't the loving, caring parents we should have been. *That's* why I kept Nanny Hardy as long as I did. I may not have liked her, but she was the one constant in your young life. How could I deprive you of that?"

Liz searched her mother's face, her eyes, unable to fully process what she was saying, her mind whirring with thoughts, memories, snippets of time she'd never consciously examined before.

Her first memories, not of her parents but of the nanny, the stern-faced woman who hadn't believed in hugs and kisses. Of being wary of the tall man she'd seen infrequently but had learned to call Daddy, and the beautiful stranger who had sometimes flitted into the nursery and then disappeared again.

All that had changed when Robbie had come, and she'd always thought it was because of him, his smiles and laughter, the love he so easily gave, that they had become a family. Now her mother was saying that wasn't the case, and Liz didn't know how to process this new information.

"All I wanted was for my children to love and admire me," her father said softly from behind them, having approached so quietly Liz hadn't known he was there.

She turned toward him, and her heart ached anew to see his face lined with worry. "I was afraid that once you heard the story you'd resent me, and that would break my heart. I… I hope you can forgive me, Eliza. I was so young, and so stupid. I didn't mean to cause any of you pain, and it's been the regret of my life to think I have."

"I hope you can forgive *us*," her mother added, laying a hand gently on Liz's arm.

"There's nothing to forgive, Dad, Mom," she said, her voice rough with the tears she was holding back. "I turned out okay, didn't I?"

It was a cry from the heart; a plea born of years of feeling disconnected, of thinking herself a disappointment to two of the people she loved most.

"Oh, baby." Her father pulled her into a hug so tight her ribs ached a bit. "You turned out perfectly. Far better than we ever deserved. And if we ever made you feel otherwise, it was probably because we were trying too hard to make up for what we'd done."

She didn't really understand what he was saying, too full of emotion to make sense of it all. But something broke free in her, releasing the kind of tenderness that cracked her hard shell of a persona only infrequently.

Leaning back in his arms, she reached up to smooth down his hair, and whispered, "Love you, Daddy."

And it was all worthwhile to see her father smile through the tears on his cheeks, as he pulled Lorelei into the circle of his arms too, for once the three of them in perfect accord.

At peace.

"'Being deeply loved by someone gives you strength, while loving someone deeply gives you courage,'" her mother murmured.

Liz leaned back, blinking away her own tears, laughter rising in her throat as she said, "Mom! When did you start quoting Lao Tzu?"

Her mother sniffed delicately. "Please continue to underestimate me. I quite enjoy it."

"She's very special," Robbie said to Cort as they watched parents and daughter embrace. "And more than special to me."

Despite his warning, Liz's brother had made no effort to "interrogate" Cort. Instead, the conversation had been general, a kind of getting to know each other Cort wasn't sure was even necessary, since it was doubtful they'd meet again. As much as he'd enjoyed parts of the day, the one thing the experience had solidified in him was that he didn't belong, at all, in this world Liz so easily navigated.

It had felt surreal to see the way these people lived; like something out of a movie, where everyone was beautiful and money was no object.

And although he'd met some nice folks, he'd also been very aware of the pointed looks he'd received, and the snubs. There had even been a few comments, not directed at him but said in such a way he couldn't help hearing, wondering what Liz had been thinking, having him there.

Cort had wondered too, more than once, during the day.

"You don't have to worry," he told Robbie. "Liz and I really are just friends."

Leaning back in his chair, eyebrows raised, the other man gave him a considering look.

"I don't know you well enough to figure out whether you're a fool or you think I'm one."

Cort shook his head, looking once more over to where Liz and her parents stood, connected by bonds so strong they were almost visible, talking quietly together. The sight made him so happy nothing else mattered. Whatever they'd spoken about had obviously bridged the divide between them, and he knew how much it must mean to Liz.

"Your sister is an amazing woman, and I..."

Love her.

It wasn't a revelation. Not really. Cort was beginning to think he'd fallen for her from that first night in Mexico, and his feelings had grown with each subsequent encounter. But it was the first time he'd allowed himself to think it, to acknowledge it, because he'd known that doing so would just increase the inevitable heartbreak exponentially.

"You...?"

Startled out of his reverie, Cort said, "I'm sorry. What?"

Robbie replied, "You said Liz is an amazing woman and were about to add something about yourself before you stopped. I was curious to know what you planned to say next."

There was no way he'd share what he'd actually thought. He cleared his suddenly tight throat and replied, "I'm honored by her friendship. It means more to me than I can express, and I'll always treasure it."

"You should." The charming, smiling façade had fallen away from Robbie's face, revealing a shrewd, serious man. "She doesn't give her friendship easily, or lightly. When she loves, she loves with her whole heart, even if she doesn't express it the way most people expect."

The mention of love made Cort's heart clench with longing, and his gaze was drawn, magnetically, back to Liz.

How beautiful she was, with her face shining with joy as she looked at her father. She wasn't smiling, but that didn't matter. Anyone who knew her well would recognize her happiness, and Cort counted himself lucky to be in that number.

It was a sublime moment, but beneath his joy for her was his own inescapable aloneness. The knowledge he'd never known, and never would know, the kind of bond these people shared, one with the others.

Robbie sighed, a contented, happy sound. "I'm glad she's made up with Dad. In the end, family's all you have, you know?"

No, I don't.

But suddenly their affair made sense to him. Liz's distance from her father had left an emotional void in her life that perhaps, in some small way, her friendship with *him* had filled. Liz had needed something, a kind of intimacy, to distract from her anger and pain.

He'd done the same with Mimi, hadn't he? Using her as a crutch after Brody's death? Was he still doing the same with Liz? It felt different. He'd drifted into the relationship with Mimi, never feeling very strongly about her, or longing to see her when they'd been apart. On the other hand, Liz filled every corner of his mind, his heart, his soul.

For a moment, just a fleeting instant, Cort allowed himself to imagine what it would mean to be truly loved by Liz Prudhomme, not just as a friend and a sexual partner but as the one person made just for her. The thought overwhelmed him, elated him before he descended, with a crash of common sense, back to reality.

He took the last swallow of the Scotch in his glass, letting the fiery liquid slip down his throat, the burn reminding him that everything in life, no matter how delicious, had an attendant pain.

And nothing, especially anything good, lasted forever.

Now that Liz was reconciled with her family, it was only a matter of time before she realized how little he had to offer, and she left him.

Everyone else of importance in his life had done it. He didn't envision her being any different.

CHAPTER SEVENTEEN

CORT WAS TOTALLY unprepared for the effect that going to Liz's brother's wedding would have on his life. In his world a wedding was just a private event, and he'd had no idea Robbie and Giovanna's would also be a media circus, with repercussions that echoed into his work life.

At first he didn't know what was causing the shift in the way some of his co-workers acted around him, and tried to ignore it. Only after one of the nurses actually came out and asked him about it did it sink in that the entire hospital knew he'd gone to Robbie Prudhomme's wedding with Liz.

It turned out there were photographs and videos of the event all over the internet. Society websites had shots of the Prudhommes and their friends, while the mainstream media and gossip sites were more interested in Giovanna and her famous friends. To cap it off, some of the attendees had taken candid shots and uploaded those too. While Cort had stayed out of most of the pictures, there were enough of him and Liz together to get the hospital tongues wagging.

The worst of it came later in the week when he was cleaning up after an emergency small bowel resection.

Dr. Malachi, the anesthesiologist, who was washing up at the other sink, said, "You're a sly one, Smith. Going for the long money shot, huh?"

Surprised and confused, Cort looked at the older man, who was grinning over at him. "Excuse me?"

"Getting in good with the Prudhommes. It's a sound investment. After all, Hepplewhite was founded by one of their relatives, and it's their money that in part funded the hospital's renovations. If you hitch your wagon to that star, you're probably guaranteed a berth for life, like our ER specialist."

There was no mistaking the malice behind the statement, but it wasn't the implication aimed at him that made Cort contemplate exactly where he wanted to punch Malachi.

Aware of the surgical nurse, who'd stopped dead in her tracks, probably too surprised to pretend to be discreet, Cort reached for a towel to dry his hands, giving himself a moment to get his temper under control.

Then he stepped into the anesthesiologist's personal space, knowing he was looming over the shorter man in what could only be considered a menacing manner. But he kept his voice conversational, as though discussing the weather.

"Are you implying that Dr. Prudhomme is anything less than a stellar medical practitioner?"

Malachi blinked up at Cort, the grin fading from his face, to be replaced with a mingled look of fear and anger. "What? No—"

"Or that she wouldn't have every hospital in the city, hell, probably the country, clamoring for her to join their staff if she decided to leave Hepplewhite?"

Malachi took a step back but was stopped short by the wall behind him. His mouth moved but no sound came out.

"I know for a fact you're not suggesting that Dr. Prudhomme or her family felt it necessary to purchase her place on the staff here. Do you know how I know that, Dr. Malachi?"

"How?" the other man said in a weak voice, when Cort raised his eyebrows and waited for a reply.

"Because I believe that would be slander, and I refuse to think that any member of staff at a hospital I work for would be capable of that."

Without waiting for a response, Cort turned and strode out of the room. Keeping his expression calm was a job in itself. Inside he was fuming and embarrassed.

Was that what people thought of him, that he was currying favor with Liz because of her family's wealth? Just telling himself those people didn't know him, so couldn't properly judge, didn't help. In reality it just fed into his own sense of unworthiness, solidifying the knowledge that he was, and would always be, an outsider, an interloper in Liz's world, and he believed she'd come to realize it too.

She had been distant since the wedding. Well, to be fair, she'd been extremely busy, back to working twelve-hour shifts and, on top of that, her parents had decided to stay in New York for a few extra days. Most of her free time was spent with them. He didn't expect that she'd want him hanging around with her parents, but Cort had hoped she'd find a little time for him. Yet, although she'd texted and they'd seen each other around the hospital, there'd been no mention of getting together.

Everything seemed to be pointing to the end of their relationship, as he'd suspected, and, as prepared as he'd tried to be for it, his heart had ached at the thought. Now, with the run-in with Malachi still fresh, and anger simmering beneath his skin, he almost looked forward to it.

It was time to end things with Liz, on his terms, before she got tired of him and told him to go. Abandoned him, the way everyone else in his life had.

At least this way he could salvage what was left of his pride, even though there was no hope for his heart.

* * *

Our love was strong enough to weather the storm of all that had happened. Made us strong enough to come out on the other side.

The words her mother had spoken at the wedding reception kept playing in Liz's head. They'd been revelatory for her. For a while, after their talk, she'd felt strange, as if the moorings tethering her to life had loosened or slipped, leaving her floating just above the ground. Everything had changed since Cort had come into her life, and she knew herself to be on the brink of a huge emotional shift. If she hadn't already gone over the precipice.

She'd needed time to sort it all out in her head, and hadn't really had the chance to do so properly, with the aftermath of the wedding and her parents' visit being extended.

Yet, in between working and time spent with her parents, she'd had a lot to ponder. Brant and Lorelei's story had explained so much, not just about why Brant had strayed but also about why she had felt somewhat disconnected from her parents. It truly was a moot point whether her character had come about through nature or nurture, but now she had no doubt it had been, at least in part, formed during those years in Nanny Hardy's care.

Knowing her parents were proud of her, even though they rarely expressed it, had also lifted a weight off her heart.

There was a sensation of being renewed, of being given a different perspective. She was still working through it but was looking forward to discussing it with Cort. In the past, she'd have called Jojo or one of her other close friends and talked to them. Now she felt as though only Cort would truly understand. After all, he was the one who'd given her the courage to speak to her mother.

Being deeply loved by someone gives you strength, while loving someone deeply gives you courage.

How true those words were, and taking the spirit of them into her heart she admitted, for the first time, that she loved Cort.

Not with the young, puppy-like devotion she'd lavished on Andrew, but with the deep, selfless, abiding love that lifted and elated, while never diminishing. Now she knew love didn't have to be a weakness but could be a river of strength.

This wasn't part of their deal, for her to fall for him, so she'd keep that to herself. It seemed unfair to burden him with her emotions. He'd made it clear that New York was just a waypoint.

Like her.

She'd texted him earlier and he'd said he'd come by, but he was late and now Liz found herself on edge. Caught up in her own ruminations and activities over the last week or so, it was only now that she realized he'd seemed a little distant.

Finally the doorbell went, and she went into the foyer to let him in.

It felt like forever since she'd seen him and, with her self-revelation fresh in her heart, she wanted to hug him, but something about his posture stopped her in her tracks.

"Hi," she said instead, hovering just inside the hallway, her heart suddenly pounding and her palms damp.

"Hello," he murmured in reply, locking the door and then turning to face her.

A cold lump developed in her stomach at his stern expression.

"Bad day?" She knew how it could be. A patient you thought you'd saved suddenly succumbing to their injuries, or one who you knew from the start was a long shot, but had hoped would recover simply couldn't be saved.

"You could say that," he replied, but didn't elaborate.

Normally she could tell what Cort was thinking, or at

least gauge his mood, but today was different, and Liz wished she knew why.

"Want to talk about it?"

Why was she being so hesitant? Normally she'd go in, guns blazing, demanding to know what had happened, but this time she didn't want to.

Cort shook his head. "Not really. And not right now. I have something else I need to talk to you about."

Silently, she led the way back into her living room and sat on the couch. Instinctively, she knew whatever it was he was about to say wouldn't be good. Bracing herself, she allowed all the changes that had come over her in the last week and a half to fade, being replaced by the cold, stoic persona she'd carefully cultivated over the years.

Crossing her legs, she looked up at him as he paced a few feet into the room and stopped. Keeping her expression noncommittal came surprisingly easily, old habits reasserting themselves without effort.

"What is it?" she asked, pleased by how cool she sounded.

"I heard from an old army buddy that they're looking for trauma surgeons, and I'm planning to reenlist."

There was no reaction inside her, except for a thickening of the ice already building in her chest.

"Hawaii?" she asked, in a mildly curious voice.

His eyebrows rose slightly, as though surprised she remembered what he'd said all those months ago.

"No, Germany."

"Well, that'll be interesting too." How distant she sounded, as if she didn't care, while inside she was dying. "Maybe the elusive Hawaii transfer will follow."

For a moment his stern façade seemed to crack, and she glimpsed something dark, painful behind his gaze. It touched something deep in her soul, melted the ice around her heart.

This was, after all, Cort. The man who'd broken her hard

shell into so many pieces she doubted she would ever truly be able to put it back together, no matter how she tried. The man who'd given her the courage to face up to her fears, comforted her when her demons had torn her apart, given her the type of uncomplicated, passionate friendship she'd secretly dreamed of but had never believed she'd find.

Taken her battered, closed heart, both soothed it and opened it wide. Reawakened her to love.

He'd never lied to her either. She'd known this day would come, and had to let him go without revealing the tears building behind her eyes, the burning pain in her heart.

For once in her life her restraint was appropriate. He didn't deserve to see her pain.

With a deep breath, she said, "Cort, I'm going to miss you. What we've shared has been so special, so real and true, at least to me. I knew this day would come, and if this is what you want, I'm happy for you. I hope you find joy on your travels."

Dark fire gleamed in his eyes for an instant and then died, and he said, "Liz, I wish I could stay longer, but I can't."

She held up her hand, stopping him. "I'm not asking you to. I made myself a promise never to expect anyone to give up their dreams for me. I know how that feels, how it can sap your determination, your courage and ambition. I… I just needed you to know how I feel."

Cort nodded, seemed set to say something more but, instead, turned and walked away.

The closing of a door had never sounded more final.

She cried then, wishing she could have told him how she truly felt. Wishing it wouldn't have made him feel badly to know she loved him and wanted him to stay.

Forever.

CHAPTER EIGHTEEN

HE SHOULD BE RELIEVED, glad that Liz had taken it so well.

Instead, his insides were in constant turmoil, and he couldn't get more than a couple of hours' sleep a night, bedeviled by memories, pain, sadness.

It was the right thing to do. He'd told her from the beginning he wouldn't be around for long, that he'd learned not to get attached to anyone. He wasn't even sure what he felt for her was love. How did you recognize something you'd never experienced? Never known?

No, he'd learned his lesson long ago.

Nothing worthwhile lasted.

Better to move on before she did, or before he couldn't.

Seeing Liz around the hospital was agony. He'd been expecting her to give him the cold shoulder, but she simply acted the same way she had all along, with cool professionalism and no drama whatsoever. The rest of the staff watched them, since the rumor mill had them pegged as a couple, and he got the impression many of them were disappointed when there were no overt displays of affection. If only they knew how many places in the hospital Liz and he had snuck to and made love!

But that was something he tried very hard not to think about. Bad enough when he turned a corner and was sideswiped by a memory of Liz, hands upraised, gasping as he held her on the edge of passion.

They'd laughed about the day they'd almost got caught in the old isolation ward, once it was far enough in the past for him to find it amusing. Liz teasing him about how angry he'd been.

If anything, it was her companionship, the shared laughter he missed the most. Liz had become such an important part of his life he was lost without her in it.

It would get better once he was out of New York City, back in the military milieu. The army had suited him. The discipline. The order. Life would go back to normal after he reenlisted.

He'd already received the paperwork from the army medical corps command. They were sitting on his desk, ready to be signed, and he'd been contacted to ask when he would be available to report for duty. He'd explained he'd need to give ample notice to Hepplewhite and had been informed the army would do whatever was necessary to assist him getting out of his current contract asap.

He'd put off signing the paperwork for weeks, although he'd made up his mind to do it. It was, he told himself, because he dreaded facing Gregory Hammond. The older man had recently been singing Cort's praises and broadly hinting that, in a couple of years when he retired as head of surgery, he hoped Cort would take his place.

His army friend who'd told him of the need for trauma surgeons had called the night before and told Cort, in rather inelegant terms, he had to make up his mind immediately.

"Time waits for no man, Cort. And the army waits even less."

Now, seeing Liz in the hallway, leaning on the nurses' station desk as she checked a chart, cemented his determination.

It was the way his heart painfully contracted and his

stomach clenched that did it. The time to move on was past. If he didn't get it done now, he might be stuck mooning over her for another five months, until his contract expired.

He didn't think he could stand it.

Getting an appointment to see the chief of surgery the next day should have been a relief. Yet he spent the entire night staring at the window of his bedroom, absolutely sure Liz's scent was still on his sheets, despite them being freshly washed.

The following morning he went in early and stood for a moment outside the hospital, looking up at the building. No matter how much he told himself he wouldn't miss it, or the city, he knew it was a lie. It had grown on him, giving him a sense of home he'd never had before.

"Hey."

And that was why.

He turned to see Liz walking toward him, the car that had dropped her off driving away.

"Hi," he replied, not trusting his voice to say anything more.

"I'm glad I saw you," she said, her cherries jubilee voice wrapping around him, enticing and arousing. Yet there was a hint of hesitancy in her voice as she continued, "I have something for you."

"Oh?"

For a moment she looked unsure, and then her chin came up and she gave him one of her straight-on, clear-eyed looks.

"Yes," she said, in her decisive way. "I… You mean a lot to me, Cort, and knowing you're leaving, I wanted to do something for you. Something you probably wouldn't do for yourself."

Mean a lot to me. The words would have made him laugh if the pain in his heart wasn't so severe. It sounded so tepid in comparison to how he felt. Standing there, her fresh, sweet scent washing over him, he just wanted to lose himself in her eyes, in her arms, her body.

He blinked, glanced away in an effort to get himself under control.

"You didn't have to do anything for me, Liz. You've done more than you can ever know."

She had taught him to love. Given him joy, and hope, and this terrible agony, knowing she would never love him back.

"I wanted to anyway."

There was something different in her voice, a dark emotion roughening the already deep tones. He looked at her in time to see her take a deep breath and push her shoulders back, as though bracing for his reaction.

"I know you said you weren't interested, and it made no difference to you, but I was talking to Robbie, and he said that knowing where he had come from had made a huge difference in his life. So I hired a private detective, and I think she's found your parents."

For a moment all the air left his body. Light-headed, he stared at her, wondering if he'd heard her correctly.

"It's not as bad as you thought, Cort. If these are your parents, and all the indications are that they are, they didn't abandon you. You were kidnapped."

There was a low wall behind him and he eased down onto it, unsure whether his legs would continue to hold him up.

"Liz…why…?"

She tilted her head, her eyebrows scrunching together in a frown.

"You deserve to know, Cort." She hesitated for a moment and then her lips firmed. "You told me you'd learned not to get attached, and I know how badly it hurt you to lose your friend, but everyone needs to have people on their side. People—family—they can turn to in times of need, or sorrow, or happiness. I… I wanted you to have that, if it was possible, even if it isn't with me."

Still numb, he took the outstretched envelope from her hand and lifted the flap. The report was several pages thick, but it started with a summary. It took him a moment to be able to focus, to make sense of the words, and gather the threads of the story.

Child Sean Gallagher, went missing from the home of his parents, Kevin and Florence Gallagher. Signs of break-in. Father's ex-wife, known drug and alcohol abuser, was also missing from the small town in Wyoming, and suspected of taking the child. The ex-wife was eventually found, deceased, in Seattle, Washington. While the child was not found with her, some articles of clothing and a stuffed animal known to have belonged to Sean were found with her body. Attempts to trace where the woman had been in the two months prior proved fruitless.

"How can your PI be sure these are my parents? What makes her sure?"

He didn't want to acknowledge the hope gathering in his chest. *Nothing good lasts forever. Don't place your hope in people, because they always let you down, hurt you. Leave you.* These were the mantras he'd taught himself, that life had taught him, and he didn't want the pain of finding out this was wrong. That this family wasn't his.

"The timing is right," Liz said gently. "And Kevin Gallagher came to the States from Ireland, while Florence is from the Shoshone tribe. The DNA matches too."

It was too much. Too unexpected. Too promise-filled.

Could it really be that once he'd had a home, been a part of a family that had wanted him, loved him, perhaps, thinking he was gone forever, mourned him? It all but broke him, thinking of it, as longing he hadn't known still existed inside his soul washed through him, like a storm.

No. That was a lie. He'd known the longing was still there. He'd felt it every time he looked at Liz, held her in his arms, experienced the passion flowing between them. That longing was what had frightened him so much, made him determined not to give in to the love.

Then her words came back to him, making his heart stumble over itself again.

She'd said she wanted him to have a family, *even if it wasn't with her.*

The fear of rejection should have made him keep his mouth shut, but hope and want and need overwhelmed him and he had to ask, "Did…did you really want to be my family, Liz?"

"I did," she said, almost defiantly, holding his gaze, even as hers filled with pain. "I never meant to love you. I knew you would leave, and I should have guarded my heart better, but—"

He didn't let her finish, just pulled her into his arms. "I'm glad you didn't. Tell me it's not too late, that the home I've found in you is still mine."

Liz didn't hesitate.

They'd wasted too much time already.

Hardly able to believe what was happening, she held him as tightly as she could.

"Of course it is. Forever," she whispered into his ear.

"I love you," he said, burying his face in her neck, neither of them caring about the other staff members coming and going nearby.

This was too important to worry about propriety and hospital gossip.

"Tell me you love me again."

"I love you, Cort. I always will. Even if you have to go."

He shook his head. "How can I give up the best thing

that's ever happened to me? I haven't signed the papers, and now that I know you love me too, I won't."

She pulled back, so she could see his eyes, and replied, "If you really want to reenlist, and you wanted me to, I'd go with you. Being with you is more important than anything else."

She needed him to know she was serious. He knew how much she loved New York, and Hepplewhite, and hoped he recognized she would give it all up for him if he wanted her to.

Cort swept a finger over her cheek.

"I don't want to reenlist, love. That was my fear making me run. Even though I've never known what love is, I knew I'd fallen for you, and was afraid of the heartache."

Tears stung her eyes as she shook her head. "You might think you didn't know what love is, Cort, but everything you do, the way you deal with people, your compassion and strength, tells me you have so much of it to give."

"It's all for you," he said, turning his hand to capture her fingers.

"Perfect," she replied. Then she took a deep breath, knowing there was one last thing they had to get out into the open. "What's been happening around the hospital…"

"You mean the speculative looks I've been getting because of your brother's wedding?"

She cringed, having heard about his encounter with Dr. Malachi. She knew he'd been subjected to sideways looks and not-so-subtle questions from some of the staff who'd seen the pictures online.

"Yes. Please don't let it bother you. People's reactions have been completely ridiculous."

He gave her a lopsided grin. "It hasn't been easy, having people question my motives regarding our relationship. But I'll get over it. You're too important to lose over something so stupid."

Liz sighed. "I'm sorry Robbie's wedding was the introduction you got to my family. It really wasn't a proper first meeting. They're all a lot more normal than that circus implied."

"You have to admit it was over the top, to put it mildly. It was like being in a movie."

"It was, but the only reason was because Robbie married Giovanna, and she's a supermodel. If he'd married Jane Brown from down the road, no one would have cared, and there certainly wouldn't be pictures all over the internet."

He leaned back slightly to look at her, his skepticism obvious, and she shrugged. "We can always avoid my family functions from now on. Or just run away somewhere where no one knows us. How about Mexico?"

Shaking his head, Cort tightened his grip. "Oh, no. I've found my version of paradise right here, and I'm not leaving. Although we could go back to the scene of the crime for a visit, to see if the honeymoon suite still lives up to its billing."

"Can we leave now?" she asked, ravenous for him, inwardly cursing having to go to work in a few minutes. "I want a chance to make sure you're convinced I'm the woman for you."

"I don't need convincing." He leaned in, so their lips were just a breath apart, teasing them both. "I'm yours, now and forever, and I'm not letting you go."

EPILOGUE

Two years later

IT WOULD HAVE been nice for it to be a quiet night for once.

Liz snorted at the thought as she strode out of one ER cubicle and headed straight for another, stripping off her blood-splattered gloves and gown as she went. Unfortunately, there had been an incident at a street carnival a couple of blocks away from the hospital, and so far they'd had a couple of stabbing victims, a gunshot victim and three people who'd been hit by a car all come in at the same time.

That was on top of the usual volume of emergency cases.

"Trauma team's on its way, Dr. Prudhomme," a nurse called out, as Liz slipped past a couple of police officers standing guard just outside the gunshot victim's cubicle.

"Thirty-two-year-old male, Sylvester McKenzie, gunshot wounds to the upper thorax and upper left thigh," the paramedic told her, as she started her examination, then listed the vitals and observations they'd made on the way to the hospital.

"Sylvester, my name is Dr. Prudhomme. I'm going to be looking after you. Can you tell me where it hurts?"

The reply was a profanity-laden rant from behind the oxygen mask, aimed at the police, the paramedics, and Liz herself.

"Hey, enough of that."

How was it that after all this time her heart still leapt whenever Cort entered the room?

Sylvester added Cort to his list of rant-worthy topics, but when Liz glanced at him, Cort just gave her a little wink before turning back to the patient.

Before long Sylvester didn't have enough breath left to rant about anything. His blood pressure started to fall too, and X-rays showed one bullet lodged in his lung. Yet it was the leg wound that worried Cort even more. Sylvester had been shot while driving his car, the bullets going through the door before striking him, and Cort suspected the lower one's trajectory might have caused serious injury.

"Here," the radiologist said, pointing to the screen. "The bullet has done damage to the femur and pelvis."

"I was afraid of that," Cort said. "We're going to have to get him stabilized enough to get him up to Angiography. I need to see what veins and arteries have been damaged before I go in there."

Liz's heart sank. Pelvic injuries were notoriously tricky.

As they headed back to Sylvester's cubicle, Cort muttered, "Can we move up our reservations if I get stuck in the OR?"

It was the anniversary of the night they'd met in Mexico, and they'd decided to celebrate. After all, they'd agreed it had been one of the best nights of their lives, and the luckiest.

"If that happens, I'll call and ask them to prepare something for takeout."

Cort looked at her and shook his head. "Only you could call one of the hottest restaurants in town and ask for takeout."

Liz gave him a wink. "I sweet-talk all the chefs and staff, so that if such an occasion arises, I'm golden."

Then Cort the lover was gone, and Dr. Smith was back; focused, cool as ice.

"Let's get him stabilized, stat. I need to know how much damage was done by that bullet and get in there to repair it as soon as possible, or we'll lose him."

After they got Sylvester stabilized, Cort headed off with him to Radiology and then from there to the OR.

When Liz finished her shift, she went up to the surgical floor to see whether they were having a nice dinner out tonight or staying in.

One of the nurses at the station said, "I think they're just finishing up, Dr. Prudhomme. Dr. Smith should be out soon."

"Thank you." She waved, going to one of the lounge areas and sitting down to wait. If they didn't leave in an hour, it would be takeout for sure. Once Cort came out of surgery, he'd let her know whether he could leave or not.

Liz stretched, suppressing a yawn. She actually wouldn't mind takeout tonight, rather than having to go home and dress up. They'd had a busy couple of weeks, with Cort's parents coming for a visit from Wyoming and his sister Misty flying in from Chicago too to celebrate Flo's birthday in New York with Cort. Unfortunately his brother Connor couldn't join them this time, since his wife was expecting their second child and, although her due date was still a few weeks away, she hadn't been given the all clear by her ob-gyn. The nice thing was that Connor and his wife lived just down the road, so to speak, in Philadelphia. Cort and Liz had already visited them a number of times, and planned to go back as soon as the baby was born.

It had been a busy time, but also a pleasure to have the Gallaghers come to stay. They were wonderful people; warm, caring, and so incredibly happy to have their son back.

They'd never given up on him, even after all those years,

and the hardest part for them was getting used to calling him "Cort" rather than "Sean."

"I'm too old to get used to a new name," Cort had said. "Plus all my degrees are in this one. It would be a huge hassle to change them, even if it were possible."

She'd heard a hint of regret in his voice, but conceded the point.

The back of Liz's neck tingled, and she twisted in the chair to see Cort coming down the corridor toward her, still wearing his surgical cap, although he'd removed the gown. It was funny how she always knew when he was around, as though an invisible string stretched between them and vibrated whenever they were close to one another.

Rising and picking up her bag, she went to meet him in the hallway.

"Takeout tonight?" she asked, even though she suspected she already knew the answer.

"Maybe just cancel altogether. He's in pretty bad shape, and I have a suspicion I'll be here quite a while longer. Chez Ramone's food isn't that great heated up at home."

She was used to it, of course she was. They both had days when plans had to be changed or abandoned, but it didn't stop her feeling a little disappointed. From the sound of it, he wouldn't be home before she had to go to bed, since she was working an early shift in the morning.

"Well, in that case, let me give you your gift now," she said.

Cort gave her a lopsided smile. "You bought me a gift?"

"Mmm-hmm," she replied, digging the brochure out of her bag and handing it to him.

He read it, a huge grin breaking across his face.

"Greece?"

"Yes. Cruising from island to island. I want to make sure we keep scratching those itchy feet of yours so you never get tempted to run away. Oh, and next year, when

Connor's baby is old enough to travel, I think we should plan a trip with both families to Ireland."

Cort shook his head then bent to give her a chaste, if slightly lingering kiss, and it was enough to heat her blood, make her want to go in for a deeper, harder one.

"There's no chance of me taking off anywhere without you, babe. I'm home to stay, right here in your arms."

"Glad to hear it," she said matter-of-factly, but she knew he could read her better than anyone, and he saw the love in her eyes. "That's the way it should be."

* * * * *

FORBIDDEN TO THE PLAYBOY SURGEON

FIONA LOWE

To my fellow Medical Romance author Annie O'Neil, who answered all my questions about London so enthusiastically and speedily. And for the laughs. Thanks! It made writing this book so much fun.

CHAPTER ONE

ALTHOUGH CLAIRE MITCHELL had been in London for a few weeks, she still pinched herself every time she stepped out onto the streets of Paddington. For an Aussie country girl, it was all a little bit surreal—like being on the set of *Mary Poppins* or *Upstairs, Downstairs*.

Dazzling white, Victorian, stuccoed terraced houses with pillared porches and decorative balconies were built neatly around tiny central gardens. This morning as she crossed the pocket-handkerchief park, passing between two black wrought-iron gates, the ubiquitous London drizzle was cheerfully absent. Tongues of early-morning light filtered down between the tender, bright green spring foliage of century-old oaks and elms. It was a far cry from the dusty, rock-hard and sun-cracked park where she'd spent her childhood. The only shade to be found at the Gundiwindi playground had been that cast by the people standing next to her.

Walking briskly, she made her way along what would be a frantically busy road in an hour's time. Right now though, the street sweepers, bakers, newsagents and baristas were the only people out offering services to a few crazy early birds like herself. Her favourite Italian trattoria had a coffee window and Tony greeted her with a cheery *buongiorno* as he handed out six lattes, neatly stacked in a cardboard carrier. 'You bring the sunshine, *mia bella.*'

Claire smiled and gave into the irrational zip of delight she allowed herself to feel. She knew the garrulous barista flirted with every female aged two to ninety-two and that his *mia bella* meant nothing. But as few men ever noticed her, let alone tried to charm her, she accepted and enjoyed his compliments as a lovely way to start her day.

She bought a *pain au chocolat* from the bakery and balanced the bag on top of the coffees as she continued to walk towards Paddington Children's Hospital, or 'the castle' as the locals called it. A bright red double-decker bus lumbered past down the narrow road. With her free hand, she grabbed a quick photo of it on her phone and immediately sent it to her brother. He was the proud owner of the Gundiwindi garage and he adored anything with an engine. Whenever Claire saw something he'd delight in, she always sent him a photo. He always replied with either a picture of her nieces and nephews or of her parents.

Unlike herself, David loved living in the small outback town where they'd both grown up. Good at both cricket and footy, he'd always belonged and thrived and he couldn't imagine living anywhere else. She, on the other hand, had been plotting to leave since she was ten years old, desperate to escape the taunts and bullying of a small-minded town that hovered on the edge of the desert and existence.

The imposing turrets of the red-brick London hospital now loomed high above her as she approached the old ornate gates. A small group of people rugged up against the post-dawn chill clutched *Save Our Hospital* and *Kids' Health NOT Wealth* signs with gloved hands. Each morning found a different combination of people in attendance. Many were parents of current patients, but hearteningly, there were some who'd been patients themselves many years ago. Together they were united and maintained a peaceful protest presence at the gates, striving to keep alive the hope that something could be done to save the hospital from closure.

'I've brought hot coffee,' Claire called out, holding up the cardboard tray as she did most mornings. Granted, she'd only been working at the castle for a few weeks but the idea of central London losing such a vitally important healthcare provider was a terrifying thought. What if the castle had already been closed when Westbourne Primary School caught fire? The thought made her shudder. There would have certainly been deaths. Even with the hospital's proximity to the school, there'd been far too many close calls. Not everyone was out of the woods yet, including little Ryan Walker.

The stalwarts at the gate greeted her and her coffees with a cheer. 'Morning, love.'

'Early again? You still on Aussie time?' one asked.

She laughed. 'I'd be going home after a day's work if I was.'

Once she'd distributed the coffees, she ducked through the gates and strode under the decorative brick archway. Behind the beautiful Victorian façade was a modern hospital with state-of-the-art equipment and an experienced and dedicated staff. There were one hundred and fifty years of history here and she was humbled to be a part of it. When she'd received the offer of a chance to train under the tutelage of the world-renowned neurosurgeon, Alistair North, she'd actually squealed in delight, deafening the very proper Englishwoman on the other end of the line.

'Now, now, Ms Mitchell,' the secretary to the chair of the Royal College of Surgeons had said primly as if overt displays of enthusiasm were frowned upon. Then, without pausing, she'd continued to outline the terms and conditions of the scholarship.

Claire hadn't cared about her unrestrained antipodean

response. If a girl couldn't get excited about such an amazing opportunity, when could she? After all, her work was her life and her life was her work, and the scholarship was a chance of a lifetime. At the time, she'd danced down the corridors of Flinders Medical Centre telling everyone from cleaners to consultants that she was going to London.

Now, as she ran up five flights of stairs, she was almost certain that if she'd known what was in store for her at the castle, she might not have been quite so excited. When she reached the landing with the large painted koala on the ward door, she smiled. Why, when all the other wards were named after northern hemisphere birds and animals, the Brits had chosen an Aussie marsupial for the neurology ward's logo was a mystery to her but she loved that they had. It made her feel a little less like an alien in what was proving to be a very unexpected foreign land.

Despite speaking English and having been raised in a country where the Union Jack still sat in the corner of the flag, Londoners were different. The brilliant Alistair North was extremely different, although not in the often restrained and polite British way. She'd been fortunate to work with talented neurosurgeons in Australia and she understood that brilliance was often accompanied by quirks. But Mr North had taken quirk and magnified it by the power of ten. All of it left her struggling to convince herself she'd done the right thing in accepting the scholarship.

Stepping into the bright and cheery ward, she noticed with a start that the nurses' station was empty. Surely she wasn't late? Her mouth dried as she spun around to check the large wall clock. The bright, red and yellow clock hands pointed to big blue numbers and they instantly reassured her. She gave a little laugh that contained both relief and irony. Of course she wasn't late—she was never late and today she was even earlier than usual. Preparation and attention to detail was as much a part of her as breathing. It had been that way since the fateful day in grade five when her small childhood world had suddenly turned on her.

Assuming the nurses to be busy with their end-of-shift tasks, she slid into an office chair and logged on to the computer. She always read her patients' overnight reports before rounds. It was better to take the extra time, learn what had happened and to have a well thought out plan than to be caught short. Just the thought of being put on the spot with the critical eyes of the medical students and junior house officers fixed upon her made her breath come faster.

The ward cared for children with a variety of neurological, craniofacial and central nervous system disorders, including those that required surgery. Although Mr North performed many different operations, his passion was the surgical treatment of focal epilepsy. It was the reason she'd fought so hard to win the scholarship and work with him, but as her brother often said in his laconic and understated tone after everything had gone pear-shaped, 'It seemed like a good idea at the time.' Right now she was second-guessing her good idea.

While she read the reports, the daytime nursing staff drifted in, busy chatting, and the medical students soon followed. Finally, the consistently late junior house officer, Andrew Bailey, arrived breathless and with his white coattails flapping. He came to a sudden halt and glanced around, his expression stunned. 'I still beat him?'

Claire, who'd just read little Ryan Walker's 'no change' report, stood with a sigh. 'You still beat him.'

He grinned. 'I must tell my father that my inability to be on time makes me a natural neurosurgeon.'

'Perhaps that's my problem,' Claire muttered as she checked her phone for a message or a missed call from the exuberantly talented consultant surgeon who had no concept of time or workplace protocol. Nope, no messages or voicemail. She automatically checked the admissions board, but if Mr Alistair North were running late because of an emergency admission, she'd have been the one hauled out of bed to deal with it.

'I heard while you and I were slaving away here last night, he was holding court over at the Frog and Peach,' Andrew said with a conspiratorial yet reverent tone.

'That doesn't automatically mean he had a late night.'

Andrew's black brows rose and waggled at her. 'I just met the delectable Islay Kennedy on the back stairs wearing yesterday's clothes. She mentioned dancing on tables, followed by an illicit boat ride on the Serpentine and then bacon and eggs at the Worker's Café watching the dawn break over the Thames. When I see him, I plan to genuflect in his direction.'

A flash of anger swept through Claire's body so hot and fast she thought it might lift her head from her neck. *I want to kill Alistair North.* Surgery was such a boys' club and neurosurgery even more so. For years she'd gone into battle time and time again on the basis of raw talent but it was never enough. She constantly fought sexism, and now, it seemed, she had to tackle ridiculous childish behaviour and the adoration of men, who in essence were little boys. Fed up and furious, she did something she rarely did: she shot the messenger.

'Andrew, don't even think that behaviour like that is commendable. It's juvenile and utterly irresponsible. If you *ever* pull a stunt like that and turn up to operate with me, I'll fail you.'

Before her stunned junior house officer could reply, the eardrum-piercing sound of party blowers rent the air. Everyone turned towards the raucous sound. A tall man with thick, rumpled dark blond hair and wearing fake black horn-rimmed glasses—complete with a large fake bulbous nose and moustache—was marching along the ward with a little girl clinging to his back like a monkey. Behind him followed a trail of children aged between two and twelve. Some were walking, others were being pushed in wheelchairs by the nurses and many wore bandages on their heads—all of them were enthusiastically puffing air into party blowers and looking like they were on a New Year's Day parade.

'Wave to Dr Mitchell,' the man instructed the little girl on his back. 'Did you know she's really a kangaroo?'

Despite his voice being slightly muffled by the fake moustache, it was without doubt the unmistakably deep and well-modulated tones of Alistair North.

A line of tension ran down Claire's spine with the speed and crack of lightning before radiating outwards into every single cell. It was the same tension that invaded her every time Alistair North spoke to her. The same tension that filled her whenever she thought about him. It was a barely leashed dislike and it hummed inside her along with something else she didn't dare name. She refused point-blank to contemplate that it might be attraction. The entire female staff of the castle might think the man was sex on a stick, but not her.

Granted, the first time she'd seen all six feet of him striding confidently towards her, she'd been struck by his presence. Unlike herself, not one single atom of the many that made up Alistair North hinted at doubt. The man positively radiated self-assurance from the square set of his shoulders to his brogue-clad feet. He wore clothes with effortless ease, their expensive cut and style fitting him flawlessly, yet at the same time finding the perfect pitch between stuffy and scruffy. Despite his posh accent, there was also something engaging and decidedly un-British about his lopsided and cheeky grin. It wasn't a smile one associated with a consultant. It would break over the stark planes of his cheeks, vanquishing the esteemed surgeon and give rise to the remnants of a cheeky and mischievous little boy. But it wasn't so much the smile that undid her—it was the glint in his slate-grey eyes. He had the ability to focus his attention on a person and make them feel as if they were the only human being on the planet.

'Welcome to the castle, Mitchell,' he'd said to her on her first day.

As she'd shaken his outstretched hand and felt his firm pressure wrap around her fingers and travel up her arm, she'd been horrified to feel herself just a little bit breathless. Her planned speech had vanished and she'd found herself replying in her broadest Australian accent, 'Thanks. It's great to be here.'

It had taken less than a week for her to realise that Alistair North's cheeky grin almost always flagged that he was about to break the rules and wreak havoc on a grand scale. She'd also learned that his eyes alone, with their dancing smoky hue and intense gaze that made the person in their sights feel like they mattered to him like no one else, were frequently used with devastating ease to tempt women into his bed.

She conceded that, perhaps, on her first day when she'd felt momentarily breathless, she'd succumbed to the hypnotic effect of his gaze. Now, after working closely with him for weeks, she was immune to its effects. She'd spent ten years slogging her way up the medical career ladder, spending more hours in hospitals than out of them, and she wasn't about to risk it all by landing up in the boss's bed. More importantly, she didn't like Alistair North, so even if he were the last man on earth, she wouldn't be tempted.

Apparently, she was virtually the only woman at the castle with that thought. Over the past few weeks she'd been stunned to find herself sought out by hopeful women seeking information about Alistair North's proclivities, or worse still, being asked to act as go-between for disappointed and sometimes furious women whom he'd dated and then hadn't bothered to call. All things considered, from his casual disregard of the rules to his blasé treatment of women, there was no way on God's green earth or in the fiery depths of hell that she was attracted to *that man*. Not now. Not never.

The stories about Alistair North that circulated around the hospital held fable qualities. If she hadn't been working closely with him as his speciality registrar, she'd have laughed on being told the tales. She'd have said, 'They've got to be the invention of an overactive imagination.' But she did work with him. Sadly, she'd seen enough evidence to know at least two of the stories she'd heard were true so she had no reason not to believe the others. As hard as she tried to focus solely on Alistair North's immense skill as a neurosurgeon and block out the excited noise that seemed to permanently spin and jangle around him, it was impossible.

Everywhere she turned, people talked about his exploits in and out of the operating theatre. Gossip about who he was currently dating or dumping and who he'd been seen with driving into work that morning ran rife along the hospital corridors. It was as if speculation about the man was the hospital's secondary power supply. What she hated most of all was the legendary status the young male house officers gave him, while she was the one left trailing behind, picking up the pieces.

No, the sensation she got every time she was in the same space as Mr Alistair North was antagonism. The man may be brilliant and talented in the operating theatre but outside of it he was utterly unprofessional. He was stuck permanently in adolescence, and at thirty-nine that was not only ridiculous, it was sad. Most of his contemporaries were married with children but she supposed it would take a brave—or more likely deluded—woman to risk all on him. The only thing Claire would risk on Alistair North was her brain. Despite what she thought of the man, she couldn't deny the doctor was the best neurosurgeon in the country.

The little girl on Alistair North's back was now waving enthusiastically at her. Claire blinked behind her glasses, suddenly realising it was Lacey—the little girl they were operating on in an hour's time. Why wasn't she tucked up in her bed quiet and calm?

'Wave back, Kanga,' Alistair North said, his clear and precise Oxford accent teasing her. 'It won't break your arm.'

Claire's blood heated to boiling point. Did the man know that kangaroos boxed? The thought of bopping him on his fake nose was far too tempting. She felt the expectant gaze of the ward staff fixed firmly on her and suddenly she was thrown back in time. She was in Gundiwindi, standing in front of the class, with fifteen sets of eyes boring into her. She could see the red dust motes dancing in the starkly bright and uncompromising summer sunshine and the strained smile of her teacher slipping as his mouth turned down into a resigned and grumpy line. She could hear the shuffling and coughing of her peers—the sound that always preceded the one or two brutal comments that managed to escape from their mouths before Mr Phillips regained control.

Moron. Idiot.

Stop it. She hauled her mind back to the present, reminding herself sternly that she wasn't either of those things. She'd spent two decades proving it. She was a woman in a difficult and male dominated speciality and she was eleven months away from sitting her final neurosurgery exams. She'd fought prejudice and sexism to get this far and she'd fought herself. She refused to allow anyone to make her feel diminished and she sure as hell wasn't going to accept an order to wave from a man who needed to grow up. She would, however, do what she always did—she'd restore order.

In heels, Claire came close to matching Alistair North's height, and although her preference had always been to wear ballet flats, she'd taken herself shoe shopping at the end of her first week of working with him. The added inches said, *Don't mess with me*. She took a few steps forward until she was standing side on to him but facing Lacey. Ignoring Alistair North completely, and most definitely ignoring his scent of freshly laundered cotton with a piquant of sunshine that made her unexpectedly homesick, she opened her arms out wide towards the waving child.

'Do you want to come for a hop with Kanga?'

'Yes, please.'

Lacey, a ward of the state, transferred almost too easily into her arms, snuggling in against her chest and chanting, 'Boing, boing, boing.'

Claire pulled her white coat over her charge, creating a makeshift pouch, and then she turned her back on Alistair North. She strode quickly down the ward carrying an overexcited Lacey back to her bed. As she lowered her down and tried to tuck her under the blankets, the little girl bounced on the mattress.

Thanks for nothing, Alistair, Claire muttered to herself. It was going to take twice as long as normal to do all the routine preoperative checks. Yet another day would run late before it had even started.

CHAPTER TWO

ALASTAIR NORTH MOVED his lower jaw sideways and then back again behind his surgical mask, mulling over the conundrum that was his incredibly perfectionist and frustratingly annoying speciality registrar. She'd more than competently created a skin pouch to hold the vagus nerve stimulator she was inserting into Lacey Clarke. Now she was delicately wrapping the wire around the left vagus nerve and hopefully its presence would effectively minimise Lacey's seizures in a way medication had so far failed to achieve.

A bit of electricity, he mused, could kill or save a life. He knew all about that. Too much or too little of the stuff left a man dead for a very long time. What he didn't know was why Claire Mitchell was permanently strung so tight a tune could be plucked on her tendons.

Based on her skills and glowing references from the Royal Prince Alfred Hospital in Sydney and the Flinders Medical Centre in Adelaide, she'd outranked twenty-five other talented applicants from the Commonwealth. With her small steady hands and deft strokes, she had the best clinical skills of all the trainees who'd applied to work with him. She'd beaten twenty-four men to win the scholarship and that alone should tell her she was the best. Surely she knew that?

Does she though?

In his speciality, he was used to fielding egos the size of Scotland. It wasn't that Claire didn't have an ego; she did. She knew her stuff and he'd seen her run through medical students and her junior house officer with a complete lack of sympathy for any whose insufficient preparedness caused them to give incorrect answers to her questions. But he was used to trainees of her calibre thinking of themselves as 'cock of the walk' and carrying themselves with an accompanying swagger.

Claire Mitchell didn't swagger, despite the fact she had the best set of legs he'd seen on a woman in a very long time. And her shoes. Good God! Her acerbic personality was at odds with those shoes. Did she have any idea how her body moved in those heels? Her breasts tilted up, her hips swung and her calves said coquettishly, *Caress me. I promise you there's even better ahead.*

Hell's bells. He had a love-hate relationship with those shoes and her legs. Did they hint at a deeply buried wild side? Would those legs party the way he loved to party? Would he even want to party with them? *No way.* Gorgeous legs weren't enough to overcome a major personality flaw. Claire had a gritty aura of steely determination and no sense of humour whatsoever.

Given what she'd achieved so far and the fact she had a ninety-nine per cent chance of passing her exams on the first attempt—an uncommon feat in neurosurgery—she should be enjoying her hard-earned position. He doubted she was enjoying anything. The bloody woman never looked happy and it drove him crazy.

As her boss, his duty of care extended only so far as making sure she was coping with the workload and her study for her fellowship exams. However, he'd spent two years living in Australia himself, and despite both countries speaking English, pretty much everything else was different. It had taken him a few months to find his feet at the Children's Hospital and get established in a social set so he was very aware that Claire Mitchell might flounder at first. Ten days after she'd started working with him, he'd found her looking extremely downcast with what he'd assumed was a dose of homesickness. The woman looked like she needed to get out of the hospital for a bit and catch her breath.

On the spur of the moment, he'd asked, 'Would you like to grab a pint at the Frog and Peach?'

Her response had been unexpected. Her eyes—a fascinating combination of both light and dark brown that reminded him of his favourite caramel swirl chocolate bar—had widened momentarily before suddenly narrowing into critical slits. In her distinctive diphthong-riddled accent—one he really didn't want to admit to enjoying—she'd said briskly and succinctly, 'I have reports.'

'There's always going to be reports to write,' he'd said with a smile that invariably softened the sternest of wills.

'Especially when *you* don't appear to write many.'

He wasn't sure who'd been more taken aback—him, because registrars knew better then to ever speak to their consultant like that, or her, because she'd actually spoken her thoughts out loud.

'I'm sorry. That was out of order,' she'd said quickly, although not in a particularly ingratiating tone. 'Please accept my apology.'

'Jet lag still bothering you?' he'd offered by way of an olive branch. After all, they had to work together and life was easier if he got along with his trainee. So far, her standoffish manner wasn't a good sign.

At his question, a momentary look of confusion had crossed her face before disappearing under her hairline. 'Jet lag's a bastard.'

It was, but they both knew right then and there she

wasn't suffering from it. She'd spent that Friday night writing reports and he'd gone to the pub determined to forget about shoes that teased and long, strong and sexy legs. Legs that should come with a warning: Toxic If Touched. Happily, he'd met a pretty midwife with a delectable Irish lilt. The music had been so loud she'd had to lean in and speak directly into his ear. Heaven help him but he was a sucker for a woman with an accent.

Claire Mitchell now snipped the last stitch and said, 'Thanks, everyone,' before stepping back from the operating table.

Alistair thought drily that after working with her over the last few weeks, he no longer had to work very hard at resisting her outback drawl. In the weeks since she'd rejected his invitation, he hadn't issued another. As long as she did her job, he overrode his concerns that she might be lonely. Of more concern to him was why he'd been working so jolly hard at trying to get her to lighten up. Hell, right now he'd take it for the win if she looked even slightly happier than if her dog had just died.

After a brief conversation with his scrub nurse, checking how her son had fared in his school athletics competition, he left Lacey in the excellent care of the paediatric anaesthetist, Rupert Emmerson. He found Claire at the computer in the staff lounge.

'That went well,' he said, pressing a coffee pod into the machine.

She pushed her tortoiseshell glasses up her nose. 'It did.'

'You sound surprised.'

She pursed her lips and her bottom lip protruded slightly—soft, plump and enticing. His gaze stalled momentarily and he wondered how it was that he'd never noticed her very kissable mouth before.

'I'm not used to children being so hyped up before surgery,' she said crisply.

And there it was—her critical tone. *That* was why he'd never noticed her lips. Her mouth was usually speaking spikey, jagged words that could never be associated with luscious, soft pink lips. He wasn't used to being questioned by staff, let alone by a trainee who was here to learn from him. If he chose, he could make her life incredibly difficult and impact on her career, but he'd learned very abruptly that life was too short to hold grudges. As far as he was concerned, in the grand scheme of things, six months was a blip on the radar.

What baffled him though was that she obviously hadn't clashed with her previous supervising neurosurgeons or she wouldn't have got this far. He struggled to align the woman at the castle with the glowing reports that had preceded her. David Wu, a surgeon of very few words, had positively gushed about the woman, calling her intuitive, skilful and courageous. It had been his recommendation that had swayed the board to offer Claire Mitchell the scholarship.

Alistair couldn't fault her surgery but he was struggling with her personality. Take this morning, for instance. Everyone on the ward had been having fun except for Mitchell, who'd looked like a disapproving schoolmistress complete with her sun-kissed blonde hair coiled into a tight knot. Like so many of his nonmedical decisions, it had been a spur of the moment thing to call out to her to wave. The moment the words had left his mouth he knew he'd done the wrong thing. It had put her on the spot and focused attention on her. He was learning that she wasn't the type of person who welcomed the spotlight.

In his defence, he'd only asked her to join in the fun because he'd found their little patient in bed, scared and trembling. He'd scooped her into his arms hoping to reassure her, and then to take her mind off things, they'd room hopped, visiting the other kids. The parade had just happened—a combination of kids being kids, some hero worship, a packet of squeakers and a little girl needing some TLC. Now Claire Mitchell had the audacity to judge it. Judge him.

'Hyped up?' he repeated, feeling the edges of his calm fraying like linen. 'Actually, I'd call it being the opposite of terrified. Lacey's spent a week being prodded and poked. She's had an MRI and a CT scan. Hell, she was attached to the EEG for two days while we recorded epileptic events so we knew which surgery to perform.'

Despite being known around the castle for his calm and relaxed approach, his voice had developed a plummy and patronising edge. 'And after enduring all of that, you'd deny Lacey a bit of fun?'

Claire's eyes flashed golden brown. 'Of course not. I'd just plan a more appropriate time for the fun.'

Her tone vibrated with her absolute conviction that her way was the right way. The only way. He remembered how once he'd been a man of absolutes and certainties and how he'd never countenanced anything ever getting in the way of what he wanted. And hadn't fate laughed itself silly over that naïve belief? Hell, it was still chuckling.

With more force than necessary, he pulled his now full coffee mug out from under the machine. Pale brown liquid spilled down the steep white sides leaving a muddy residue. 'There's a lot to be said for spontaneity, Claire.'

Her eyes dilated as if he'd just shocked her by using her first name. 'We'll have to agree to disagree on that, Mr—' She quickly corrected herself. 'Alistair.'

Good God. Frustration brought his hands up, tearing through his hair. He'd been telling her from day one to call him 'Alistair.' She'd never called him 'sir'—probably the anti-establishment Australian in her prevented her from doing that—but she'd stuck with 'Mr North.' Every time she called him by his title he responded by calling her by her surname to drive home the point. He knew it was childish and very public school, but even so, she still didn't seem to be getting the message.

He really didn't understand her at all. Hell, he couldn't even get a read on her. Every other Australian he'd ever met or worked with tended to be laid-back, easy-going and with a well-developed sense of the ridiculous. When he was a kid, he'd grown up listening to his great-grandfather recounting the antics of the ANZACs during the Second World War—brave men who didn't hesitate to break the rules if they thought any rule was stupid. What in heaven's name had he done in a previous life to be lumbered with the only dour and highly strung Aussie in existence?

'Would you like to insert the ventricular peritoneal shunt in Bodhi Singh?' he asked, returning his thoughts to work, which was a lot more straightforward than the enigma that was Claire Mitchell.

'Really?' she asked, scrutinising him closely as if she didn't quite believe his offer.

That rankled. How was it that the woman who normally couldn't detect a joke now misread a genuine offer? 'Absolutely.'

Her mouth suddenly curved upwards as wonder and anticipation carved a dimple into her left cheek.

So that's what it takes to make her smile. For weeks, he'd been trying all the wrong things.

'Thanks,' she said enthusiastically. 'I'd love the opportunity.'

The tightness that was so much a part of her faded away under the brilliance of a smile so wide it encompassed her entire face. Along with her tension, all her sharp angles disappeared too, softened by the movement of her cheeks and the dazzling sparkle in her eyes. It was like looking at a completely different person—someone whose enthusiasm was so infectious that everyone vied to be on her team.

Pick me! Pick me!

What the hell? This was worse than a momentary thought about her gorgeous legs. Utterly discombobulated, he dragged his gaze away from her pink-cheeked face that danced with excitement, and far, far away from that come-hither dimple that had his blood pumping faster than necessary. He'd spent weeks trying to make her smile, and now that he had, he knew he must make it stop. It was one thing to wish that for the good of the patients and workplace harmony his speciality registrar be a little more relaxed. It was another thing entirely to find himself attracted to her as a woman. Hell, he didn't even like her. Not. At. All.

He'd never been attracted to someone he didn't like before, but that conundrum aside, there were many reasons why any sort of attraction was utterly out of the question. First and foremost, nothing could happen between them because he was her boss and she was his trainee. Fortunately, he knew exactly how to quash any remaining eddies of unwanted desire and kill off all temptation without any pain or suffering to himself.

'Good,' he said to her, tossing the dregs of his coffee into the sink. 'I'm glad you're on board, because I promised to have lunch with the new and very attractive burns-unit house officer. Inserting the VP would make me late.'

Her tension rode back in as fast as the cavalry into battle and her eyes flashed so brightly he needed sunglasses to deflect the glare. 'You're having lunch instead of operating?'

He gave a practised shrug—one that said, *What of it?* 'I've got complete confidence in your ability, but please, do page me if you need me.'

'I wouldn't dream of interrupting you,' she snapped.

Her previous lush mouth was now a thin, hard line and Alistair was thankfully back in familiar territory. Nothing about this Claire Mitchell was remotely attractive and his body reacted accordingly, which was to say, it didn't react at all. 'Excellent,' he said, as much to himself as to her. 'I'm glad we've got that sorted.'

Without another word, he left the room and strode towards the lifts. He'd spend the unexpected extra time with Ryan Walker's parents. It was the least he could do.

A few days later, Claire was handing out her morning coffees to the dawn crusaders at the hospital gates when she got chatting with a delightful man in his seventies. With his Cockney accent that reminded her of Eliza Doolittle's father in *Pygmalion*, he told her he'd been born 'a blue baby.'

'Me 'art's plumbing was all wrong like. Lucky for me, the castle 'ere had a pioneer in 'art surgery, otherwise I'd 'ave been dead a long time now.' Reg flicked his thumb towards the original ornate building. 'I've got a lot of love for the old girl. She gave me a chance to 'ave a bloody good life. One of me kids was born 'ere when she come early and the docs patched up the others when they broke bones. Me grandkids were all born 'ere and me first great-grandkiddy's due on Guy Fawkes.'

'It sounds like the castle is your family's hospital,' Claire said, thinking about the affection in the man's voice.

He nodded enthusiastically. 'Too right. That's why I'm 'ere every mornin'. All us Landsburys are on the rota right down to the little tackers. If that lot in suits close 'er down, it'll be a bloody disgrace.'

Claire was about to agree when she heard her name being called. She excused herself and turned to see Victoria Christie, the petite and dark-haired paramedic who'd galvanised everyone into action by starting the Save Our Hospital committee. With rapid flicks of her fingers, Victoria was motioning her over.

Bidding Reg goodbye, Claire crossed the cobblestones with care, regretting her heels. She reminded herself that her extra height would be necessary soon enough when she did rounds with Alistair. 'G'day, Vicki.'

'Hello, Claire. How are things?'

It was a broad question that really didn't demand a truthful answer but Claire had an unexpected and utterly disturbing urge to confide in the woman about how hard she was finding working with Alistair North. The thought unsettled her. She'd never been a woman who had a lot of girlfriends, and truth be told she usually got along better with men than women—which was fortunate given she was working in a male-dominated speciality. But it was immensely competitive so any friendships that had formed were always constrained by that reality.

She'd tried friendships outside of medicine but people didn't understand the crazy hours. Her frequent failures to turn up at events due to being delayed at work frustrated them and she noticed that it didn't take long for the invitations to dry up altogether. It killed relationships too, or at least it had played a big part in her and Michael's demise.

There was more to it than just your job.

She pulled her mind fast away from difficult thoughts and concentrated instead on trying to work out why women had to run in a pack and share the most intimate details of their lives with each other. She did have two close girlfriends and she'd always considered them enough, but Emma and Jessica were in Australia juggling toddlers, babies, partners and a burgeoning women's health clinic. She missed them, and these last few weeks at the castle had thrown her for a loop. Never before had she felt so at sea in a job and she had no one to talk to about her baffling boss.

How could one man generate such disparate feelings? She lurched from admiration to antipathy and back again, although right now admiration was fast losing its gloss. In Australia, she'd worked under crusty old neurosurgeons who barely knew her name and when they did deign speak to her it was to bark out instructions. It hadn't always been a pleasant experience but at least it was predictable behaviour. They'd played by the archaic rules set down a hundred years ago and she'd just put her head down and got on with the job. So why was she struggling to do that with Alistair North?

Because he doesn't play by the rules.

And wasn't that the truth! The man drove her to the point of distraction with his lack of attention to detail outside of theatre. Sure, she was his trainee, but along with her clinical work she was carrying his administrative load as well as her own and it was wearing her down. She'd been working ridiculously long hours trying to manage the paperwork and she didn't know how much longer she could trade sleep to keep up. Last week, with an enormous sense of guilt, she'd offloaded some of it onto her house officer. Andrew had accepted it without question, because that was the system, but part of her had wanted to explain. The rest of her had overruled the idea. Since leaving Gundiwindi, she'd held her secret close so it couldn't be used against her. She'd got this far and as soon as she qualified she'd be home free.

Meanwhile, she was barely treading water with the added report load, and combined with her own exhaustion and the Pied Piper incident on the ward two days ago, she'd lost her temper. Oh, how she regretted that she'd given in to fatigue and frustration. It had been beyond unwise but what worried her even more was her current pattern of behaviour. For some reason, when she was in Alistair North's company, she lost her protective restraint.

Not once in her career had she ever spoken back to her consultant, and now with the end of her fellowship in sight, it wasn't the time to start. But as each day passed, she felt more and more like a smoking and steaming volcano ready to blow. To try and keep herself in check, she'd started clenching her fists when she felt her frustrations rising.

As a result, her palms had developed permanent dents in them. She'd discovered if she focused on the sharp digging pain she was less likely to say something she'd regret. It didn't always work and she'd clearly seen his displeasure at her criticism of his approach with Lacey. But instead of disciplining her, he'd rewarded her by letting her operate.

This unexpected offer had both stunned and thrilled her. At the time, she'd hoped it meant she'd finally passed his test of attempting to drown her under a sea of administrative work. That his offer for her to operate solo meant he'd finally recognised her clinical skills and they were entering the next phase in their working relationship. For a few delicious moments she'd floated on air and then reality had hit. His offer for her to operate had been pure expediency. The playboy had a lunch date.

That moment was the first time she'd ever doubted his professionalism. Even then, the suspicion wasn't straightforward. Back in Australia, she'd had opportunities to insert VP shunts and she was competent in the procedure. He would have known that, so the fact he wasn't going to be in the operating theatre with her wasn't exactly abandoning his patient. Yet he'd admitted to going to lunch!

So, you'll lambast him for telling the truth when he could have created excuses like your previous bosses?

Sick of the endless loop of contradictory thoughts, Claire gave herself a shake. 'Today's a new day,' she said cryptically to Victoria's question, 'with new things to learn.'

'Alistair's a generous teacher.'

'He's certainly generous,' she said, fighting the urge to purse her lips in disapproval.

Victoria laughed and her chestnut ponytail swung around her shoulders. 'Our Alistair certainly loves women. That's what I wanted to talk to you about.'

Unable to hide her astonishment, Claire blinked at the pretty paramedic. *Not you too!* If the hospital grapevine was to be believed, Victoria and Dominic MacBride were very much together. 'Oh?' she asked cautiously.

Victoria's face lit up with enthusiasm. 'You've heard about the hospital ball?'

For anyone not to have heard about the ball, they'd have to have been living under a rock. Posters graced every noticeboard inside the hospital, and outside they'd been pasted on the poster pillars along the main road. Invitations had been sent to the past and present medical and auxiliary staff and one massive wall in the cafeteria had been covered with an enormous banner declaring the Spring Fling ball to be *the* social event of the season. The chatter about it had even managed to dent the football conversations about which team would be playing in the FA Cup final in a few weeks.

'I think I may have seen a poster about it somewhere,' she said with mock thoughtfulness.

Victoria missed the joke and continued in earnest. 'It's our first major event and we're hoping to raise fifty thousand pounds. The thing is, we really need Alistair to attend. If he doesn't, it's going to affect ticket sales.'

Claire laughed and then stopped as she caught the expression on Victoria's face. 'You're serious?'

'Deadly. He told Dominic that things were—' she raised her fingers into quotation marks '—complicated, which is code for he's broken some poor deluded girl's heart once again.' She let out a long sigh. 'Why they even think they could be the one to get him to commit is beyond me. The man is Peter Pan. Anyway, we really need him at the ball because we plan to auction the seat next to him. Women will have the chance to sit next to him for one of three courses. We're also selling his dance card. Your job is to make sure he attends.'

'I doubt I can make Alistair North do anything he doesn't want to do,' she replied honestly.

Victoria shot her an understanding smile. 'Alistair was

raised right and he went to the right schools. As a result, he has a social code of conduct that he sticks to. He will go to the ball if he's your date.'

Claire's intake of breath was so sharp it sent her into a paroxysm of coughing. 'I can't ask my boss out,' she said, her voice rising sharply.

Victoria shrugged as if the fact Alistair was her boss was immaterial. 'Of course you can. We all have to do our bit to save the castle,' she said pragmatically. 'Besides, it's all about how you word the invitation. Guilt him into it if you have to. Tell him it's imperative there's a show of strength from Koala Ward. He can't really argue against the expectation that as head of the department he should be there.'

The thought of having this conversation with Alistair North was enough to make her hyperventilate. 'Victoria, I really don't think—'

'Do you know how much the community will suffer if the hospital's sold?' Victoria's hands hit her hips, elbows akimbo. 'Keeping the castle open means everything to me, to the staff and to the patients. We're expecting to raise at least a thousand pounds by auctioning off his dance card, plus all the money we'll get for selling the seats next to him.'

Oh, how she wanted to rush to the ATM right this second and withdraw the cash but the idea of eating next month took precedence. 'I can't promise you—'

'Yes, you can. And you will,' Victoria said with the sort of authority in her voice usually reserved for recalcitrant patients. She reached out her hand and gave Claire's arm a gentle squeeze. 'And all the children and families in the district will thank you.'

Claire, who towered over the brunette, couldn't comprehend how someone so petite could be such an indomitable force. 'That's blackmail,' she said weakly.

Victoria smiled. 'No. It's preventing a travesty. We're

all mucking in to save our wonderful hospital for generations to come. This is your small contribution.'

Small? If this was small, she hated to think what a big request would look like. Claire was keen to do her bit, but she knew that Victoria had just well and truly dropped her into the muck right up to her neck.

CHAPTER THREE

CLAIRE STOOD AT the end of Ryan Walker's bed and chewed her lip. She had expected the little boy to have improved much faster than this. When he'd arrived at A & E barely conscious after being hit on the head by a falling beam at the Westbourne Primary School fire, Dominic MacBride, the castle's trauma surgeon, had immediately called her and Alistair in to consult. They'd ordered a CT scan that showed Ryan had sustained a fractured skull. Fortunately, there was no displacement of bones but there was a tiny associated subdural haematoma.

Rather than rushing in with guns blazing, she'd totally agreed with Alistair's conservative treatment plan. They'd worked closely with Rupert Emmerson, the anaesthetist, who'd sedated and ventilated Ryan. Alistair had inserted an intracranial pressure monitor and she'd inserted a central line, administering a mannitol infusion to decrease any associated brain swelling from the injury. The small haematoma hadn't diminished in size but neither had it grown. As a result, Ryan remained ventilated and his condition was still in a state of flux.

Yesterday morning, in a moment of frustrated despair during teaching rounds, she'd asked Alistair if she'd missed anything. Despite the large group of students gathered around the little tacker's bed, Alistair's pewter-grey eyes had zeroed in on her as if they were the only two people in the room.

'If you've missed something, Mitchell, then so have I.'

'Shall we do another MRI?'

'He had an MRI two days ago. While his observations remain the same it's not warranted. You have to ask yourself why you're doing the test.'

Because I have to do something. Doing nothing feels like giving up.

'Surely there's another option?'

Something she'd been momentarily tempted to think was sympathy had crossed his face but it vanished the moment he opened his mouth.

'There is. We wait.'

Wait? That wasn't something. That was sitting on their hands. 'And what if he doesn't improve?'

His shoulders had risen and fallen. 'That may be the reality.'

No. 'I don't like that reality,' she'd said briskly as if being terse would change it.

He'd given her a brief sad smile before returning his attention to the group of students. 'Who can tell me the elements of the Glasgow Coma Scale?'

'I swear he squeezed my hand before,' Ryan's mother said, her voice breaking into Claire's thoughts. Louise's anxious face was lined with two weeks of worry. 'That's a good sign, isn't it.'

It wasn't framed as a question—it was a solid statement. Louise needed to reassure herself that her little boy really was showing signs of improvement when in fact he was neither improving nor deteriorating. It was the limbo that was so disconcerting and heartbreaking, especially when neither she nor Alistair could pinpoint the reason.

Claire didn't want to upset the traumatised woman but

she didn't attach the same significance to what was likely a muscle spasm. 'He's very heavily sedated, Louise.'

Claire checked his vital signs as she did twice each day. *No change.* She wrote up a drug order to override the one that was about to expire and then she turned her attention to Louise. Gunmetal-grey shadows stretched from the mother's eyes down to her cheekbones. Claire was familiar with the signs of relatives at the end of their rope.

'How are you sleeping?' she asked, despite the signs that the woman wasn't sleeping very much at all.

The exhausted mother shrugged and tilted her head towards the rollaway bed. 'It's got springs in interesting places.'

'We can get you another one,' Claire offered, having no idea if that was even possible. With all the talk of the probable sale of the hospital land and relocating the facility to one of the home counties, the powers that be weren't spending any money. If push came to shove, she'd buy a rollaway bed herself. At least it would feel like she was doing something other than this interminable waiting.

Louise sighed. 'To be fair, it's as much the disturbed sleep as anything. I wake up every time the nurses do their hourly check.'

'Would you consider taking a night off?' Claire asked carefully. She'd learned to tread very gently with families.

'I doubt I'd sleep any better at home.'

'Your GP can prescribe some sleeping tablets. Believe me, eight hours sleep in your own bed would do you the world of good.'

Louise gave her head a brisk shake. 'I want to be here when he wakes up.'

'I understand.' She pulled up a chair and sat, putting herself at eye level with Louise. 'The thing is, Ryan doesn't have to be alone. I'm sure there's someone in your extended family you could ask to give you a break? You know, so both you and Colin can get a full night's sleep.'

Louise glanced between Claire and her redheaded son, whose freckles seemed darker than ever against his porcelain-white face. A tear spilled over and ran down her cheek. 'I'm beyond making decisions. My mind feels like it's encased in a wet, London fog.'

'Then let me make the decision for you.'

She looked uncertain. 'I've never felt this exhausted in my life. It's like fatigue's not only invaded my soul but it's set up residence. All I want to do is curl up under the duvet and sleep for a week. I want to forget about the fire and how it turned my life on its head in an instant. But how can I? This is my new reality. Ryan can't leave and forget. If I go home, aren't I letting him down?'

Claire had heard variations of this story from grieving parents many times before. She gave the woman's knee a gentle pat. 'If you don't look after yourself, Louise, you risk getting sick. If you fall apart, then you'll be away from Ryan a lot longer than twelve hours.'

The enervated mother suddenly sagged as if utterly defeated by a fortnight's emotional trauma and associated sleep debt. Her weary moss-green eyes met Claire's. 'If he wakes up while I'm at home, you must call me.'

'Of course.'

'Thank you.' The woman visibly brightened. 'Perhaps my leaving will trigger him waking up. You know, like when you take an umbrella with you every day and it's always dry but the moment you leave it at home it rains.'

Claire couldn't quite see the connection.

'I've been here for days,' Louise explained, 'and nothing's changed. It stands to reason that if I leave, he'll sit up and start talking.'

A worrying sensation roved along Claire's spine and she had to resist the urge not to wince. 'Medicine doesn't really work that way, Louise,' she said gently. 'Would you like me to contact your GP about the sleeping tablets? And I can ask the ward clerk to call you a taxi.'

'Thank you. That would be great.' Louise leaned over, brushed the hair from Ryan's forehead and kissed him. 'See you soon, buddy.' She smoothed his hair back into place and then stood up. 'Promise me, Claire, you'll telephone if he wakes up.'

'I promise,' Claire said easily. 'Wild horses couldn't stop me from giving you good news like that.'

Alistair high-fived Tristan Lewis-Smith. 'Way to go, Tris,' he said with a grin.

The kid had just whooped him at virtual tennis—twice—but he didn't care. He was too busy rejoicing in the fact that the ten-year-old had been seizure free for a week. That hadn't happened in two years and it was moments like these that reminded him that what he did each day mattered. Hell, it reinforced his mantra that every single day mattered and life should be lived to the full.

He'd almost lost the opportunity to do that, and when he'd woken up in the coronary care unit, he'd vowed never to forget how life could change in a heartbeat—or the lack of one as the case may be—and how close he'd come to death. He'd been blessed with a second chance and he never took it for granted. He was thrilled to be able to give Tristan a second chance at a normal life.

'Right-oh, mate.' He pulled down the sheet and patted the centre of the bed. 'Time to tuck in and pretend to read or the night sister will have my guts for garters.'

Full of beans and far from quiet, Tristan bounced onto the bed. 'You're just saying that because you're scared if you play another game I'll beat you. Again.'

'There is that,' Alistair said with a grin. 'Hurry up. I've got somewhere I need to be.'

Tristan scrambled under the covers. 'Nurse Saunders said you couldn't stay long because you've got a hot date.'

'Did she now?' Funny that Lindsay appeared to know more about this hot date than he did. He found himself automatically tucking the sheet around the little boy, only this time an odd feeling of something akin to emptiness accompanied it.

He immediately shook it off. He had no reason to feel empty or lonely. Life was good. He had a job he loved and a spacious and light-filled apartment just off the Portobello Road that he'd filled with curios from his world travels. Three years ago, he'd added to his property portfolio and bought a pretty stone cottage surrounded by fields of lavender in Provence. When he was there, he revelled in the sensory delights of sunshine, hearty Mediterranean food and great wine. He visited at least once a month, either alone or with a companion depending on whether or not the woman he was dating was still focused on having fun. The moment a woman started dropping hints about 'taking things to the next level' she was no longer welcome in France. Or in Notting Hill for that matter.

He loved women but he didn't do next levels. It was better to break a heart in the early days, well before things got serious, than to risk shattering a life, or worse, lives. His childhood was a case in point, and furthermore, no one ever knew precisely the duration of a second chance.

Surprised by the unexpected direction his musings had taken him—he didn't do dark thoughts and he certainly wasn't known for them—he left Tristan's room and contemplated the hour. It wasn't quite eight. As it was a Thursday night there'd be a sizeable hospital crowd at the Frog and Peach and he'd be welcomed with open arms for his dart skills. Oddly, the thought didn't entice. He had an overwhelming urge to do something completely different. Something wild that would make him feel alive.

Parkour in the dark?
Alive not dead, thank you very much.

Still, parkour in daylight this coming weekend was worth investigating. He pulled out his phone and had just brought up a browser when he heard, 'G'day, Alistair.'

Astonished, he spun around at the sound of the broad Australian accent. Although he'd heard Claire Mitchell use the informal Aussie greeting with other people, she'd always been far more circumspect with him. Well, with the exception of one or two lapses. In general, he knew she tried to be polite with him and that she found it a struggle. Did it make him a bad person that he enjoyed watching her keep herself in check? The woman was always buttoned up so tightly it wasn't surprising she cracked every now and then.

Now she stood in front of him with her hands pressed deep into the pockets of her once starched but now very end-of-day limp doctor's coat. Her hair was pulled back into its functional ponytail and a hot-pink stethoscope was slung around her neck. A tiny koala clung to her security lanyard along with a small pen on retractable elastic. Her utilitarian white blouse and medium length black skirt were unremarkable except that the skirt revealed those long shapely legs that taunted him.

Her feet were tucked into bright red shoes with a wide strap that crossed her instep just below her ankle and culminated in a large red button that drew the eye. He suddenly understood completely why Victorian gentlemen had waxed lyrical over a fleeting glimpse of a fine ankle.

He scanned her face, looking for clues as to why she was suddenly attempting a colloquial greeting with him. 'G'day, yourself,' he intoned back, with a fair crack at an Aussie accent.

Behind her sexy librarian-style glasses her eyes did that milk and dark chocolate swirly thing he always enjoyed and—was she blushing?

'Do you have a minute?' she asked, quickly pushing her glasses up her nose as they continued walking towards the lifts.

'Always. Problem?'

'Um.' She surreptitiously glanced along the corridor, taking in the nurses' station that was teaming with staff. She suddenly veered left into the treatment room.

Utterly intrigued by this uncharacteristic behaviour, he followed. 'Shall I close the door?'

She tugged hard at some stray strands of her hair before pushing them behind her ears. 'Thanks.'

He closed the door and flicked the blinds to the closed position before leaning back against the wide bench. Claire stood a metre or more away, her plump lips deliciously red. He shifted his gaze and— *Damn it!* His eyes caught on a fluttering pulse beating at the base of her throat. She really had the most gloriously long, smooth neck that just begged to be explored.

That's as may be, but remember, most of the time she's a pain in the ass. Not to mention she's your trainee.

'Alistair,' she started purposefully, and then stopped.

'Claire.' He couldn't help teasing back. He'd never seen her at a loss before and it was deliciously refreshing.

She took in such a deep breath that her breasts rose, stressing the button he was pretty certain sat just above her bra line. Was it delicate sheer lace or plainly utilitarian? It was his experience that plain women often wore the sexiest underwear.

With that mouth, she's hardly plain.

As if on cue, the tip of her tongue peeked out, flicking the bow of her top lip.

His blood leapt.

She cleared her throat. 'I hope you won't take this the wrong way but…'

Trying to look utterly unaffected by her, he cocked one

brow and reminded himself of all the times she'd been critical of him. 'My sensibilities haven't stopped you from giving me your opinion before.'

This time she definitely blushed, but somehow she managed to wrestle her embarrassment under control with dignity. 'True, but that was work. This doesn't exactly fall into that category. Although I suppose it does technically if you—'

'You're babbling,' he said, hoping it would force her to focus. At the same time, he had an absurd and unexpected need to rescue her from herself.

Her head jerked up so fast he was worried her neck might snap but then she hit him with a gimlet stare. He forced himself not to squirm as an unsettling feeling trickled through him. Did she see straight through the man he liked to show the world? Had she glimpsed the corner edge of the bubbling mess he kept securely sealed away?

'As the head of the department of neurosurgery,' she said tightly, 'I think it's important you lead by example and attend the Spring Fling.'

The Spring Fling? Surely he'd misheard. 'You mean the neurosurgery spring symposium?'

She shook her head and once again the blush bloomed on her cheeks. She swallowed and that damn tongue of hers darted out to moisten her lips. This time as the zip of heat hit him, he pushed off the bench to try and shake it off.

'I mean the fundraising ball,' she said slowly, as if the words were being reluctantly pulled out of her.

He couldn't resist. 'Are you inviting me to the ball?'

Her eyes widened in consternation. 'No!' For a moment, indignation spun around her before fading with a sigh and a fall of her shoulders. 'I mean perhaps. Yes. In a manner of speaking.'

His mouth twitched. 'It's good to know you're so decisive.'

Her chin shot up, jabbing the air. 'You can tease me all you like, Mr—Alistair, but you know as well as I do that at the bare minimum there should be a neurosurgery staff table at the ball.'

Damn it to hell. She was absolutely right but how had she found out he wasn't going? He'd been keeping that bit of information to himself, more out of embarrassment than anything else. A couple of months ago, just before Claire had arrived, he'd had a particularly tough day. He'd lost a patient—a two-year-old boy with a brainstem glioma—and for some reason he'd avoided the sympathetic eyes of his staff at the Frog and Peach. He'd hit a trendy bar in Soho instead, and in retrospect, he'd consumed one whisky too many.

It had been enough to scramble his usually accurate *crazy woman* detector. As a result, he'd allowed himself to be tempted by the Amazonian features of Lela. The thirty-year-old was a fitness instructor as well as being a part-time security guard. They'd had a lot of fun together until he'd realised her possessive streak wasn't limited to bedroom games.

He knew the ball committee had flagged the idea of auctioning off the chairs next to eligible bachelors. Usually he'd have been fine with the concept and embraced it, but he'd been worried Lela might turn up and cause a nasty public spectacle. Or worse, buy the ticket. To save himself, and the hospital, embarrassment he'd decided not to attend the ball but to make a sizeable donation to the cause instead. The only person he'd mentioned this plan to was Dominic.

Stupid, stupid, stupid! The paediatric trauma surgeon had obviously broken the bro code and told Victoria. What was it about a man in love that made him prepared to throw his friend under the bus just to stay in sweet with his lady? Now the *i*-dotting and *t*-crossing Claire Mitchell was calling him out on a perceived lack of social etiquette.

He ploughed his hand through his hair. He'd been raised on etiquette, and the irony that an Australian, with their supposedly classless society, was reminding him of his social responsibilities almost made him laugh. Perhaps he could turn this whole Lela-and-the-ball mess around and use it to his advantage.

'Let me get this straight,' he said with a lazy smile. 'You're prepared to spend an evening with me just to make sure I do the right thing?'

This time she was the one to raise an eyebrow. 'As your second-in-command, I can't expect you to attend the ball if I'm not prepared to attend.'

'Ah, yes, that sucker duty gets you every time.'

She stiffened. 'But it seems you're often immune.'

Ouch. Her words tried to scratch him like the sharp tip of a knife, but he didn't need to justify himself to her. He was very well aware of his duty. Ironically, duty had arrived in a rush just after he'd vowed to make the most of every new day that had been gifted to him. It was the juxtaposition of his life.

'None of us are immune, Claire. It's just I try to have a bit of fun too.'

She narrowed her eyes. 'And you're inferring that I don't have fun?'

Not that I've seen. 'Have you had any fun since arriving in London?'

She looked momentarily nonplussed. 'I…um…yes. Of course.'

Liar. But he was planning on having some fun with her right now and killing two birds with one stone. 'Excellent. I can certainly promise you fun at the ball. Especially considering how you've gone above and beyond the call of duty and bought the seat next to me.'

'What?' She paled, her expression momentarily aghast, and then she rallied. 'I don't get paid enough for that.'

'Brutal.' He exaggeratedly slapped his chest in the general area of his heart, his long fingers grazing the lower edge of his pacemaker. 'And here I was thinking I was your date. I tell you what. I'll pay for both of our tickets.'

'That won't be necess—'

'It's the least I can do,' he interrupted, waving away her protest. 'I imagine it was Victoria who dropped you right in it.'

She grimaced. 'You're not wrong there.'

He made a huffing sound more at the absent Dominic than her. 'The good thing is you'll be saving me from having to play nice all evening.'

Effrontery streaked across her face. 'Well, when you put it like that, I can hardly wait,' she said drily.

Her sarcasm was unexpected and delightfully refreshing and he heard himself laugh. He wasn't used to a woman viewing an evening with him as a trial. The women he dated erred on the appreciative side and often went to great lengths to make him happy. Not Claire Mitchell.

A streak of anticipation shot through him. Without realising it, she'd just thrown down a challenge. He wasn't totally convinced she was even capable of having fun and he had a sudden urge to know what she looked like when she was in the midst of a good time.

She'd smile like she did when you let her operate solo. Remember how you felt then?

He disregarded the warning that it was probably unwise to be looking forward to the ball quite this much.

'So will you be picking me—' His phone rang with the ICU ringtone, and as he pulled it from his pocket, Claire's pager beeped.

'North,' he said, answering the call just as Claire mouthed to him, 'ICU?'

Listening to the nurse on the other end of the line, he nodded at Claire and opened the treatment room door. As she walked quickly past him, her crisp scent of the sea drifted back to him and he was suddenly back on Bondi Beach when his life had been simpler and there had been few restraints placed upon it.

'We're on our way,' he told the worried nurse. Stepping out into the corridor, he followed Claire down the fire escape, taking the fastest way to ICU.

CHAPTER FOUR

CLAIRE WALKED OUT of the operating theatre, tugging her mask from her face. Her hand shook so much that her toss missed the bin and she had to stoop to pick up the mask. Even then it took her two more shots to land it.

Get a grip.

'You all right, Dr Mitchell?' Cyril, the night cleaner, asked. Apparently, he'd been working at the castle for forty years and as well as keeping the operating theatre suite clean he took a keen parental interest in the junior staff. 'You look a bit shaky.'

'Nothing a cup of tea won't fix,' she lied breezily, not trusting herself to let his concern touch her. She couldn't afford to fall apart. Not yet anyway. Not when her job was only half finished.

She walked into the doctors' lounge, which at ten in the evening was thankfully empty. She needed and wanted privacy to make this call. Picking up the phone, it took her two attempts to get the number right as her mind kept spinning off and practicing what she was going to say. As the phone rang in her ear, she concentrated on slowing her breathing and her wildly hammering heart.

'Hello,' a sleep-filled voice croaked down the line.

'Louise.' Her voice sounded unsteady and she tried to firm it up. 'It's Claire Mitchell. From the hospital.'

'Claire!' Ryan's mother's voice was instantly alert. 'You're calling me? Oh, my God,' she said half laughing, half crying, 'it's just like the umbrella story. You told me to come home and now you're calling. He's awake, isn't he? Colin, wake up. It's Ryan.'

Claire's stomach lurched so hard she had to force the rising tide of acid back down her throat. 'Louise,' she said firmly but gravely, trying to signal to the woman this call wasn't the positive one she craved. 'Ryan's not awake.'

'What?' She sounded confused. 'Then why are you calling?' she asked angrily.

Claire thought about the desperately ill little boy who was lying surrounded by all the latest medical technology. 'Ryan's condition has deteriorated.'

'No!'

Claire flinched at the pain contained in one small word.

'You said you'd call me if he woke up.' Louise's accusation was loud and clear. In the mother's mind, Claire had broken a promise to her.

'I'm sorry to have to tell you that Ryan's had another bleed. We rushed him to theatre and we've just operated on him.'

'So, this is a just a little setback? He's going to be all right?'

Claire bit her lip so hard she tasted blood. 'Unfortunately, it was a big bleed. It caused his brain to swell and it was necessary to remove a small part of his skull to ease the pressure. It's called a craniotomy.'

'He's got a hole in his head?'

The rising disbelief and trauma in Louise's voice wound through her like poison. 'The bone flap's being stored in a freezer at the hospital until the swelling in Ryan's brain has subsided. When that happens, we can reinsert it.'

'Are you saying that his brain's open to the air? That can't possibly be a good thing.'

'He'll wear a special protective helmet while the bone flap's removed.'

There was a long silence followed by a sharp intake of breath. 'He's not going to have brain damage, is he?'

This was the question Claire always dreaded. 'We won't know the exact situation until the swelling in his brain has diminished.'

'How long will that take?'

'I'm sorry, Louise, but right now I can't say. It's too hard to predict.'

She heard the sound of a duvet being moved and feet hitting the floor. 'Why didn't you see this coming? Why didn't you stop it?'

The words whipped and lashed Claire, playing on her days of misgivings that they were missing something. 'I know this is very hard for you—'

'Hard!' Louise barked down the phone, her voice so loud and outraged that Claire jumped. 'Do you have children, Claire?'

Don't play this game. You'll be the one left bleeding. Even if Louise had been a friend instead of a patient's relative, Claire wouldn't have confessed her one regret. Somehow, by pursuing the toughest medical speciality to prove to herself, Gundiwindi and the world that she was capable and intelligent, she was suddenly thirty-four, alone and with the chance of motherhood rapidly diminishing.

Alistair walked into the lounge and threw her a questioning glance as he cast tea bags into mugs.

Claire turned away from his penetrating gaze, which despite her determined efforts to stay on task had the uncanny ability to derail her concentration every single time. It both bothered and confused her. She'd always been known for her intense focus and her ability to block out all unnecessary distractions. Over the last few years, her consultants had told her that her natural attention to detail was a perfect trait for a neurosurgeon.

No one outside of her family knew that skill wasn't natural at all but borne from necessity and honed by sheer determination and bloody-mindedness. It rarely let her down. Even during what she'd considered the 'heady days' with Michael, when she'd thought he loved her, her focus hadn't faltered. However, under the assault of Alistair North's clear, iron-ore-grey eyes, it wobbled precariously.

'Louise,' she said, centring her thoughts. 'Ryan's being transferred back to ICU now. When you and your husband arrive at the hospital, Mr North and I will be here to answer all your questions. Just ask the staff to page us.'

She finished the call and slowly lowered the receiver onto the cradle. She knew she should stand up but she wasn't certain her shaking legs would hold her.

'Tough call,' Alistair commented as he opened the fridge.

'I've had better.'

'Do you take milk and sugar in your tea?'

Despite her surprise at his offer, her head fell back to rest on the couch as exhaustion caught up with her. 'Just milk.'

'You look like you could do with some sugar.'

She suddenly craved something sweet. 'Do you have chocolate?'

'Surely in the six weeks you've been here you've learned that any chocolate that enters this room vanishes in five minutes.' He rummaged through the cupboards and then gave an unexpected woot, holding up a red-and-black box. 'Will chilli and chocolate shortbread suffice?'

She had a ridiculous and overwhelming urge to cry at his unanticipated thoughtfulness. 'Awesome.'

He walked over to her carrying two mugs of tea and balancing the box of biscuits on the top of one of the mugs. 'Here you go.'

There was no sign of the teasing playboy or the supercilious consultant. In her overwrought state, she couldn't make sense of the change and that troubled her. She stuck to what she knew best: work. 'We should have done that MRI.'

Her words tumbled out loaded with blame. 'We should have done more. We caused this.'

'Hey,' he said, his grey eyes suddenly stern. 'We did not cause this. We both operated on him and we both saw exactly the same thing. This bleed was hidden by the original haematoma. That's why it wasn't showing up on the scans. On the plus side, if he'd bled anywhere else instead of in ICU, he'd probably be dead.'

Culpability pummelled her so hard it hurt and she was unable to control her belligerent tone. 'How is that supposed to make me feel better? He wouldn't have been in hospital if it weren't for the fire. We're supposed to pre-empt disasters like this. Now he's sicker than when he arrived.'

'Not necessarily,' Alistair said with frustrating logic and calm. 'The craniotomy gives him the possibility of recovery. We've done everything we can to give him a chance at the best possible outcome.' His face softened into friendly lines. 'I know this sucks, but it's just one of those god-awful things that happen sometimes.'

'I don't accept that,' she said so emphatically her hand jerked. Hot tea spilled over the rim and onto her skin. 'Ouch!'

He immediately removed the mug from her hand. 'I'll get you some ice. Meanwhile, open wide.' He shoved a shortbread into her mouth.

For reasons she couldn't fathom, she'd done as he'd asked and obediently opened her mouth. Now, more out of surprise than anything else, she bit into the soft, buttery, chocolate goodness and embraced the kick of chilli. It shocked her senses in a much-needed way and she wiped her tea-covered hand on her scrub. A large red welt with a white centre rose fast on the base of her thumb accompanied by a furious sting. Wearing surgical gloves was going to hurt for the next few days.

Alistair returned with an icepack wrapped in a red-and-white-checked tea towel. His large hand folded the pack around hers and the burn of the ice tangoed with the burn of his hand. He lifted her left hand and placed it over the pack. 'Hold that there for ten minutes.'

'Thanks.' Irrational tears threatened again along with an equally irrational sense of loss as he removed his hand. *What the hell was wrong with her?*

'Shortbread sugar starting to hit?' Alistair asked, his brow furrowed with mild concern.

Not really. Her head was spinning and she felt strangely adrift and utterly drained. It was as if a decade of fatigue had just sideswiped her. She'd been working so hard and for so long doing everything on her own, proving she was as good as or better than her peers, and fighting harder than anyone to stay on top that she wasn't used to anyone looking out for her. Right now, nothing was making sense, especially this version of Alistair who was being remarkably kind.

Her entire body sagged heavily and it took almost more effort than she had to keep herself upright. She had a ludicrous urge to drop her head onto his shoulder and take shelter there, sleeping for a week.

Have you completely lost your mind? You're at work. He's your boss and just no. *Got that?*

Aghast that her jumbled thoughts had somehow managed to get to this point, she tried squaring her shoulders in an attempt to summon up her professional decorum. Not once in her career had she ever lost control at work and tonight wasn't the time to start—especially not in front of Alistair North. No, the moment the ten minutes was up, she'd stow the ice pack in the freezer, bid Alistair a crisp goodnight and head home to bed for a much-needed sleep. Everything would make sense again after a good night's sleep.

And if it doesn't?

She'd worry about that if and when it happened.

Alistair rubbed the back of his neck, slightly bewildered and definitely disconcerted by this version of Claire Mitchell sitting next to him on the couch. Her reaction to what had been a routine craniotomy was out of proportion and out of character. When he'd first met her, he'd picked her as being meticulous, ambitious and with a 'take no prisoners' approach to work. It wasn't that she didn't care—she was indeed empathetic—but she always put the medicine first. Surely Ryan Walker's unexpected deterioration couldn't have been the first time she'd been faced with an unanswerable medical conundrum?

Whatever it was, it was obvious it had upset her greatly. As her consultant, it was his job to help her work through it. But how? He sipped his tea and pondered the matter until a possible solution came to him.

'Would it help if we took Ryan's case to peer review? I doubt they'll disagree with our treatment plan but the process will reassure you that we did everything we could.'

'Peer review doesn't have to deal with Ryan's parents,' she said, her voice cracking. Her shoulders slumped. 'Louise Walker hates me.'

Ah. So Claire Mitchell wasn't just about protocol and paperwork after all. Underneath her automaton tendencies and prickly exterior existed a regular person. For whatever reason, something about Ryan's case had got under her skin. He knew all about that. At some point in every doctor's career, one patient would touch them more than the others. 'Louise Walker is a terrified mother.'

'I know.'

Her eyes, now as round as huge saucers of warm caramel, looked at him. He got an unanticipated urge to dive right in. *That won't help matters. You don't really like her.* Baffled, he blinked and then as his vision came back into focus he saw her beseeching distress urging him to understand.

'I made Louise leave the hospital today. I insisted on it.'

He rushed to reassure her and at the same time get himself back on solid ground. 'And rightly so. The woman was exhausted.'

Her fingers plucked at invisible balls of lint on her scrubs. 'She made me promise to call her if Ryan woke up.'

Worry pulled tightly behind his eyes. 'Promises are always fraught…'

Her chin, which he'd noticed tended to tilt up sharply whenever she felt under attack, barely lifted. 'I'm not a novice.'

'No.'

'And of course I'd have called her if Ryan woke up. It was hardly an unprofessional assurance.'

Suddenly, his veil of confusion lifted. With piercing clarity, he saw exactly where this was going. He felt for her—he really did. 'When you rang Louise just before, she thought—'

'That I had the first piece of good news in two weeks.' She sucked her lips in tight and blinked rapidly. It wasn't enough to prevent a tear escaping and running down her cheek beyond the reach of her glasses. She crooked the forefinger of her uninjured hand and brushed it away.

Bloody hell. Unlike a lot of men who froze in the presence of a distressed woman, he was always moved to assist, which was why he'd already made his registrar a cup of tea. But now, seeing the usually stitched-up and almost too-together Claire Mitchell falling apart in front of him sent a visceral spike of pain into him, cramping his gut. 'Why didn't you ask me to make the call?'

Her free hand curled into a tight fist and her chin dropped towards her chest. 'You were very clear about it being my job.'

'Bloody hell, Claire,' he said softly, the words coming out on a puff of air. He felt like the worst boss in the world. 'I don't understand. You've queried me and judged my opinions more than once in the past few weeks. Why on earth did you decide this telephone call was the *one* thing you weren't going to question?'

'All I know,' she said so softly he needed to strain to listen, 'is that I've destroyed Louise Walker. I've made her pain ten times worse.'

Her head rose and her woebegone expression ate into him like acid on paper. It was as natural as breathing to put a hand on her shoulder. 'You haven't destroyed her,' he said quietly.

Her head fell forward onto his shoulder and he patted her gently on the back. 'Deep down you know that. You're just having a rough night.'

She made a muffled noise that sounded half like denial and half like a hiccough. He smiled at the very normal snorting sound coming from someone he'd thought kept a wide distance between work and her emotions. He found himself stroking her hair, the fine strands like silk against his palm. With her head now resting under his chin, the scent of cinnamon and apples drifted upwards.

Memories flooded back—a large homey kitchen warmed by the continually heating Aga, the beatific, round face of Cook and the aroma of brown sugar and butter. Everything he associated with the comfort of childhood was centred on that kitchen. Not once in his wildest dreams had he ever imagined it wouldn't always be there waiting for him when he returned home from boarding school. Twenty-six years had passed and he still missed it.

Claire raised her head, her cheeks blotchy and her eyes red-rimmed. Her gaze was fixed doggedly on the wet patch on his shirt and her small hand patted it as if the action was enough to dry it. 'Oh, God. I'm so sorry.'

The pads of her fingers warmed his skin through the fine cotton. 'No need to apologise,' he said, intending to sound hearty and encouraging, but the words came out husky as if he was suffering from a cold. 'Worse things have happened to my shirts.'

'The thing is, I've never done anything like this at work before.' She sounded utterly poleaxed. 'You must think I'm a total basket case.'

'No.' He knew he should say more. He should tell her that everyone has a bad day occasionally, that doctors are human too, and some cases have a deeper impact than others. But her heat was weaving through him and creating so much havoc that he was having trouble remembering his own name, let alone articulating anything beyond a single syllable. In a desperate attempt to regain his equilibrium, he caught her hand, encasing it in his, stopping her jerky strokes.

She stilled for a moment and stared at his white hand covering her tanned one and then, slowly, she lifted her face to his. Her liquid eyes were a mirror to her embarrassment, confusion and sorrow. Once again, he wanted to make her feel better, because anyone who worked in medicine had spent time in that dismal place and it was dangerous to linger there too long. He was about to say, 'Tomorrow's another day,' when he glimpsed something indefinable beyond the chaotic swirl of emotions. The shadows told him it wasn't new. In fact, it had the intransigent look of an indelible stain that no amount of soap, salt or methylated spirits could remove.

Was it doubt? Fear? Inadequacy? *Surely not.* But whatever it was, it hit him hard in the solar plexus and held on tight like a lasso. *Whatever it is, it's wrong. It shouldn't be part of her. It doesn't belong there.*

The need to vanquish this malignant thing and banish it from her eyes—from her soul—pulled him down towards her. His lips touched her damp cheek in a consoling kiss and the tang of salt zipped into him. He was about to pull back when her head turned and suddenly his mouth was softly touching those plump, ruby-red lips. They were soft and tear-cooled. He tasted the heady essence of bergamot.

Stop now.

He was about to pull back when her lips opened infinitesimally. He was immediately rushed by the unexpected spicy zap of chilli. Hot. Sizzling. One hundred per cent aroused woman. His breath left his lungs and for a moment he was rendered utterly still, unable to think, move or feel.

The tip of her tongue flicked against his lips so lightly and so quickly that his brain couldn't decide if it had even happened or if he was imagining it. But his body knew. Good God, it knew. He dropped his arms to her waist and hauled her in against him before opening his mouth and welcoming her in.

She came to him without a moment's hesitation, filling him completely. Her tongue explored, her teeth nipped, her heat and flavours exploded through him until he was nothing but a river of pulsating sensation. Her free hand wound its way through his hair, her fingers digging into his scalp as if she needed to hold on to something to keep herself tethered to earth.

He understood exactly. Kissing her was like being in free fall. He returned her kiss with one of his own—deep, thorough and practiced until he heard a low guttural moan coming from Claire. Usually that sound made him smile and reinforced not only that he knew exactly what he was doing but that he was the one in total control.

Not this time.

His usual measured composure with women was unravelling faster than a skein of wool in the paws of a cat. He had the strangest awareness that somehow she'd turned the tables on him completely. What had started out as a quick and reassuring kiss to console her was now a kiss that was stripping him of the protective layers he'd spent five years cementing into place.

Break the kiss. Now. Right now.

But his body overruled him again, craving what was on offer and seizing it like a drowning man grips a life preserver. He slid the utilitarian black band from her ponytail, and as her hair fell to her shoulders in a sun-kissed cascade, it released its treasured aroma of spices and apples. Golden strands caressed his face and he breathed deeply. Claire's sweet behind was now in his lap—he had no idea if he'd pulled her there, if she'd climbed in or if it was a bit of both. It didn't matter. All that mattered was here, now and her.

Her hand cupped the back of his neck, her fingers splayed. His hand, which had been gripping her hip, now slid under the loose top of her scrubs. His palm instantly tingled as it touched warm, smooth skin. He spider-walked his fingers along her spine, absorbing every rise and dip until he reached the wide strap of her bra.

He'd never considered any piece of lingerie a challenge—more like an inconvenient barrier that he dismantled easily every time. His fingers rested on the hooks and he was just about to flick and twist when Claire ripped her hand out of his and hauled her mouth from his lips. It all happened so fast that he shivered from the loss of her intoxicating heat.

Her lips, now bee-sting pouty and puffy from kissing and being kissed, gave her a sexy aura he'd never suspected even existed underneath her uptight personality. But despite how deliciously alluring it made her, it was the way her mussed hair fell softly, framing her face that got to him. It made her look younger than her years. She suddenly seemed fragile and vulnerable as if she expected the world as she knew it to end any second.

In that instant, he knew the exact direction her thoughts had taken. He was her boss and she was his trainee. Hospitals had rules about this sort of thing to protect both parties from sexual harassment charges. Without meaning to, they'd both fallen over the line together, but there was no power play happening on either side. He'd stake his life she was as surprised as he was that the kiss had even happened.

'It's okay, Claire,' he said, wanting to put her at ease, but his voice was rough, raspy and the antithesis of soothing.

'Okay?' Her voice rose with incredulity and her beautiful eyes reflected her turmoil. In a flurry of uncoordinated movements, which included her knee pressing into his inner thigh, she scrambled out of his lap as fast as if he was on fire and she was about to go up in flames too. The entire time she kept her arms outstretched in front of her as if she was scared he was going to try and touch her.

'I… This… It.' Her left hand covered her mouth for a moment before falling away. 'Nothing about any of this is okay.'

Still dazed from her kisses and with the majority of his circulating volume residing in his lap, he struggled to move beyond the basic functions of his reptilian brain. He tried a second time to reassure her. 'I meant, we're both adults.' He shrugged. 'Things happen.'

She shook her head so hard and fast that her hair whipped around her head in a golden wave. '*Nothing* happened.' Her voice trembled along with the rest of her. 'Do you understand? Absolutely nothing.'

As his blood pounded thickly through his body defy-

ing her words, both their pages beeped. The sound stopped
Claire's flight to the door. 'Oh, no. The Walkers are here.'

'Right.' His voice sounded a long way away as his body
lurched from lust to logic and the doctor overrode the man.
Hell, he needed some time. 'I'll meet you in ICU in five
minutes.'

Relief and embarrassment tugged at her cheeks. 'Yes.
Good. Fine. I'll be there.' She disappeared into the corridor.

Well, that went well, Alistair. Blowing out a long, slow
breath he rubbed his face with his hands and tried to fathom
how something so incredible had ended so badly.

CHAPTER FIVE

'DECAF THIS MORNING, please, Tony.'

The friendly barista shot her a disbelieving look. 'Is not coffee, *mia bella*.'

She gave him an apologetic shrug. 'Please.' The last thing she needed was caffeine. It was barely seven and she was running on adrenaline. Her heart pounded, her chest was so tight breathing felt like lifting weights, she was as jumpy as a cat and she felt the telltale burn of reflux. That was always the stress marker.

Occasionally, when she thought work was going well, she'd be surprised to get the liver-tip pain telling her that her body wasn't as calm as her mind. Today, she didn't need her medical degree to know the exact cause of her extreme agitation. She'd relived the reason over and over and over last night until exhaustion had somehow managed to claim her, providing a few hours of fitful sleep.

She'd woken with a start to a foggy dawn and the weight of reality crushing down on her so hard and heavy she was surprised she wasn't lying on the floor. Real life had decisively ended a wonderful dream where she'd felt unusually safe and secure. A utopia where she'd been able to be herself without the constant and nagging worry that someone was going to find out that despite all her hard work she was always only one step away from failing. Those tantalisingly peaceful feelings had vanished a second after she'd woken. Tranquillity had been torpedoed by the visual of her nestled in Alistair North's lap, kissing him like he was the last man standing after the apocalypse.

She'd jumped her boss. *Oh, God, oh, God, oh, God.*

Hours later, she still wasn't totally certain how it had happened.

Oh, come on. Be honest. Bottom line, you abandoned your principles, you opened your mouth and took what you wanted. You sucked Alistair North's marrow into you like he was oxygen.

She barely recognised the woman she'd been last night, and she knew if it had been an option, she'd have climbed inside the man. Never before had she let go like that, giving up all thought and reason, and existing only for the streaming sensations of bliss that had consumed her. It was if she'd been drawing her life force from him. She'd certainly never kissed anyone with such intensity before.

You've never been kissed like that before.

Her mind retreated from the thought so fast she almost gave herself whiplash. Truth be told, despite her thirty-four years, her kissing experience was fairly limited. During her teenage years, her brother's footy mates had considered her far too bookish and reserved to bother trying to kiss and her peers thought she was weird for studying so hard, so when she'd left Gundiwindi bound for Adelaide Uni, she'd been a kissing virgin as well as a sexual one.

It had only taken one medical students' society party to remedy the kissing situation. She'd discovered that having a tongue shoved unceremoniously down her throat by a drunk second year had been enough. Then and there she'd determined to wait until she met someone who, A, she actually liked and, B, had some experience and panache in the art of kissing.

Michael had literally walked into her life five years later

when she'd been hiking the Milford Track in the spectacular South Island of New Zealand. After two days spent laughing and talking together, and with him proffering the occasional hand to balance her as she crossed creeks and clambered over fallen trees, he'd kissed her on the sandy shore of Milford Sound with the backdrop of the indomitable Mitre Peak.

It had been the most romantic thing she'd ever experienced. For a while, all of Michael's romantic gestures had deluded her into thinking she was worthy of love after all. When the cracks started appearing, the more she worked to shore them up, the worse things had got. His parting words still haunted her. *You're too hard to love, Claire.*

Her alarm had chosen that moment to shrill, pulling her thoughts sharply and blessedly away from the past and dragging them firmly into the present. She'd run to the shower and left the flat half an hour later, walking directly to Tony's in the ubiquitous London mist.

The barista handed her the usual half dozen coffees pressed snugly into their cardboard carrier along with one extra. 'What's this?' she asked as her left hand wrapped around the single cup.

'A proper latte, *doctore.*'

'But, Tony, I wanted decaf.'

He tapped the cup with a *D* scrawled on it. 'Is here. But you drink it and I know you wish you get your usual.'

'Thanks.' He wasn't to know that if she were any more wired she'd shatter. She handed over some pound notes but he waved them away. 'The doctors at the castle, they fix my Serena when she born with her bad foot. Sick *bambinos* need the hospital. I happy to help.'

'That's very generous of you. I know the protestors on the night shift appreciate your coffee.'

She heard the gentle clearing of a throat behind her— the British equivalent of *Hurry up.*

'Bye, Tony.'

'*Ciao, bella.* You have a good day, yes.'

A good day. Oh, yeah. It was going to be one for the ages. More than anything she wanted a time machine so she could return to last night and change everything that had happened, starting with preventing little Ryan Walker from having a large brain bleed. At least the gods were on her side today in as much as it wasn't an operating day. The thought of having to stand next to Alistair—*Mr North, Mr North, Mr North.*

You're kidding yourself if you think using his title is going to give you any protection.

It's all I've got.

That and hiding from him as much as possible. Only she knew hiding was a pipe dream. The whole point of her scholarship was to work hand in glove with the man and learn as much from him as she possibly could. Last night, she'd left the hospital the moment the difficult interview with the Walkers was concluded. In fact, she'd been the first one to leave, with a brisk goodnight to her consultant in front of the distraught parents, blocking any chance of him saying anything to her about the kiss.

The only reprieve she had today was that straight after rounds he was working from home, preparing his paper for the neurosurgery symposium.

Yesterday morning when she'd read that entry in the electronic diary, she'd rolled her eyes. In not unexpected fashion, he'd left it pretty much to the last minute to get it done. If she'd been presenting a paper, she'd have had it fully edited, bound and memorised a week ahead of time because medicine had a habit of throwing curve balls. All it took was a couple of emergencies or some staff illness to throw out a timeline. She always padded her deadlines with a lot of wriggle room, as much to allow for her own set of learning challenges as well as for external ones.

Today, however, there was no eye rolling at Alis— Mr North's laid-back procrastination, only unbridled relief. It meant the only time she had to see him today was at the ICU and Koala Ward rounds. Given they'd be surrounded by staff and students and their focus would be on patient care, how hard could that be? He was hardly going to say anything to her about last night in front of everyone and she sure as hell wasn't going to mention it. Not now. Not ever. In regards to last night, her plan was to pretend and subsequently believe that it had *never* happened. She could only hope that Mr North felt the same.

Lost so deeply in her thoughts, she was surprised to find she'd arrived at the hospital. As she distributed the coffees, she made sure to mention to everyone they were a donation from Tony's Trattoria. Chatting with the protesters and learning more and more stories about the legacy of the castle was fast becoming a favourite part of her day and she listened with delighted fascination. A woman was telling a tale about her grandfather who'd been a surgeon during the Second World War. Claire was so busy listening to how he'd risked his own life to save others by operating in the basement of the hospital during the Blitz that she lost all sense of time.

Hearing someone's watch chime the hour, she gasped. *Late!* She hurriedly excused herself, ran through the gates, pelted up the D wing stairs, flung herself through the door and arrived on Koala Ward a panting and gasping mess.

Andrew Bailey gave her a wide-eyed look. 'You okay?'

She was desperately short of breath but she dug deep and summoned up a husky 'Fine' as she tried to fill her lungs with air. At the same time, she worked on quelling the rising tide of frantic dread that threatened to swamp her like a massive wave at Coogee. Being a few minutes late for rounds with a consultant who considered ten minutes after the hour as being 'on time' wasn't an issue. Being twenty minutes later than her usual arrival time was a disaster. It meant she had no time to read and memorise the overnight reports. It meant she'd be flying blind during rounds.

Panicked, she rounded on her house officer. 'Have you read the reports?'

'Was I supposed to?' Andrew asked, half bemused and half confused. 'I thought that was the point of rounds.'

Still trying to catch her breath, she huffed loudly and caught the injured look in her generally congenial junior's eyes. He was absolutely correct—for most people that was the case. 'True, but it never hurts to be ahead of the game and impress the consultant.'

A grin broke across his round face. 'Is that why you're here early most days?'

She dodged the truth with the skill of a secret keeper. 'Something like that.'

The rumble of many feet against the linoleum floor made her turn. Alistair North was striding along the corridor with the nurse unit manager and the nursing and medical students hurrying along behind.

Claire pressed her glasses up her nose and blinked. Alistair North didn't ever wear a white coat but he generally wore one of what she'd come to realise was a selection of fine wool Italian suits. Generally, he started the day in a jacket and tie, although the ties were never serious. They were almost always prints of animated characters from kids' TV shows, which the little patients loved. Claire's favourite ties were from a fundraising range sold by the castle's auxiliary. Some clever clogs had come up with the idea of printing the children's drawings of doctors, nurses and auxiliary staff onto silk. She particularly liked the one of a doctor wearing a head torch and a big smile.

Just admit it. You like that one because it's Alistair.
Not if my life depended on it.

By late afternoon most days, he was seen on the ward

in scrubs, or if it was a non-operating day, he'd have discarded the jacket and tie. An open-necked business shirt was as casual as she'd ever seen him, but today there was no sign of a suit, nor smart casual weekend wear or even jeans. He was striding towards them wearing a T-shirt that stretched across his wide chest and perfectly outlined the rise and fall of his pectoral muscles. The shirt read *Epilepsy Warrior Run*. Her gaze instinctively dropped.

Damn. No compression tights.

Shut up! She hated the zip of disappointment that wove through her that the rest of his body wasn't delineated in fine detail by tight fabric. His running shorts, however, only came to mid-thigh, giving her plenty of opportunity to admire his taut quads.

Look up, look up, look up.

'Morning, Mitchell. Bailey,' he said with his usual nod of greeting. 'Missed the two of you at boot camp this morning.'

'Boot camp, sir?' Andrew said faintly. The rotund house officer wore the look of one who went to great lengths to avoid any sort of physical pursuit.

'Yes, Bailey. All Koala Ward staff are participating in the Epilepsy Warrior fun run. Morag—' he turned to the highly efficient unit nurse manager '—you sent the diary entry to everyone about this morning's training session?'

'Of course,' she said briskly in her thick Scottish brogue.

Claire pulled out her phone and immediately saw the reminder on her screen. Her stomach fell through the floor. She'd been so obsessed by the fact she'd landed in Alistair's lap last night and tickled his tonsils that she'd totally forgotten about boot camp.

Andrew's face drained of colour. 'Surely someone needs to be on duty on—' he read the black and purple writing on his boss's T-shirt '—the tenth. Happy to volunteer, sir.'

'Already got that covered, Bailey,' Alistair said in a tone

that brooked no argument. He swung his clear sea-grey gaze to Claire.

Be professional. She clenched her fists and willed herself not to drop her gaze. Willed herself to act as if this was just a regular morning instead of the one after her worst ever career folly. Memories of last night—of the way his eyes and then his mouth had fixed on hers—rolled back in, foaming and bubbling like a king tide.

Let it go. It didn't happen.

Oh, but it did. She had the sweet and tender bruises on her lips to prove it.

Now, faced with all six foot of him standing there in front of her wearing athletic gear and with the scent of his cologne invading her senses, it was increasingly difficult to focus on her plan to banish every delicious thing that had happened between them. *Remember the embarrassment. Remember he's your boss. That will do the trick every time.*

'It's not like you to forget an appointment, Mitchell,' he said, using her surname in the British public school way as he did occasionally. 'It's important we all attend for team spirit,' he added politely.

Despite the well-modulated parameters of his very British accent, she heard the unmistakable tone of an order. Was this his way of saying that he agreed with her that last night was an aberration? That it was a shocking mistake they both needed to forget and move on from? That it was over and done with and she needed to remember that the cohesion of the workplace team always came ahead of everything?

Please let it be so. 'We won't let you down again,' she said brightly. She sent up a plea that Alistair had caught her double meaning and knew that she understood they were both on the same page about last night. 'We're looking forward to the next boot camp, aren't we, Andrew?'

Andrew stared at her as if she'd completely lost her mind. 'Wouldn't miss it,' he said glumly.

Alistair grinned and clapped his hands together once. 'Excellent. Let's start rounds.'

As they walked towards the first bay, Morag handed Claire a tablet computer. Archie McGregor's medical history was open on the screen, but before she could silently read the first sentence, Alistair was saying, 'Lead off, Dr Mitchell.'

Eight sets of eyes swung her way. Even before her mouth had dried, her tongue had thickened and her throat had threatened to close, the words on the screen had jumbled into an incomprehensible mess. Long ago voices boomed in her head, deafening her.

Moron. That girl's a sandwich short of a picnic.

Panic eddied out from her gut and into her veins, stealing her concentration. She broke out in a cold sweat. Her greatest fear, which lurked constantly inside her and was never far from the surface, surged up to choke her. *You knew you'd get found out one day. This is it.*

No! She'd fought too hard for it to end like this. She'd set up strategies so this situation would never happen to her and she wasn't about to let years of sacrifice go to waste and have it fall apart now. Not here in London where it was too easy for people to make cheap shots at her being a colonial. Not when she was the recipient of one of the most prestigious scholarships on offer for neurosurgery. Not when she was so close to qualifying.

Think!

'Actually,' she said, shoving the tablet at her junior houseman with a hand that trembled. 'Archie is Dr Bailey's patient. He admitted him overnight.'

Andrew, who'd accepted the tablet without question, glanced at the screen. 'Archie McGregor, age seven, admitted last night post-seizure and with suspected juvenile myoclonic epilepsy. Observations stable overnight and...'

Claire wanted to relax and blow out the breath that was

stalled tightly in her chest but she didn't have any time to spare. As Andrew was fielding a battery of questions from Alistair, she was trying to calmly and surreptitiously read the next patient's history.

An hour later she was helping herself to a delicious currant bun from the nurses' breakfast platter. As she bit into the sticky sweetness, she gave thanks that she'd not only narrowly avoided disaster, she'd also survived the round. Alistair had appeared happy with both her and Andrew's treatment plans and now, emergencies excepted, her boss was gone for the day. She was thankfully home free. She had some medication charts to write up, some test results to read and then, fingers crossed, she was going to take advantage of the relative calm and spend some time in the library studying.

'Oh, good.' A very familiar voice rumbled around her, its timbre as rich and smooth as a Barossa Valley cabernet sauvignon. 'There you are.'

Shock stuck the sticky bun to the roof of her mouth and she tried desperately to dislodge it with a slurp of tea. The hot liquid went down the wrong way and she coughed violently, trying to get her breath. The next minute, Alistair's face was pushed in close to hers with his brows pulled down sharply.

'Can you get air?'

She shook her head but he misunderstood and the next minute the side of his hand sliced down between her shoulder blades like a karate chop. The snaps on her bra bit into her skin. 'Ouch.'

'Good,' he said, cheerfully reappearing back in front of her. 'I need you alive today.'

'Just today?' she said waspishly as the tangy scent of his sweat hit her nostrils. She worked hard at resisting the urge to breathe in deeply. 'I rather like being alive every day.'

'As do I. Live every day as if it's your last.'

She took a careful sip of tea. 'I've often found people who say that use it as an excuse to be selfish.'

His smile faded and a line of tension ran along his jaw, disappearing up behind his ear. 'That's a very jaundiced view of humanity.'

She welcomed the familiar antagonism vibrating between them and relaxed into it, giving thanks that everything was back to normal. 'Not at all. It's merely an observation about how some people live their lives with little thought or regard for how their actions impact on others.'

His eyes darkened and he looked as if he was about to say something when he suddenly helped himself to a currant bun. She was oddly disappointed that he wasn't going to take the discussion further. Sparring in a robust debate with Alistair North was far safer than confiding in him.

Or kissing him.

She suddenly felt stranded standing there in the small pantry. She was far too aware of him and how his mouth, which had savoured hers so thoroughly last night, was now relishing the currant bun. Too aware of how his tight behind was pressed hard against the bench and how his long, running-fit legs stretched out in front of him. She suddenly wanted to invoke the staff dress code she'd been lectured on during her orientation program.

He raised his hand to his mouth and one by one he meticulously licked the sugar from the bun off his fingers. She swallowed a gasp as her body clenched and then sighed in delight. The memory of how he tasted was burned on her brain—spicy with a hint of citrus zip. And hot. Oh-so-flaming hot.

I thought the kiss never happened so why are we doing this?

She cleared her throat. 'I best go and write up the medication changes.'

'Bailey can do that.'

'Excuse me?'

He pushed off the bench. 'Get Bailey to do the medication changes and chase up the test results. I've got some far more interesting work for you.'

A skitter of excitement whipped through her. There'd been a rumour going around that a charity in India was making overtures to the castle in regards to separating a set of conjoined twins. Being part of the multidisciplinary team from the planning stages through to the massive operation and postoperative care would be the chance of a lifetime.

'Oh?' she said, far more casually than she felt.

'We're giving a paper at the spring symposium.'

A streak of surprise was followed by a trickle of dread. 'We?' She hated that it came out on a squeak.

He nodded. 'It's the tradition across all the medical departments that the specialist registrar in his or her last year of their fellowship always gives a joint presentation with their consultant.' He scratched his head and his brow furrowed. 'Did I not mention this to you when you first arrived?'

No! 'You did not,' she said, trying to sound calm. The dread was now spinning her stomach and sending out wave upon wave of nausea. 'This is the first I've heard of it.'

'Oh, well, not to worry,' he said with a grin that held a modicum of contrition. 'Lucky it's quiet so we should meet tomorrow's deadline.'

'Tomorrow.' Her screech of disbelief could have given a sulphur-crested cockatoo a run for its money. 'But the symposium's still weeks away.'

'The papers are due tomorrow. The admin staff need time to print and bind them and prepare the handouts for the attendees.'

'We can't write a paper in a day.' She hated the squeak in her voice.

'Of course we can,' he said with all the easy confidence of someone who'd never had to think twice about reading or writing. 'Some of the best papers I've ever written have happened at that adrenaline-fuelled last-minute deadline.' Memories filled his handsome face. 'It's such a buzz to pull an all-nighter and finish as the fingers of dawn are lighting up the city.'

The very idea made her gag. 'That's not the way I work,' she countered, desperately clutching at straws. 'I mean, we don't even have a topic.'

'Of course we've got a topic,' he said, sounding amused. 'I wouldn't do that to you.'

'I guess I should be thankful for small mercies,' she said sarcastically.

'I'm sorry it slipped my mind, Claire. Your predecessor, Harry Banks, was supposed to write the paper, but as you know, he left us the moment things started looking rocky for the castle.' His face filled with kindness. 'I'm aware you like things to be ordered and just so, but believe me, stepping out of your comfort zone every now and then makes you feel alive.'

Oh. My. God. He was serious. He honestly thought he was doing her a favour. Her heart thumped so hard she was sure he must hear it. 'What's the topic?' she asked weakly.

His face lit up. 'Epilepsy surgery's the most effective way to control seizures in patients with drug-resistant focal epilepsy. I've got all the data. It's just a matter of assembling it and stringing it together with some well-chosen case studies. Don't panic. Most people prefer to attend the summer symposium on the Continent. The spring one's the smallest of the three. Think of it as a test run. If the paper's well received there, we can work it up into something bigger for *The Lancet*. Too easy.' He laughed. 'Isn't that what you Aussie's like to say?'

'Something like that,' she said faintly. The task he was

asking her to undertake would be a significant one for most people, but for her the short time frame made it monumentally huge. Hopefully, she could find a quiet corner in the library where she could spread out the data and work her way through it slowly and methodically. 'I guess I better make a start, then.'

'Excellent.' He gave her warm smile. 'Give me fifteen minutes to grab a quick shower and then meet me in my office.'

No, no, no! Working alongside Alistair risked exposing her secret and she'd do anything to prevent that from happening. With a decisive movement that said *all business*, she pushed her glasses up her nose. 'I'll work in the library.'

He tilted his head and gave her a long and questioning look. Somehow, despite feeling like a desert plant wilting under the intense scrutiny of summer noontime heat, she managed to hold his gaze.

'It makes far more sense to work in my office,' he said, breaking the long silence. 'All the data's on my computer and there'll be far fewer interruptions and distractions there.'

Fewer distractions? She stifled a groan. Her much-needed day of physical distance from Alistair North had just imploded and sucked her down with it. Now, she faced spending the working day with him in the close confines of his office. Every breath she took would carry his musky scent. The air around her would vibrate with his bounding energy and any inadvertent brush of shoulders or hands, which invariably happened when two people worked in close proximity, would only serve to remind her how amazing the strength of his toned muscles and the tautness of his skin had felt last night under her hands.

All of it was one enormous distraction, but in relative terms, her irrational attraction was the least of her worries. Her biggest problem was the challenge of hiding the fact she found data analysis and large writing tasks difficult. Under extreme pressure, it was almost impossible. If her boss discovered that, it could jeopardise her scholarship. She swallowed hard. There was only one solution—she had to get creative and make sure he never discovered her secret.

CHAPTER SIX

ALISTAIR STRODE ALONG Praed Street carrying a plastic bag containing take-away containers of Tandoori Chicken, Rogan Josh, curried vegetables and naan bread. The pungent aromas of the food made his stomach juices run and he picked up the pace. So much for a quiet day—he hadn't even managed lunch and he couldn't wait to tuck into the spicy delights.

It was eight in the evening and he'd been away from the office for hours. He hadn't intended for that to happen. In fact, when Dominic MacBride had telephoned at ten interrupting his writing day, he'd told him that a policy and procedures meeting didn't come under the banner of life or death. Today that was the only criteria that would get him to leave the office.

It was Claire who'd insisted he attend the meeting and raise the issue of referral waiting times. All had been dangerously pushed out since the staffing levels at the hospital had been decimated. 'The board needs to know their current actions are risking lives. I'd go but they won't listen to me. You've got FRCS after your name so surely that gives you more clout.'

'I doubt they can see past the dollar signs,' he'd said with a sigh, 'but you're right. It's worth a shot.'

He and Dominic had spent a frustrating few hours getting nowhere with the board and he'd been on his way back to the office when Morag called. 'Sorry, Alistair, but the Walkers are asking to see you. They're insisting upon it.'

He'd gone direct to ICU and the afternoon had rolled away from him as he'd dealt with a variety of issues. Truth be told, he should have called Bailey in to deal with most of them as they came under the banner of house officer jobs, but he'd been feeling generous. He could still remember how fraught life was as a junior doctor so he'd reinserted a central line and performed a lumbar puncture. He'd rather enjoyed the hands-on medicine, although that hadn't prevented a slight flicker of guilt that his largesse was a form of procrastination. As much as he disliked statistics, he knew he should be back in the office helping Claire with the difficult job instead of leaving her on her own to deal with it.

Given how horrified she'd both looked and sounded when she'd learned about the project, he'd been expecting to hear the return of her clipped and critical tones along with a lecture on time management each time he'd called her to notify her of yet another delay. However, on all three occasions all she'd said was, 'No worries. These things happen. Things are going well at this end.'

Ten minutes ago, just as he'd been paying for what he'd planned to be their dinner, she'd sent him a text.

No need to return to the office. Job done. Enjoy your evening.

He'd read it twice, trying to absorb the surprising and oddly dismaying text. He couldn't believe she'd finished the paper so quickly and without his help. Then again, he supposed if anyone was capable of knocking out something so complicated in a short space of time, it was probably Claire Mitchell. He'd tried to shrug off the unreasonable level of disappointment that they wouldn't be having dinner together. He'd been looking forward to returning to the office, sharing a curry, working on the paper and proving to her they were both adults and capable of being in the same room together without kissing each other.

No need for that. You've already done it.

He'd spent a restless night lurching between reliving the amazing and mind-blowing kiss and the unsettling feelings that stirred inside him whenever he recalled Claire's utterly appalled and slightly panicked post-kiss expression. As a result, he'd done his very British best at the interview with the Walkers last night and again this morning to sweep last night under the carpet and show Claire that everything was as it had been prior to the kiss. On one level he knew he should be pleased and relived that she regretted the incident. After all, they worked closely together and a fling wasn't conducive to workplace harmony, not to mention the fact it would break a dozen hospital rules. But then again, he wasn't used to anyone looking at him with such abhorrence. He felt a crazy need to prove to her that he was more than capable of respecting her wishes on the *nothing happened* front even though something incredible had taken place. He still couldn't reconcile the fact that prickly, terse Claire Mitchell could kiss a man better than his wildest fantasy.

He gave a wave to the evening protestors who were warming themselves around a brazier and then switched the take-away food bag to his other hand. For a brief moment he toyed with the idea of texting Islay Kennedy and inviting her to share the curries, but then his stomach growled. Hell, he was famished and he didn't want to delay. Taking the lift to level five, he punched in the security numbers and entered the consulting suite. After six each evening the lighting reverted to power-saving mode and the corridor was low-lit. He walked past a series of closed doors— the offices of his colleagues—and stopped in front of his, surprised by the spill of light coming from under the door. He turned the handle and stepped inside.

Holy— The first thing he saw was Claire Mitchell's sweet behind. She was leaning over his desk and the soft fabric of her dress fell in such a way that it perfectly outlined the two orbs of her cheeks. The memory of those curves pressed hard into his lap last night sent a raft of delicious sensation thrumming through him, heating his blood and making his palms itch. All he wanted to do was walk up behind her, pull her back into him and feel her pressing against hard him.

Good God! What the hell was wrong with him? This wasn't a role-play fantasy with a consenting partner. He was at work. She was his trainee and all of his thoughts were utterly inappropriate. He closed his eyes for a moment, concentrating hard on reducing his breathing from ragged to normal.

When he opened his eyes he avoided looking at the kryptonite that was her behind. Instead, he noticed her bare left foot was flat on the floor, her right knee was pressed into the seat of a chair and she was leaning over his desk. Her sun-gold hair had fallen free of its usual black band, cascading in shimmering waves across her shoulders. She held her arms outstretched in front of her, taking her weight on the heels of both hands, and her glasses dangled from the fingers of her left hand.

As his gaze strayed from her glasses, he noticed the paper. Papers to be exact. His entire office looked like someone had placed a fan in front of a ream of white A4 and turned it on full tilt. Pages spilled from the desk to the floor, some were stuck to the wall and others had migrated to his other desk and completely covered the green-tooled leather. Each page was filled with some sort of black printing—from graphs and tables to double-spaced words.

'Did it snow paper while I was gone?' he quipped as he quietly closed the door.

Claire swung around, shock etched deeply on her face and her colour as white as the paper. 'What are you doing here?'

'It's my office,' he said equably as he set down the take-away bag. 'More to the point, why are you here? You sent me a text saying you were finished.'

Her chin rose—a sure sign she was on the back foot. 'I thought I was done but I got caught up with a bit of tweaking.'

He snorted and swept his arm out to encompass the room. 'Tweaking? This looks like you're stuck smack bang in the mud-sucking middle.'

Something akin to panic crossed her face. 'And if I am?'

'It's exactly where I expected you to be.'

For a moment, her body went deathly still and then she abruptly shoved her glasses back on her face. 'You know?' she demanded in a voice that was half accusative and half defeated.

Know?

Then, as if someone had just poked her hard between her scapulas, her shoulders rolled back into a straight, sharp line and her nostrils flared. 'So this was deliberate? Some sort of macabre joke? Or worse? Sophisticated bullying to get back at me for last night? To put me in my place?'

Bullying? What the— He held up his hands as if a gun was being pointed menacingly at his head. 'Hang on just one damn minute, Dr Mitchell. That's a very serious accusation.'

She swept an arm through a pile of papers, sending them fluttering to the floor. 'And this is a serious setup. I can't believe how badly you want me to fail.'

Fail? His temper surged at her abhorrent claims. Every part of him screamed to carpet her here and now for insubordination and character assassination, but something about the tension pulling sharply at her features and the desolation in her eyes quelled his anger. The furious boil reduced to a slow and cross simmer. Once again he'd glimpsed those same malignant shadows clinging tightly where they didn't belong.

He sighed and dropped his arms, letting them fall loosely to his sides. 'Something's clearly upset you to make you behave like this but I'm at a loss as to what it is. When I said you were in the mud-sucking middle, I was referring to that moment in a project everyone experiences when you're suffering from information overload.'

She stared at him from behind her tortoiseshell glasses, intently studying his face. It was like she was trying to decode his words and match them up with his expression and tone of voice. He pressed on. 'That place in a project that demands you commence putting the data into a coherent form but the precise place to start eludes you.'

He tried for a wry smile. 'To be honest, I was very surprised to get your text saying you were finished. I expected you to only just be starting the narrative.'

For a moment she made no sound and then her face crumpled and a long, low moan escaped across her ruby-red lips. She sank onto the chair and dropped her face into her hands. 'Oh, God. No.'

The ragged sound carried old pain and it echoed around the quiet office before returning to cloak her in a toxic cloud. More than anything he wanted to reach out and touch her but then he remembered what had happened the last time he'd offered comfort. He decided that discretion was the better part of valour. He'd feed her instead.

As he silently dished up the food, she mumbled something, but given her faint volume, he assumed she was talking to herself rather than to him. Handing her a bowl of curry and some naan bread, he said, 'Want to tell me what's going on?'

Her hand shook as she accepted the bowl. 'Not really, no.'

'Put it this way. I was being polite.' He pulled up a chair and seated himself opposite her. 'You don't have an option.'

With a jerky movement, she set the bowl down on the desk. 'I can't eat knowing you're about to revoke my scholarship. Just do it and get it over with.'

He felt like he was watching a play where he'd missed act one and he was now totally muddled in act two. 'I haven't any intention of revoking your scholarship, although God knows why not, Claire Mitchell. Ever since you arrived, you've pushed the envelope and all of my buttons. You are by far *the* most challenging trainee I've ever worked with.'

She sucked in her lips. 'I… You…' She sighed and her head dropped. 'Sorry.'

It was the first time one of her apologies actually sounded sincere. Looking at the top of her bent head, he was still at a loss as to what was going on. 'I'm not sure you realise that you're also the most talented trainee I've ever had the fortune to work with.'

Her head rose slowly but her distinctive chocolate-brown brows had drawn down into a frown of doubt and anxiety. Yet again he was convinced she didn't come close to believing him. Exactly why, he had no idea. Nor did he understand why she was so convinced he'd been acting against her best interests. That accusation burned hot and cut deeply. In his private life he'd had women hurl accusations at him ranging from *commitment-phobe* to *heartless*, but at work he prided himself on equality and fairness. No one had ever suggested otherwise.

Looking for clues, he wracked his brain and tried to think of something he may have done or said to give her that impression. As he drew a blank, the mumbled words she'd spoken earlier suddenly sounded in his head as clear as a bell on a windless day.

Everything's falling apart just as I always knew it would.

Why, with a track record of successes, did his most talented trainee believe she was going to fail? He'd bet his last pound that whatever or whoever had caused those tormenting shadows of hers was connected to this eroding self-belief. He was determined to find the source.

'If we're to continue working together, Claire, I need to know two things. Why you texted me saying you were finished when obviously you are nowhere near, and more importantly, why you would even entertain the thought I had set you up to fail?'

From the moment Alistair had stepped into the office, Claire's heart had picked up its pace and now it was beating so quickly and erratically that she was light-headed and dizzy. She still couldn't wrap her head around how rapidly things had unravelled. Not that she'd ever been in control of the project, but she'd been convinced she was in control of keeping Alistair far, far away from the office for the bulk of the day. Except now he was here and she was backed into a corner of her own making. The only available escape route was ripping out her soul.

His words *'You're exactly where I expected you to be'* had not only left her feeling utterly exposed, they'd hauled her backwards into the dark abyss that was her school days in Gundiwindi. She hated the emotions the past always generated. When she'd combined them with her determination that no one was ever going to bully her again, she'd lashed out, only to discover Alistair had no idea about her secret. No one got away with incorrectly accusing their boss of a heinous crime without having to face the consequences. This was her Armageddon.

Everything she'd worked so hard to achieve was about to

shatter into a thousand irreparable pieces and she only had herself to blame. Lacing her fingers together tightly, she fixed her gaze on the tip of his left ear. 'I'm—' she forced the word up and out through a tight throat '—dyslexic.'

He looked utterly taken aback. 'Are you sure?' Doubt rang in his very precise accent.

'Your daughter's not going to amount to very much, Mr Mitchell.'

'Moron.'

'You're a very lazy girl. Accept that you belong in the remedial class.'

'Dumb ass.'

Against the harsh memories of the past, a bark of laughter fully loaded with derision broke out of her, raining down on them both. 'Oh, believe me. I'm more than sure. Dyslexia's been my constant companion since I started primary school.'

'But…'

Confusion shone in his eyes. A part of her wanted to hug him that he'd been clueless about her condition. The rest of her ached with embarrassment that she'd got herself into the situation where she was forced to tell him.

'I don't understand,' he finally managed to say as he ran a hand through his hair, making it even messier than usual. 'If you have this disability, how on earth have you got this far in your career?'

She shrugged. 'Sheer bloody-mindedness and a photographic memory.'

This time he laughed—a great booming sound that twirled around her with reassuring gravitas. 'Well, you do have bloody-mindedness in spades.'

She smiled weakly. 'Um, thank you, I guess.' She didn't know what else to say.

'Determination can carry a person a very long way.'

Unwanted tears pricked at the back of her eyes and she

blinked furiously, refusing to allow them to form, let alone fall. 'When you're told often enough that you're useless, it can go one of two ways.'

Respect flared on his face. 'And you chose success.'

She thought of her years of struggle and for the first time she glimpsed what she'd achieved in a new light. 'I suppose I have.'

'I'd say you definitely have.' He gave her a contemplative glance. 'Why didn't you tell me about the dyslexia?'

She tossed her head. 'I refuse to be defined by it.'

'But you are.'

His words crashed into her, making her chest cramp in twisting pain. She'd spent years proving she was no different from anyone else and she wasn't about to accept his view. 'No. I. Am. Not. You said yourself you had no idea I was dyslexic.'

'That's not what I'm talking about. All of us are an amalgam of our experiences.' The skin on his bladed cheeks momentarily tensed and then relaxed. 'You live with a learning disability. I imagine that isn't always easy.'

'No,' she said softly, appreciating his insight on that point if not on the other.

'Exactly how hard is it? Was it?'

The question made her flinch. 'I don't waste time thinking about it.'

Although a flash of sympathy lit up his eyes, his mouth straightened into a taut line. 'Perhaps not consciously, but I think it all came out to play today when you accused me of bullying.'

The sternness of his voice didn't hide his hurt and it ate into her. 'I'm sorry. I should never—'

'I don't want an apology, Claire,' he interrupted briskly. 'But I require an explanation as to why you would make that leap.'

She knew she owed him the truth but that didn't stop

her feeling as if she was about to rip herself open from the inside out. *Just do it and get it over with.* 'I grew up in a tiny outback town where sport ruled and there was no tolerance for being different. Not only was I myopic, I struggled to learn, which made me a sitting duck for cruel kids.'

'Bullies?'

'Yep.' A long sigh shuddered out of her. 'Although, in retrospect, it wasn't the kids who were the worst offenders. I had an ally in my brother, who was a well-respected football player. He stomped on anyone who stole my glasses and pinched my books. By the time I left primary school, I had amassed a lot of one-liners. A clever putdown confused most of the boys who were all brawn and no brains.'

'I can imagine,' he said with a knowing smile. 'I can see where you honed your acerbic skills.'

Her cheeks burned with embarrassed heat as her mind spun with confusion. She'd been so rude to him and yet here he was actively listening and trying to understand. As much as she disliked talking about her life prior to university, she wanted to honour his interest and hopefully hold on to her job.

'The saying "Everything's there but it's wired differently" is my brain. Spelling and reading have always been a challenge. I had trouble linking the sound of a word to the letters on the page. When I was little, there was no reading recovery program and as the years went past I slipped further and further behind.

'I was accused of being lazy and not putting in the effort. Teachers took to saying, "You're nothing like your brother," and it was easier for them to label me the difficult child. Mum and Dad tried to help but as I was frustrating qualified teachers, it wasn't surprising that my parents eventually accepted what they'd been told. Eyes were constantly rolled in class when I struggled to read out loud and I never gained my pen licence. By the end of primary school, nothing was expected of me. Everyone assumed the moment I turned fifteen, I'd leave school.'

His leaned forward slightly. 'What changed?'

'A guardian angel called Strez.' She smiled and gave a self-deprecating laugh. 'Mr Strezinski. He was a Polish migrant who spoke four languages. I have no idea how he landed up at Gundiwindi High or why he agreed to teach typing and woodwork. Fortunately for me, I took both subjects. He saw something in me no one else did. He lent me audiobooks so I could hear the English texts while I read along. Without having to agonise over every word, I could hear the themes and analyse the text. He suggested I type my assignments.'

Her heart swelled as it did whenever she thought of Strez. 'I'll never forget the day I got a B+ on an essay. I was both over the moon about the mark and white with fury that I had to prove to the teacher I hadn't plagiarised the work. Strez helped me devise strategies, like chewing gum, to help me focus and using headphones to block out extraneous noise. Most importantly, he was the one person who truly believed in me.'

Alistair nodded and a lock of hair fell forward. He brushed it aside. 'He sounds like a true mentor.'

She looked up into his eyes, which in the low light were the colour of silver moonbeams dancing on water. 'He changed my life. Without his help, I'd never have passed Year Twelve, let alone got into medicine. He released me from all of Gundiwindi's preconceived ideas.'

His brow's rose questioningly. 'But not, I think, from its legacy.'

She considered the statement. 'I've never thought about it in those terms. You may have a point.'

This time he gave a bark of laughter. 'There's no *may*, Claire. I see it in your eyes. There's a part of you that still believes you're that struggling little girl.'

'That's because I am.' The words shot out before she could catch them back. *Idiot!* She hated feeling so vulnerable in front of him. 'You're the first person outside of Gundiwindi to know I'm dyslexic. I only told you to try and save my job.'

A sympathetic look similar to the one he'd shown her last night flashed across his face. For a moment she yearned for a touch of his hand and immediately thought better of it. She couldn't trust herself not to lean in and repeat last night's kiss, and *that* was totally out of the question.

He moved abruptly, picking up her curry from the desk and pressing it on her. 'Eat this before it goes cold.'

She gratefully accepted it, having discovered that not being fired on the spot had revived her appetite. She was suddenly ravenous. Using the garlic naan, she scooped up some curry and savoured the subtle flavours.

'Part of me can understand why you've kept it quiet,' Alistair said. 'Medicine's fiercely competitive with a take-no-prisoners approach.'

'And I learned that hard lesson in the Gundiwindi playground. Never expose a weakness or you get trampled. Like anyone with a secret, I've gone to great lengths and become very good at hiding it. Today was no exception.' She huffed out a breath and looked him straight in the eye. 'I didn't want you here working alongside me. I couldn't risk you seeing how I have to read things twice to decipher them and once more to memorise them.'

His high forehead creased into deep lines. 'So that's why you told me you'd completed the job. You wanted to keep me away.'

She nodded and he added drily, 'Well, that answers my question as to why you were so unexpectedly conciliatory about my extended absence today.'

She gave an apologetic shrug. 'When you arrived back here and said you expected me to be in the mud-sucking middle, I thought you'd deliberately given me this task to expose my biggest weakness and my worst fear.'

Understanding rolled across his face. Ruefulness followed immediately, settling in the lines around his mouth and eyes. 'My general dislike of statistics combined with my procrastination became your worst nightmare.'

'The project isn't the nightmare.' She hurried to reassure him. 'It's the short timeline.'

He helped himself to more Tandoori Chicken. 'So what I've interpreted as officious organisation is in fact one of your coping strategies?'

She nodded slowly. 'I need time to read and memorise. I can't leave anything to the last minute.'

'And I leave everything to the last minute.'

'Why is that when it must make things more difficult for you?' she asked, genuinely interested.

A muscle in his cheek twitched unexpectedly. 'Because life's far too short to spend so much time doing stuff I don't enjoy.'

And there it was again—his selfish streak. A strand of disappointment wound through her with more intensity than she cared to experience. What did it matter to her if he was a fully paid up and card carrying member of the *live for today and for me* club.

'The first thing I did when I qualified was activate the fine tradition of all consultants and dump the bulk of the boring paperwork onto my trainees.' He suddenly winced and rubbed the back of his neck. 'Hell, Claire. No wonder we've been crossing swords. I've exhausted you.'

Guilt slugged her. 'I should have told you I was struggling, but now you know why I didn't.' She gave him an apologetic shrug. 'All of the above. The thing is, in my previous positions I've never had to deal with quite so much paperwork. Brain surgery is so much easier than reading and writing. As for public speaking, I fear death less.'

He laughed. 'Dyslexia aside, you're not alone there.' His expression sobered. 'Despite—or perhaps because of—your dyslexia and the type of brain you have, you're an excellent neurosurgeon.'

Gratitude flowed through her and for the first time she actually accepted and believed in the compliment. 'Thank you. Surgery's spatial and kinaesthetic learning.'

'The practical component is, but what about all those years of lectures?'

'Like I said, I have a visual memory. Just don't ask me to write anything quickly or my *"p"*s will become *"b"*s and vice versa, along with a lot of other words spelt backwards. Oh, and never get me to navigate because I can't follow a map, and don't expect me to identify left or right without making my left hand into an *L*.'

He grinned. 'I'll remember that.'

She watched his open and friendly face and saw kindness reflected there. Other consultants would have summoned security to march her off the premises for her earlier behaviour. Although she'd hardly enjoyed his insistence she tell him about her dyslexia and school days in Gundiwindi, she appreciated it because it had saved her job. Sure, the man had a selfish side but how could she have ever thought he was shallow? Or that he wanted her to fail?

'Claire, I meant what I said about you being best trainee I've ever had. I can teach you and make you even better, but if we're going to make this work, we need to be a team. We need to be on the same page.'

Her heart added a beat. 'I came close to throwing away my chance, didn't I?'

'Put it this way. You're lucky you're so talented and that I'm so easy-going.' He gave her a wink as he set down his now empty bowl, wiped clean with the bread. His face settled into serious lines. 'Is there anything else you're finding difficult about working with me?'

Her mouthful of curry stalled mid-swallow as their shared kiss flashed like a neon light in her mind.

He means aside from the fact your body goes on hyper-alert whenever you think about him. Aside from the fact you kissed him senseless.

She cleared her throat. 'Ah, no. Um, well, not that I can think of right at the moment.'

His eyes did that intense staring thing that made her feel as if he could see down to her soul. 'Are you sure?'

'Absolutely,' she said, trying to sound cool, calm and detached instead of a quivering mess of liquid lust. 'But I give you my word that I'll discuss any problems with you if and when they arise.'

A wide and reassuring smile broke across his face and she saw immediately why his little patients and their parents trusted him implicitly. Almost everything she'd ever believed about Alistair North had just been turned on its head.

'I'm glad we've had this conversation. It's important we're on the same page and it's going to make the ball a much more enjoyable evening.'

The ball. Her stomach flipped. So much had changed between them since she'd insisted he attend the ball and he'd turned the tables on her by buying her ticket. Thank goodness she'd already told Victoria to seat her on the opposite side of the ten-seat table from Alistair. The width of the table meant conversation between them would be impossible.

Seriously? You're worried about conversation? Be worried about the close proximity of a bloke who will rock a tux.

'Indeed,' she somehow managed to say and sound professional.

'Excellent. Consider this conversation your first staff assessment, which, by the way, you've passed. I'll get around to writing up your report, but first, I have a paper to write before nine tomorrow morning.'

An hour ago she'd have been tempted to take a crack at the chaos his procrastination had caused him, but given how generous he'd been to her that would be grossly unfair.

He scratched his head and blew out a sigh as he took in the sea of papers. 'Where to start exactly,' he said quietly as if he was thinking out loud.

As wonderful as the idea of sleep was, she'd have to be blind not to notice the dark rings under his eyes. She didn't have a monopoly on a sleep debt and to walk away now and leave him dealing with the project after he'd just gone beyond what was expected of an understanding boss wasn't something she could do.

'To the uninitiated it looks like a mess but I promise you there's a system.'

'I believe you, but thousands wouldn't,' he said with a laugh in his voice. 'Were you able to draw any conclusions from the data?'

'I was.'

'Thank goodness.'

This time she laughed. 'I'll tell you what I discovered, if you convert it into flowing words that are spelt correctly.'

'You're on.' He opened up a new document on his computer. 'And there's a silver lining to all of this, Claire.'

'There is?'

'Sure.' He gave her a bone-melting smile. 'At the end of a long night, we'll be rewarded with a perfect view of dawn breaking over London.'

She tried not to think about the fact that she had a perfect view in front of her right this minute.

CHAPTER SEVEN

LONDON HAD PUT on a warm, starlit evening for the Paddington Children's Hospital fundraising ball and from the balcony overlooking the Thames the scent of gardenias wafted on the air. The evening was in full swing—the dance floor was crowded, some potential couples seeking a quiet tête-à-tête lingered on the curve of the elegant art nouveau staircase and the liveried staff busily cleared away the remnants of the main course.

The opulence and grandeur of the nineteenth century Paris salon–styled ballroom was equally matched by the massive floral arrangements of white roses, gardenias and hydrangeas as well as by the crowd. Alistair was used to seeing his staff in their PCH uniform or scrubs. He was used to seeing Claire in her utilitarian white blouse, black skirt, white coat and with her hair pulled back in a ponytail. He sure as hell wasn't used to seeing her in a full-length ball gown with her hair piled up onto her head in a way that emphasised her long and slender neck. A neck that just screamed to be kissed.

Many of the women wore strapless dresses exposing acres of skin and generous cleavages that drew and glued the gazes of most of the men in the room. Usually, he'd have enjoyed the spectacle—hell, he'd probably have toyed with the idea of later in the evening burying his face deep into their pillow softness—but not tonight. Somehow, Claire, in her high-necked sleeveless gown with its beaded bodice and full skirt, was sexier than all of them put together. The combination was doing his head in and the irony of the evening wasn't lost on him either.

Two weeks ago when he'd insisted on bringing Claire to the ball it had been a personal challenge to see if the buttoned-up woman with the acerbic tongue was capable of enjoying herself. Back then his plan had been to crack her façade, get her to smile and, as her boss, show her that there was more to life than just work. Fate, however, had thumbed its nose at him again.

Of all people, he knew better than most how life could change in a heartbeat. Or, in his case, a lack of one. With that information etched onto his heart and soul it stood to reason that he should have anticipated how much could happen in two weeks. He had not. Tonight, he was faced with the reality of change.

For starters, there'd been *that* kiss neither of them was acknowledging and then they'd had their frank conversation in his office. Since that night, the stressed-out and snarky woman he'd thought was Claire had almost vanished. Tonight, in her place, was a woman he barely recognised inside or out.

Since he'd learned about her dyslexia and they'd pulled a companionable and constructive all-nighter on the paper for the symposium, the two of them had reset their working relationship. Now that he understood her struggles with the written word, he'd taken back the lion's share of the report writing, leaving her with an amount she assured him she could handle. With more sleep, the dead weight of hiding a secret being lifted and a workload she could manage, Claire Mitchell's general demeanour had softened. In the last fourteen days, without even trying, his professional respect for her work and his admiration for what she'd achieved against steep odds had tipped the scales. He liked her.

That's not a crime, he told himself before his subconscious could berate him. *I liked her predecessor, Harry, too.*

But you didn't kiss him.

He had no comeback to that. All he knew was that if Claire was going to the same lengths as he was not to act on the wide current of attraction that arced between them every time they stepped into each other's orbit, then she was well down the road to insanity. This thing between them lived and breathed. It flickered and flared like firelight and it tantalisingly danced and sparkled like sunshine on water. No matter how hard he tried to ignore its pull, it never completely disappeared. It was playing merry hell with his concentration.

When he was alone, his thoughts were full of her and when they were together at work he was like a cat on a hot tin roof. Simple things like the brush of fingers on his hand when he passed her a pen or when he accepted her offer of a cup of coffee took on cataclysmic proportions. Any inadvertent touch set off rafts of sensation that tumbled over and over each other, racing along his veins until he was on fire with a thirst for her that couldn't be slaked. His body, which craved release, ranted at him all the time to *just do it.*

It took more willpower than he'd ever imposed upon himself before not to throw caution to the wind, spin her into his arms and kiss her senseless. Hell, just the other day during surgery she'd reached over him and to avoid an inadvertent touch he'd pulled back so fast that he'd upended a tray of sterilised instruments. The scrub sister was yet to forgive him.

He wasn't used to holding back. Hell, what was the point when the future couldn't be predicted and any day may well be his last. He'd always acted on intoxicating zips of attraction between him and a woman. If Claire had been any other woman and she'd kissed him with that same intense abandon, he knew without a doubt they'd have spent the rest of the night burning up the sheets. Instead, they'd shared the oddest fortnight, lurching from strict professional courtesy to relaxed moments of friendship. All the while the unacknowledged attraction simmered so strongly between them that he didn't know if he was coming or going. Tonight was no exception.

'Oh. Hello,' Claire said with a friendly—if slightly hesitant—smile as she passed him walking back from the dance floor.

Strands of her golden-blonde hair had escaped from the pile atop her head, her cheeks were flushed pink and her contact-lens-covered caramel eyes were almost obliterated by her dilated ebony pupils. She looked like she'd just been tumbled onto her back and ravished. His blood dived to his groin and he grabbed a glass of water from a passing waiter, drinking it down fast to stifle a groan.

'It's warm, isn't it?' She took a proffered glass of water too. 'I've danced with Dominic and Matthew but thank goodness I only have to dance with Andrew once. My toes couldn't take much more.'

'Hmm,' he managed, frantically channelling thoughts of the icy cold streams in the Scottish Highlands where his father had started teaching him to fly-fish. Thoughts about the effect the chilly water always had on his body.

Although he'd paid for her ticket to the ball, he hadn't spent very much time with her this evening, which was both a good and a bad thing. She'd refused his offer to pick her up and drive her, insisting instead on meeting him here. When he'd arrived, he'd looked for her but he'd soon been absorbed into a group so by the time he reached their allocated table and discovered that Victoria had seated them on opposite sides of the large round, it was too late to do anything about it.

He'd spent the entrée and main course flanked on one side by a chatty physiotherapist and on the other side by the ward pharmacist. Both were perfectly delightful and interesting women and on another night he'd have probably enjoyed their company immensely. But tonight, every time he'd heard Claire's tinkling laugh—yes, the woman had actually laughed—he'd wanted to lunge across the table and throttle Duncan MacKinnon.

If anyone was going to make Claire laugh, it was going to be him. If anyone was going to show her how to have fun, it should be him, except he hadn't had the chance. The moment the meal had finished, the dancing had started and Victoria had sold him off like he was meat on a slab. He'd danced for an hour straight, fending off a dozen invitations from sexy and beautiful women. It both surprised and worried him that he hadn't been tempted by any of them. What the hell was wrong with him?

You know exactly what's wrong with you. Ethics and blue balls.

'Does Victoria know you're hiding behind the aspidistra instead of being out on the dance floor?' Claire asked with a teasing glint in her beautiful eyes.

This time he gulped champagne. From the moment he'd first laid eyes on her tonight, he'd recognised that off-duty Claire was a very different woman from Dr Mitchell. Out from under the mantle of responsibility and the pressures of her dyslexia, the need for her to control everything had faded. If anything, tonight she had a look of wonder about her, as if she couldn't quite believe she was at the ball and she was absorbing every moment. None of it was helping him control his libido in any shape or form.

'I'm not hiding. I'm taking a break.'

She laughed. 'Poor, Al. What a tough gig, having beautiful women throw themselves at you.'

Al? 'You have no idea,' he said tightly, thinking about

the battle that currently raged inside him. The beautiful woman he wanted wasn't throwing herself at him, and unless she did, he couldn't have her.

Lighten up, mate. Forcing himself to smile just like he'd been doing all evening, he said, 'But one must do one's bit to help save the castle.'

'You Brits break me up,' she said, laughing. 'Keep calm and dance on?'

'Something like that,' he said, thinking that he hadn't known calm since he'd kissed her.

'Victoria, Rosie, Matt and Robyn have done an amazing job pulling this together. Apparently, their photo's going to be in the paper tomorrow, so hopefully donations will flood in.' She gazed up at the ceiling with a starry-eyed look, taking in the intricate plasterwork and gilt. 'All of this is so far removed from the Gundiwindi Mechanic's Institute hall I keep thinking I'm dreaming it.' She swung her gaze to his. 'Did you know that Anna Pavlova once danced here and that Fred Astaire danced on the roof with his sister?'

He loved the awe that wove across her face and he had a crazy desire to try and keep it there and never let it fade. 'How do you know all this?'

'I stumbled across a photographic exhibition,' she said enthusiastically. 'Once, there was a leopard in this stunning Belle Époque room. Can you imagine?'

'Well, us crazy Brits like to shake things up a bit now and then,' he said with a grin.

'Alistair.' A voice with an Irish lilt called his name from the dance floor. A Cornish accent followed it. 'Come dance with us.'

'Yes, do,' a chorus of accents from around the British Isles sang across the ballroom.

The Koala Ward nurses were excelling at having fun, but the last thing he wanted was to be back in that pawing crush. He smiled at Claire. 'I wouldn't mind seeing those photos.'

'You're just saying that to avoid the tipsy nurses.'

Absolutely. 'As a Londoner, I think it's imperative I catch up on the history of this esteemed establishment.'

She gave an exaggerated eye roll and a lightness shot through him. 'Exactly where do I find this exhibition?'

'Downstairs. You cross the foyer, go left at reception, take the first right and there's a set of double doors—' She laughed. 'It's probably just easier if I show you.'

Yes, please. He stepped back, allowing her the space to move past him and then it was just good manners to rest his hand lightly on the small of her back to guide her as they negotiated their way across the crowded room.

'Alistair, old man,' Lionel Harrington, a retired paediatric surgeon, called out to him with a definite slur in his voice.

Claire slowed and Alistair leaned forward, saying quietly into her ear, 'Keep going or we'll be stuck with loquacious Lionel for the next half an hour.'

She immediately picked up the pace, walking determinedly against the crowd who were now returning for dessert. Instead of summoning a lift, she picked up her skirt and with a smoothness of motion that belied her high heels she almost sailed down the stunning staircase.

He had a flash of Cinderella running away from the Prince and he hurried down after her. He automatically turned towards the foyer but she grabbed his hand and pulled him through a door and down a corridor. It wasn't decorated in quite the same grand style as the rest of the hotel and he had a sudden thought. 'Are we allowed back here?'

Her hand paused on the door handle of a set of double doors and her eyes danced. 'Put it this way. There's no sign saying that we're not.'

He laughed, loving that she was living for the moment. She immediately shushed him. Using what he assumed was the staff entrance, he followed her into a large room. Large crates, ladders and other equipment were scattered around the room and half of the space was hung with framed photographs of various sizes.

He picked up a flyer that had spilled from a box. 'It says it opens on the fourth.'

'How lucky are we to get an advanced peek,' she said, eyes shining as she tugged him towards an enormous black and white photo. 'Ta-dah!'

He did a double take. 'Is that a five-foot cake balanced on an elephant that's standing on a gondola?'

'I know, right?' she said, laughter lacing her voice. Dropping her hand from his arm, she peered forward to read the information plaque next to the photo. 'And it says it was lit by four hundred paper lanterns.'

He had to fist his hand so as not to snatch hers back. 'I'm quite taken with the twelve thousand carnations and the swans.'

She shook her head in amazement. 'I can't even wrap my head around such extravagance.'

Side by side they wandered slowly up and down the room taking in the photos of famous people. Bogart and Bacall, and Marilyn Monroe, represented Hollywood royalty. There was a very young Christian Dior surrounded by five models dressed in intricately beaded ball gowns. Personally, he didn't think any of them looked as amazing as Claire.

'Here's one for you,' he said, pointing to a portrait of the famous Australian soprano, Dame Nellie Melba. It was taken when she was young and she was pressing a fan coquettishly to her cheek. 'The hotel's chef invented peach Melba to honour her triumph at Covent Garden.'

Claire laughed. 'I bet it was far more extravagant than

the Gundiwindi pub's best efforts of some canned cling peaches served with half-melted ice cream.'

'You forgot the raspberry sauce.'

'There's raspberry sauce in peach Melba?'

'Good heavens,' he said with faux shock. 'What sort of Australian are you if you don't know that?'

'Obviously a dessert-ignorant one. I guess I'll be forced to remedy the situation.'

He had a sudden flash of her mouth closing around a spoon and slowly sucking ice cream off it. He was abruptly very hot and finding it hard to breathe. Tugging at his collar, he loosened his bow tie.

One of the last photos in the collection was taken during the Second World War. 'I can't imagine dancing while the bombs fell,' Claire said softly.

He could. Dicing with death was a way of life for him with his unreliable heart. 'Why not enjoy yourself to the very last?'

She gave him a sideways look. 'More of your live-for-the-moment mantra?'

'Sure. Just like we're living for the moment now.'

A small frown creased her forehead. 'I hardly think sneaking in here is very dangerous.'

'Oh, I don't know…'

She tilted her head, looking at him from those glorious eyes of hers. Her perfume, which always reminded him of sunshine, summer days and freedom, pulled at his restraint. So help him, he should have stayed upstairs and danced with the giggly nurses instead of coming down here with her. But here they were, alone for the very first time this evening, and all he wanted to do was wrap his arms around her. He wanted to haul her in against him, feel her body pressed against the length of him and lose himself in kissing her until nothing else existed but their touch.

You know you can't do any of it.

He never prevaricated or second-guessed anything but this was new territory for him. This was Claire and he was her boss. Until she gave him a sign that she felt exactly the same way he did, that she would welcome his touch, nothing could happen.

'How can this possibly be dangerous,' she said briskly with a hint of the terse Claire from two weeks ago.

He knew her well enough to recognise the tone she used when she was stressed. Was it because she could feel this thing leaping and writhing between them, desperate to be satiated? *Please.* He gazed down at her and said softly, 'I think you know exactly how dangerous it is for us to be alone in this room.'

Alistair's impossibly deep voice flowed around Claire like dark, melted chocolate—decadent, enticing and blissfully sinful. She knew exactly how dangerous it was for her to be standing mere millimetres away from him and his rock-hard body. A body her fingertips had committed to memory just over two weeks ago and itched to touch again.

You had a plan. Why didn't you stick to it?

So much had happened between them since the evening she'd invited him to the ball and all of it made her head spin. Back when she'd issued the invitation, all he'd been to her was an infuriating and exasperating boss. Since then, she'd seen more sides to him than a polygon. When she combined it with *that* kiss, it made him—for her at least—the most dangerous man in London. It didn't matter how great he'd been about her slightly unhinged behaviour around the Walker case or his empathy and practicality about her dyslexia, or that she now recognised in him values and ethics that she admired. No matter how much her body ached to touch his again, they were still in the power dynamic of boss and trainee.

To that end, she'd gone to great lengths to protect herself

from doing something she'd regret at work. Tonight, she'd had a simple and foolproof plan for the evening—never be alone with Alistair. She'd known that outside of the protective framework of the hospital and their defined roles she might be tempted, so she'd strategised for it. She'd started by politely refusing his offer of a ride to the hotel and until now she'd only talked to him in the ballroom surrounded by three hundred people.

Why in heaven's name had she brought him down here?

She blamed the dress and the hotel. Tonight was like stepping out of her prescribed life and into a magical world of pretend. It had started the moment she'd stared disbelievingly at the woman who'd faced her in the bedroom mirror. She'd hardly recognised herself. The boutique owner on a little road just off Oxford Street deserved a medal for convincing her to buy this frock. The little girl from dusty Gundiwindi had ridden to the ball in a London black cab, which in her book was as amazing as a pumpkin carriage being drawn by white horses. The moment the hotel's doorman had swept open the cab's door and she'd stepped onto the green carpet, she'd been treated as if she was someone special. Someone who mattered. That was her ambrosia.

The opulence and grandeur of the surroundings had called to her and she'd been like a kid in a lolly shop. She'd gone exploring, making her way noiselessly along thickly carpeted corridors and peeking behind closed doors. When she'd stumbled into the half-hung exhibition, she'd been so excited about discovering the living history of the luxurious hotel that she'd wanted to share it with someone. It had totally messed with her plan. So here she was, alone with Alistair, and although his hands were by his sides and not a single cell of their bodies touched, the electricity that buzzed and fizzed between them could light up London and the home counties.

For the first time, the look in his eyes was unguarded.

The professional interest that usually resided in the grey depths whenever he looked at her—a glance that occasionally morphed into moments of a friendly gaze—had vanished. In its place, the flames of unadulterated lust burned brightly. Danger and desire swirled with an intoxicating pull.

Her body responded to it, leaping with a need to match his. Fleetingly, she wondered why he'd dropped his guard. Why now?

It's this hotel. This dress. This night. None of it's real life.

Exactly. So take what's on offer because it will vanish with the dawn.

She swallowed and dug to find her voice, not quite believing she could be so daring. 'You once accused me of not having fun. This hotel, with all of its stories, almost demands I step outside of my real life and do something outrageous for a night.'

His eyes flashed silver. 'It would almost be disrespectful not to honour the hotel's reputation as a host to many clandestine lovers.'

Tingling delight swooped through her and she was dizzy with the idea that he wanted her as much as she wanted him. But memories of Michael, along with a deep-seated need to protect herself and her scholarship, made her say, 'This has nothing to do with work. What happens in the hotel stays in the hotel.'

Tension coiled through his body, radiating from the jut of his jaw and out across the square set of his shoulders, but still he didn't move to touch her. 'I promise you, Claire. It won't spill into our work world. It's your decision. If you have any doubts…' His husky voice cracked. 'Are you absolutely certain you want this?'

Her heart rolled oddly at the concern in his question and she plucked at the organza of her full skirt. After working with him for weeks she recognised him to be an honourable man. She trusted him and knew that he'd never coerce her or use this night against her. She met his gaze. 'Tonight's all about fantasy, right?'

He made a low growling sound in the back of his throat. It made her feel strangely powerful and she rose on her toes to kiss him. For two long weeks she'd replayed the juxtaposing touch of his mouth on hers—soft and firm—and the searing heat of his lips that lit her up from the inside out. She couldn't wait another second for his taste to invade her.

Knowing his mouth was millimetres from hers, she closed her eyes and leaned in. Her lips hit air. As disappointment whipped her, Alistair grabbed her hand. He pulled her so fast towards the double doors that she almost tripped. 'What are you doing?' she asked, frantically trying to keep her balance.

'What the hell do you think I'm doing?' He wrenched open the door.

'I thought you were going to kiss me.'

He stopped and gently cupped her cheeks, his palms warm against her skin. 'If I kiss you here, Claire,' he said raggedly, 'I won't be able to stop.'

The little girl inside her squealed, twirled and clapped her hands. 'Really?'

'Yes, really.' He dropped his forehead to gently rest against hers. 'I've wanted to kiss you from the moment I saw you across the other side of the crowded ballroom. I'm not ruining this fantasy of ours by getting charged with indecent exposure. We're getting a room.'

'But Marlene Dietrich apparently—'

But he was already towing her across the foyer towards the reception desk. With one arm clamped firmly around her waist, keeping her tightly pressed against him, he said in a crisp, polite and plummy voice, 'We'd like a room for the evening.'

The receptionist—his name badge said he was Daniel—

didn't bat an eyelid. Nor did he ask about their luggage or lack of it. 'These functions can be quite exhausting, sir. I'm sure you'll find everything you need in Room 613.' After running Alistair's credit card through the machine he gave them a wallet containing two key cards. 'Just insert the card into the lift, sir, and press six. Enjoy your evening.'

At that precise moment Claire developed a fondness for what up until now she'd always considered starchy, British manners.

'Thank you,' Alistair said as he turned her and briskly marched them both to the lifts.

The journey to the sixth floor was interminable with the lift stopping at almost every floor. Their slow progression added to her frustration that Alistair was holding firm to his resolve that he wasn't going to kiss her until they were inside the room. 'You're crushing my hand.'

'Sorry.' He gave her a tight and apologetic glance before dropping her hand and hitting the number six button another three times.

She used the tortoise-like passage of time to slip off her shoes. When the lift doors finally opened on their level she picked up her skirt and her shoes, stepped out into the corridor and ran. Just as she'd found their door, Alistair caught her around the waist with his left hand and with his right he inserted the card into the lock with a quick in-out action.

'You've done that before.'

'Never with quite the same level of desperation,' he said with an ironic edge. He pushed open the door.

Together, they tumbled into the room, and as the door clicked shut quietly behind them, he kissed her.

Unlike that first time in the lounge, there was nothing slow about this kiss. It held two weeks of frustration and tightly leashed lust that now spilled into her with an urgency that chased along her veins. As it scooped up her desire and merged it into a molten ball of need, it detonated bursts of wonder. The explosions lit her up until her body was a pleasure dome of sensation and her legs threatened to buckle out from under her.

In a sea of organza and tulle she fell back onto the king-size bed, bringing Alistair down with her. Her hands tugged at his bespoke jacket, pushing it off his shoulders, and as he shrugged out of it his mouth didn't leave hers. Somehow, despite the fact his kisses had reduced her body to a puddle of vibrating need and her mind to mush, she managed to get her fingers to work. She undid the buttons of his waistcoat and popped the studs on his shirt and collar. Finally, after clawing at a flurry of white material, her palms pressed against hot skin, corded tendon and rock-solid muscle. *Bliss.*

As she ran her hands across his chest she heard herself make an involuntary moan. Alistair pulled his mouth from hers and gazed down at her with a wide grin on his face. 'Having fun?'

Her cheeks burned and she reminded herself that as much as he wanted her for his own enjoyment, she wanted him. He was hers for this night and it would be silly to waste precious time by being embarrassed. 'You bet I'm having fun,' she said, lifting her head and laying her mouth over his left nipple. She flicked out her tongue, tasting the hard nub, and then she sucked him into her mouth.

He gasped and his entire body flinched. 'Vixen,' he muttered, and as she laughed his hands moved frantically across the bodice of her dress. She could barely feel his touch through the detailed beading and corsetry and her laugher faded. She wanted his hands on her skin. His mouth on her skin. She wanted—

'Bloody hell,' he said through gritted teeth. 'I'll get gravel rash from all this beadwork.'

'The zipper's on the—' She suddenly had a face full of organza and tulle, but before she could fight the material, Alistair's mouth nipped gently at the tender skin of her inner thigh.

'Oh.' She gasped and writhed in delight as his tongue flicked and his mouth sucked, all the while moving closer and closer to her hot and aching centre. Her breath came short and sharp as the delicious assault continued and it wasn't until silver spots flickered behind her eyes that she flipped the skirt over and panted, 'Need. Air.'

He extricated himself. 'I was just having fun,' he said with a wicked glint in his eye. 'Just like you.'

Laughing, she sat up. 'In the fairy tales, they never mentioned how the Princess got out of her gown for the Prince.'

'Going on history and the lack of underwear back then, I think the Prince just pulled up the skirts and helped himself while the Princess lay back and thought of England.' As his fingers found the tag of the dress's zipper, he kissed her gently. 'But I want to see and feel all of you.'

'So do I.' She reached for his belt and as her hand brushed his erection she suddenly flashed hot and cold. *Contraception.* 'You've got a condom, right?'

He paled. 'No.'

'What?' Panic and surprise took her voice up an octave. 'I thought you—'

'Never leave home without one?' He grimaced. 'Don't believe all the hospital gossip, Claire. This—' he flicked his long, dextrous fingers between them '—is an unexpected gift.'

His lack of a condom was in a way gratifying—he hadn't planned on having sex with anyone else—as well as devastating. They might not be having sex this evening after all.

'Mind you,' he said tightly as he strode to the bathroom. 'It might be a gift that doesn't get fully unwrapped.'

No. As she jerkily pulled open the bedside drawers on both sides of the bed, she heard him muttering, 'Bloody hell. There's enough shower gel here to wash an army.'

She reached into the second drawer expecting her fingers to touch a book but instead she felt a plastic case. 'Alistair.'

He stuck his head out of the bathroom, his messy hair wild from the ministrations of her fingers. 'What?'

'Apparently, in the tradition of a hotel that's infamous for catering to the rich and famous, there's an aptly named "fun pack."' Laughing with delight, she waved it at him. 'Daniel wasn't wrong when he said we'd find everything we need. It's all here, plus breath mints.'

'Thank God for British ingenuity and organisation.' He walked back to the bed and the mood lighting cast tantalising shadows on his naked chest. 'Now,' he said with a sly grin, 'let's get you out of this dress.'

He made short work of the frock, freeing her in less time than it had taken her to pour herself into it and then he was gazing appreciatively at her new French lace bra and matching knickers. She sent up a vote of thanks to the sales assistant who'd encouraged her to buy them, despite the fact she'd spent far too much money.

'Don't think I don't appreciate lingerie, because I do,' he said, his eyes fixed on the demi-bra. 'It's just, right now I'd appreciate it more off you than on.'

With a proficiency she didn't want to examine too closely, he quickly divested her of her underwear. Attempting to match him, she unhooked his trousers and pushed his pants and underwear down to his ankles. He kicked them off and a thrill spun deep down inside her at the glorious sight of him before her—delineated pecs, washboard-flat abdomen, the tantalising trail of dark blond hair that arrowed down to the prize, which jutted out towards her, erect and ready.

I caused that, she thought in wonder, but before another thought could form, he'd killed the lights and was pulling her down onto the bed, rolling her into him in a tangle of limbs. His mouth honoured her, starting with her lips and then trailing along her jaw and down her neck before his tongue traced the hollow in her throat.

She shivered in delight, never having known such delicious sensations, and as much as she wanted to run her hands up and down his back and feel him too, she didn't want a moment's distraction from revelling in his touch. Besides, his mouth had closed around the aching and tingling flesh of her breast. An arrow of need darted deep, sharp and erotic, lifting her hips to his and bucking against him. Seeking him. Sliding her slick and ready self against him.

He groaned and raised his head. 'If you want me to go slowly, that's not the way to encourage it.'

'Fast, slow, I don't care.'

'God, Claire,' he ground out. 'I'm serious.'

'So am I.' Her heart hammered. 'Ever since that kiss I've—'

'Wanted this so badly I can't even think straight,' he said hoarsely.

'Yes.' She breathed out the word. 'Oh, yes.'

From the lights of the city that cast shadows in the room, she saw the agony of holding back glowing deep in his eyes. Her body thrummed so fast with need that her muscles quivered, desperate to close around him. She pulled her hands out of his grasp and picked up one of the distinctive blue squares. 'We've got more than one condom and we've got the night.'

'In that case, who am I to argue?'

She kissed him as she slid the condom along his silken length. Reminding herself this was her fantasy, and that he was hers to use for her pleasure, she rolled him over onto his back.

He rolled her straight back, capturing her hands again. 'I've fantasised for a long time about your legs wrapped high around me.'

She was awestruck. 'You have?'

'Do you have any idea what those shoes you wear do to me?' His voice was hoarse.

'I can put them on if you want?'

'Next time.' His voice was hoarse.

She gripped his waist with her legs, crossing her ankles above his back and he entered her tantalisingly slowly. Millimetre by millimetre, in and out, gently gaining depth until he filled her completely, she was almost screaming with frustrated pleasure. An unexpected sob left her lips.

He instantly tensed and concern pierced the fog of lust in his eyes. 'Are you okay?'

She tightened around him. 'I'm more than okay.'

It had been such a long time since she'd had sex. Since she'd experienced bliss quite like this.

It's never been like this.

Her hips rose as she matched his rhythm, welcoming the length of him stroking her. She wanted to kiss him but sensation was taking over and her head thrashed from side to side as ecstasy built. The noise of their panting breaths fell away as the edges of her mind started to blur. Nothing existed except his touch and the addictive bliss that drove her on, promising euphoria. Her body spun ever upwards—twirling, rising, seeking and craving the ephemeral delight.

With a shout of wonder, she was lifted high out of herself, shattering into a thousand shards of silver that rained down all around her. As she fell back to earth, he jerked over her, crying out her name. As she raised her head to kiss him, she tasted salt and the joy of her own tears.

CHAPTER EIGHT

ALISTAIR COULDN'T STOP grinning but he knew he had to wrestle down the desire to beam from ear to ear before he arrived at the castle. If he didn't, his joie de vivre would invite nudges, winks and comments from all the usual suspects—like the porters who'd say, 'You're looking happier than you deserve to, guv.'

And he was happy. Ridiculously happy, but no one at the castle could know the reason for his good spirits. Especially not Robyn. As head of surgery, she'd have his guts for garters and the Royal College of Surgeons would be none too pleased either if they got a whiff of anything untoward. Not that either he or Claire considered what had happened between them to be anything other than marvellous.

After making love twice—the first time hot and explosive, the second time deliciously slow but oddly more intense—they'd fallen asleep. He'd woken to find her head on his chest and her hair strewn all over his body. Normally when he had sex with a woman, he tended to leave her bed soon afterwards, but with Claire's words—*one night*—clear in his mind, along with being in the neutral territory of the hotel, he'd fallen asleep and had slept surprisingly well.

He blew a few strands of her hair out of his mouth and nose, but his tickling breath must have woken her. She'd opened her sleep-filled eyes and a moment later—the exact second she'd remembered where she was—they'd dilated into pools of caramel sauce. It was as natural as breathing to stroke her hair. 'Good morning.'

She smiled, although it held hesitancy at the edges. 'Hi.' She raised her head so she could see the bedside clock and then gasped. 'No. Nine-fifteen? This is a little awkward.'

It should have been very awkward but for some reason it wasn't.

'Why?'

She sat up quickly, pulling the sheet with her. 'Oh, you know.' She gave an embarrassed laugh. 'With the dawn comes the unforgiving light.'

He laughed. 'You look deliciously sexy and sleep rumpled to me. I tell you what. We can always keep the curtains closed and pretend it's still the night.'

Two hot-pink spots appeared on her cheeks and she groaned. 'Is that a polite way of saying I have the remnants of last night's makeup halfway down my cheeks and wild and crazy bed hair?'

He thought she looked beautiful. 'Nothing that a shower won't repair,' he'd said, kissing her gently. 'Tell you what. Let's have a shower and some breakfast before we open the curtains and concede the night's over.' She stared at him for a long moment, her face giving away nothing. A stab of disappointment pierced him. 'Or not.'

She blinked a few times before making a sound that was half laugh and half discomfiture. 'Um… Al.'

All his life he'd been called Alistair and it was rare that anyone ever shortened it. If they did, he promptly corrected them, but there was something about Claire's accent, and the intimacy the contraction implied that kept him silent. 'Yes?'

'The dawn also brings reality. My disposable contacts are long gone and I don't have my glasses. Everything's out of focus. To be honest, I can't see much further than my fingertips.'

He laughed and pulled her in close. 'You don't have to see, Claire. Just feel.'

'Is that an invitation?'

'Could I deny a half-blind woman anything?'

She smiled the smile of a woman who'd just been given a box wrapped up in tissue paper and a bow, and she slid her hands up into his hair. Her fingers delved deep, firmly exploring his skull.

'Are you taking up phrenology?' he quipped.

Her fingers moved forward to his forehead. 'With this prominence, you'd be considered benevolent.'

'That's definitely me.'

She raised her brows as if disputing his claim, but the look in her eyes didn't match it. She continued her exploration, slowly tracing the orbit of his eyes before the stubble on his cheekbones slowed the progression of her fingertips. She traversed the length of his nose, drawing a little circle on the tip and then she outlined his lips and traced his jaw. As her fingers left a spot, she kissed it.

He relaxed into her light and gentle caresses and his mind slid away from all thought, sinking blissfully into the sensations and absorbing every single one of them. She moved her hands to the column of his neck and using both thumbs in a soft massage she swept outwards from the centre until she reached the base of his throat.

His now languid body pressed heavily into the mattress and his mind emptied, conscious of nothing except the pleasure of her touch. Her fingers were drawing delicious small and continuous 'e's along both of his clavicles, moving slowly but surely out towards his shoulders.

A shot of adrenaline pierced his languor and he thrust out his left hand, immediately capturing her right. He had no problem with Claire, the woman, touching him, but

Claire, the doctor, was another matter entirely. He sure as hell had no desire to talk about what she was about to feel and instantly diagnose with her fingers. She'd ask questions—questions he didn't want to answer—and not only would it summarily end her delicious exploration of him, it would end their magical time together on a sour note. He had no intention of allowing that to happen.

Thank goodness she couldn't see very well. He pressed her hand to his mouth and kissed it before using his tongue to tickle her palm. She laughed and the musical sound surrounded him before sliding under his skin. As it trickled along his veins, he had the strangest sensation—something that made him feel different somehow—but with a beautiful and naked woman sitting astride him, he didn't pause to give it any thought.

Very slowly, he sucked one of her fingers into his mouth before releasing it and turning his attention to the next one. With each flick of his tongue, he felt her thighs tense and relax against his own and felt himself harden against her. As he released her pinkie finger he pressed her hand on his belly with her fingers splayed downwards.

She shivered and without hesitation she took the bait exactly as he'd hoped she would. Her attention was focused far from his shoulder and her fingers and mouth explored him until he begged for mercy. She rolled a condom on him and he rolled her under him.

Afterwards, they'd shared a tub and he'd cradled her back against him, keeping her hands firmly away from his chest. They'd blown bubbles of bath gel like little kids, delighting in the rainbow of colours as the bubbles floated above them. Food had followed and he'd consumed the largest breakfast he'd eaten in a very long time. He'd been unable to convince her that kippers were a treat.

'Bacon is a treat,' she'd said, savouring two poached

eggs. 'Pancakes and maple syrup are a treat, but oily smoked fish? Not so much.'

'All that omega-3 is good for your joints and helps ward off Alzheimer's.'

'You forgot to mention reducing the risk of heart disease and stroke.'

He hadn't forgotten at all. His failure to mention the top two health risks had been deliberate. Not that omega-3 could have prevented his cardiac condition, but it could help stave off other complications.

'I prefer to get my daily dose of omega-3 from nuts.' With a theatrical shudder of her white-bathrobe-clad shoulders, she pushed the plate of kippers back towards him. 'Be my guest and eat mine.'

'Well, if you're forcing it on me...' He'd speared it with his fork before enjoying the fish on hearty seed-laden toast.

'Perhaps kippers are a bit like Vegemite,' she said reflectively.

'How so exactly?' he asked, wondering about the connection between the ghastly black stuff Australians loved and the cold-water fish.

'To enjoy either of them, perhaps you have to be raised on them from an early age.'

'You might be right,' he said with a grin. 'I ate kippers a lot growing up. They were Cook's favourite breakfast food.'

Her coffee cup stalled halfway to her luscious mouth. 'Cook?' She blinked. 'You grew up with a cook?' Her disbelief rode across her face and settled in her startled and out-of-focus gaze.

He regretted the slip of his tongue. What the hell had made him mention Cook? Trying to shrug away all the disparate emotions that always hit him when he thought about Englewood, he said with feigned easiness, 'We lived in the country.'

She laughed. 'And that's your explanation? In Australia,

living in the country and having a cook are not automatically connected. Next you'll be telling me you had a nanny and you went to boarding school.'

'Guilty on both counts, I'm afraid.'

'And it keeps happening,' she said, sounding slightly bewildered.

'What keeps happening?'

'Me, feeling like I've stepped into the middle of an English novel from my childhood.' She slathered jam onto a croissant. 'I grew up in a town ringed by red dust. I'm the daughter of a mechanic and a secretary. My mother was an anglophile and she read me all the classics like *The Secret Garden*, *Wind in the Willows*, all the Roald Dahl stories and, of course, A. A. Milne. The idea of having a cook and a nanny was the stuff of stories, but you actually lived it. Tell me, did you have a secret garden?'

'There was a walled garden, but it wasn't very secret.' He gave a wry smile. 'My father used to tease my mother that she only married him for the garden. She certainly loved it and my earliest memories are playing hide-and-seek with her there.'

Claire's eyes lit up. 'Do your parents still live in the great house in the country?'

He tried to stave off the flinch but it came anyway. Not for the first time today, he gave thanks that Claire was extremely short-sighted without her glasses. 'No. Dad died when I was thirteen. Due to a complicated family will, we had to leave.'

'Oh.' Her hand shot out and rested over his. 'I'm sorry.'

'It was a long time ago,' he said, sliding his hand out from under hers and refilling their coffee cups.

She frowned. 'Thirteen's a tough age to lose your father.'

Yes. 'Fortunately, I had some excellent housemasters at school.'

She rubbed her temples and he swooped into action, needing to prevent her from asking anything else about his father. 'Headache?' he asked.

She nodded at him with a resigned smile. 'As wonderful as all of this has been, I need to get home to my glasses.'

'In that case…' He rose and pressed a button. The curtains smoothly opened to reveal a Sunday full of sunshine. They both squinted into the light.

'Oh, God,' Claire suddenly moaned. 'I have to go out into broad daylight in an evening gown.'

'No, you don't.' He pulled her to her feet and kissed her hair. 'I've bought us both a souvenir to remember our night.'

She grimaced. 'I'm not sure wearing the hotel bathrobe home is any less incriminating than the dress.'

'O ye of little faith,' he said, tucking some damp strands of her hair behind her ear. 'We're leaving wearing a set of monogrammed hotel gym gear.'

'They sell that?' She laughed. 'I love this hotel.'

He'd agreed with her.

That had been nineteen hours ago. The last words she'd said to him before she hopped into a cab were, 'See you at work, Mr North.'

'Morning, guv,' one of the porters greeted him as he entered the hospital.

'Morning, Amos.'

'Heard you had a good weekend.' The porter tapped his nose as if he was privy to some private information. Alistair tensed for moment but relaxed when Amos said, 'Saw your photo in the paper with that pretty nurse Ms Hobbes.'

'It was my job to dance with all of the nurses,' he said easily, telling the truth. 'And I went home alone.'

Disappointment flashed across the man's face. 'That's too bad, guv. Next time, eh?'

Alistair grinned and kept walking. When he arrived on Koala Ward, his team were waiting for him, including Claire. He knew she would have arrived half an hour ago to read the files.

She gave him the same quietly restrained smile she'd given him for the past two weeks—well, at work anyway. With her hair pulled neatly back in a ponytail, a fresh white coat and glasses perched on her nose she looked exactly the same as she'd always looked. Rising to her feet, she picked up her stethoscope and swung it around her neck. The bell came to rest on the V of her blouse and it snagged his gaze. Immediately, the memory of a sheer lace bra that left little to the imagination hit him so hard his blood swooped to his groin.

'Morning, Mitchell. Bailey.' His normal greeting sounded strained and he cleared his throat. 'I want an update on Ryan Walker.'

'He's not triggering the ventilator yet,' Claire said as a small frown made a V on the bridge of her nose. 'We're continuing with the treatment of sedation, ventilation and parenteral nutrition.'

'That's all we can do at the moment,' Alistair said. 'Right, Bailey, your turn.'

After the ward round finished and he'd spoken to the Walkers, he ducked into the nurses' tea room and grabbed a cheese and ham croissant. He needed the fuel before a busy morning in outpatients. He'd just brushed the last crumbs off his fingers when Dominic MacBride telephoned him.

'We need you and your registrar down here for a consult. Sooner rather than later if possible.'

'On my way.'

As he ran down the stairs, he was surprised to meet Claire on the third floor. 'On your way to A & E?'

She's hardly going to the circus.

She nodded. 'Yep.'

He opened his mouth to say, *I had a great time with you*, which was what he usually said to a woman he'd slept with and wanted to see again. He promptly swallowed the words, remembering he'd promised her what had happened wouldn't spill into their work world. Right now, they were clearly at work. He frantically sought for something else to say but pulled up blank.

What the hell was wrong with him? He was British, for heaven's sake. He'd been raised on polite small talk. It was a relief to arrive at the ground floor. He pushed open the heavy fire door for her. As she slipped past he breathed in deeply, drawing in her scent that reminded him so much of summer days on the Côte d'Azur. The tang of grapes, the softness of lavender and the refreshing fizz of lemon shot through him and he had to fist his right hand so as not to wrap it around her waist.

In the corridor, he fell into step next to her when Claire's brisk pace suddenly faltered. She abruptly stepped sideways as if she was avoiding something and bumped into him, knocking him off balance. He automatically gripped her hips to steady himself. As he did so, he noticed a man standing stock-still in the middle of the hallway staring straight at him and Claire.

It took him a moment to recognise who he was, but as his hands fell away from Claire, he realised it was Thomas Wolfe. He hadn't seen the paediatric cardiologist in years, so why the hell was he staring at them as if he'd just come face to face with his worst nightmare?

The painful intensity of Thomas's gaze gave Alistair pause, and without thinking he glanced over his shoulder. Rebecca Scott, the transplant surgeon, stood behind them, her face pale and tight.

'North. Mitchell.' She gave them a brisk nod of acknowledgment before striding past them. Without saying another word, she skirted around Thomas Wolfe and exited the corridor.

For a moment Thomas didn't move. Alistair was about to break the uncomfortable silence with a 'Good to see you again, Thomas,' when the man spun around, punched open the large plastic doors to A & E and disappeared.

'Wow. ' Claire's face was full of curiosity. 'Who was that?'

'Thomas Wolfe. He's a cardiologist. Worked here years ago. I got a memo this morning saying he's back. God knows why when the storm clouds of closure are hanging over the castle.'

'That's as may be,' Claire said thoughtfully. 'But something pretty big's going on between him and Rebecca. If looks were a loaded gun, one of us would be dead by now.'

'They used to be married.' He blew out a long sigh. 'Guess it must have been a messy divorce.'

'That's an understatement,' Claire said with a shiver. 'It's a perfect example of why people who work together shouldn't…'

Her cheeks pinked up, reminding him of how she'd looked two nights ago. More than anything he wanted to kiss her. 'Get married?' he said quickly, before she could say, *Have sex*. 'I absolutely agree with you, but surely that doesn't preclude enjoying each other away from the hospital.'

'I think we demonstrated that was possible.' Her clipped tone was at war with her expression.

'Then why are you sounding like it was a science experiment where we proved a hypothesis?'

She gave him a rueful smile. 'We agreed to one night.'

A spark of hope lit through him. 'We can always agree to one night again. Hell, we can agree to one night as many times as we wish.'

'Alistair,' she said sadly. 'That spontaneous woman on Saturday night wasn't the real me.'

He wouldn't accept that. 'I think that woman's always been very much a part of you.'

'You're just saying that so I agree to another night.'

'I'd love another night with you, but what I said isn't a line.' He really wanted to touch her but they were standing in a busy corridor and she deserved better than becoming the next topic on the hospital grapevine. 'I think that impetuous and risk-taking woman's been hampered by your dyslexia and buried by its secret.

'But it's not a secret any more, and more importantly, not everything in life can be planned.' He was intimate with the truth of that statement. 'Nor should it be because overplanning can deny you opportunities.'

He held his breath and waited for her to disagree or tell him to go to hell but she didn't say anything. Instead, she shoved her hands deep into the pockets of her white coat and rocked back on her fire-engine-red heels.

When she met his gaze again, the whirlpool in her eyes had stilled to a millpond. 'So, you're suggesting that outside of work I could benefit from some more practice at being spontaneous.'

He grinned, delight lighting through him. 'I'd be very happy to help you.'

'In that case,' she said with a tinkle in her voice, 'I'll be in touch.'

'When?' He tensed as the needy word left his lips. The moment was utterly foreign to him. He wasn't the one who ever asked a question like that—it was the domain of all the women he dated.

'When I'm feeling impulsive.' A momentary flash of lust mixed with promise in her beautiful eyes. And then it was gone and she was pushing her glasses up her nose and turning away from him saying, 'They're waiting for us in A & E.'

He watched her walk towards the plastic doors feeling slightly discombobulated. She'd just done to him what he'd done to so many women before her. He didn't like it one little bit.

CHAPTER NINE

CLAIRE SLIPPED OUT of bed and took a moment to watch a sleeping Alistair gently snoring. She smiled at him tucked up in pyjamas, finding it odd that he always wore them or a T-shirt in bed. She put it down to a British idiosyncrasy.

Padding out of the room, she pulled a throw rug around her shoulders, sat on the couch and reluctantly opened her computer. The recently unleashed woman who was living for the moment reprimanded her.

You have a man in your bed other women would fight you for. Why aren't you in there with him?

Because I've been having so much fun the last three weeks I'm behind with studying.

Pffp!

The pleasure-seeking woman pouted, sat down and crossed her arms as if she was taking part in a sit-in demonstration.

You've still got time.

Claire visualised the calendar and wasn't as convinced. Ever since she'd made that first booty call to Alistair on the Monday night after the ball, they'd met at least three nights a week. Sometimes she called him and sometimes he called her, but either way, they always seemed to end up in her flat rather than his. She was working on not letting that bother her, because this thing they shared was just sex. Did it really matter whose bed they tumbled into?

She'd gone into this affair with her eyes wide open. Her goal was to loosen the reins on her need to control everything in her life and to practise some spontaneity. And it was paying off—she'd definitely improved. Of course, she'd never be as laid-back as Alistair was at work but she was giving him a run for his money outside of it. They were having fun and enjoying each other and that's all it could be. Even if Alistair hadn't been the perennial bachelor everyone knew him to be, she wasn't easy to love.

Claire forced her attention to the podcast about endovascular coiling of an aneurysm, but as the professor's words droned on, her mind drifted. *Why is he a bachelor?* That thought had been popping into her mind more frequently of late, especially after days like yesterday. Alistair had texted her just as she'd finished handing over to Andrew at noon. She and her junior house officer were sharing a Saturday shift and she'd worked the morning. *If you're free, I've got a plan.*

As his plans so often occurred under the cover of darkness and involved them being horizontal, she'd been a bit stunned when he'd picked her up saying, 'I thought it was time you were a tourist.' He'd pointed the car towards the Thames and half an hour later she was standing in a pod on the London Eye. As the cantilevered observation wheel slowly rotated, she'd taken in the awe-inspiring view with her very own tour guide.

'This is amazing. I'm so excited I don't know where to look first.' Her back was snuggled into Alistair's chest and he had his arms wrapped firmly around her.

'Start with the easy and close stuff. There's Big Ben and the House of Commons.' He lifted his right hand and pointed. 'That big block of flats is Buckingham Palace and closer to the river is Horse Guards. That big column—'

'Nelson in Trafalgar Square.'

'Well done. Now cast your eye beyond the bridge and what can you see?'

'Our favourite hotel.' She smiled a secret smile and tilted her head back until he was looking down at her with a sexy gleam in his eyes. A delicious shiver roved through her, setting off tiny fires of desire. 'That was a great night.'

He kissed her and she started to turn into him before she realised they were sharing this pod with strangers. 'It was one of my best nights,' he said throatily before reverting back into tour guide mode. 'Keep your eye on the river and you can see Tower Bridge and the Tower of London.'

She could see their familiar shapes but it was a modern building that caught her eye. 'What's that glass and black steel building?'

'The Gherkin. It's office space and apparently its design style is neo-futuristic.'

Claire laughed. 'Looks more like a rocket to me. I think I prefer the older buildings.'

It was a gloriously sunny day without a skerrick of the famous London fog. She could see for miles. 'Where were the Olympics held?'

'Stratford.' He pointed in the direction.

'And where did you grow up?'

He didn't instantly respond. It seemed to her that a tiny gap had just opened up between their bodies, interrupting what had been one continuous head-to-toe touch.

He eventually said, 'It's further than the eye can see.'

'Show me the general direction.'

The gap closed and his warmth was once again trickling through her without any little darts of cool air. 'My mother lives in Little Wilbraham.' As the pod dropped in height he pointed in the same general direction as Olympic Park. 'It's a tiny little village south-east of Cambridge.'

She remembered him telling her he and his mother had

been required to move house when his father died. 'Has that been home since you were thirteen?'

'I've always considered it more Mother's house than mine.'

'Why?'

Did she remarry? Did you feel usurped? Did you clash with your stepfather?

She found herself hoping he'd reveal something so she could flesh out the vague sketch she'd drawn in her head of his childhood. Currently, he knew a lot more about the child she'd been than she knew of him.

'I suppose it's because I spent more time at school than I ever spent at Rose Cottage,' he said reflectively. 'We always spent part of the summer abroad, and once I'd finished school and went up to Oxford, it become a place I visited on short stays. Home's my flat in Notting Hill.'

The flat she'd never been invited to.

He suddenly spun her around in his arms and gazed down at her, his grey eyes dancing with anticipation. 'Are you ready for your next surprise?'

'There's more?'

'Of course there is. You deserve a London day out and it's my privilege to provide it.'

Her heart suddenly wobbled rather precariously in her chest. She kissed him quickly, forcing herself to concentrate on how warm his lips felt against her own rather than how very close she was to the edge of a cliff and a flashing orange danger zone sign.

Hand in hand, they'd exited the pod and walked back to the car, before re-crossing the Thames and making their way to Hyde Park. Alistair had produced a wicker basket complete with a rug, china plates and cups, champagne glasses, silver cutlery and cotton napkins. They'd picnicked in style by the Serpentine, sipping champagne, feasting on Scottish smoked salmon inside crusty buttered bread and peeled quail eggs and cheese. As they ate, they talked about the books they'd read, music they enjoyed, current political scandals and the many differences yet shared similarities between their two countries.

When Claire was almost certain she couldn't eat another thing, Alistair had delved back into the basket and with a 'Ta-dah!' produced two slices of chocolate and salted caramel layer cake and a Thermos of hot water to make tea. After they'd licked their fingers of every trace of chocolate and were utterly replete, they'd both fallen asleep in the treasured London sunshine.

Of all the times they'd spent together, yesterday afternoon had felt the most like a date. When Alistair had suggested they head home, she'd almost said, 'To your flat?' What had stopped her?

She thought about it and she couldn't get past her gut feeling that the question would have caused awkward tension. She hadn't wanted to ruin what had been a perfectly lovely afternoon. When it came to talking about himself and his family, he seemed surrounded by a taut reserve that doubled as a permanent *Approach with Care* sign. So she hadn't pushed that they go to his flat. Instead, she'd agreed with him that heading home to Bayswater was a great idea.

In the glowing cerise and violet fingers of the setting sun that streamed through the window, they'd made love. *No, you had sex.* Sex was their thing—their selfish, living for the moment thing—when they lost themselves in pure pleasure and in each other. He always started by gently pulling her hair out of her hairband and removing her glasses and then he'd kiss her long and leisurely until every part of her quivered like a taut string under the ministrations of a bow. Each time they had sex, she determined yet again to keep her glasses on because Alistair didn't require soft focus in any shape or form. She ached to see all of his perfection in sharp relief, but the moment he kissed her, she lost all coherent thought, her glasses vanished and she found she didn't care at all.

As darkness had settled over the flat, declaring the day truly gone, and the lights had flickered on both inside and out, he'd pulled on his shirt and she'd prepared herself for his goodbye. Instead, he'd said, 'I make a mean omelette.'

'Do you?' she'd asked, tracing a line from his hand, along his forearm and up towards his shoulder.

'I do.' He captured her arm and pulled her to her feet. 'Come on. You can be my sous chef.'

He hadn't been exaggerating his skills—he did indeed make a fabulous omelette. After eating the savoury delight, they'd cuddled up on the couch—she with her head on his chest, he with his arm looped casually around her—and he'd made stealth moves on her popcorn. The entire afternoon and evening had been scarily normal. Anyone outside on the street who'd paused to peer in through the window would have thought they were a regular couple.

We are so not a couple. Couples share more than sex.

They shared stories, and although she'd told him about her dyslexia and growing up and he'd certainly mentioned that his father had died when he was young and he'd spent his adolescent years at boarding school, there was something in the way he'd revealed the information that told her it was just the tip of the iceberg. And yet he was a kind, generous and thoughtful man, so why was he still a bachelor?

And just like that, she was back to where she'd started and nowhere near close to knowing what made Alistair North tick. *There's a reason for that. And he doesn't want you to know it.*

This thing they shared was nothing more than a hedonistic fling. She knew she was just another woman in a long line with many before her and just as likely many more after.

It's fine. I'm using him to practise being spontaneous and impetuous.

Then why do you want to see his flat? Why do you want to know where the estate with the walled garden is? Where he spent his childhood? Why do you want to discover the date of his birthday and if he's a good son to his mother?

I don't want that. I only want his body.

A sound not dissimilar to hysterical laughter sounded faintly in her mind and she shoved the ear buds harder into her ears. She restarted the podcast and this time she listened intently to the lecturer as if he was the only voice in the world.

An hour later she felt a tap on her shoulder and she glanced up to see Alistair standing behind the couch, freshly showered and fully dressed. She pressed pause on the podcast as a sigh of disappointment rumbled through her. She'd have loved him to be padding around her flat wearing nothing more than a towel looped low on his hips so she could watch the play of bunching muscles dancing under his skin. But the man was always pulling a shirt on and covering up.

'Good morning.' With a sexy smile, he bent down and kissed her full on the mouth. 'You're up early for a Sunday.'

The shimmers and tingles from his kiss spun through her, making her feel far more alive and happy than she could remember. 'Exams are less than six months away.'

A slight frown pulled down his brows. 'I've been distracting you.'

She pressed her hand against his cheek. 'In the best possible way.'

He kissed her again but this time it was devoid of the usual intoxicating heat. Instead, it was infused with gentleness and something else she couldn't place. 'I'll leave you to get on with it.'

Despite knowing that she needed to spend the day studying, she was filled with a disproportionate sense of despondency. She was about to say, 'Thanks for yesterday,' when he said, 'I'll go and grab some fresh clothes and return with pastries and coffee from Tony's. Then I'll quiz you on...' He squinted down at her screen.

'Aneurysms.' Somehow, she managed to pluck the word out of her stunned mind.

He nodded, his face full of empathy. 'Tricky buggers, aneurysms.' Then he kissed her on the top of her head and said, 'Back soon,' before disappearing out the door.

As it clicked shut behind him, she stared at it, trying to make sense of what had just happened. Alistair had offered to help her study.

So? Nothing odd or unusual about that. He's a neuro-surgeon.

But there was everything odd and unusual about it. Consultants didn't help their registrars study—that wasn't in the job description.

Neither was having sex.

The sex has nothing to do with work.

And it didn't. They'd both kept the two utterly separate. During work hours they didn't text or call each other and when they were alone they were too focused on enjoying each other to talk about work. But this offer to help her study came on the back of yesterday's generosity and thoughtfulness. It made her heart lurch dangerously close to the rickety safety rail balanced on the crumbling precipice.

If she wasn't careful, she was at very great risk of falling in love with Alistair North. Not only wasn't it part of the plan, it was exceedingly hazardous. Loving Alistair wasn't an option because she risked far more than just her job—she risked her heart.

As she recommenced the podcast yet again, the droning voice of the professor seemed to whisper, *It's too late.*

* * *

Alistair stood at the scrub sinks looking out through the glass and saw the broad back of Matthew McGrory bent over a trolley. As the plastic surgeon straightened and the porter wheeled the patient into the operating theatre, Alistair glimpsed the serious burn to the child's face.

Matthew then came barrelling through the double doors, his athletic build making short shrift of the plastic doors. 'Hello, Alistair,' he said in his gentle Irish brogue so at odds with his rugby player bulk.

'That burn looks nasty,' Alistair said as he lathered up his arms. 'How did it happen?'

'He's one of the Westbourne Primary School kids. Name's Simon Bennett.' Matthew flicked the taps on with his elbows. 'Poor bloody kid. It's tough enough that his parents' drug habit came ahead of him and that he's basically growing up in foster care, without the added burden of disfigurement by a facial burn.'

'You using spray-on skin?'

He nodded. 'Aye. It's phenomenal and that burn is much improved. Today I'm debriding an infection on his arm. It's best done in theatre. Rupert gives him a light GA and it minimises his pain.'

'The fallout of that fire's still haunting us,' Alistair said, thinking of Ryan.

'It is,' Matthew said quietly, 'but it also proved how much the castle's needed here in central London.' He rinsed off his arms. 'By the way, the fundraising committee owes you a debt of thanks. It was good of you to let Victoria sell off every part of your night to raise money.'

'No problem.'

'Did you at least meet someone you liked? Someone to have fun with?'

Alistair immediately thought of Claire and how much fun they'd had—were still having. He opened his mouth to give the usual quip—a standard shared between two men who have no desire to be tied down—but the words stuck in his throat. He put it down to his promise to Claire to keep their affair secret and out of the hospital.

'Mr North,' a nurse interrupted. 'Patient's under and we're ready when you are.'

'On my way,' he said, stepping back from the sink with both arms raised and a silent vote of thanks to the nurse.

'No rest for the wicked, eh?' Matt said, a friendly glint in his eyes.

None indeed.

Claire paced outside the lecture theatre, clutching her notes and the accompanying USB stick that held her presentation. As she walked, she concentrated on keeping the rolling nausea at bay. The day she'd dreaded had arrived and she was about to stand up in front of her peers and their consultants.

'I've arranged for us to present first,' Alistair had said to her two days ago at the end of a long operating list. 'After all, neurosurgery's the elite surgery and deserves top billing.' What he didn't say, but was clearly implied was, 'That way you get the presentation over and done with early and you can relax and enjoy the others.'

His discretion and kindness had just about undone her. He knew how much standing up in front of people terrified her and he'd done his best to try and minimise her trauma. It had taken everything she had not to throw her arms around him there and then in front of the theatre staff and shower him in kisses of gratitude. Instead, she'd said a brisk, 'Sounds like a plan,' from behind her surgical mask and hoped he saw her thanks clear in her eyes.

His eyes had twinkled as he'd said, 'Don't be late, Mitchell.'

The scrub nurse had laughed. 'Alistair, that's the pot

calling the kettle black. You could take a leaf or ten out of Claire's book.'

Andrew Bailey, surrounded by a crowd of other junior house officers, walked past Claire and gave her the double thumbs up. He was clueless to the fact she was working very hard on keeping from throwing up the piece of toast and black tea she'd only half managed to finish at breakfast. Despite having committed the presentation to memory, she'd been up since five a.m., going over it *one more time* at least five times more.

She checked her watch. Where was Alistair? *Please don't be late today. Please.* The previously full corridor was now empty as everyone had entered the lecture theatre to take their seats. The toast hit the back of her throat and she gagged, forcing it back down.

What was wrong with her? This was even worse than the last time she'd had to present in Australia. Back there, no one had known about her dyslexia and she'd not only laboured under keeping it a secret, she hadn't received any support from her consultant. Today she was secure in the knowledge of Alistair's respect and understanding and yet she was desperately close to throwing up. It didn't make any sense. Then again, nerves rarely did.

Closing her eyes, she tried to focus on long, slow deep breaths so she could harness some desperately needed calm.

'Are you ready, Claire?' Alistair's voice sounded quietly behind her.

Her eyes flew open and she spun around as frustration and relief tangoed fast in her veins. 'You're late!'

He checked his watch. 'I'm a minute early.'

'A minute isn't early,' she heard herself screech. 'It's barely on time.'

He raised his brows. 'Have you ever known me to be a minute early?'

Against the noise of her thundering heart booming in

her ears and the agitation of her mind, she clearly heard, *No, not once*. He'd made a huge effort for her. Her heart lurched and she completely let go of the pretence that she liked him but didn't love him. It streamed away like the rush and gurgle of bath water racing down the drain. When Alistair made gestures like helping her study and arriving early, it was impossible not to feel her love for him fill up her heart and spill over into her soul.

Joy and heartache collided, crashing together in her chest. *I truly love him.*

'However, if you're going to stand here arguing the point with me, we will be late,' he said with envious ease, infuriating logic and absolutely no idea of her inner turmoil.

Her unwise love for him mixed in with her fear of public speaking, spinning her stomach like a tumble dryer. 'I think I'm going to throw up.'

'Nonsense, you're going to be fine,' he said with British exactitude. 'You're prepared. You know the work inside out, and if the worst happens, which it won't, I'm right there beside you.' He stretched out his arm towards the door and gave her a reassuring smile. 'Shall we go in and dazzle with them our findings?'

Claire didn't know if she was happy or sad that the symposium was over. Alistair, true to his word, had stood next to her but there'd been no need for him to step in—she hadn't faltered once. On Alistair's flippant but sound advice, she'd pictured the audience naked and it had helped. Whether it was that, her preparation, Alistair's presence or a combination of the three, it had carried her past her terror.

For the rest of the day, she'd floated on a sea of praise. Robyn Kelly, the head of surgery, had sought her out at lunch to congratulate her and strongly urged her to submit the paper for consideration at the international neurosurgery conference. Andrew had pumped her hand so enthu-

siastically that her shoulder still ached and she'd overheard
Dominic MacBride telling Alistair that he wished his specialist registrar was as switched on as Claire.

Her boss had quipped, 'Of course she's brilliant. I taught
her.' The man she loved had said quietly to her during the
applause, 'Well done. We'll celebrate tonight.'

It was the first time he'd ever referenced their affair at
work and rather than sending rafts of anxiety thudding
through her, a warm glow of anticipation spread instead.
When she stacked up all the little acts of caring he'd shown
her over the past weeks, was his breech of their pact part of
a growing affection for her? She hugged the thought tight as
she closed her heart and mind to the warning. *He's known
as the playboy surgeon for a reason.*

The afternoon sped by quickly with a full outpatients'
clinic and now it was six in the evening. She'd called by
Koala Ward to check for any outstanding IV orders and
medication updates, and thankfully all was quiet. Her stomach rumbled, the noise reminding her that she'd not really
eaten very much all day. This morning's nauseous nerves
had killed her appetite and most of lunchtime had been
spent fielding congratulations, leaving no time to eat. She'd
munched on an apple during the dash to outpatients. It
wasn't surprising she was now famished.

As she was rostered on until nine, she needed to stay
close to the hospital but the thought of the cafeteria food
suddenly made her feel queasy. Decision made, she grabbed
her bag and said to Morag, 'I'm just popping over to the
Frog and Peach to grab some dinner.'

'I'm glad you're accepting the house officers' invitation.'
The older woman gave her a motherly smile. 'There's more
to life than work, Claire.'

'I'm a specialist registrar with exams looming,' she said
with a wry smile. 'There is no life outside of work.' But as
she spoke the words, she knew them to be a lie. Over the

last few weeks, she'd most definitely had a life outside of the hospital. 'Page me if you need me.'

'I'm sure we'll cope without you for half an hour or so. I recommend the pulled pork nachos. They serve it with their famous pale ale barbecue sauce. It's delicious.'

'Thanks for the tip.' She didn't bother to mention that Andrew had invited her for a drink at the end of her shift, not dinner. Although she appreciated the offer, the moment she could get away for the night she was heading straight home.

Home to Alistair. As she crossed the road to the pub, she felt the grin of pleasure stretch across her face and her body leap in anticipation. He'd messaged her about a late supper featuring chocolate sauce. As much as she liked licking chocolate sauce from the top of ice cream and cake, she had a fervent desire to lick rich, dark chocolate sauce off Alistair.

Her cheeks immediately heated at the thought and she laughed. Six months ago, she could never have imagined herself being so sexually adventurous but practising being spontaneous was paying off in spades. *It's not that. It's Alistair.* And she knew it to be the truth. She'd had boyfriends before and there'd been the year with Michael, but no one had ever made her feel as accepted, safe and loved as Alistair. It meant she had no need to hold anything back and as a result she'd thrown herself heart and soul into this affair. She was utterly and deliciously in love.

Earlier in the day when she'd realised she loved him, gut wrenching worry had pulled at her, but not now. She'd gained an odd sort of peace in the knowledge that she loved him. Instead of trying to plan and control everything, instead of telling him how she felt or trying to find out if he felt the same way, she was just going to savour the feeling and the evening. After all, what did Alistair always say? Live every day as if it's your last.

The pub was a glorious historic building that had been in continuous operation since being built in 1823. Claire always laughed when she was told it was a young pub—it was still older than the oldest pubs at home. In typical English style it featured dark wooden panelling, ambient lighting, comfortable chesterfield couches and a dartboard. The noise from the Thursday night crowd came out to meet her as she stepped across the threshold and much of it was emanating from a spirited game of darts between the junior house officers and the hospital porters. Not surprisingly, the porters were winning.

She was depositing her dripping umbrella in the umbrella bin when a waitress walked past balancing four plates of delicious-looking food. She breathed in the aroma of meat, battered fish, chicken and cabbage and her stomach suddenly lurched, vanquishing her hunger. She gagged and her hand flew to her mouth. She gulped in air but the kitchen door opened again and this time the sight of the food had her turning and dashing into the ladies'.

A rotund woman in her forties glanced up from applying lipstick. 'You all right, love? You look a bit peaky.'

Claire didn't dare open her mouth until she was inside the cubicle. When she did, her stomach heaved its meagre contents up into the bowl. When there was nothing left to vomit, she flushed the toilet, closed the lid and then sat shakily on the closed seat, feeling sweat beading on her top lip and under her arms. The rest of her shivered.

A tap came on the door. 'You all right, love?'

Claire raised her head from her elbow-propped hands. 'I will be. Thanks for asking.'

'Was it sumfink you ate? The food 'ere's usually top-notch.'

'I've hardly eaten anything today,' she said, thinking about this morning as she opened the door of the stall. 'I woke up feeling nauseous but that was because I was nervous about work.' She flicked on the taps and splashed her face with water.

'I think it's probably more than just nerves, love. Either you've got a bug or a baby.' The woman laughed as she checked her hair in the mirror. 'Every time I was pregnant, the smell of fried food and cabbage always did me in.'

'I can't possibly be pregnant,' she said, thinking how she and Alistair had always used condoms.

The woman handed her some paper towels and her expression held a worldly air. 'Unless you've 'ad your tubes tied, love, or you're not getting any, there's always a chance of being up the duff. My old man 'ad the snip and nine months later I 'ad me third. At least you can find out fast these days. There's a pharmacy across the road.' With a final check in the mirror, she turned and walked back into the pub.

Claire stared at herself in the mirror. A pale face with dark rings under her eyes stared back. Surely she'd just picked up a bug? She worked with children and earlier in the week there'd been a minor outbreak of gastro on the ward. Even with best practice of hand washing, it only took one child to sneeze or cough on her to transfer the infection. That had to be the culprit of the nausea and vomiting. She couldn't possibly be pregnant—she'd had a period just a couple of weeks ago.

You had a light period.

I've been burning the candle at both ends.

A flutter of panic filled her and she forced it down. She was being ridiculous and letting an off-the-cuff comment by a stranger put the wind up her. Feeling sick and off-colour all day had a perfectly reasonable explanation. She was understandably tired because she hadn't slept well worrying about the presentation. This morning's nausea had been stress and she'd vomited just now because she was overhungry and exhausted. Or she'd picked up a virus. Either way, she was *not* pregnant.

However, the pharmacy the woman mentioned would sell jellybeans and electrolyte solution, both of which were good for gastro. She left the bathroom and retrieved her umbrella. Just as she stepped back out into the rain her phone buzzed with Koala Ward's number. Sam Riccardo was fitting. The jellybeans would have to wait.

CHAPTER TEN

CLAIRE LAY IN the dark bedroom snuggled up with Alistair in a languid fog of bliss. The champagne he'd bought sat unopened in the fridge next to the untouched celebration cake and the chocolate sauce. It wasn't that she didn't appreciate his efforts—she did, very much indeed. It was just that once she'd stepped into the flat, into his arms and he'd told her how amazing she'd been this morning before proceeding to nuzzle her neck and tell her the things he'd been wanting to do with her all day, they'd both lost interest in the food and the drink.

Her phone rang, bringing reality back into the room. With a groan, she rolled over to the bedside table and picked up the glowing device. 'It's the hospital.'

'I thought you were off-duty?' Alistair stroked her hair.

'I am.' She swiped the screen, silencing the ring tone. 'Claire Mitchell.'

'It's Andrew.' Her junior house officer's voice came down the line sounding decidedly shaky.

'You sound dreadful. What's up?'

'I've got a temperature and I've been throwing up for an hour. I need to go home but I'm on call tonight. I've rung three other people but two of them have the same bug and the other is covering for one of them. My patients are stable but can you cover if needed?'

Gastro. Andrew has gastro. She gave herself a virtual high five. 'Sure. Tell the ward and the switchboard and then go home.'

'Sorry, Claire.' He made a gagging sound. 'Got to go.'

He rang off abruptly, and although Claire knew she should be sympathetic, she started to laugh. It bubbled up on a wave of deliverance, and although she tried to stop it, that only seemed to intensify the feeling. Tears streamed down her cheeks, her belly tightened and her whole body shook as she was utterly consumed by amusement and abject relief.

Alistair gave her a bemused smile before rolling her under him. His warm grey eyes stared down at her. 'What's so funny?'

'Andrew's got gastro.'

He frowned at her, his expression confused. 'And that's funny how?'

She wiped her cheeks on the sheet and tried to curb her laughter. 'It's not funny for him.'

'But it is for you?'

She smiled up at him, eager to share the joke. 'I threw up tonight at the Frog and Peach and a random woman in the bathroom asked me if I was pregnant. Of course I knew the suggestion was ridiculous but just for a short time I was a little rattled. But Andrew has gastro and quite a few other castle staff have it too. So you can see why it's funny.'

She expected him to laugh with her and then tease her about being obsessive but instead his face tightened along with the rest of his body. He rolled away from her.

'I don't think the idea of you being pregnant is funny in any shape or form.'

She gave a wry smile. 'It was really more like a momentary possibility than an idea.'

'Jeez, Claire.' He suddenly grabbed his shirt, pulling it on jerkily before he reached out and switched on the lamp.

'That's semantics. You know that both scenarios would be a total disaster.'

Would it? A tiny part of her thought being pregnant might be the most wonderful thing to ever happen to her. Her practical side conceded that a pregnancy right now wouldn't be ideal but there was something in the aristocratic way he'd said 'disaster' that made her spine tingle.

'We're two adults having sex, Alistair. Contraception has been known to fail. Although we both know it's small, there's always an inherent risk.' She gave a light laugh. 'You're the one who's always saying not everything in life can be planned.'

He swung his feet to the floor. 'Children are the one exception.'

For someone who was impetuous, it seemed an odd thing to say. She sat up and pressed her hand gently against his back. 'But you're so great with kids. I'd like to think that if we'd had an accident and I was actually pregnant, we'd be a team.'

He lurched abruptly to his feet, moving away from her so quickly that her hand was left hanging in the air. 'A team? As in parents?' Incredulity dripped from the words, landing on her like scalding water and blistering her skin. He shook his head so hard that strands of his thick hair rose off his head. 'No. That is *never* going to happen.'

His emphatic words struck her with the biting sting of an open-handed slap and her heart cramped so tightly it was hard to breathe. Michael's words, which had faded to silence over the last few weeks, roared back loudly and in surround sound. *You're too hard to love, Claire.*

'I see,' she said grimly, feeling the sudden need to cover up. Pulling on her pyjamas, she stood, pointing a shaking finger at him accusingly. 'So basically, I'm good enough for you to screw but I'm not good enough to be the mother of your children.'

He flinched and his face pulled into a grimace. 'I didn't say that. Don't put words in my mouth.'

'I'll just use the ones you inferred, then, shall I?'

'Claire.' His usually tender voice now spoke her name on a warning growl.

'Fine,' she said bitterly, hugging herself to try and stop the shaking. To try and silence the insidious voice of relationships past. 'Tell me exactly what it is that you're saying.'

He sighed, the sound patronisingly reasonable. It was the same sound people used when they believed they were dealing with a difficult person. 'Why are we arguing about a hypothetical situation? You're not even pregnant.'

Because you started it. The common childhood expression burst into her brain but the feelings behind it were anything but childish. 'Because if I was pregnant, we'd need to have this conversation.'

'This is crazy, Claire. It's all about *ifs* and *buts* and it's not worth our time.'

But suddenly it was very much worth her time because she'd glimpsed something that scared her. 'What if I was pregnant?'

'You're not.' The words quivered with barely leashed restraint.

'No, but what if I was?' She scanned his face, trying to read it. 'What would you say?'

He suddenly looked wary. 'Would it matter?'

'Of course it would matter.'

He stared at her as if she was someone he didn't recognise. 'Are you telling me that if you were pregnant, you'd want to keep it?'

It. The pronoun battered her like a barrage of needles piercing her skin with sharp and biting stings. How could one tiny word emote so much? How could two innocuous letters combined draw such a precise line in the sand and place them clearly on opposite sides? To her, a pregnancy was a longed-for baby and the reactivation of a dream she'd believed to be covered in dust. To him, it was just an amorphous *it*.

'Of course I'd want to keep it.'

Horror and bewilderment streaked across his face. 'Why?'

She didn't have to think twice. 'Because it would be our child. Because I love you.'

He went deathly still and his handsome face lost its healthy colour, leaving behind a tinge of yellowy-green. 'You don't love me, Claire.'

The softly spoken words fell like the blow of a hammer. They shattered any remaining delusional daydreams she may have been clinging to and they shattered her heart. 'I think what you meant to say was that *you* don't love me.'

He started pacing jerkily around the small room. 'This thing we've been sharing is fun, Claire. It's not love.'

She wasn't prepared to lie. 'For me it's been both.'

His hand tore through his hair and his face crumpled. 'Good God, Claire. No.'

She hated the crushing waves of despair that rolled in on her, bringing with them all the reminders that no matter what she did, or how hard she tried, it was never enough to be loved. Her breath came in short jerky pulls and she felt as if she was folding in on herself and collapsing down into a dark pit of hopelessness.

Her legs trembled like jelly to the point she reached out to the wall for support, but then her knees suddenly locked. Like a life preserver being thrown from a ship to a drowning person in a choppy sea, she saw and heard a collage of moments spent with Alistair.

You're a very good neurosurgeon.

It's your decision. If you have any doubts at all…

Don't believe all the hospital gossip, Claire.

Are you okay?

I think that spontaneous woman's always been very much a part of you.

I'm right there beside you.

You deserve a London day out and it's my privilege to provide it.

It was one of my best nights.

Her mouth dried in shock. She may not have a vast experience of men, but she'd lived with Michael. During their year together all he'd done was find fault with her in so many ways and, oh, how he'd loved to tell her. She worked too much. She studied too much. Her friends were boring. She micromanaged their lives. She was inflexible. She stifled him with her need to control every minute detail. The list had gone on and on.

Right there and then she realised with the clarity of a fine-cut diamond that Michael had only considered their relationship in terms of himself. None of it had been about her, her feelings, her wants or her needs. Yet in a few short weeks, Alistair had considered her and cared for her in more ways than Michael had managed in a year.

Did Alistair love her but not recognise what he felt as love?

The thought snuck in and took hold, sending down a deep and anchoring root. If that was the case and she took her hurt and walked away now just to avoid the possibility of further pain, she might be abandoning an opportunity for happiness.

And if he doesn't love you?

Isn't it better to have tried and failed than to never have tried at all?

Yes. No. I'm scared.

It can't be worse than it is already. It might even be better. Fight for him. Open his eyes.

Tugging at the base of her pyjama top, she sucked in a deep breath. 'Actually, Alistair, the answer is yes. I do love you. I didn't intend to fall in love and the fact that I have lies squarely at your feet.'

'What?'

'You've only got yourself to blame.'

Bewilderment hovered over every part of his lean frame. 'What the hell are you talking about?'

She mustered an attempt at a smile. 'You've been so kind to me. You care.'

'Well, of course I bloody well care.' He agitatedly rubbed his stubble-covered jaw with his palm. 'I care for every woman that I date. That doesn't mean I've loved any of them. It doesn't mean that I love you.'

Her armour pinged with the hit but she pressed on. 'Will the world end if you admit that you love me?'

'Look, Claire,' he said in a voice she'd heard him use with junior staff at the hospital. 'You've got this all wrong. Somehow you've tangled up professional courtesy and mentoring with the fun we've been having. I can assure you, none of it is love.'

A distance she'd not seen before took up residence in his eyes. 'I'm not looking for love, Claire. I thought we were both very clear on that topic from the start. I've got a great career and a good life. I've got a flat in Notting Hill, a house in Provence and I can do what I want when I please.'

She pushed her glasses up her nose and stared him down. 'You forgot to mention the German sports car.'

'Exactly,' he said as if he thought she was being helpful. 'It's not designed for a baby seat. When you add up everything I have, why would I want to tie myself down by getting married and becoming a father?'

You're thirty-nine. Why wouldn't you want to?

'It's an impressive list of possessions,' she said, trying to sound calm, when in reality desperation was clawing at her. 'There's just one flaw with your argument. Your job, your houses and your car won't love you like a family.'

His eyes immediately darkened to the steely colour of storm clouds bursting with rain and tinged with the red of outback dust. 'Like your family loved you?'

The attack was swift and lethal but as the pain seared her she somehow scrambled to tell the truth. 'My parents loved me, Alistair. They just didn't know how to help me.'

He grunted as if the explanation made no difference. Suddenly it was her turn to see everything through a red haze. 'I think that comment has far more to do with you than with me. Your father died when you were at a vulnerable age and your mother packed you off to boarding school. Is that love?'

'Don't you dare presume to think you know anything about me and my family.'

Anger radiated off him with the ferocity of a bushfire and she almost raised her hands to try and ward off the scorching heat. His reaction spoke volumes and she'd stake her life she was close to whatever it was that had him placing possessions ahead of people. 'The reason I don't know anything is because you won't tell me,' she said as calmly as she could. She reached for his arm. 'You helped me, Alistair. You listened and you didn't judge. Let me return the favour. Please let me help you.'

He spun away from her, breaking their touch. 'I don't need any help. Unlike you, there's nothing wrong with me.'

Visceral pain ripped into her, stealing her breath and spinning the room. The past tried to rise up and consume her but it stalled. Without a shadow of a doubt, the man who'd just hurt her so comprehensively wasn't the man she knew and loved. That man had always respected her. He'd given her opportunities and choices. Out of the work environment they were equals, so what the hell was going on now?

He's hurting.

But exactly what was hurting him and why, she had

no idea at all. Whatever it was, it was old and gnarly with deeply tangled roots. It lived inside him, and the more she pushed to get close, the more it would lash out and slice her until all that was left of her was a bleeding mess of heartache and pain. She'd be the one left suffering.

Self-preservation knotted inside her. She'd worked too hard to allow him to destroy her fledging self-confidence and the irony of that thought wasn't lost on her. It had been Alistair's acceptance of her that had taught her to value herself. She jutted her chin. 'I never took you for a coward, Alistair.'

As he pulled on his trousers and slipped his feet into his shoes, his mouth tugged down at the edges, thinning into a hard line. It accentuated his cheekbones, making them blade-sharp in his face. 'I was perfectly fine before I met you, Claire. I'll be perfectly fine when I walk out this door.'

He quickly grabbed his wallet, phone and car fob before storming past her. 'Of all the women I've ever fooled around with, I thought you were the one who truly understood because you put work ahead of everything. Us having sex was all about you learning to be spontaneous and having some hard-earned fun.' He laughed bitterly. 'And you were doing so well. I thought you were more like me after all.'

She jerked her chin high. 'You mean emotionally shutdown and hiding behind a collection of possessions?'

He threw her a filthy look, which she met head-on and batted straight back at him. 'Believe me,' she said cuttingly, 'I'm not that sad.'

Stalking to her front door he hauled it open. In the brief moment before he slammed it shut, the sound of tyres squelching on a wet road and the distant toot of a train drifted into the flat—the sounds of a perfectly normal London night. Only none of this came close to normal. This was the end of friendship, hopes and dreams.

The door closed with a thwack and a thick wave of silence rolled inside, enveloping her. Alistair was gone. He'd left her without so much as a backwards glance. He'd also left her love—abandoning it casually on the couch, on the bed and on every surface in the flat. It lingered in the air she breathed and the sense of loss overwhelmed her. She sank to the floor and let her tears flow.

'Morag!' Alistair roared through the closed door of the unit manager's office. His day was going to hell in a hand basket and it wasn't even ten o'clock in the morning.

Things went to hell last night.

But he wasn't spending any more time thinking about how things between him and Claire had gone pear-shaped so quickly and so unexpectedly. He'd spent the dark wee hours consumed by it, trying to work out how he'd missed the telltale signs. Good God, he had a thesis in detecting signs from women wanting marriage and babies but he had missed the clues. Claire was just like all women and she wanted what he couldn't give her. 'Morag!'

Her dark-haired head appeared around the door thirty seconds later. 'Did it slip your mind that you can walk the twelve steps from here to the nurses' station if you wish to speak with me?'

'Humph,' he grunted as he opened a filing cabinet drawer. 'I'm going to France.'

Surprise crossed her face. 'When?'

An hour ago. 'Tonight if I can get a booking on the Eurostar. Where the hell are the leave forms?'

Morag walked calmly into the office, smoothed her uniform and sat down. 'Alistair, didn't you read the memo from the board?'

He riffled through the neatly labelled manila folders. 'Which one? They've been coming in thick and fast ever since the proposed merger with Riverside.'

'The one where they cancelled all leave requests because we've barely got enough staff to keep operating as it is.'

He didn't care about any of that. He had to get out of the castle and he had to get out now. He needed the space and serenity that Provence always offered him. He needed to find his equilibrium. He desperately needed to find the solid foundations he'd rebuilt his life on after almost losing it five years ago. 'Surely that doesn't include consultants.'

She gave him a pitying smile. 'I know it's a rarefied atmosphere up there at the top of the tree, but this time you have to slum it down here with the rest of us. The board isn't paying for annual leave and nor is it paying for covering staff. France will have to wait until your next three-day weekend.'

I can do what I want when I please. His haughty statement from last night came back to bite him. *You know your job never allows you to take off at a minute's notice. Your weekends in France are blocked out at the start of each year.*

He closed his eyes to the spotlight on the fact he did plan some things. 'If the board's not spending any money, then what about this rumour that Robyn's flying in some hotshot Italian paediatrician?'

'The duke?' Morag grinned. 'Apparently they've been good friends since medical school. He's coming as a PR favour to Robyn and using his own coin.'

He sighed, seeing his out closing fast.

'Besides,' Morag continued, 'even if the board was approving leave you couldn't go today. Both Bailey and Mitchell are down with gastro along with three of my nurses.'

Claire's not in. He hated the relief that he didn't have to face her today. Hell, he shouldn't need to feel relief. She'd been the one to move the goalposts on him and change every single rule of their game. If she hadn't done that, if she hadn't pushed him about babies and about his family, then he wouldn't have needed to speak. He wouldn't have said the unforgivably cruel thing to her that fear had driven out of him.

Hell, he could still see her beautiful but tortured face every time he closed his eyes. It made him sick to his stomach. He wanted to apologise to her but if he did she'd expect an explanation from him as to why he'd said what he said. That would immediately take them back to square one, more arguing and even more distress. He'd survive but he wasn't sure she would. He didn't want to risk it. He couldn't bear to hurt her all over again.

No, it was better to say nothing and make last night the clean break. She'd nurse her pain into a fulminating rage towards him, which would grow into hatred and loathing. The result would be abhorrence, which would keep her far, far away from him. He expected her letter of resignation to arrive in his in-box by the end of the working day. All in all, it was the best possible outcome for both of them. With his condition and his family history, he couldn't offer her marriage and babies and she deserved to be free to find someone who could.

His mind threw up a picture of a faceless man and a flash of bright green light burst behind his eyes. He squeezed them shut against blinding pain and automatically rubbed his temples with his forefingers.

'Is there anything I can help with, Alistair?' Morag asked, her usually taciturn tone softening.

A new heart. 'No. There's nothing for it but to get out there and be junior house officer, registrar and consultant all rolled into one.'

'Be extra meticulous with hand washing,' Morag said, following him onto the ward. 'We don't need anyone else getting this bug.'

CHAPTER ELEVEN

CLAIRE MUNCHED ON dry biscuits and reread a list she'd started at three a.m. when she hadn't been able to sleep. That had been twelve hours ago and no matter which way she came at it, she couldn't get the list to clearly state what she willed it to. What she wanted more than anything was to jump online and book a flight back home to Australia. She wanted to put seventeen thousand kilometres between her and Alistair and the constant reminder that he didn't love her. She tried to find some reassurance in the fact he didn't love someone else either, but that only made her feel desperately sad for him. For some reason he seemed hell-bent on not allowing himself to love anyone.

The thought of spending another three months working side by side with him most days made it hard to breathe but the thought of giving up her scholarship and returning home a failure was worse. She'd fought so hard for the scholarship and the prestige that went with it, and besides, she still had things to learn. Trying to explain to her family why she'd given up London when she'd talked excitedly about it for months would take more energy than she could muster. Trying to talk her way around the fact she'd left the tutelage of Mr Alistair North at job interviews back in Australia would be equally hard. The panel would give her uneasy looks and ask the hard question, 'Why, when you were so close to qualifying, did you throw this opportunity away?'

When she heard the truth embedded in the words—*I'm putting a broken heart ahead of my career*—she knew what she had to do. Right now, in the detritus of her personal life, her career was the only thing she had left to hold on to and guide her. The scholarship lasted ninety more days, less if she subtracted her rostered days off. She sipped her lemon and ginger tea and sat a little straighter. She could do this. She would do this. In fact, she'd start as soon as she stopped throwing up.

Actually, she hadn't thrown up since last night, and although she'd felt a little nauseous this morning, it had passed by ten and she'd wolfed down a big breakfast. She'd be back at work bright and early in the morning but meanwhile she'd check her roster and count the actual number of days she had left at the castle. Opening her calendar on her computer she looked at the whole year displayed in four neat columns. Blue denoted today, green was days off, yellow was payday, purple was when her rent was due each month, brown was the fast approaching date of her exams and red was her period.

All of it made for a heartening and colourful display that was balm to an organised person's soul. Just glancing at the planner made her feel secure and slightly more in control. Who needed spontaneity? There was no pattern to it, which by its nature was not at all reassuring. Cross-referencing with her roster, she clicked her mouse and added in her days off for the next six weeks.

Job done, she sat back and enjoyed seeing the patterns all the different dots created. She suddenly lurched forward closer to the screen and adjusted her glasses, blinking at a red dot. Her period had been due on the tenth. She knew for a fact it hadn't come on that date. It had come earlier but she'd been too busy being spontaneous to realise quite how early it had come.

And it was very light.

Her stomach rolled. *Implantation bleed.* The thought she'd dismissed so easily yesterday was a lot harder to shift today. Was what she thought was a light dose of gastro not gastro at all? Was she pregnant? Was what would constitute Alistair's disaster and her not unwelcome surprise a reality?

Or not. It wasn't like her period was always clockwork regular. There'd been times when it was a bit hit and miss, and after all, she'd moved continents and was working long hours in a stressful job. Plus, they'd always used condoms and to her knowledge no condom had broken.

There was that one time you straddled him before the condom was on.

She bit her lip. Was that all it took?

Her contraceptive lectures reverberated in her mind. *Oh, yes, it actually took less.* She tasted blood. If she was pregnant, Alistair had made it very clear to her that he didn't want to have a child with her.

It's not you, she promptly reminded herself, determined not to let past beliefs pull her down. She knew that all the way to her soul. Alistair didn't want to have a child with anyone. *So why does he work with kids?* So often, people who didn't want children were uncomfortable around them and avoided them as much as possible. Alistair not only worked with them, he was relaxed around them and he had the special skill of being able to calm a sick and terrified child. He'd ace fatherhood so why didn't he want children?

No answer was obvious and none made any sense. She couldn't help but wonder if all of it was connected to losing his father. She was intimately acquainted with childhood beliefs getting tangled up in adult lives and skewing them. Alistair had helped her see that in her own situation but he wasn't allowing her to help him. He refused to let anyone get close enough to offer any insight.

She was under no illusions. The reality was that if she were pregnant, she'd be embarking on the difficult but rewarding path of a single, working mother.

And if you're not pregnant?

I'll be relieved.

An empty feeling ringed with sadness tumbled through her, leaving an ache everywhere it touched. She gave herself a shake. Of course she'd be relieved if she wasn't pregnant. She had to be, didn't she?

'Argh!' The sound reverberated around the flat. There were too many *what-ifs* on both sides of the argument. There was only one definitive way to end this constant circular process and find out for certain if she was pregnant or not. Grabbing her phone, her keys and her handbag, she dashed out of the flat.

Yesterday, Alistair had welcomed the extra workload generated by Bailey and Cla—Mitchell's absence as it meant he hadn't had to think about anything other than work. Not that he needed to think about anything other than work right now, he reminded himself crossly, swiping the air savagely as he played solo virtual tennis in the quiet Koala Ward's lounge.

He'd spent the evening playing with the kids but they were all tucked up in bed now having been hustled away by the night nurse who liked the order of routine. He should have gone home then but the thought of an empty flat had kept him in the lounge playing game after game. He was determined to beat the machine. Determined to get thoughts of Claire out of his head.

Damn it, she wasn't the first woman he'd broken up with. She wouldn't be the last.

Other breakups didn't touch you. This one has.

He refused to acknowledge that. Hell, he'd dated other women for longer than he'd dated Claire so he had no reason to be affected by this breakup. The two of them wanted different things out of life. She had a choice in wanting a family, but he did not. End of story. Move on. Find someone else to have fun with. It wasn't like there weren't plenty of candidates to fill Claire's place.

Just this morning, he'd been called down to do a consult in the cardiothoracic ward, and while he was trying to locate the child in question, he'd come across Maddie, the pretty and chatty physiotherapist he'd sat next to at the ball. She was working with Penelope, the cute little girl with the sunny disposition who'd been in and out of hospital all her life. She'd become one of the cute-as-a-button, tug-at-the-heartstrings faces of sick children in the *Save Paddington's* campaign. Her photo, along with others, was on posters and billboards all around town.

Penelope, who was wearing a pink tutu, lay with her head and chest tilted downwards while Maddie's cupped hands postured and percussed her patient's chest, loosening mucous and easing the child's breathing.

'Hello,' Penelope said with a big smile. 'You're not one of my doctors.'

He smiled at her precociousness. 'I'm Alistair. I'm a brain doctor.'

The child considered this. 'My brain works really well. It's my heart and lungs that don't work so good.'

'Hello, Alistair,' Maddie had said with a wide smile as if she was protecting him from a difficult reply. 'Where have you been hiding lately? I haven't seen you since you stole my bread roll at the ball.'

'Oh, I've been busy,' he said, feeling oddly self-conscious. Part of him wanted to say, *With Claire*. 'You know how it is.'

'I do.' She smiled again and this time her chocolate eyelashes fluttered at him. 'But all work and no play makes for a very boring life. I'm a big fan of breaking up the work with a bit of fun. I've heard you're of a similar mind?'

You bet I'm having fun. Claire's throaty voice filled his head and he found himself comparing Maddie's flirting green eyes with Claire's studious yet sexy caramel ones. The physiotherapist's came up lacking. 'I better go and find Olivia McDermott,' he'd said, backing quickly out of the room.

A few short weeks ago he'd probably have taken Maddie up on her offer. *Before Claire.* Feeling warm, he loosened his tie and took another swipe at the virtual ball, thrusting his arm out hard and fast. Now, it was officially *After Claire*, except the damn woman was still at the hospital. All day yesterday he'd waited for her resignation to ping into his in-box, planning to expedite her leaving as quickly as possible. It hadn't arrived. The first thing he'd done when he'd hauled himself out of another fitful night's sleep this morning was to check for the email. It still hadn't come.

Despite that, he'd been stunned an hour later when he saw her standing next to Bailey, waiting for him on the ward. Her oval face had been slightly paler than usual but determination had squared her shoulders, rolling down her spine and spearing through her gorgeous—ridiculous—high heels to plant her firmly in place. All of it had said, *I'm not going anywhere.* It had rendered him momentarily speechless.

He hated that she'd said, 'Good morning, Alistair,' before he'd been able to give his usual nod and greeting. From that moment, he'd felt as if he was on the back foot for the rest of the round and that she'd been directing the play. Hell, even Bailey, who looked like death warmed up, had been less distracted than him.

At the end of the round when everyone had scattered

he'd found himself asking her quietly, 'Are you sure you're well enough to be back at work?'

'Absolutely,' she'd said with a return of the crispness that had been such a part of her when she'd first arrived from Australia. Then she'd looked him straight in the eye and added, 'I plan to make the most of my remaining seventy-two working days here at the castle.'

His mouth had dried at her announcement that she wasn't leaving. She was going to be at work five days a week for the next three months and he couldn't do a damn thing about it. But he knew women and a jet of anxiety streamed through him. 'You do know that your staying makes no difference to us?'

Her eye roll was so swift and strong that the floor felt like it had moved under his feet. 'No need to worry, Alistair. You made your feelings abundantly clear. Besides, I learned from the master on how to clearly separate work and play without any inconvenient overlaps. I'm here because it's the best place for me to learn. Everything else is immaterial.'

And he *was* the master, so why in heaven's name did his mind keep slipping back to the fundraising ball and the subsequent nights they'd shared. *Because it was good sex.*

This time his subconscious gave an eye roll.

If it was just about the sex, why do you treasure the laughter and time shared on the picnic by the Serpentine? Why did you watch a chick-flick with her on the couch? Why did you spend whole nights at her flat? You've never done that with a woman before.

Anger stirred and he swiped the air again with an even harder thwack, sending the virtual ball scudding back across the screen. It suddenly looked out of focus and he blinked to clear his fuzzy vision. Was it rather warm in here? He threw off his tie without missing a point.

Remembering fun times with Claire didn't mean anything more than that he liked her and enjoyed spending time with her. When had that become a crime?

And what do you fondly remember doing with McKenzie, Islay, Rebecca, Eloise and Leila? Shall I go on?

Shut up.

He served with gusto, slicing through the air so hard his arm hurt. Sweat beaded on his brow. He leaped around the lounge, volleying the virtual ball, determined to beat the damn machine.

Will the world end if you admit that you love me?

Claire's distinctive voice with its rising inflection was so loud in his head she may as well have been in the room with him. *Yes, damn it. It will.* He couldn't love her because if he did, then his carefully constructed new world—his post-ironman world—would tumble in on itself and bring with it all of the old pain. Pain he'd already endured once before. Pain he didn't intend to deal with again and he sure as hell wouldn't inflict it on anyone he loved.

And you love her.

The reality hit him so hard he felt light-headed and the room spun. The game buzzed at him, telling him he'd missed a shot. He started over, serving fast and faulting. He blinked away double vision, suddenly feeling unbelievably tired and cloaked with an overwhelming sense of fatalism. What did it matter if he loved Claire? Nothing good could come of it so there was no point telling her. He'd survived worse and he'd survive this. In seventy-two days she'd be gone.

'Alistair?'

Heat and cold raced through him at her voice but he didn't turn. Instead, he kept playing despite feeling that with each shot it was increasingly difficult to raise his arm. 'Claire?'

'Is it possible to add Harrison Raines to tomorrow's surgical list?'

'Fine.' He took another swipe with the plastic racquet and the room listed sideways. He staggered, fighting to stay upright.

'Are you okay?'

'Fine.' But the word echoed in his head. He didn't feel fine at all. The edges of his mind filled with grey fog. The racquet fell from his hand and he reached for the back of the couch to stop himself from falling.

Terror gripped him. Memories assaulted him. It had been a long time but he knew this feeling. He tilted sideways.

'Alistair!' Claire yelled his name as he fell.

After that everything was a blur as he slipped in and out of consciousness. He heard the thud of shoes on linoleum. Felt Claire's hand on his throat, seeking his pulse. Heard her say, 'God, his pulse is twenty-eight.' He recognised Bailey's voice yelling to get the crash cart.

'Alistair.' Hands shook him. 'Al. Do you have pain?'

Claire's beautiful face floated above him and he tried hard to fix it so it was still. He couldn't manage it.

Was this it? Had his borrowed time come to an end? *No!* He didn't want to die, but he already felt disconnected from his body as if he was on the outside and looking down on everyone frantically trying to save him. With a monumental effort he tried again to bring Claire's beautiful face into focus. Behind her sexy thinking-woman's glasses, her eyes burned with terror and pain. He wanted to change that.

It was suddenly vital to him that his last word to her wasn't a terse, 'Fine.' He didn't want her to remember their last real conversation when he'd cruelly said, 'Unlike you, there's nothing wrong with me.' Oh, the irony.

'Claire.' His voice sounded far, far away but she must have heard him because she lowered her head to his.

'It's okay, Al,' she said frantically. 'I refuse to let anything happen to you. You're going to be okay.'

He wanted to lift his hand to her cheek and feel her

soft skin against his but he lacked the strength. 'I...
Love... You.'

The last thing he heard before his hearing faded was her
choking cry and then everything went black.

CHAPTER TWELVE

As Claire stared at the contents of the St John's Hospital vending machine, she knew down to the tips of her toes that she never wanted to relive the last few hours ever again. *Not quite.* She smiled as she dropped coins into the machine. She'd happily relive hearing Alistair say quietly but clearly, 'I love you.' Was there anything more truthful than words spoken by a man who thought he was dying? She didn't think so. He loved her and she'd been right about that; however, it brought cold comfort when she'd been desperately worried she might never have the opportunity to hear him say them again.

Selecting orange juice, cheese and biscuits, and chocolate, she sent up another vote of thanks that by a stroke of luck or, as Thomas Wolfe had said to her, due to 'the mountain of unrelenting paperwork' that he'd still been at the castle at ten-thirty last night. Not only had he accompanied Alistair in the ambulance, he'd been very generous to her. As she wasn't family, without his consideration she'd have been denied any information about Alistair's condition and certainly not been allowed in to see him. Not that she'd seen him yet, but she lived in hope. Meanwhile, Thomas had reassured her that the surgery had gone well.

Along with Alistair's collapse had come a lot of answers to unasked questions. Why he was so hell-bent on living for the moment, although it seemed an excessive response to his condition. Then again, who was she to judge?

She unwrapped the thick and gooey chocolate-coated caramel bar and just as she bit into it a nurse walked over and enquired, 'Dr Mitchell?'

'Thaff's me,' she stuttered, using all her facial muscles to haul her teeth out of the caramel.

The nurse caught sight of her food stash and shot her a sympathetic smile. 'You got the five a.m. sugar drop? I get it too. Always feel a little bit nauseous at this time of the day.'

Claire nodded, still battling the quicksand-like properties of the caramel.

'Mr North's just waking up now,' the nurse continued. 'As his mother isn't due to arrive until midmorning, Dr Wolfe said you could sit with him.'

Bless you, Thomas. 'Thank you.'

They walked the length of the ward from the waiting area to the nurses' station and the nurse pointed to the door opposite. 'He's in there. I'll be in shortly to do his observations.'

Claire opened the door and stopped abruptly just inside. Alistair, always so vital and full of life, lay semi-upright in the narrow hospital bed. A sheet was pulled up tightly to his waist and a white hospital gown took over from there covering his torso to his Adam's apple. His face held slightly more colour than the cotton but not by much. Wires connecting him to the monitor snaked out from under the gown along with the IV that was connected to a pump that buzzed and purred. The rhythmic beep of the monitor, representing each life-giving heartbeat, broke the silence of the room.

Although she'd seen similar scenarios over and over since her first hospital visit as a medical student all those years ago, this was the first time someone she loved lay connected to all the high-tech machinery. Her heart beat faster in her chest and it took every gram of self-control she had not to rush over and throw herself at him and say, 'You scared me so much.'

Besides the very unwise idea of body slamming anyone who'd just undergone surgery, she knew that words like *You scared me* and *Never do that to me again* were not going to work in her favour. Alistair loved her but that hadn't stopped him walking away from her once before. She wasn't giving him a single excuse to do it a second time.

Walking slowly, she sat herself in the chair by the bed and slid her hand into his. He stirred, his head turning, and his eyes fluttered open. 'Welcome back.' She smiled, squeezed his hand and added softly, 'I believe you love me.'

Alistair's mind fought the pea-soup fog that encased it as he watched Claire's mouth move. Then her words hit him and everything rushed back. The virtual tennis. His dizziness. His almost certain belief that he was dying.

I love you.

His hand immediately moved to his left shoulder, his fingers frantically feeling for the small box-like device that had been part of him for the last five years. The shape and scar he'd hidden from Claire. All he could feel was adhesive tape and discomfort.

'It's gone,' Claire said matter-of-factly. 'Thomas removed it.'

He didn't understand. If Thomas had removed his pacemaker he'd be dead. But he couldn't be dead because he could feel the warmth of Claire's hand and the softness of her skin against his. 'If it's gone, what's keeping me alive?'

'The world's smallest pacemaker. It's wireless, and it's sitting snugly in your right ventricle doing its job perfectly.'

'Wireless?' He knew he sounded inane but he was struggling to piece everything together.

She nodded and squeezed his hand again. 'Tell me. Exactly how long had you been playing virtual tennis when I arrived to find you on the verge of collapse?'

He thought back and automatically scratched his head, noticing the IV taped to the back of his hand. 'I'm not sure. Some of the kids wanted a tournament so I organised it and I played too. We started before dinner and kept going until Sister Kaur hustled them off to bed. I suppose I stayed a little bit longer after that.'

She made a sound that was half a groan and half despairing laugh. 'Alistair, that adds up to about five hours.'

He shrugged and the stitches in his shoulder immediately pulled. *Ouch*. 'So? I had the time. It's just swiping a plastic bat through the air. It's not like I was lifting weights for hours on end.'

She dropped her head for a moment before lifting it and pushing her glasses up her nose. She gazed at him, her eyes full of love and affection with a hint of frustration. 'I know it wasn't weightlifting or rugby but substantial repetitive action for that length of time isn't recommended for people with pacemakers.'

The events of the evening came back to him and he started joining the dots. 'I should have gone home but I was procrastinating. I didn't realise how long I'd been trying to beat that bloody machine.' *I was too busy thinking about you.* 'Did I damage a lead?'

'Thomas will explain it all to you but he thinks it's more likely you exacerbated a fault. The good news is your new pacemaker's titanium. There are no leads and the battery and pulse generator are all combined into one tiny device the size of a pill.'

He glanced at the monitor and saw the perfect run of sinus rhythm. 'It's working.'

'It's working very well indeed.' She winked at him. 'So now. Back to the fact that you love me.'

The relief at being alive took a hit from reality. God,

how was he going to get out of this situation without hurting her? Without hurting himself. 'I thought I was dying.'

She didn't flinch and she didn't break her gaze. 'I know.'

A long sigh shuddered out of him. 'Now that you know all about my secret time bomb, you can understand why me loving you doesn't change a thing.'

She pursed her lips. 'I disagree. I think it changes everything.'

He threw his arm out towards the monitor and the pump. 'You saw me collapse. You worked on me. You know I could die at any moment and I refuse to put you through that.'

'So, what? We just live miserable lives apart and when I die before you at ninety, then you'll realise what a dumb idea this is?'

He pulled his hand away from hers, needing to break the addictive warmth that promised what he couldn't have. 'I'm not going to live until ninety.'

'You don't know that.'

But he did. 'Claire.' He sighed again. 'You deserve a long and happy life with someone who can give you healthy children. Someone who will be around to see them grow up. I can't promise you either of those things.'

Her mouth pursed. 'The pacemaker overrides your SA node's propensity not to fire. With that sorted and without pesky leads getting in the way of your—' she made quotation marks with her fingers '—"live for the moment" obsession of playing virtual tennis for five hours, then the odds are in your favour to live a long life.'

He dropped his gaze, wishing it were that simple.

Suddenly two deep lines carved into her intelligent brow. 'It's not just the pacemaker, is it?'

Every other time she'd pressed him for information he'd been able to deflect or walk away. Today was different. He wasn't just physically trapped in a hospital bed hooked up to equipment; he was also trapped by his declaration of love.

'This is something to do with your father, isn't it?'

His heart raced. 'Why did I fall in love with a MENSA member,' he muttered darkly.

She gave a wry smile and raised his hand to her lips. 'Because I'm good for you and you're good for me.'

And he recognised the truth in her words but it wasn't enough to convince him that he should drag her down with him. 'Dad dropped dead at forty-seven from a myocardial infarction.'

'That's young.'

'Exactly. It dramatically changed my life and my mother's. We didn't just lose Dad, we lost our home and everything familiar. My grief-stricken mother retreated into herself and it took her a long time to tread a new path without him. She did the best she was capable of doing but I ended up fatherless and half motherless for many years. I wouldn't inflict that on any child.'

He'd expected her to offer soothing murmurs but instead she asked perfunctorily, 'Did he have an arrhythmia like you?'

'Not that we knew, but given he just dropped dead with no warning, it's safe to assume that he did.'

She frowned. 'So, no episodes of dizziness? No pacemaker?'

'No,' he said irritably. 'I thought I'd established that. He was fit and healthy and then he was dead.'

She ignored his terse tone. 'How old was his father when he died?'

'Seventy-five.'

'Heart attack?'

'No. Tractor accident.'

'Alistair, have you ever read your father's autopsy report?'

He was getting sick of the interrogation. 'Of course not. I was a child.'

'Exactly,' she said emphatically, her eyes suddenly shining. 'You were a kid.'

'You're not making any sense.'

'Okay.' She tucked some hair behind her ears. 'Do you remember when I was telling you about my fabulous mentor, Strez, and how he freed me from Gundiwindi's preconceived ideas? You said, "But not from its legacy."'

He didn't know where she was going with this but he did remember the conversation. He answered with a reluctant, 'Yes.'

'I think you're suffering from a legacy too.' She leaned in closer. 'Even though you're now a qualified medical practitioner, the trauma of losing your father at a vulnerable age has blinkered you to the facts. I think you've made a massive non-scientific leap that connects your father's early death with your heart block. The result is an erroneous belief that you'll die young too.'

'It's not unreasonable—'

'It is. The statistics don't support it. Thomas told me you have a two per cent chance of dying from your heart condition. That's way better odds than crossing Piccadilly Circus at rush hour.'

Her words beat hard against his belief that he had a faulty heart just like his father. A belief cemented by the crusty cardiologist who'd said five years ago, 'You can't fight genetics, son.'

'That may be but it doesn't rule out me passing on a faulty heart to a child.'

'And I could just as easily pass on my dyslexia.'

Frustration bit him. 'That's completely different.'

'Yes, it is.'

Her acceptance surprised him and he studied her. She

immediately speared him with an intense look that belied her words and made him squirm.

She continued briskly. 'We don't know yet if your condition's inherited or if there are other factors. Want to tell me exactly what happened five years ago?'

He sighed. 'I was working really long hours and training for an ironman competition when I had my first episode of heart block.'

'Athlete's heart syndrome?'

'Yes and no. It's complicated.'

'You need to talk to Thomas and get all the facts, but I know for certain that my dyslexia's inherited. My grandmother and great-grandfather never learned to read. There's a chance a child of ours may have learning challenges.'

A child of ours.

The thought tempted and terrified him in equal measure. He fought back. 'Why don't you get this?' he asked tersely. 'Dyslexia's not a life-threatening condition.'

She folded her arms across her chest. 'It is if it's not treated.'

He snorted. 'No one ever died of dyslexia.'

'People with low self-esteem and no hope die every day,' she said softly, the message in her words sharp and clear.

'We wouldn't allow things to get to that,' he said quickly, stunned by his strong need to protect a child that didn't even exist. 'We'd be on the lookout for any signs of dyslexia. We'd make sure they had access to early intervention. They'd get all the help they needed to thrive.'

'Of course we would,' she said evenly. 'And in exactly the same way, we'd get be on the lookout and get an early diagnosis and intervention for any child of ours who had a cardiac arrhythmia.' A smile wove across her lips. 'I think that's called checkmate.'

'Claire,' he heard himself growl. 'It's not that simple.'

'Alistair,' she sighed. 'It really is. With your pacemaker,

your heart's pumping life through you just as it's been doing without error for the last five years, but you're not taking full advantage of what technology's offering you. You can let irrational fear continue to rule your life and keep everyone at arm's length or you can take a chance, embrace love, accept some low-level risk and share your life with me.

'The choice is yours.' Without waiting for him to reply, she rose to her feet and left the room.

Her words filled his head, duelling with his long-held beliefs about his life and the decisions he'd made long ago. Not once in five years had he ever questioned them. Hell, he'd accepted his fate and got on with his life, so why was he even considering what she'd said?

Because you've never been in love before.

How could it be so simple and so bloody complicated? Claire painted a picture of a life with her and children—a life he wanted badly, but either way he risked hurting her.

'Alistair.' Thomas Wolfe strode energetically into the room wearing a grey suit, a crisp white shirt and a pale blue tie. He'd obviously been home and acknowledged the new day with fresh clothes. Only the shadows under his eyes hinted that perhaps all wasn't quite as it appeared. 'Good to see you're awake.'

Alistair grimaced. 'I hear I have a state-of-the-art pacemaker.'

'The silver bullet.' Thomas's eyes lit up. 'It's a great invention. And you can play as much virtual tennis as you want, although at thirty-nine, your shoulder might object.'

Alistair sat up a bit higher. 'You're not that far behind me, old man.'

'Indeed.' Thomas's smile was wry. 'The good news is your cardiac enzymes and ECG are both normal. Your groin will feel a bit sore for a few days and you can't walk until tomorrow, but other than that, you'll be feeling yourself again very soon. No need to let this hiccough slow you down.'

'Hiccough?' He heard the disbelief in his voice.

'It's unfortunate the lead became damaged but you were close to a battery replacement anyway. In a way, you did yourself a favour. This pacemaker is a huge leap forward in the treatment of heart block, and apart from not being able to go scuba-diving or joining the armed forces, your life's your own.'

Was it? Immediately, Claire's accusation that he'd made a massive non-scientific leap about his condition burned him. 'My father died suddenly at forty-seven.'

'Of an MI?'

'I always assumed.'

Thomas checked the tablet computer in his hand. 'Your cholesterol's low, your blood pressure's in the normal range and you don't smoke. All of it puts your risk factor for an MI as very low.' He rubbed his neck. 'Your father could have died of an aneurysm or numerous other things. If it was an MI, then I think you've inherited your mother's heart genes. If you can get hold of your father's medical history, I'd be happy to take a look. Meanwhile, you having problems is not something I'd be betting any money on.'

Again Claire's voice sounded loud and clear in his head.

You can let irrational fear continue to rule your life and keep everyone at arm's length or you can take a chance, embrace love, accept some low-level risk and share your life with me.

A feeling of lightness streaked through him almost raising him off the bed and he stuck out his right hand. 'Thank you, Thomas. You have no idea how much I appreciate your straight-talking.'

'Any time.' Thomas shook his proffered hand. 'I'll see

you in the morning before you're discharged but any other questions just call me.' He turned to leave.

'Thomas, before you go, can I ask you a favour?'

One of the hardest things Claire had ever done was walk out of Alistair's hospital room yesterday morning but she'd felt it was her only option. It was that or hit him over the head in frustration. Or beg. She certainly wasn't going to beg. The old Claire may have begged but Alistair had taught her that she didn't need to beg anyone for anything. The lesson wasn't without irony.

Still, she'd been sorely tempted to beg but she'd fought it. In her mind, two things were very clear. The first was that Alistair loved and valued her. The second was that if they were to have any chance at happiness, Alistair had to come to his decision freely and not be cornered or cajoled into committing to her. She also knew that his love for her was a big part of the problem. He didn't want to hurt her and yet by protecting her from life—from his life—he was hurting her ten times over.

'How's the boss?' Andrew asked as they stripped off their surgical gowns.

'If he takes his doctor's advice, he'll be back at work next week.'

'So we can expect him here tomorrow, then.' Andrew winked at her. 'I imagine he's got women lining up to look after him so perhaps he will stay away for the week.'

A bristle ran up Claire's spine. 'The man needs to rest, Andrew.'

He grinned. 'Sure. But hey, what a way to rest.'

Claire hit him with the folder she was holding. 'Go and check your patients in recovery.'

He held up his hands in surrender. 'Yes, Mum. On my way.'

She walked to the doctors' lounge and made herself a

late-afternoon snack to keep her energy levels up. She was eating a plate of cheese and biscuits when her phone rang. 'Claire Mitchell.'

'Thomas Wolfe, Claire. As Alistair's indisposed, I was wondering if you could help me out.'

'Ah, sure. Do you have a patient who needs a neuro consult?'

'In a manner of speaking. He's a high-profile private patient and coming here's difficult with the…um…'

'Picket line,' she supplied as her thoughts roved to a possible celebrity child.

'Exactly,' Thomas said firmly. 'They're sending a car. What time suits you?'

'I'll be free in an hour.'

It suddenly occurred to her that perhaps it was a royal child, but as she opened her mouth to ask, Thomas was already saying, 'Excellent. I'll get the porter to buzz you when the driver arrives.'

'Can you give me some de—?' The line went dead. She waited for him to call her back or send a text but nothing came. A skitter of excitement raced through her at the idea of a very top-secret patient. At least it would take her mind off Alistair.

The car wasn't a limousine nor did it have any distinctive crest or signage on it, so Claire wasn't able to glean any clues about the mystery patient from her transport. When she'd quizzed the driver he'd replied that he wasn't at liberty to disclose who'd ordered and paid for the car.

Despite the evening traffic, the drive was thankfully short and soon enough she was standing on the porch of a Victorian town house with a royal-blue door. She rang the recessed brass bell and waited, her curiosity rising and her stomach churning. She probably should have eaten more before coming. She listened intently for footsteps. About thirty seconds later she was still listening. She was about to ring the bell again when the door opened.

Her stomach rolled and she felt her eyes widen. 'Alistair?'

He stood in front of her wearing faded jeans and a button-necked light wool jumper that lit his grey eyes to a burnished pewter. His hair was its usual messy chic and the addition of a five o'clock stubble shadow on his cheeks made him sexier than ever.

'You're not a celebrity child.'

A momentary look of confusion crossed his face. 'Ah, no. Was I supposed to be?'

'Thomas led me to believe…' Actually, Thomas hadn't given any details at all. She'd jumped to those conclusions all on her own. 'Never mind. You've been discharged,' she said, stating the obvious and trying to keep calm when all she wanted to do was hug him tightly. 'You've got your colour back,' she said crisply.

'I feel pretty good. How are you?' A familiar frown creased his brow. 'You look tired.'

She wanted to bask in his concern for her but she'd done that before and it hurt too much. Now, far too much was at stake. 'Yes, well, it's been a big few days.'

He gave her a wan smile. 'It has. Please come in.' He stepped back from the doorway so she could enter but as she passed him she could smell his delicious shower-fresh scent and her heart raced.

She immediately tried to slow it down. The only thing being at his house meant was that he wanted to talk to her. What he planned to say would either cause the crack in her heart to break open for good or it would heal it.

'Go through.' He indicated she walk the length of the hall and she was very aware of the noise her heels made clicking against his polished floorboards. It echoed into the strained silence.

She entered a large, light-filled space that combined a

kitchen, dining area and family room that opened out onto a walled garden. The evening was warm and the sweet perfume of wisteria drifted in through the open French doors. So this was his house? It wasn't the soulless stainless steel and chrome bachelor pad she'd imagined. If anything, it looked of a style and design that was ripe to be filled with the children he was too scared to have.

'I thought we could sit outside?' he suggested politely.

From the moment he'd opened the front door he'd been the perfect host, and if he were going to continue in the same vein when there was so much at stake, she'd go mad. With a shake of her head, she set her handbag down on the dining table next to a vase overflowing with roses, scented lilies, daisies and hypericum berries. They were a beautiful arrangement and most likely get-well-soon flowers, although she wondered at the pink and mauve colour palette for a man.

'I'm a firm believer of ripping a sticking plaster off fast.'

His brows drew down. 'Sorry?'

'Alistair.' His name came out on a sigh. 'I don't want to go through the charade of you offering me a drink and something to eat and then breaking my heart. Just do it now and get it over and done with.'

He looked disconcerted as if they were actors in a play and she'd just gone off-script. He pulled out a chair for her.

'I don't need to sit down if I'm leaving in a minute.'

He rubbed the back of his neck and glanced out towards the garden before looking back at her. 'You're not making this easy.'

She shrugged. 'I didn't think that was my job.'

'No.' He drew in a deep breath. 'I love you, Claire.'

She steeled herself against the thrill that traitorously stole through her. 'I know you do. But for us those three words are hardly reassuring.'

'I'm sorry, Claire…'

Her heart quivered and she found one hand clutching the edge of the table and the other curling around her belly as it lurched and rolled.

'I've been a fool and...'

What? His words began to penetrate her fog of despair. She clawed back her concentration and watched him carefully.

His eyes held sorrow. 'If I had my time over I'd have handled everything differently. I'm standing here before you now begging you to take a chance and risk sharing your life with me.'

For a moment, her astonishment seemed to almost stop time and then her heart leapt at his words—her words. He was saying to her exactly what she'd said to him in the hospital. 'You want to embrace love?'

He reached out his arms. 'I want to embrace love. I want to embrace you and a life together.'

More than anything in the world, she wanted to rush into his arms but something—survival—kept her rooted to the spot. 'And children?' She asked the question softly, barely daring to speak the words out loud for fear they would bring her world crashing down on her again.

'Yes.' He nodded slowly. 'That is, if we're fortunate enough to have them. You're right, Claire. If our kids face challenges, we'll be there with the resources to help.'

Relief and joy—so sweet and strong—surged through her making her sway but still she held herself back from the security of his arms. It was important to her—to them both—that she understood exactly how he'd got to this point. 'What happened to change your mind?'

'You happened.' He stared down at her while his left hand stroked her hair. 'Five years ago, when I collapsed and got the pacemaker, I saw it as a second chance at life. I also believed it came with a very big condition. I couldn't risk having kids and there are very few women out there who don't want the full package of marriage and children. So I focused on work and having fun. When a woman tried to get too close, I broke things off. It was always that easy until I met you.'

'I've always been difficult,' she said, half joking and half serious.

A slow smile broke over his handsome face. 'You're the most wonderfully difficult woman I've ever had the plea-sure to know. You're also the only woman I've ever fallen in love with. It threw me so completely that I've behaved abominably.'

The only woman I've ever fallen in love with.

All those beautiful women who'd preceded her and yet it was her—the woman with the learning challenges and a lifetime of idiosyncrasies—she was the one he loved. He wanted to share his life with her come what may. Make a future with her.

Tears pricked the back of her eyes and she raised her hand to his cheek, welcoming the feel of his stubble graz-ing her palm. 'You were scared.'

'I can't believe how close I got to losing you.' His voice cracked and he cleared his throat. 'Thank you for coming to the hospital and talking sense to me.' His forehead touched hers. 'Thank you for loving me.'

She blinked rapidly as her legs trembled. 'Thank you for loving me.'

His arms wrapped around her, pulling her in so close and tight she could barely breathe. 'Claire?'

'Yes.'

He set her back from him so he could see her face. 'Will you do me the honour of becoming my wife?'

His proposal stunned and thrilled her and she found her-self struggling to speak. 'I… That's…I… Yes,' she finally managed to splutter out. 'Yes, yes, yes.'

He grinned at her, his face alight with love. 'Thank

goodness for that.' Cupping her cheeks in his hands, he tilted her head back and kissed her with firm, warm and giving lips.

She sighed into him, letting him take her weight and absorbing the solid feel of him against her. His touch and feel radiated love, support and infinite generosity. When he eventually broke the kiss, he said, 'By the way, these flowers are for you. A peace offering for my stupidity. I don't mind if you throw them at me.'

She gave an unsteady laugh as she tried to unpack everything that was happening—how hopelessness had been turned on its head to become happiness. 'I can't throw them at you. That would be a waste. They're too beautiful.'

'So are you.' He kissed her again. 'Will you come outside into the garden? Please.'

The entreaty in his voice made it impossible to deny him. 'I think it's probably safe for me to do that now.'

He grinned and gripping her hand he tugged her across the room and out into the garden. A silver champagne bucket stood on a table and protruding from it was the neck of a bottle of champagne with distinctive gold, orange and black foil. A platter of antipasti covered in a fine net cloth sat beside it along with two champagne flutes.

He gave her a sheepish look. 'I'd planned to propose to you out here. I wanted to do my very best to make it as romantic as possible. Make it something you'd remember.'

His love and care circled her in warmth. 'And I went and threw a spanner in the works. Sorry.'

He laughed. 'Hey, I still got the girl so I don't mind at all.' He removed the foil covering on the top of the champagne bottle and then his long, surgical fingers popped the cork. The fizzing liquid quickly filled the fine crystal glasses.

When he'd set the bottle back into the ice bucket, she

stepped into his arms and ran her hands through his hair. 'You've got more than just me.'

He gazed down at her. 'In-laws, you mean? My mother's keen to meet you, and we can take a trip to—'

She pressed her fingers to his lips as she shook her head. 'I don't mean my family. I mean our family.'

He looked increasingly bewildered so she took pity on him. 'It turns out I didn't have gastro.'

His eyes widened into silver moons. 'You're pregnant?' Hope and awe tumbled from his whispered words.

'Six weeks.' She couldn't stop a broad smile despite knowing she needed to urge caution. 'It's still early days and you know that anything could hap—' She gave a squeal of surprise as her feet suddenly left the ground.

Alistair spun her around and around, his face alight with sheer delight. 'You're amazing. This is amazing.'

She threw back her head and laughed, revelling in more joy than she'd ever known. The circular motion eventually caught up with her and she suddenly gripped his shoulders. 'Feeling sick.'

He stopped abruptly and set her down on the chair. 'Sorry. Drink this.' He picked up the champagne and then laughed and put it down again. 'I'll get you something else.'

When he returned a short moment later the world had stilled on its axis and she was feeling a little better. She accepted the glass of apple juice he'd poured into a champagne glass.

Squatting by her side, he picked up his champagne flute. 'To my darling Claire, for opening my eyes and giving me back my life.'

She leaned in and kissed him, her heart so full it threatened to burst in her chest. 'To my darling Alistair, for opening my eyes so I can appreciate my strengths and skills.'

'You're most welcome.' He grinned up at her. 'Someone wise once told me that we're good for each other.'

'And don't you forget it. I love you, Alistair North.'

'I love you too, Claire Mitchell. Here's to a life lived to the full. To facing challenges head-on and to the joy of children.'

She thought about what they'd taught each other. 'To enough routine to make life enjoyable and enough spontaneity to keep it fun.'

They raised their glasses and clinked. 'To the future.'

And then he kissed her and she knew she was home.

EPILOGUE

'DO YOU THINK international travel with children comes under the heading of spontaneity and fun?' Alistair asked with a wry smile as he tramped along a wide, golden sand beach with a baby carrier on his back.

Claire laughed as she adjusted the baby carrier on her own back. 'Nothing about travelling with babies and all of their associated gear can be called spontaneous.'

'Their creation, however, was both spontaneous and fun,' Alistair teased as he slid his hand into hers and squeezed it.

'It was.' She leaned in and kissed him on the cheek. She was more in love with him now than on the day she'd said, 'I do,' in the beautiful stained-glass chapel at the castle and she was absolutely stunned that it was even possible. 'Bringing the twins to my homeland is fun.'

The twins—a boy and a girl now eleven months old—squealed in delight. Thrashing their arms wildly, they touched hands now that their parents were walking close enough so they could reach each other from their carriers.

Claire breathed in the fresh, salty air and felt peace invade her bones. She enjoyed London but she loved Australia and its wide-open spaces more. She couldn't quite believe she—*they*—were here in Queensland. The last nineteen months had been momentous. Two weeks after Alistair had proposed, he'd accompanied her to the routine pregnancy ultrasound. As she lay on the table with her hand encased in Alistair's, excitement on hearing the baby's heartbeat had turned from joy to shock and back to joy again when they'd heard two heartbeats.

'Twins? But how?' she'd asked inanely.

Alistair had laughed. 'Any twins in your family?'

'Dad has twin brothers.'

'There you go,' he'd said, kissing her on the forehead. 'Now this is the sort of inherited condition I can get behind.'

Being pregnant and studying for her exams had been tough but with her study regime and Alistair's help—both practical and emotional—she'd passed. The good news had arrived just before she'd gone into labour. A paediatrician had been on hand at the birth to check for any cardiac irregularities but both children were declared to have healthy hearts. Their six-month check-ups had all been normal and they were kicking goals on all their developmental milestones, although Claire noticed Emily did things just that little bit earlier than Noah. It was typical girl power.

Parenthood had brought with it both joy and delight along with exhaustion, but she and Alistair were used to functioning on limited sleep courtesy of years of working in hospitals. It didn't faze them too much. They'd become experts at walking the floor, bouncing the pram and driving around London in the wee small hours, all sure-fire ways to get unsettled babies back to sleep. The biggest surprise—and the most appreciated—had been Alistair's decision to cut back his work hours so he could be around more for hands-on help. Claire, loving motherhood but missing work, took up the two days a week that Alistair had dropped. It was a perfect solution. Just recently, with the twins close to their first birthday, they felt they'd found their groove and had decided to bring them out to Australia to meet her parents as well as taking a well-earned beach holiday.

At the prospect of the twenty-four-hour journey, Alistair had said, 'We're either brave or stupid.'

'We're both,' she'd said, kissing him with gratitude. 'And I love you for it.'

A pacific gull and a cormorant swooped over the gently breaking waves and then dived, probably having just spotted a school of fish and dinner. The sun, now a vivid orange ball of fire, dropped low to the horizon, shooting out fingers of red and yellow flames that lit up the scudding clouds. Claire felt the chill in the breeze for the first time.

'We should probably take them home.'

'Dinner, bath, bed?'

'For us or them?' she teased.

His eyes darkened just the way she liked. 'Twins first and then us.'

'I'll hold you to that.' They turned around and walked back towards the beach access track. Not able to hold back her sigh, she said, 'I can't believe we've only got one day of our holiday left.'

'What if we stayed?'

She laughed and gave him a gentle elbow in the ribs. 'You're just procrastinating because you don't want to face the flight back to London.'

'Well, there is that,' he said with a grin, but then his expression sobered. 'I'm serious, Claire. What if we stayed and worked in Australia? I enjoyed my time in Sydney as a registrar so I know what I'm in for. I've loved this holiday and I love this country. Your mother's besotted by the twins—'

'There's not a big call for neurosurgeons in Gundiwindi,' she said, thinking of her dusty hometown.

'True, but there is in Brisbane. The city's only a few hours' drive away for your parents, which is a lot closer than London. Plus, your dad's talking about retiring closer to the coast.'

'Is he?'

'He told me they'd been looking at properties in the hinterland.'

Her mother had mentioned something in passing along those lines but she hadn't thought anything of it because she couldn't imagine her father ever leaving Gundiwindi. The idea of having her parents closer for support was very tempting, as was the opportunity for the twins to grow up with grandparents. 'But what about your mother?' she asked, trying to be fair. 'If we stay here, then she misses out.'

'You know as well as I do Mother's not really a natural at being an extra-pair-of-hands type of a grandmother. She prefers children when they're older. We'll Skype her each week and buy a big house with a large guest room and an en-suite. She can fly out anytime she wants to visit. But I can pretty much guarantee she won't do that until they're at school.'

Anticipation and excitement started to bubble in her veins. She stopped walking and turned to face him. 'You've really thought about this, haven't you?'

'I have.'

'What about our friends and colleagues? The castle? Won't you miss the old girl?'

'Paddington's always going to have a place in my heart, because it's where I met you. But times change and we need to change with them.'

She'd never asked him to consider moving to Australia because they'd met in London. 'You'd really do this for me?'

'It's not a hardship, Claire. Yesterday, when you were at the beach with your parents, I made enquiries at Brisbane's public and private hospitals.' He stroked her face. 'Would you like to go into private practice with me in Brisbane, Ms Mitchell?'

Marvelling at how lucky she was to have him in her life,

she didn't have to think twice. 'Yes, please.' Throwing her arms around her neck, she kissed him, welcoming the future and all it had to offer.

* * * * *

SUMMER WITH A FRENCH SURGEON

MARGARET BARKER

To my wonderful family, who give me continual love,
inspiration and happiness.

CHAPTER ONE

EVER since she'd been tiny, Julia had always made a special point of trying to appear confident. Well, with three older brothers to boss her around she'd had to be tough to survive. Still, glancing around now at her fellow trainee surgeons, she felt decidedly nervous. Since her disastrous marriage to Tony—who'd done his best to destroy whatever confidence she'd had—her life had been an uphill struggle to even get back to how she'd felt as a teenager, competing against her brilliant medical-student and qualified brothers.

Coming here, to France, to further her surgical career was the first step on her long journey back to self-confidence. And, in fact, looking out of the taxi as she had been driven down the hill just now towards St Martin sur Mer, she'd been in seventh heaven as she'd absorbed the wonderful scenery spread out in front of her. The stunning view had made her forget any apprehension she'd had about taking this big step.

She'd found herself overwhelmed with nostalgia as she'd seen the undulating sand dunes spilling down onto the beach and behind them the small, typically French hotels, cafés *tabac*, restaurants, shops and houses clustered near the high-tech hospital. She'd felt the excitement she'd known as a child when her French mother and English father, both doctors, had brought the whole family here for a couple of weeks every summer holiday.

She brought her thoughts back to the present as the eminent professor of orthopaedic surgery strode into the room. She caught her breath. Wow! Bernard Cappelle looked much younger than she'd expected and very... handsome? She paused, surprised by the turn of her wicked thoughts. It had been a very long time since she'd noticed any man in that way.

He was more than handsome, he was charismatic. Yes, that was more like it. He was oozing the sort of confidence she longed to acquire. Well, maybe, just maybe in another ten years, when she was an eminent surgeon, she would stride into a room and silence would descend as her students stared in awe at their professor of surgery, as was happening now with the great Bernard Cappelle.

If she hadn't made a concrete decision to hold off relationships since Tony had bled her dry of all desire for emotional commitment of any kind she would have allowed herself to fancy Bernard Cappelle.

In your dreams, girl! No chance! She wouldn't let herself even fantasise about him. Good! That meant she could concentrate on making the most of the six-month course without wasting her energy on emotional dreams about an unattainable man who wouldn't even notice her.

The awesome man cleared his throat as he looked around the assembled doctors. Ah, so he was possibly a bit nervous? At least that meant he had a human side.

'Hello, and welcome, ladies and gentlemen. I hope that…'

Bernard Cappelle began by welcoming them to the Hopital de la Plage, which would be their place of study and work for the six-month course. He explained they would study an orthopaedic operation theoretically before they moved on to the practical aspect of observing and assisting in Theatre. They would also be expected to assist with the pre- and post-operative care of the patients and also work in *Urgences*, the accident and emergency department, on occasion if required.

Julia took notes but realised soon enough that she'd read most of this in the brochure she'd studied carefully before applying. So she allowed herself to study the man who was to lead them all to the final exams, which would give them a prestigious qualification that would be a definite help to her in her desire to become a first-class orthopaedic surgeon.

She sat back in her hard and uncomfortable chair, probably designed to keep students awake. There were ten students on the course, Dr Cappelle explained. He'd chosen them from their CVs and was confident from their qualifications and experience that they were all going to give the next six months one hundred per cent of their available effort. He paused for a moment and his eyes swept the room before alighting on Julia in the front row.

'Are you happy for me to speak French all the time, Dr Montgomery?' he asked in heavily accented but charming English.

She was taken aback by suddenly being the centre of attention. Everyone was waiting for her reply. She swallowed hard. 'Yes, yes, of course. My mother is French, my father English, so I'm bilingual.'

'Then if you are happy I will speak in French…' He went on to explain that he was much happier when speaking French. 'And you are not intimidated by being the only lady in the class?'

She sat up straight, trying to look bigger than she actually was. 'Not at all. I was brought up with three brothers who did their best to intimidate me but without success.'

There was a scattering of sympathetic laughter. She was quaking in her shoes but making a valiant effort not to show it. She wished he would take his eyes off her and attention would focus on someone else.

'Excellent!'

A student sitting nearby spoke out in a clear distinct voice. 'Why is it, sir, that women orthopaedic surgeons are few and far between?'

Bernard Cappelle appeared to be giving the matter some thought. 'Good question. Could it be that the fairer sex are more delicate and possibly wary of taking on a profession that requires a certain amount of strength on occasions? What is your view, Dr Montgomery?'

'I have to say,' she continued boldly, forcing herself to display a confidence she didn't feel, 'I'm surprised to be the only woman on the course. I've never found, during my early career so far in orthopaedics, that being female is a disadvantage. When you're operating the patient is usually sedated in some way…I mean they're not likely to struggle with you or…'

Her voice trailed away as her depleted confidence ebbed and flowed.

The student who'd begun the discussion broke in. 'And there's always some hunky big, strong male doctor hovering around a fragile lady, hoping she'll ask for his help so that he can muscle in and...'

She missed the end of his sentence because the entire group was now laughing loudly. Ha, ha, very funny... she didn't think. She waited until the laughter died down before taking a deep breath and speaking in the clear, concise, correct French her well-spoken mother had always insisted she use.

'Gentlemen, you can be assured that I never take advantage of my so-called fragility. My brothers took me to judo classes when I was very young. I was awarded a black belt as soon as I was old enough to qualify and the skills I learned have often come in handy. So, as you can see, I only need to call for help when it's absolutely necessary.'

'Bravo!' Dr Cappelle said, admiration showing in his eyes. From her position in the front row she could see they were sensitive, a distinctive shade of hazel. Phew, she was glad she'd had to practise the art of being strong from an early age. Her show of pseudo-confidence was turning into the real thing, although she realised that had she known she would be the only woman on the course she might have hesitated before signing up.

Well, probably only hesitated for a short while. Looking around, she knew she could handle these young doctors, whatever they tried on. She'd learned a lot about men in the last few years. Basically, they were still boys, feeling as daunted as she was at the prospect of the exacting course they'd signed up to.

'I'm now going to give you a tour of the operating

theatres we use here at the Hopital de la Plage. Some of them will be in use and we won't be able to go inside en masse. May I suggest you make a note of the areas you aren't able to see today so that you can find a more suitable time to inspect them at a later date?'

Before they all filed out, the professor asked them to call him Bernard. He said that he didn't hold with titles in a teaching situation, explaining that it was easier for him to get to know his students if there was always a warm atmosphere, especially in tutorials like today. He looked around the room as if to judge the collective re-action of his students to this unexpected statement.

There was a stunned silence. Julia felt slightly more at ease with the great man when he said that but as she glanced around the room she knew that her fel-low students weren't taken in. Bernard Cappelle some-how managed to remain aloof even while he spoke. She sensed an aura of mystery surrounding him, which made him seem distant, brooding, definitely enigmatic, approachable in a professional situation but with cau-tion. Yes, his students would call him Bernard because he'd requested they do so but at the same time they would be wary of him. So would she but for several reasons, some of them decidedly inadvisable given her past history!

Being in the front row, she went out first and found Bernard walking beside her. He seemed very tall. She wished she'd put her heels on but hadn't realised they were going to trek round the hospital.

'You don't mind if I call you Julia, do you?'

He had such a deep, sexy, mellifluous voice. She was going to have to be very firm with herself to eliminate any sign that she felt an attraction to him. There, she'd admitted it. Well, power plus charisma, plus a barely discernible twinkle in the eye, which undoubtedly accompanied a wicked sense of humour, all added up to a desirable package that she certainly wasn't going to attempt to unwrap. Bernard could teach her his professional skills and knowledge and that was all she wanted from him.

Besides, he was probably married, bound to have a stunning wife waiting for him at home. Although married men were often ready for a fling and flings were another thing totally off her agenda.

'Yes, you can call me Julia.' She didn't even smile, making it seem as if she was doing him a favour.

'Good.'

They were now going inside one of the theatres, which Bernard had told them was not in use that afternoon. There was gleaming, bright high-tech equipment everywhere she looked. She was really going to enjoy working in a place like this.

At the end of the afternoon tour Bernard took them down to the staff cafeteria, where the conversation drifted from the equipment they'd viewed and the endless possibilities of a teaching hospital of this calibre to their previous experience and what they hoped to get out of the course that would be relevant to their future careers.

Somehow she found herself next to Bernard again. She wondered if he felt he had to protect her from the attentions of her fellow students in spite of the fact that she'd made it quite clear she wanted to be treated in the same way as all the men on the course.

'So, do you think you're going to enjoy working here, Julia?'

'I don't know whether *enjoy* is quite the right word.' She took a sip of her coffee. 'I intend to get the most out of it but I realise it's going to be hard work.'

'You look like the sort of person who enjoys hard work—determined, tough, doesn't give up easily. From your CV you seem to have led a busy life both in and outside hospital. Am I right, Julia?'

She nodded. 'I suppose so—at least, that's what people have told me concerning my professional life. I've been focussed on my medical career throughout my adult life.'

'Did that give you enough time for your private life?'

'My private life? Well…'

She broke off. She wasn't going to notify her teacher that she'd come to the conclusion she had a serious flaw in her personality—her inability to handle her time outside the pursuit of her career. Especially in her inability to recognise a complete and utter swine when she thought she'd picked the man of her dreams. She turned her head away from him so that he wouldn't notice the misty, damp expression in her eyes that would give him an inkling of her intense vulnerability since the suffering Tony had inflicted on her.

Looking round the almost deserted cafeteria, she noticed that the majority of her fellow doctors were drifting out through the door, having been told that the rest of the day was theirs to orientate themselves around the hospital or do whatever they wanted.

She had been planning to escape back to the small study-bedroom she'd been assigned in the medical quarters and sort out her luggage. She felt that would be the safest option open to her now, instead of having a discussion about her least favourite subject.

She stood up. 'If you'll excuse me, Bernard, I'm going to make use of this free time to get my room sorted out.'

It sounded trite to her own ears but the last thing she wanted so early in the course was to be interrogated by her boss on the delicate subject of her private life.

As he rose to his full height there was an enigmatic expression on his face. 'Of course, Julia.'

He escorted her to the door. She turned left towards the medical residents' quarters. He turned right towards the theatre block.

She walked swiftly down the corridor. At the entrance to the door to the residents' quarters she found one of her colleagues waiting for her. She recognised him as the one who'd had most to say for himself. Tall, dark and good looking in a rugged sort of way, very self-assured.

He smiled, displaying strong white teeth as he stretched out a hand towards her.

'Dominic,' he said, as he shook her hand in a firm grip.

She reclaimed her hand. 'Julia.'

'I know. Some of us are having an impromptu meeting at the bar round the corner and we'd like you to join us if you could spare the time.'

'Well, my room needs sorting and—'

'Julia, we've all got things to do but...' He broke off and began speaking in English. 'All work and no play isn't good for you.'

She smiled at him. She needed to stop taking herself so seriously and it would be good to get to know her colleagues.

'OK. I'll come but I mustn't stay too long.'

'Don't worry. We're all in the same boat.'

'Ah, it's good to be outside in the fresh air.' Julia revelled in the warm early evening sunshine as they walked out through the hospital gates.

Across the road there were still families on the beach, children running into the sea, which she knew would still be a little chilly in the spring.

'Café Maurice Chevalier,' she read from the sign outside the café restaurant Dominic took her to.

She could see some of her fellow students grouped around a large table outside. Two of them were already pulling up another small table and a couple of chairs. There was a bottle of wine on the table. Someone poured her a glass. Dominic went inside to the bar, returning with another bottle and some more glasses.

Dominic went round the table, topping up wine glasses. They all raised their glasses to cries of '*Santé!*'

'Cheers!' said Dominic, proud of his English.

'Cheers!' everybody repeated, laughing loudly.

Names were bandied about and she managed to put names to faces. Pierre, Christophe, Daniel, Jacques, Gerard and Paul were the most vociferous. Dominic seemed to have been elected leader of the group. Julia was secretly glad she'd got brothers who'd shown her how to join in when she found herself in all-male company.

'This place was here when I was a child,' she said,

during an unusually quiet moment. 'I used to sit outside and watch the sun going down with my parents and my brothers. It's good to be back here.'

'I should think it's good to escape from the attentions of our grumpy old tutor,' Dominic said. 'I saw him deep in conversation with you. How did he come across on a one-to-one basis?'

'To be honest, I don't know what to make of him. All I hope is that he's a good teacher.'

'Oh, he's a good teacher,' Dominic said vehemently. 'But he's a hard taskmaster. Apparently, he went through a difficult divorce and he's sorting out custody of his six-year-old son at the moment.'

'How do you know?' Pierre asked, screwing up his eyes against the glare of the setting sun.

Dominic grinned. 'I came here a week early to get the feel of the place. Unlike Julia, I've never been to this part of France before. I was born in Marseilles. I chatted up one of the nurses—'

Loud guffaws around the table greeted this.

'And found out a lot about Professor Grumpy. There's a rumour that he's going through a bad time at the moment, touchy about his divorce and tends to take it out on his students if they don't come up to scratch. But he's a brilliant surgeon and teacher, much admired by his colleagues.'

'Well, that's all I need to know,' Julia said, putting her hand over her glass as Christophe came round with another bottle.

'Ah, don't be too complacent,' Dominic told her. 'It's also rumoured that he doesn't think women make good surgeons.'

All eyes were on her now. She found herself filled with dread. Not only was she desperate to make a good impression on her new teacher but she was battling with an insane attraction towards him. Could it be true he didn't like women surgeons? So why had she been the only woman chosen for his exclusive course?

She looked out over the beach to the sand dunes at the corner of the bay, breathing slowly until the feeling of dread disappeared. She would cope. She would have to. She turned her head to look up at the magnificent hill behind them. She didn't want negative thoughts to spoil the beautiful sunset that was casting a glow over the hills, just as she remembered from her childhood.

She glanced round the table. 'My tutor in England told me I'm a good surgeon,' she said quietly. 'It's what I want to do with my life. And I'm not going to let a grumpy tutor spoil my career plans.'

A cheer went round the table. She felt she'd been accepted, just as her brothers' friends accepted her.

She stood up, smiling at her colleagues who had now become her friends. 'I've really enjoyed myself but I must go.'

'I'll come with you, escort you back.'

'No, you stay and have another drink, Dominic. It's not far.'

He pulled a wry face, but let her go off by herself.

She walked quickly, pausing as she went round the corner to look up at the sun dipping behind the hills. It had almost disappeared but a pink and mauve colour was diffusing over the skyline. She remembered how she'd once thought it was a miracle that the sun could disappear behind the hills and reappear from the depths of the sea in the morning. Her father had explained about the earth being round and so on but she'd still thought it was a miracle. Still did!

She turned her head and looked out at the darkening sea. There were fireflies dancing on the black waves, illuminating the scene. It was truly romantic, though not if you were all alone surrounded by strolling couples and families taking their children home to bed. She reminded herself that this was the life she'd now chosen, to ensure that she pursued her chosen career to the height of her destiny.

A smile flitted across her lips as she told herself to lighten up. It was a bit early to be having grand thoughts about her destiny.

Oh, yes, she was going to enjoy her evening now that she'd calmed her wicked thoughts and got herself back on the journey that she'd set herself. There would be time enough for romance, marriage, babies and everything else she wouldn't allow herself until she'd established her career.

CHAPTER TWO

ALMOST three weeks later Julia was sitting outside Bernard's office, waiting for her turn to have a one-on-one meeting with him about her progress to date. She was studying the printed sheets that Bernard had handed out at the last tutorial. It was difficult to believe that the first month of their course was almost over. The days had flown by during which they'd all been bombarded with work assignments, essays to write on the theories behind various orthopaedic operations and actual operations to observe in Theatre.

Whilst in Theatre they had to make copious notes, all of which needed to be written up in their own time. The notes then had to be transformed into a coherent observation of the operation, including their own comments and criticisms. These were emailed to Bernard as soon as possible. In no time at all they received an assessment of their work with much criticism from him. She knew she wasn't alone in being the recipient of his scathing comments.

They'd also undertaken sessions in the *Urgences* department, the French equivalent of Accident and Emergency, where they had to do minor operations and treatments on emergency cases, observed and assessed by the director of *Urgences*, Michel Devine. He in turn reported back to the twitchy Bernard.

When Dominic had told everybody that Bernard was reputed to be a hard taskmaster, he had been spot on! She'd been so naive three weeks ago. She hadn't believed she would have to work under such pressure.

Just at that moment Dominic arrived in the corridor and plonked himself down beside her.

'What time's your endurance test?'

She frowned at him. 'Shh. He'll hear you.'

'Don't care if he does. I feel like walking out. It's time he cut us some slack. We're all qualified and experienced doctors, for heaven's sake. Who does he think he is, treating us like—?'

The door opened. 'Good morning, Julia. Dominic,' their taskmaster said, glancing severely at Dominic.

Julia followed Bernard inside and sat down on the upright chair in front of the desk. She wasn't afraid of him, she told herself as he went round to the other side and glanced at the screen of his computer. She reckoned all the information on her was there. Everything she'd ever done since aspiring to take on this arduous course.

He looked across the desk at her and at last there was eye contact with him. She couldn't help the frisson of excitement that ran through her as she looked directly into those dark hazel eyes. Why was she being so perverse in finding herself attracted to this man who'd made the past three weeks such an endurance test for her?

'How are you finding the course, Julia?'

No smile, just that piercing stare that was causing

shivers to run down her spine. Shivers she couldn't possibly analyse.

She took a deep breath. 'It's relentlessly tiring...but exceptionally interesting and frustrating at the same time.'

He frowned. 'In what way is it frustrating?'

'Well, you haven't yet let me loose in Theatre so I can do some actual surgery. I'm getting withdrawal symptoms from all this theorising.'

Was that a brief twitching of the lips or the beginnings of a contemptuous smile on his face? Whatever it was, it died immediately as he looked intensely displeased with her.

'Julia, you will appreciate that I have to make absolutely sure that if I let one of my students 'loose in Theatre', as you put it, that the patient will be in capable hands.'

'Yes, of course, I do appreciate that, but I've had a great deal of experience in Theatre and—'

'So I'm told,' he interrupted dryly. 'Your tutor in London, Don Grainger, gave you an extremely glowing reference, outlining some of the orthopaedic operations you have performed.'

She brightened up at this piece of news. What a treasure Don Grainger had been during her medical-school days and after graduation.

'So,' Bernard continued in the same dour tone, 'during this illustrious career you're pursuing, how much experience have you had of hip replacements?'

Oh, joy! At last she was definitely on home ground! She began to elaborate at length on the hip replacements she'd undertaken, at first assisting before moving on to operating under supervision.

He interrupted to ask questions as she enthused about how she loved to remove the static, painful joint and replace it with a prosthesis. His questions concerned the types of prostheses she'd used, which she preferred and if she enjoyed following up the after-care of her patients.

'But of course I enjoy seeing my patients after I've spent so much time with them in Theatre. Seeing the patient before and after surgery, making sure they're getting the best possible after-care, is all part of the buzz a surgeon gets.'

'Buzz? What do you mean by this?'

In her enthusiasm for the subject she'd gone into English. Embarrassed at getting so carried away, she began to speak French again to dispel the wrinkles of concern that had appeared on his brow. 'It's the wonderful excitement of taking away pain and suffering and restoring a new, more active lifestyle to a patient. Not exactly what I meant but something like that.'

They were both silent for a few moments. The clock on the wall ticked away the seconds, reminding Bernard he had another student to see. He wished he didn't find this one so fascinating. Was it her enthusiasm for the subject or was it something he shouldn't even be thinking about every time he met up with her? She was his student, a career woman, and he was a family man. Never the twain should meet!

He put on his stern tutor expression as he stood up to indicate the interview was over.

'Send Dominic in, please.'

She turned and walked to the door, anxious to escape from the inquisition and the conflict of emotions she was experiencing.

'How was it?' Dominic asked as she came out.

She shrugged her shoulders. 'I've no idea how it went,' she whispered. 'Good luck!'

The next day she was still none the wiser. If anything, she was now feeling even more frustrated. She really was getting withdrawal symptoms from being just a cog in the machinery of this difficult course. She needed to actually make a major contribution to an interesting operation in Theatre, feel the buzz of satisfaction she was used to getting when an operation was a success and the patient's state of health vastly improved.

She looked up from the notes she'd been studying as Bernard walked in and took his place at the front of the tutorial room. The chattering between the students died down as ten pairs of eyes focussed on their professor. She thought he looked slightly worried this morning as he glanced around the room.

'Good morning.' A slight nod of the head in her direction as he acknowledged her, seated, as she had been so far this course, in the front row.

Bernard's serious expression didn't change as he began to explain what would happen that morning. They had admitted a patient three days before who had been on the waiting list for a hip replacement. Apparently, the lady in question was from a medical background herself. She had elected to have her operation under general anaesthetic and in the interests of furthering the education of the budding surgeons in Bernard's group she had agreed that her operation should be used for teaching purposes.

'Surgery begins at eleven this morning.' He seemed to be directing his statement right at her.

Why was he still looking at her? She tried to shrink down in her seat. He raised his eyes again to address the now apprehensive students.

'I shall be performing the operation with the help of a qualified and experienced junior surgeon and one of my students.'

He was looking at her again. She swallowed hard.

'I have deliberately given you no warning of this because there will be times in your future careers when you will be called upon to operate at short notice and I wanted to see how you handle the added adrenalin that sometimes causes panic amongst the less suitable candidates.'

He smiled. Thank goodness! It was as if the sun had come out. She shifted awkwardly in her seat, sensing that he was about to make an important announcement.

'The reason I sent out a questionnaire before you arrived here, asking about previous experience of hip replacement surgery, was to ascertain who might be a likely candidate for the first operation of the course. Several of you indicated varying degrees of competence. I consider that some of you would be perfectly capable of being my second assistant this morning.'

He read from a list, Julia holding her breath apprehensively after she heard her name read out.

'There's no need to be worried. We are a teaching hospital with excellent insurance.' His smile broadened. 'There is a stipulation that patients must be chosen with care and must agree to everything that might happen during their surgery. The patient we will operate on this morning is a retired surgeon herself and fully co-operative. Now...'

He paused and looked around the class. 'Who would like the opportunity to work with me this morning?'

Talk about adrenalin pumping! Her heart was pounding so quickly she felt everyone in the room would hear it. This was the opportunity she should seize on. The opportunity she'd asked Bernard for. The old Julia would have been leaping to her feet, desperate for the experience. These days she could feel real fear whenever opportunity knocked.

Seconds dragged by. Nobody had moved. Several throats had been cleared, including Bernard's. She could feel his eyes boring into her. What had her father always told her? Feel the fear and do it anyway.

Her hand shot up, seemingly having a life of its own. Every fibre of her body was warning her to hold off, not to stick her neck out, but this was why she'd come here. To challenge herself and banish her insecurities. She could do this! Raising her eyes tentatively towards the rostrum, she was rewarded by a look of intense pride.

Bernard knew he'd goaded her on that morning. He'd deliberately put her to the test and she hadn't failed him. He'd already seen for himself how knowledgeable she was about her passion but, from what he'd learned during their brief time since she arrived, she was a student who needed her confidence boosted. And this could only be done by subjecting her to difficult and demanding situations that required top-class skills, diligent training, impeccable qualifications and endless energy. The ability to carry on long after your whole body was experiencing real physical weariness, if required.

Though he didn't doubt that intellectually she was probably streets ahead of her louder colleagues he worried that she might not be physically strong enough at times. He would have the same concerns with any female student. A fact that had made him consider hard about offering her a place on this course. If he was honest with himself, he'd only admitted her to the course as a favour to his old friend Don Grainger. Don was no fool. He wouldn't have put her forward to take the course if he didn't think she was a natural surgeon.

But Julia still had to prove herself to him. Although he trusted his old friend, he needed to be in Theatre with her himself to actually make a sound judgement.

He composed his features back to the completely objective, professional tutor he was supposed to be. But it was difficult to hold back the elation he felt now that his plan had worked. The teacher in him wanted to build up her confidence, which he surmised had for some reason taken a knock somewhere along the way. The fact that he found her impossibly attractive must be dealt with as a separate issue, which couldn't in any way colour his professional judgement of her.

'Thank you, Julia. Would you meet me in the ante-theatre at ten-thirty, please? We shall be using the teaching theatre where those of you not required on the lower surgery area will sit on the raised seats behind the transparent screens. You will be able to hear everything, take notes and ask questions at the end of the operation.'

Julia dealt with the moment of panic that suddenly

came over her. She needed to escape and scan her notes. She mustn't leave anything to chance during her debut in Theatre. And she wanted time to check out the patient. That was always important. She wasn't dealing with an abstract. This was a human being who deserved respect so perhaps it would be possible to…

Thoughts tumbled through her mind as she hurried to the door, only to find that Bernard was waiting there for her.

'Would you like to meet the patient?'

She gave a sigh of relief. 'That's definitely on my check list…along with everything else I need to do.'

'Don't worry. There's plenty of time.'

She revelled in his smooth, soothing voice and remembered that he must have had to go through difficult situations to reach the heights of his profession. She had a lot to prove to him so she felt intensely nervous because he still hadn't thawed out with her. Could she work alongside him without making a fool of herself?

She squared her shoulders. She would do the best for the patient, as she had always done, and Bernard's opinion of her didn't matter. Oh, but his opinion of you does matter, said a small, nagging voice in her head.

'You look nervous, Julia,' he said, as if reading her thoughts. 'Take a deep breath. Now let it out. That's better. I wouldn't let you operate on my patient if I didn't think you were capable, extremely capable according to your previous tutor.'

She felt as if she'd grown taller already and much stronger. Her thoughts were clearing and she could feel a list of priorities forming in her head.

He led her along the corridor, speaking now in a gentler tone than he usually used. She felt comforted, supported both physically and mentally. His arm brushed hers as they walked together and she was surprised by the sparks of attraction his close proximity aroused. Not an easy situation to be in. Nervous of Bernard because he would be judging her performance in Theatre, concerned about their patient and surprised at the frequent frissons of attraction towards her boss. This was going to be an intensely difficult situation.

He had a difficult job as tutor to ten students who had begun to regard him as the enemy. But she was beginning to view Bernard differently. Again she felt a tingling down her spine and knew she mustn't give in to this strange insane feeling that was forcing itself upon her.

'You see, Julia, in most hospital situations the surgical team meet the patient before they operate, don't they? So I do like my students to be involved in the pre-operative and post-operative care of their patients, working alongside the full-time hospital staff.'

She felt her clinical interest rising along with the added interest engendered by simply being alongside this charismatic man. On this, her surgical debut day, when she wanted to use her skills and knowledge as best she could, she was also trying so hard not to let her personal interest in him get in the way.

'Yes, as I told you, I would very much like to meet our patient. You said she was a surgeon?'

'An extremely eminent surgeon here in France. As a student I was very much in awe of her.'

'So you've known her a long time?'

He smiled as he looked sideways at his demure companion, looking so fresh, so young, so infinitely…he checked his thoughts…capable. Yes, she was capable. That was all that mattered.

He composed his thoughts again. 'I feel we shall experience full co-operation from our learned colleague. She was a great help when I was a young student in Paris.'

They walked together along the corridor, he adapting his stride to her slower pace. In the orthopaedic ward Bernard led her into one of the single rooms.

'Hello, Brigitte. How are you this morning?'

The patient, who was seated in a comfortable armchair by the window, smiled and put down her newspaper.

'Bernard! I'm very well, thank you, and so relieved that I'm going to have my operation today.'

He introduced Julia as a well-qualified doctor from England who was working towards a career in orthopaedic surgery.

'Julia has had a great deal of surgical experience. She has been mentored by our esteemed colleague Don Grainger and comes to us with his own high recommendations.'

The patient smiled. 'High praise indeed from Don.'

'Well, he's been Julia's tutor since medical school and he wrote in glowing terms about her capabilities. So much so that I've decided to tell my designated assistant to remain on standby in the theatre. I may or may not need him. How would you both feel about that?'

Brigitte leaned forward towards Julia. 'I would be delighted to help you up the career ladder in any way I can, Julia. After the operation—at which, of course, you must assist—we must have a long chat. I truly miss my days in surgery but my arthritis cut my career short. I like to keep up with the latest developments, though.'

Bernard was waiting for Julia's answer. 'And how do you feel about assisting with the surgery, Julia?'

'Very honoured.' She felt confident. Why shouldn't she be, with such generous support from the patient and professor?

'Excellent!' Bernard smiled.

Jeanine, the orthopaedic sister, came in to explain that they were about to prepare their patient for surgery. Did Bernard wish to do a further examination? He said he would like a few minutes to show his assistant the extent of the arthritic damage to the hip. Brigitte, walking with a stick, made her way back to her bed and lay down with a thankful sigh of relief.

She pointed out the most painful areas of her leg, which were around the the head of the right femur. Bernard held up the X-rays so that Julia could see the extent of the arthritic erosion and they discussed the method they were going to use to remove the damaged bone and replace it with a prosthesis.

Leaving the patient to be prepared for Theatre by the nursing staff, Julia still felt slightly apprehensive but at the same time she realised how lucky she was to be given an ideal situation like this in which to move forward, gathering confidence along the way. At the same time she would not only be furthering her career, she would be easing the pain and improving the health of a patient, which was why she and all the members of her family had joined the medical profession.

She walked towards the medical quarters. She needed

a few minutes of peace and quiet to gather her thoughts and focus on the operation in front of her. She no longer felt the need to check her notes. Every bit of knowledge she needed was stored in her brain. She'd assisted at a hip replacement before on several occasions, actually performing part of the surgery with an experienced surgeon hovering nearby, watching her every move, ready to stop or correct anything he didn't approve of.

It wouldn't be any different this time, except that it would be Bernard who would be doing the hovering. And this affinity she felt with him, this desperation to please him was something that unnerved her. It wasn't just that he was her chief in this situation. It was something more than that. Something definitely emotional. An emotional connection. And she was trying to avoid emotion.

Where relationships were concerned she didn't trust herself, judging by her track record. At least she should leave all emotion outside the door of the theatre and concentrate all her training and expertise on doing the best for her patient.

Bernard was waiting for her when she nervously pushed open the swing doors of the ante-theatre. He gave her a smile of encouragement.

'OK?'

She smiled back with a confidence she didn't feel— yet! It would come back to her as soon as she started working. Concentrate on the patient, she told herself. Don't think about yourself. Remember the last time you assisted at a hip replacement. The outcome was excellent. The patient survived to live a useful life—and so did you!

She scrubbed up. A nurse helped her into her sterile gown.

'We're ready to begin, Bernard,' the anaesthetist said over the intercom.

They were ready. Julia was aware of the bright lights as she followed Bernard into the theatre. Indistinguishable faces appeared as blurs through the transparent screen. She made her way towards the motionless figure on the theatre table aware, not for the first time, that going into Theatre felt very much like going on stage.

She was so involved during the operation that she had no time to worry about herself. Her concentration was taken up completely by the task in hand. She found herself working harmoniously with Bernard. Sometimes he would nod to her across the shrouded figure on the table, indicating that she should perform the next stage while he supervised. All the procedures came back to her immediately as her fingers deftly performed what was required.

Time flew by and it seemed only minutes before she was finishing the final sutures. At that point she suddenly became aware of Bernard's eyes on her as they had been during the entire operation. She placed her final used instrument on the unsterile tray, which a theatre nurse was preparing to remove. As she did so she glanced up at Bernard's eagle eyes above his mask. She thought he was smiling but she couldn't be sure as he turned to speak to the theatre sister and began giving her instructions on the immediate after-care of their patient.

There was nothing more for her to do in Theatre. It was all over and she'd survived, and more importantly so had Brigitte. The patient was now being wheeled into the recovery room. As she made her way out through the swing doors, Bernard came up to speak to her.

'I think a debriefing session would be a good idea this evening, Julia.'

As he held open the swing door and followed her out, she allowed herself to admit that the sparks of attraction she'd felt as his gloved hand had brushed hers during the operation had been difficult to ignore. And when she'd looked up once to the eyes above the mask she'd had to take a deep breath to remain focussed and professional.

She looked up at him as they walked together along the corridor. 'Yes, that would be very helpful.'

'Come along to my office about six.'

He was pushing open the door of his office as he spoke as if anxious to be alone again. The door closed behind him and he walked across to his chair. He had to admit to himself that Julia really was a natural. Everything that Don had said about her was true. What Don had failed to mention about his prize student was how attractive she was.

What was it about Julia that made him feel so physically moved when they were together? Even in Theatre, the place where usually he was at his most professional, he'd felt sparks of attraction. That time when he'd passed her an instrument and their gloved hands had briefly touched... He shouldn't be thinking like this!

He had a difficult ex-wife to deal with, a wonderful six-year-old son who should be his priority. He shouldn't even be allowing these insane thoughts to enter his mind. He leaned back in his chair and took a deep breath. That made it worse because he was sure he could still smell that subtle perfume that lingered around her.

Was he going mad? He switched on his computer and forced himself to begin writing up his notes on the operation.

Walking down the corridor, Julia had no idea what impression she'd given Bernard during the operation. He'd given her no indication of his assessment of her performance as he'd closed the door, seemingly anxious to get away from her.

Her confidence, which had been high in Theatre, was now wavering but she reminded herself of the way he'd reassured her all the way through the operation. Now that she had time to reflect, she thought he'd even smiled into his mask on occasion and nodded approval as she'd used her initiative. And she was almost sure she'd heard him whisper, 'Well done!' as she'd finished the final suture—or had she imagined that?

But did it matter what Bernard thought of her performance? If she was satisfied that she'd given it one hundred per cent and made life easier for her patient then that was what really mattered, wasn't it? Seeking approbation from Bernard was not why she'd come here.

She walked away purposefully. She would make notes, be ready to ask questions and take the criticisms that would help make her a better surgeon in the future.

At six o'clock she was standing outside Bernard's office, waiting for the second hand to reach the top of her watch.

'Come in!'

He was sitting at his desk. He stood up and came towards her as she closed the door, motioning her to sit in one of the armchairs placed near the window. He took the other one and opened a file of notes. She put her briefcase on the floor at the side of her chair after taking out her own small laptop.

'So how do you think the operation went, Julia?'

She cleared her throat and launched into the questions she'd prepared, going through all the steps of the operation from the first incision to the final suture.

He answered all her questions carefully and lucidly while she made notes on her laptop.

She leaned back against the back of the armchair as he answered her final question, and looked across at him. The expression on his face gave nothing away for a few seconds until he relaxed and gave her a studied smile.

'Excellent! I like a student who has everything under control both during and after the operation. I've no doubt you'll make a first-class surgeon.'

She breathed a sigh of relief. She'd sensed his approval but until that moment she couldn't be sure she hadn't been imagining it.

She smiled back. 'Thank you, Bernard. So, do you have any questions for me?'

'Just one.' He hesitated. He really shouldn't say what was uppermost in his mind. But he planned to be very careful if he felt himself giving in to the wrong emotions.

'It's been a long and intense day. Your trip shouldn't all be about work, however. You are a visitor to France after all, so may I buy you a drink at the Maurice Chevalier?'

She hesitated for a couple of seconds. She doubted very much that Bernard had extended this invitation to any of her fellow students, but his offer had been very formal. She would be foolish to try and read too much into it. Finally she smiled and nodded her agreement.

As she closed her laptop and put it back in its case she was aware of the now familiar tingling feeling running down her spine. Apprehension?

Yes, but it was something more than that, she admitted as she felt the light touch of Bernard's arm as he ushered her out through the door.

CHAPTER THREE

THE Maurice Chevalier was deserted when they first arrived. Julia breathed a sigh of relief. The last thing she wanted was to seen by her fellow students socialising with their tyrannical boss. She had mixed feelings about her motivation in accepting his offer to buy her a drink. Yes, he was thawing out towards her. But would her colleagues think this was favouritism? And should she be alone with him in a social situation given the insane feelings she'd been experiencing?

Very soon a trickle of sunset worshippers gradually filled up most of the tables overlooking the sea. She folded her white cashmere sweater on her lap as she sat down and breathed in the scent of the sea and this unspoiled stretch of the coast that she loved so much.

It was turning a bit chilly now that the sun had disappeared behind a cloud so she would soon have an excuse to wear the new sweater that she'd fallen in love with when she'd been doing some last-minute panic buying in London . She didn't usually spend so much on clothes but she'd salved her conscience by convincing herself that anything that would boost her depleted confidence was a definite asset.

'What would you like to drink, Julia?'

'I'll have a Kir please, Bernard.'

He nodded before going inside to the bar, returning shortly with her crème de cassis and white wine aperitif and a pastis with ice and water for himself.

She smiled as he placed the drinks on the table. 'Thank you. I used to come here as a child with my parents and brothers when we were on holiday. My mother used to drink Kir. I knew it was a very grown-up drink but she allowed me a small sip. I loved the taste of the blackcurrant juice mixed in with white wine. As soon as I was old enough I tried one for myself and that became my favourite aperitif in the evenings.'

'To your grown-up Kir, Julia.' Bernard smiled as he raised his glass to her. He thought she looked so lovely now with the sun low in the sky on her face. What an enigma she was! To think that she had performed so self-assuredly in Theatre today and yet here she was reminiscing so naively about her childhood.

She smiled back as she took her first sip. 'Mmm! So reviving after a long day in hospital!'

'You deserve it after your performance this morning. I was proud of you—I mean, you're one of the students I selected from a large number of applicants who wanted a place on the course so it's good to know you didn't let me down.'

He hastily drank from his glass of pastis with ice, adding some water so that he wouldn't become too exuberant. He didn't want Julia to misinterpret his remarks. She might think he…well, he fancied her in some way. Perish the thought, he lied to himself, knowing full well that she was a most attractive woman and he'd better be careful or he might go overboard in his admiration.

But putting that aside, he told himself sharply, trying to leave his admiration out of the equation, whenever he discovered a talented student he found it very satisfying, euphoric almost! But he'd better hold back with the praise so that Julia would work hard throughout the course and not let him down. And he must also be aware that his delight in her achievements had to remain totally without emotional attachment.

Nevertheless, it was certainly true that he found himself drawn towards her in a way that a professor shouldn't think of his student. They were both adults, yes, but he mustn't let this attraction he felt affect his professional judgement of her during the months of hard work ahead.

He looked across the table. 'So tell me, Julia, what made you apply for this course?'

She hesitated before answering. 'Well…er…having survived a disastrous marriage that had been a total mistake, I felt it was time to make a fresh start and get on with my career. My family background also contributed to my decision. Mum and Dad, who'd planned to be surgeons when they were in medical school, had then taken a more practical route to become general practitioners because they fell in love, married when my eldest brother was on the way and…'

She broke off and took a deep breath. 'Sorry, Bernard, you don't need to know all this.'

'Oh, but I do. It's fascinating! Your story is similar to mine, in fact. I too come from a medical background where my parents gave up their ambitions in favour of family life. Please go on.'

She felt relieved she wasn't boring him. 'Well, as I

told you before, GP parents and three brothers, now surgeons, meant I had to be a high achiever to get myself heard in the family. Fortunately I enjoyed studying my favourite subjects. Only when I hastily married Tony after a whirlwind courtship and found it so difficult to find the time for study did I question the sanity of becoming a surgeon.'

She leaned back against her chair, her eyes temporarily blinded by the sun low in the sky, setting behind the hillside that swooped down into the sea. She delved into her bag for her sunglasses.

'That's better.'

She paused to gather her thoughts. How much should she tell him? He was a good listener, seemed interested, but was he simply being polite?

'At times I despaired of my exhausting role of wife, stepmother, medical student...'

'So you hadn't qualified when you married. Why didn't you wait until...?'

'I thought I was madly in love! I'd never been in love before and the wonderful euphoric sensations I experienced when I first met Tony swept me along. For the first time in my life I entered a world that was quite different from my own.'

Bernard looked puzzled as he watched the vibrant expressions on her face. 'In what way was it different?'

'Tony was a very successful man, having made enormous profits in the building and property business, proud of the fact that he'd come from a deprived background and made something of himself. Money meant everything to him. He lived and breathed doing deals, buying expensive clothes for himself, for the children and for me. He told me he'd outgrown his first wife, she was lazy, an ex-model who'd let herself go and wouldn't keep up with his aspirations so he'd set her up in an expensive house where she could bring up their two children. He'd bought a luxurious flat in London where he could continue his wheeling and dealing.

'I found out later that his wife had divorced him because of his womanising, realising that she was happier without him. She'd been hoping for a huge divorce settlement but she was still waiting. Of course, I didn't know any of this when I first saw him at the opera.'

'The opera?'

She smiled. 'Oh, it was a business deal he was doing with a client and he clinched it by taking this man and his wife to a performance of *La Bohème*. Anyway, I'd gone along with a group of fellow medical students and we were queuing at the bar in the interval, trying to get a drink.

'Tony was in front of me and put on the charm when he gathered that we were all medical students. He insisted on buying everybody a drink before whisking me off to his table and introducing me to his business friends as a young doctor. With the benefit of hindsight I know I shouldn't have allowed myself to be swept away by an unknown man who liked to flash his cash but I was still young, impressionable, and having had a cloistered childhood this whirlwind from another exciting world seemed the epitome of sophistication.'

'But what about your own friends? Didn't they think…?'

'Oh, they were happy to accept the free drinks but they thought I'd gone mad…which actually I had, for the first time in my life! I'd always been so careful to toe the line and do everything my mother and father told me…especially my mother. She'd insisted I mustn't marry until I was well established in my career. She used to constantly tell me about how she'd sacrificed her ambitions and forced herself to be content with life as a country GP, married to a GP, struggling with a huge workload whilst bringing up a family.'

She looked across the table at Bernard, who was hanging on her every word. She took a deep breath as she remembered her totally out-of-character stupidity in those early days of her relationship with the charismatic but totally unreliable Tony.

'You see, I was totally blown away by Tony's charismatic aura. I'd never seen anyone like him before except on TV or in a film. Looking back and remembering, I can't believe how gullible I was in those days. I feel as if I'm remembering something that happened to someone else, a little sister if I'd had one, someone with no experience of real life—which, in a way, was exactly how I was. I couldn't take my eyes off this tall, handsome character in the well-cut, expensive suit who seemed to demand attention from everybody who was listening to his deep, sexy voice.'

She paused as the weird memories from her past came back to her.

She took a deep breath as she watched Bernard's reaction. Yes, he was a good listener and definitely seemed to want her to continue.

'Tony was proud of the fact that he was a self-made man who'd come from a poor background. At the time I just couldn't help admiring him and then the admiration blossomed into something more dangerous and I fell for him, hook, line and sinker, whilst enjoying the fact that he seemed attracted to me.'

'So he was impressed by the fact that you were a medical student?'

'Oh, he thought I was a good catch. He told me during our disastrous marriage that he'd thought I must be from a wealthy family because we were all doctors. How wrong he was! Our education was the top priority to my parents and that made a big hole in the family budget.

'What I didn't realise was that his business deals were getting fewer and further between and he needed to find a wealthy wife to help keep him in the lifestyle he'd got used to during his successful years. My parents met him for the first time at our registry office wedding. My mother could hardly disguise her dislike of him and she made no secret of the fact that I'd let her down badly. That hurt…that really hurt.'

Her voice faltered as she remembered the angst she'd suffered, knowing full well that it was all her fault, knowing she'd hurt her mother who'd given up so much to raise her family. She shifted in her seat, pulling the sweater around her shoulders as she glanced away from Bernard towards the beautiful seascape in front of them. Maybe she should stop talking about her past and give him a chance to recover from his busy day.

'Bernard, you're a good listener but I don't want to bore you.'

'Please continue! I'm fascinated. I can see where you're coming from now. I do like to take an interest in the background of my students. As you say in England, it helps if I know what makes them tick, isn't it, Julia?'

'Yes, you got that exactly right, Bernard. You're finding out what makes me tick.'

He leaned across the table. 'I can tell you already, having known you only a couple of days. You're aiming for the top and it isn't easy, believe me. You'll reach the next peak and what will you find? Another peak to climb!'

He broke off. 'Please do go on. So you married this man from a different world? Were you happy at first?'

'Well, for the first few weeks of our marriage Tony boasted to all his associates—I won't call them friends because they were mostly hangers-on intent on helping themselves to his dwindling cash—about his clever young wife who was going to be a doctor. But the problem was that he thought I could pass my exams without spending time studying, be the perfect stepmother to his children when they came to stay at weekends, be a good hostess to his clients—and I quickly realised it wasn't possible. That's when it all turned nasty. His attitude completely changed. He seemed to think that by shouting at me he could turn me into superwoman, perfect in everything he wanted me to do for him.'

'You have another saying in England—marry in haste, repent at leisure. Isn't that right?' Bernard was watching her reaction. 'Was that what happened?'

'Exactly! He changed completely once the ring was on my finger and he realised my family hadn't endowed me with money. One of the things he told me before we married was that having fathered twins who were then five, a boy and a girl, he didn't want any more children.

It was a struggle to come to terms with that because I'd always hoped I would have children of my own when I'd established my career.

'I subjugated my own desires for parenthood by immersing myself in taking care of my stepchildren. I loved those two as if they were my own and it was a terrible wrench when we split up and I lost all contact with them.'

Bernard noticed the emotional waver in her voice as she said this. Yes, he could see she would adore starting a family. Warning bells were ringing in his head. He mustn't get too familiar with her.

'So what caused you to split up?'

'It was pressures of my work and trying to take care of my stepchildren. Tony, not being from a medical background, just didn't understand. I adored the children, bonded with them and began to put them before my medical studies, but Tony was still dissatisfied with the amount of time I could spare him. He began to look elsewhere.

'Everything came to a head one fateful weekend just six months after we were married. I was trying to get to grips with some revision in the study and was working on my computer when he flung open the door and told me to leave all that medical stuff and get into some expensive clothes. It was important that I should get out of my scruffy tracksuit and tart myself up so that I looked drop-dead gorgeous. He'd been speaking to a prospective client and he was taking him and his wife out for lunch. The wife, apparently, was a real doll and knew how to dress so I'd better make the effort.'

She took another deep breath as the awful memories of that occasion came flooding back.

'I pointed out that I had an exam on the Monday and I needed to study...'

She broke off as she remembered how miserable she'd felt. Bernard put his hand across the table and laid it over her slender fingers. 'Julia, you don't have to tell me if it's too awful to remember.'

She swallowed hard. The touch of his fingers and his obvious concern for her unnerved her. Careful! Be very careful. Don't mistake sympathy with emotional involvement.

'Tony told me he was fed up with seeing me studying. I was no fun any more. And then he blurted out that he'd met somebody else. He wanted a divorce.'

'So...what did you do?'

'To be honest, I'd had enough and it was a blessed relief to think that I could walk away from the hell that my life had become. I asked him to have my things sent to the medical school. He said he would make all the necessary arrangements for my stuff to be sent wherever I wanted. I took my laptop and a few books, went back to the medical school and tried to concentrate on the exams looming after that disastrous weekend.'

'You must have felt...'

'I felt relieved to escape from Tony.' She shivered at the bad memories that still haunted her, often preventing her from sleeping in the night. 'But terribly sad to lose contact with the children.'

They sat for a few moments in silence. Bernard had been deeply moved by the story of her marriage. He could see how she would need her confidence to be boosted at every possible moment. But he mustn't go overboard. Mustn't allow emotion to take over. Yet he didn't want to cut short the evening and they both needed a meal after their long day.

'Let's go inside and have something to eat. That's if you'd like to,' he added. 'Maybe you've got other plans tonight, meeting up with friends from the group or…'

'No plans tonight except to relax.' She smiled up at him. He was already standing, looking down at her.

He led the way. Inside, the warmth of the sun had made the place feel cosy and inviting. He held out her chair for her. The waiter came along and Bernard asked what the *plat du jour* was.

'Always best to get the main dish that's been cooked that day in these small places, don't you think?'

She felt very comfortable with him as he ordered the coq au vin for them. It came in a large casserole dish. Bernard dug the large serving spoon into the centre and helped her to a generous portion.

'Hey, steady on!' she said, reaching across to touch his wrist. A shiver went down her spine, a quite different shiver to the cold one she'd experienced outside. She felt they must have met somewhere before in a former life. She put both hands back in her lap.

'Did you live near here when you were a child, Bernard?'

He passed her plate across to her. 'I was born just five miles from here, up there in the valley beyond the hills. My grandparents were farmers. The farm is still there, but my father decided he wanted to be a doctor. He went off to medical school in Paris—like I did—and after qualifying he did a course in general practice so that he could come back to our village and fill a very real need. He set up practice in a room at the end of the house and my mother acted as receptionist and nurse besides running the family. She had trained as a nurse in Boulogne but she was born in the village.'

She swallowed a spoonful of the delicious chicken casserole. 'Did you have brothers and sisters?'

He shook his head sadly. 'No, my mother wanted to have more children but it didn't happen. She died of ovarian cancer when I was six.'

'That must have been awful for you and your father. However did you cope?'

'My father employed a lady from the village to help out as nurse, receptionist and housekeeper but it was hard for him to adapt. He also employed her daughter Marianne to help her mother with the housekeeping and look after me. She's still working up there at the farm just as she did when she was sixteen. She took care of me from the time I was six and when she married in her late teens her husband moved in to work on the farm. They became part of the family.'

He hesitated for a moment as if to compose himself. 'I was fifteen when my father died. He'd never been the same since my mother's death. He went through the motions of being a competent doctor but one harsh winter he succumbed to a bout of influenza that turned to pneumonia. I think he simply lost the will to live without my mother.'

They were both silent for a while, engrossed in their own thoughts as the delicious, home-cooked food revived them.

Bernard cleared his throat and put down his spoon.

'I always wanted to marry someone who would be my soul mate as my parents had been together,' he said huskily. 'But it didn't happen. Like you, I was mistaken about the partner I chose—or did she choose me?'

He gave her a whimsical smile. 'If only I could turn the clock back. Apart from the fact that I wouldn't have had my wonderful son, Philippe, if I hadn't met Gabrielle.'

She leaned back in her chair, watching the sad expression that flitted across his face. The young families around them were departing now, mothers ushering their offspring out of the door as fathers paid the bills. It was all so nostalgic. Why couldn't she have replicated something like this? Why couldn't Bernard?

It wasn't just that both of them were career minded, both aiming to climb the peaks to the top of their chosen profession. It was possible to have a career and a family—but not yet! The timing was wrong. She mustn't get ideas about the rapport building up between them. She mustn't fantasise about developing a meaningful relationship with Bernard.

'How often do you see your son?'

'As often as I can escape from my work. I'm going to Paris this weekend to see him. Philippe lives with Gabrielle in her mother's house, which is very convenient. His grandmother dotes on him and has been a tower of strength to all of us when my wife was…well, lacking in maternal instinct and hell bent on—'

He broke off. 'No, you don't want to hear all the sordid details of our less than perfect marriage.'

She wanted to say, Oh yes, I do. She liked to hear about other people making mistakes in their lives. It made her feel in some way that she wasn't the only naive idiot where relationships were concerned. But she remained silent

'I'll get the bill.' He signalled for the waiter. Suddenly he was turning back into the professional as his thoughts turned to the work ahead.

'I've asked Dominic to assist me tomorrow in Theatre. He came to me this afternoon and said he would be happy to assist. It just so happens I've got to do a knee replacement tomorrow morning so I'll be able to put him through his paces. He's had a lot of experience but wasn't brave enough to volunteer for the first operation of the class.' He stood up and moved round to hold the back of her chair. As they walked to the door he said, 'Thank you for setting the ball rolling today, Julia. You'll be a difficult act to follow.'

As they walked back together towards the hospital she was aware of his hand hanging loosely by his side. She so wished he would take hold of hers but she realised he was in professional mode again. Just as well when she'd decided to keep a rein on her own emotions.

'I've got to do some work,' he said briskly, not trusting himself to relax his guard as they stood together outside the main door of the hospital. He did have work to do in his consulting room but he was trying to ignore his real feelings. What he wanted to do was whisk her back to his rooms in the medics' quarters and… No, don't go there, he told himself as he looked down at her beautiful face turned up towards his.

'So have I,' she said quickly, knowing full well that all she wanted to do was have a hot shower and climb into bed. The shower should help to take away the mad emotions running through her mind and her body, but would she be able to sleep?

'Goodnight, Julia. See you tomorrow.'

He bent down and brushed the side of her face with his lips, telling himself they were off duty now and hospital protocol had no place in this private moment. He mustn't give anyone cause to think that he was favouring one of his students because he wasn't. But he couldn't bear to let her go without some brief contact. Anyway, it was normal to exchange kisses on the cheek in France after spending the evening with a pleasant companion.

She walked quickly in the opposite direction from his consulting room, taking the long way round to her study-bedroom in the medics' quarters. She didn't look back.

He watched the slight, slim figure in the beautiful white sweater and figure-hugging black trousers turning the corner at the end of the corridor. He'd better wait a few moments before he made his way to his own study-bedroom, where he planned to sleep that night. He felt too tired to drive out to the farm and he'd had a couple of glasses of wine with the meal. He could go and do some work in his consulting rooms but he didn't think it would be easy to concentrate tonight.

He realised the nurse on Reception was watching him. He hoped he'd given Julia enough time to disappear into her room.

He let the water cascade over him as he soaped himself with shower gel. His mind was buzzing with conflicting ideas. It was going to be so difficult to keep his growing admiration for Julia under control. He had to remain totally professional. But that was easier said than done.

He stepped out of the shower and reached for a towel. He'd hoped the hot water would help to put him in a steadier mood. It had been a long time since he'd felt like this. As he dried himself and threw the towel towards the laundry bin he recognised the symptoms only too well. It wasn't necessary to have medical qualifications to recognise that he was very attracted to Julia. And he wanted to go along with this mad, wonderful feeling. But it could be disastrous!

He climbed between the cool sheets, kicking at the corners where the maid had tucked them in. That was better. One of the perks of being a consultant was that you had daily maid service and a decent-sized room. He thought of the tiny room where Julia would be cloistered and hoped she was comfortable. She would have forgotten all about him and knowing how conscientious she was she would be reading up about knee-replacement operations.

He put his hands behind his head and leaned back against the pillow as he thought about how she had suffered with her marriage. He would have liked to talk about his own marriage with her but had decided against it even though he just knew she would have lent him a sympathetic ear. But he'd never told anyone the full story of what had gone wrong with Gabrielle. He'd been every bit as gullible as Julia! But at least he had his adorable son, Philippe, to dote on—the one good thing to have come from that ill-advised union.

Which reminded him about the latest bombshell his ex-wife had dropped recently. She was planning to get married again. The prospective husband was rich apparently but also considerably older than she was with grown-up children from a previous marriage and he didn't want a young child around the house. So she'd asked him to have Philippe live with him.

Bernard knew he would be absolutely thrilled at having Philippe with him. He'd already planned ahead so that the new arrangement would work. Philippe could stay at the farm during the day with Marianne, go to the local school as he'd done, make friends in the village. He felt the excitement rising at the prospect. But it was tinged with apprehension about how Veronique, Gabrielle's mother, would react.

His ex-wife hadn't yet told her mother of her plans. It would be too cruel to simply take Philippe away. He was like her own son and she'd poured all her considerable maternal love into his upbringing to the age of six. He would have to make sure Veronique came over to see Philippe and that he took his son to Paris as often as he could.

He could feel the doubts creeping in already and knew that if he was really honest with himself the situation was far from solved. Ah, well, he'd have to contend with that problem this weekend when he went to Paris. Meanwhile, he'd better try to get some sleep.

He allowed himself to think about Julia as he closed his eyes, alarmed at the physical reaction surging through his body. If only he'd been able to bring her back here, make love to her and then fall asleep with her in his arms.

He knew that it was going to take an effort on his part but he had to stop thinking like this, definitely try to see her only in a professional situation. Yes, that was what he should do. But whether he could keep to this resolution was a different matter.

CHAPTER FOUR

As JULIA showered in the tiny bathroom tucked away in the corner of her study-bedroom her thoughts turned to the day ahead. Hard to believe she'd been here more than a month. The last five weeks had flown by so quickly as she'd tried hard to put all her energy into adapting to her new situation.

She stepped out of the shower and grabbed a large fluffy towel. A whole weekend stretched ahead of her. Two whole days when she was going to try and catch up on her sleep, do some work on the notes she'd taken during Bernard's tutorials and then spend some time outside in the glorious June sunshine.

For the past few weeks she'd spent far too much time indoors, in Theatre and in the wards, seeing the pre-operative and post-operative patients in her care. On two occasions she'd been called in to help out in the *Urgences* department, the French equivalent of Accident and Emergency. She'd enjoyed all her work, giving all her energies and expertise to the patients and ensuring she learned and made notes on every important medical experience to store up for future reference.

But as she pulled on her jeans and a favourite old black T-shirt she knew she'd neglected her own health and strength in her desire to embrace every situation in her new life. It was something her parents had constantly chided her about. But it had been a case of 'Do as I say, not do as I do.' She'd long ago realised she was inherently disposed to using up her energy and then falling back on her frazzled nerves with an empty tank of petrol—just like her parents and brothers.

Nevertheless, she had work to do this morning before she could play. She sat down at her desk and reached for her laptop and the notebook that was always in her bag. She tried to put as much information straight onto the laptop but in many situations where she had a hands-on approach this was impossible.

She particularly enjoyed Bernard's tutorials because they seemed to be the only times she saw him nowadays—when they were in a professional situation. He'd definitely thawed out with all of his students and she'd noticed he'd gained their respect now that they appreciated how much he wanted them all to succeed.

She'd been particularly amazed—and gratified!—when he'd praised her in front of all the students, saying she'd made him reassess his opinion of female orthopaedic surgeons. 'I've no doubt now that Julia is inherently talented and a natural at this type of surgery.'

She'd been delighted by his praise, but slightly apprehensive. She worried that her fellow students would tease her for being teacher's pet. She needn't have worried on that score because they crowded aound her at the end of the tutorial, congratulating her. Those who'd watched her debut performance were especially complimentary.

Dominic had actually kissed her on both cheeks,

and as she glanced at their tutor on the rostrum she'd seen him frowning with disapproval. Strange. She didn't know what to make of that. Dominic was ever the flamboyant one of the crowd and she'd made a point of discouraging any advances. While she enjoyed spending time in Dominic's company, if she was honest with herself it was Bernard's attentions she longed for.

She wondered what he was doing this weekend. She knew he'd been off to Paris to see his son on the weekend after they'd enjoyed supper together at the Maurice Chevalier. She'd looked forward to his return but on the Monday morning, as they'd worked together, he'd seemed distant, preoccupied even. During a coffee break, when all her colleagues had been with them, she'd plucked up courage, hoping to break the ice, and asked him if he'd enjoyed his weekend. He'd answered briefly that, yes, it had made a change from hospital life.

From the pained expression on his face she'd deduced it hadn't been a total success. But there had been something else in his manner towards her. Without being overtly cold, he was putting her at arm's length, as it were. Making it obvious that perhaps he regretted being so warm towards her after her debut performance in Theatre. At least, that was how she'd taken it. So she'd thrown herself into her work and reined in her emotions, which, yes, she admitted it now, had been getting out of control.

But it hadn't been easy. She was still plagued by embarrassing thoughts about him. Thoughts that had nothing to do with real life and never could become reality…could they? She was like a teenager with a crush on the teacher! She should get out more, which she was definitely going to do this morning after she'd done some work on her notes.She sighed as she opened up and began reading the scribbled notes, remembering how she'd hung on every word as Bernard had delivered an off-the-cuff mini-lecture about performing amputations a couple of days ago. The importance of preparing the patient both physically and mentally. And then the after-care, the importance of listening, referring the patient to the best professional care. She'd been totally enthralled by his sympathetic approach, by the stories he'd told them about his secondment as an army surgeon in a war zone overseas. Some of his descriptions of what that had entailed had brought tears to her eyes because she'd found herself thinking she was so glad that he hadn't had to have a limb amputated.

That beautiful body of his—well, she assumed it was magnificent beneath the well-cut suits. Occasionally when he took off his jacket and rolled up his sleeves in a practical situation she'd seen muscles that looked as if they should be on one of those statues she'd seen when she'd wandered around the Louvre in Paris.

She made a determined effort to gather her thoughts and get back to the real work in hand.

A couple of hours later she got up from her desk and pulled on her jeans and a T-shirt. Scraping her long blonde hair into a ponytail, she hurried out of her room, anxious to get on the beach before it got too hot.

In a room not too far away down the corridor that was reserved for senior staff Bernard was also working on his laptop. He was transcribing notes for a paper he had to deliver at a conference in Paris soon. He'd been putting it off as he'd had to spend a lot of time with his students during the last month. They were an intelligent group and the work was enjoyable but time consuming.

He glanced at his watch. Good thing he'd started early that morning. He'd still have to finish off the paper while Philippe was here. He'd promised to take him to the beach. Perhaps if he took him there this morning they could go up to the farm, have lunch and then he could work for a couple of hours while Marianne took care of Philippe.

He phoned the farm. Marianne was delighted with the arrangement he proposed. 'Yes, take Philippe to the beach for the good sea air before you come out here for lunch. Your rooms are ready, of course. See you soon, Bernard!'

He started to get ready for the arrival of his son. Philippe's car, driven by the uniformed chauffeur, would arrive soon from Paris. This was one of the perks that Gabrielle had got used to since she'd begun dating the wealthy Frederic—her soon-to-be husband.

Julia walked briskly down to the beach. As the warm summer breeze fanned her cheeks she felt reinvigorated. This was exactly what she needed today. Fresh air. No work. No worries!

She skipped down the wooden steps that led onto the sand and broke into a gentle jog. As her breathing improved to a steady rhythm she increased her pace to a gentle run. Mmm, it was good to know her limbs hadn't seized up as she worked endlessly in hospital! She ran towards the sea and began to follow the shoreline.

'Julia?'

She turned at the sound of a man's voice. A little way up the beach a man in a T-shirt and shorts was digging a moat round a sandcastle. A child was helping him.

'Bernard?' She stood still, panting to get her breath back.

Bernard stopped digging and leaned on his spade. 'I don't mean to disturb your run but I'd love you to meet my son.'

She smiled as she walked up the beach towards him. He came towards her. Her heart, which had increased its rate due to her running, was now beating even more rapidly.

The young boy followed behind.

'Hello.' She smiled down at the young boy who turned to his father, looking up at him adoringly whilst waiting to be enlightened as to who the lady was.

'This is Julia, Philippe.'

Philippe extended his hand towards her. 'Hello, *mademoiselle*.'

She gave the charming boy a big smile. 'Oh, please call me Julia,' she said in French. 'Have you come from Paris this morning?'

Bernard watched her easy rapport with his son. It gave him a warm feeling but warning bells rang. Julia was only here for six months. He mustn't allow a rapport to build up between them. Philippe would be sad when she had to leave. So would he!

'Yes, I came by car. Are you a doctor here, like Papa?'

'Yes, I'm a doctor but I'm also a student on the course

that your father is in charge of. I'm learning how to improve my surgical skills.'

'Oh, yes, Papa has told me all about it. I'm going to be a surgeon when I grow up.'

'Are you?'

'Papa tells me I'll have to work very hard if I want to be a surgeon. Papa works hard all the time. Look at the castle he's building for me, Julia.'

'It's beautiful! A real work of art.'

'What's a work of art?'

'Well, it's something that's beautiful.'

'I've been digging the moat round it and piling the sand on the castle while Papa made the work-of-art bit at the top. I'm going to run down to the sea now and bring back some water in my bucket.'

Julia smiled down at the eager young boy. 'If you start digging a channel down to the sea, the incoming tide will flow into it and come all the way up to the moat round your castle.'

Wide eyes stared up at her in amazement. 'Will it really, Julia? Will you help me?'

She'd been totally unaware that Bernard had been watching with mixed emotions the two of them getting on so well together. He could feel the poignancy of the encounter and the feelings he was experiencing were difficult to understand.

She glanced across at him, her maternal instincts making her want to spend time with this adorable child but at the same time wondering how Bernard would feel. To her relief he was smiling fondly at the pair of them.

'That's a brilliant idea, Julia. Are you sure you can

spare the time? I know your tutor has a reputation for pushing you hard!'

She smiled back at him. 'I'm giving myself the whole day off to recharge my batteries.' She turned back to the little boy, who was still waiting for her answer. 'I'd love to help you, Philippe. Have you got a spare spade?'

Bernard picked up a large plastic bag and passed her a spare spade.

'Thank you.'

His hand, covered in sand, felt rough as it touched hers. She looked up at him and her heart seemed to stand still. She allowed herself to look into his eyes for a second longer before she turned back to his son.

'Come on, Philippe. Let's show Papa how hard we can work together.'

Bernard leaned against his spade as he watched Julia take his son to the edge of the sea. As they sprinted together she looked so young. Her long blonde hair had escaped the band she'd tied round it and was flowing over her shoulders. He couldn't help thinking how much more attractive she looked now than when she had to imprison it in a theatre cap. And, heaven knew, she had a serious effect on him in Theatre even without that tantalising hair showing!

He shouldn't be thinking like this. How many times had he reprimanded himself for breaking his self-made rule of no commitment ever again? And before his eyes he could see the rapport developing between Julia and Philippe.

They were digging their channel now. The tide was coming in and beginning to trickle into it. Throwing aside all his reservations about relationships, he ran down the beach to join them. This was what he needed. Some carefree relaxation. If Julia could give herself a day off, so could he.

The channel grew much quicker now with three of them working together. In no time at all it had reached the moat of the castle and water was trickling in, slowly at first and then more quickly.

Bernard put the finishing touches to the crenellated edge at the top of the castle before reaching into the bag for a small boat.

'Here you are, Philippe. See if your boat will sail round the castle now.'

'Oh, it's brilliant! Look at my boat, Papa!' The little boy was clapping his hands with delight, stopping occasionally to push the boat if it got stuck in the side of the castle. 'Round and round and round and...'

'That was a brainwave of yours, Julia,' Bernard said quietly. 'I can see you've done this a few times.'

She smiled. 'I have indeed. And on this very beach. But the tide's coming in very quickly now so Philippe had better make the most of it. Not long before you'll have to pack up and leave. I'll help gather up your things.'

Together they gathered up the plastic beach toys and Bernard stuffed them back into the large bag. A particularly strong surge of water flooded the moat and he called out to Philippe that they would have to go now.

'No, Papa, I don't want to go!'

Another surge of water swirled around Philippe's ankles. 'OK! I'm coming.'

Philippe ran to his father for safety, putting his arms around his legs. Bernard hoisted him up onto his shoulders and picked up the bag then they all hurried up the beach.

'I've got my car parked on the promenade. I'm taking Philippe up to my farm. Julia, can I give you a lift back to hospital or are you going to keep running on the path up there now that the tide will soon be in? Alternatively...'

He hesitated only a second before putting to her the idea that had been forming in his mind.

'Would you like to come up to the farm with us as you've given yourself a day off from the tyranny of your endless work schedule?'

'Oh, Julia, please say you'll come! I can show you the sheep and the cows and the—'

'That sounds really exciting, Philippe.' She shouldn't accept this invitation but she desperately wanted to. She salved her conscience by telling herself that it would be good for Philippe to have someone other than his father to amuse him. 'Thank you, Bernard, I'd love to see your farm.'

'Hurrah!'

Bernard had already justified his invitation by telling himself that Julia obviously loved children and might like to amuse Philippe while he got on with some work that afternoon. He led the way up the steps and along the promenade to the car.

Philippe had slipped his little hand inside Julia's and was chatting happily to her about the farm, the animals and all the other delights of the place that was his home when he was with his beloved Papa.

'You don't mind sitting in the back, I hope? Philippe

is happier there if he's got someone to talk to and you both seem to have a lot to discuss.'

'Oh, we've got a lot to talk about, haven't we, Philippe? So, did you drive yourself over from Paris this morning?'

Philippe giggled. 'I'm only six.'

'Oh, I thought you were much older.'

'Philippe is six going on sixteen, actually.'

She smiled, positively glowing at the attentions of father and son. Bernard was leaning through the door of the car, checking on Philippe's seat belt and pointing out hers. He was very close as he leaned across to check on both of them. As he straightened up and prepared to close the car door their eyes met and Julia felt a frisson of pure excitement mingled with apprehension running through her. She felt emotionally warm and cosseted and decided to simply go with the flow for a few hours. No point worrying too much about where all this might be leading

There was absolutely nothing wrong with them being friends, she decided. But as she looked up at the expression on Bernard's face she held her breath.

His expression was one of total admiration as he looked at her and she could feel her confidence zooming higher. Bernard was so good for her professional confidence. She remembered how he'd praised her in front of her colleagues. That had given her ego a much-needed boost after the knocks she'd taken in the past. This was what she needed, a totally platonic friendship. The fact that she was only here for just over four more months and shouldn't be building a rapport with Bernard's son was still at the back of mind, but for today she shelved the problem. A day off was a day off from worry.

Bernard drove them out onto the main road.

'I'm going to drive as soon as I'm old enough, Julia. Thomas was explaining about his car this morning when we came down this hill. It's such a clever car, it changes gears all by itself. Papa has to change his own gears in this car, don't you?'

'It makes me feel more in control.' Bernard shifted down a gear as the hill grew steeper.

'Thomas says he'll teach me to drive when I'm older.'

Bernard remained quiet. Who knew what the future held? There were so many hurdles to negotiate in the new situation that his ex-wife had thrust upon them.

Julia was also confused about the man Thomas but she didn't want to ask questions. It was Philippe who provided a clue.

'Thomas took his cap off when we got outside Paris. Mummy likes him to wear it when he takes us shopping. He's Frederic's chauffeur.' He leaned towards Julia. 'I think Mummy is going to marry him soon—well, she keeps telling me she is. I hope we don't have to move into his house. It's so quiet and Frederic won't let me use his computer. I was only looking at it one day when he came in and he got really cross with me. I wasn't going to play games on it or anything like that.'

Bernard pulled into a parking area saying that this was a good place to admire the view. There was a tight feeling in his chest. The revelations that his son made every time he saw him made his heart bleed. The sooner he finalised the custody preparations and got Philippe over here, the better. He got out of the car and opened the back doors.

'Wonderful view, isn't it?'

Julia heard the emotion in his voice and saw the sad expression in his eyes. She could only guess at the situation that had developed in Bernard's life and he was obviously deeply concerned about his son's welfare.

Bernard was taking hold of Philippe's hand as he jumped out onto the grass. 'Keep hold of my hand, Philippe. I don't want you to roll down the hillside and end up in the sea.'

Philippe giggled. 'That would be fun!'

'Do you know, Philippe, I used to stand here admiring the view with my *papa* and mummy when I was younger?' Julia said.

'Really! Papa told me that you live in England.'

'Oh, I do live in England but we used to spend our holidays in France. My mother is French and my father is English. My mother was keen we should speak French all the time when we were in France so we would enlarge our French vocabulary.'

She broke off as she noticed the puzzled expression on the young boy's face. 'Sorry, Philippe, I keep forgetting you're only six. What I'm trying to say is that we needed as much practice as we could get to make sure we spoke good French. My grandmother lived over those hills there in Montreuil sur Mer.'

She pointed her finger towards the hills they'd travelled over so often.

'We used to stay with her when I was small and after she died we continued coming over to France and staying here on the coast for our holidays.'

Bernard was smiling across at her appraisingly.

She smiled back. He looked like a man who was also taking a day off from his worries.

'Philippe is so intelligent I'm speaking to him as if he were much older,' she said quietly.

'I entirely approve. I do the same myself. Expand his knowledge as much as you can if he's interested. If he gets bored he'll switch off. It's a fascinating world if he's with the right people while he's growing up.'

Philippe was anxious to be included in the conversation again. 'So, Julia, when did you learn to speak French properly like you do now?'

She thought hard. 'I sort of learned it alongside learning to speak English—as a child. It seemed natural to speak English to my father and French to my mother. My brothers learned in the same way.'

'How many brothers have you got?'

'Three brothers, all older than me.'

'They must be very old. Are they as old as Papa?'

'My eldest brother, John, is about the same age as your father, I think. One time when we were standing here John started walking down that steep slope when my parents weren't looking. His trainers slipped on the wet grass and he tumbled a long way down the field until he managed to stop.'

'Was he hurt?'

'No, but his clothes were all grass stained and muddy. My mother wasn't too pleased.'

Philippe giggled. 'It must be fun, having brothers to play with. Frederic, Maman's fiancé, has got a few grown-up children but I don't think he likes them very much. They don't come to see him. He's very old, you see, and he gets tired.'

Julia looked across at Bernard. As their eyes met she could see his desolate expression deepen. Poor Bernard! She wanted to lean across the top of Philippe's head and give him a big hug—in a totally platonic, friendly way, of course. She mustn't lose sight of the fact that she'd come out to France for a fresh start and here she was becoming involved with another ready-made family, just as she had with Tony.

But Bernard wasn't like Tony. Nobody could be as bad as Tony. But what did she know about men? Only that if they wanted you they were charming and attentive at first. When they were fed up with you they moved on to someone else.

'Come on, let's all get back in the car. There's a storm brewing up over the sea.' Bernard was pointing out towards the horizon. 'Can you see the white flecks on the top of the waves, Philippe?'

'Yes, it's so exciting. The white flecks on the waves look like white horses riding over the waves. Oh, look up there, Papa! The sky's getting all dark. Where's the sun gone? Can't we wait here till it really arrives, Papa?'

'It's better to get to the farm so we don't get wet.'

Bernard drove over the brow of the steep hill and started down the other side. The road was narrow with tortuous bends. He drove carefully because the rain was now pelting down and hailstones were bouncing on the slippery road.

'I remember coming over into this valley as a child and seeing that village down there! Difficult to see it in all this rain but I know it's there.'

Bernard switched on the car lights, hoping that if another vehicle drove towards him it would also have its lights on.

'We can't see the farm in this bad weather but we'll soon be there. It's on the other side of the village.'

It was a difficult but short drive down the hill. The rain began to ease off as they drove through the village. Bernard pointed out various landmarks—the village school, the *tabac*, the *alimentation*, which sold groceries.

'There's no *boulangerie* these days. A van comes over from the next village and delivers the bread to the *dépôt de pain*—that building over there, which doubles as the newsagent.'

They were soon driving out of the village towards the farm. The gate was open. Smoke was curling from a chimney.

'Strange to see smoke from a chimney in June,' Julia said.

'We have an ancient wood stove in the kitchen, which is never allowed to go out.'

'I help Marianne put wood on the stove when I come to stay with Papa. Look, there she is.'

A plump, middle-aged lady was coming towards the car, carrying a large umbrella.

Bernard got out and took charge of the umbrella. 'Philippe, you go into the house with Marianne. I'll bring Julia under the umbrella I've got in the boot of the car.'

She felt a firm arm going around her waist as she moved towards the kitchen door. They were sheltered from the rain by the umbrella but as she splashed through the puddles she glanced down at her mud-splashed workout clothes.

'Oh, dear,' said Bernard. 'Looks like your clothes have taken a bit of a beating.'

Julia laughed. 'Are you trying to say I look a mess?'

His grip tightened around her waist as he steadied her advance towards the kitchen door. Rain was dripping from the edge of the umbrella all around them but for a brief moment she felt as if they were the only people in the world. He'd pulled her to a halt and was looking down at her with such a strange expression on his handsome face. She felt her heart beating madly.

She knew this was another of those magic moments in life that she would never ever forget. For a brief moment she allowed herself to think that nothing else mattered except this magic feeling that was running through her.

'Papa, hurry up!'

'We're coming, Philippe.'

CHAPTER FIVE

JULIA wiggled her bare toes in front of the lively flames in the wood-burning stove as she sipped the mug of hot coffee that Bernard had just put into her hands before settling himself amongst the squashy cushions beside his son.

'I can do that, Julia!'

'Do what, Philippe?'

She looked across at the other side of the stove and watched as the small boy wiggled his toes much faster than she could. He was curled up in a corner of the old sofa, snuggling up to Bernard, who was looking more relaxed than she'd ever seen him.

She smiled at the pair of them. 'You're much more supple than me, Philippe.'

The young boy giggled. 'That's because I like running about in my bare feet. Maman won't let me go without shoes in Paris but when I come home—I mean to this home, my real home—Papa doesn't mind, do you?'

Bernard put his coffee mug in a safe place on the hearth out of reach of Philippe's arms, which rarely stayed still when he was enjoying himself.

'That just depends on the weather. It wouldn't be a

good idea to wade across the farmyard while it's still raining, would it? You saw the state of Julia's jeans and shoes when she came in, didn't you?'

Philippe put his head on one side while he considered his father's words. 'You know, Papa, I think Julia should have taken off her things in the car so she wouldn't have spoiled them.'

'Maybe I didn't want to arrive in the kitchen half-dressed.' She took another sip of her coffee, feeling a nice, warm, thawed-out feeling creeping over her.

'Oh, it wouldn't have mattered, would it, Papa? You see people with no clothes on all the time, don't you?'

Bernard looked across at Julia with a whimsical expression on his handsome face. 'I do indeed, son. But not usually beautiful young ladies like Julia. I have to say, though, that Julia's own trousers are a much better fit. Kind as it was of Marianne to wash them, these baggy jeans tied up with an old belt look most comical on her.'

She gave him a wry smile. 'Oh, very funny! Are you trying to tell me I look frumpish now?'

'Julia, you would look good in an old sack.'

She felt overwhelmed by the admiration that shone from his eyes. She realised he was flirting with her, probably feeling safe because his son was with them.

Philippe was obviously enjoying being part of a grown-up conversation. Suddenly, he jumped up.

'Shall I get a sack, Papa? I know where Gaston keeps a whole pile of them in the barn. We could cut some holes for her arms and then Julia could put it over her head. Then we could all play at dressing-up, couldn't we? Would you like that, Julia?'

She pretended to be considering the offer, keeping half an eye on Bernard, who looked as if he was going to say something outrageous. Keeping a serious expression on her face, she said, 'I think you might get a bit wet, Philippe, if you go out to the barn.'

'Oh, yes, the rain!' Philippe stared across at the kitchen window where the drops of rain seemed even bigger as they lashed at the panes of glass. 'When will the rain stop, Papa?'

Bernard shrugged. 'Soon, I hope. We'll have to play a game that doesn't involve going outside until the weather improves. Would you like to find one of your board games that the three of us could play together?'

He looked up at Marianne, who'd just returned from organising the washing in the utility room alongside the kitchen and was waiting to say something to him.

'Bernard, I heard you talking about the weather. I was about to suggest we have an early lunch because the weather report says things are likely to improve…'

Julia gathered that the weather report on television had predicted there would be dry weather and sunshine in the afternoon. Marianne had a chicken casserole in the oven, which she could serve up in a few minutes.

'Excellent! Let's have an early lunch.' Bernard stood up and moved across to Julia. 'Be careful you don't trip up in those baggy pants.'

He held out his hand, which she took, not because it was required to steady herself but simply for the feel of those firm, enticingly capable fingers in an off-duty situation. Marianne said she'd laid the table in the dining room. Bernard, still holding her hand, led her down a stone-flagged corridor to the front of the house, which had a good view of the garden.

Philippe skipped along beside her, chattering all the time. She was glad none of the young boy's conversation required an answer because she had suddenly become overwhelmed by the warm feeling of the intimacy that was developing between the three of them. She felt she was enveloped in a family situation that seemed perfectly natural.

'I want to sit next to Julia, Papa!'

'That's strange, so do I.'

'She can sit between us, can't she?'

Bernard led her to the table where a beautifully laundered white cloth had been placed. The silver cutlery shone in the light from the chandelier hanging over the centre of the large round table.

'It's not often we need to have the light on during the day,' Bernard said, glancing out at the darkened garden with low black clouds overhead.

He held out a chair for her. Philippe sat down quickly beside her. Bernard smiled. 'It's a good thing we have a round table. My grandparents bought this table for my parents when they were first married.'

Marianne bustled in and placed the chicken casserole in front of Bernard.

'Enjoy your lunch!'

'Thank you!'

Bernard began serving out portions of the delicious casserole. Throughout the meal the warm rapport between the three of them continued. The conversation flowed, the food was exceptionally good and only

Philippe noticed, as he put down his dessert spoon, preparing to leave the table, that the rain had stopped.

'Papa, the weather report was correct. Here's the sun!'

He waved his arms excitedly at the sun, which was now shining through the windows as they left their places in the dining room.

Julia was feeling replete, having enjoyed a good helping of the chicken casserole and farm-grown vegetables followed by a home-made apple pie. Philippe had enjoyed joining in the conversation and she found she loved the sound of his young voice making interesting comments, asking questions, always giving a positive aspect to what they were discussing.

He seemed older than six but that was possibly because he'd had to get used to different situations during his short life. She hoped Bernard would elaborate at some point about why his marriage had been as disastrous as he'd implied. It couldn't have been his fault. He couldn't have brought about a divorce…not with his generous personality and wonderful parenting skills. His wife must have been in the wrong.

She remembered how, glancing up at Bernard as she'd finished her apple pie, she'd seen him looking at her with an enigmatic expression. Had he any idea how overwhelmed she was by the warmth of the situation they'd created that day, just the three of them? It was the first time she'd felt she belonged somewhere since she'd left her own family home.

Bernard suggested a grand tour of the farm, if he could enlist the help of his son as a fellow guide perhaps? After all, he knew the interesting places as well

as his father now that it had become second home
to him.

Philippe readily agreed to help his father show Julia
around. They started with the barns. The smell of the
hay in one barn took her right back to her own childhood.

'My brothers and I had some friends who lived on a
farm. We used to spend lots of time there in the school
holidays and the barns were wonderful places to play
hide and seek in.'

Philippe said children in France also played that
game but he hadn't got any friends to play it with when
he was here and there weren't any barns in Paris.

Oh, dear! Julia wished she hadn't started talking
about her childhood. Obviously, neither Bernard nor his
son had experienced the enjoyable if sometimes chaotic
family situations she'd had. Once more she thought how
sad for Bernard that his marriage had been a disaster.
He was a brilliant father.

They walked up the hill to see the sheep grazing on
the hillside and talked to Gaston, Marianne's husband,
who was mending a wall. The affable, middle-aged man
was happy to show them his wall-making techniques
and smiled encouragingly at Philippe, who was a willing pupil.

'We'll have you up here, helping me out, when you're
a bit bigger,' he told Philippe. 'Would you like that?'

'I'd like to stay here all the time. It's much better
here than in Paris.'

As they were going back down the hill, Philippe
skipping happily ahead of them, Bernard spoke quietly to Julia.

'You've no idea how relieved I was when Philippe just said he'd love to live here.'

'I'm sure he would. It's a wonderful place for a child.' She hesitated. 'You aren't thinking of…?'

'I'll tell you later.'

Philippe was running back up the hill. 'Papa, Julia, look, there's a rabbit by the side of that wall. Can you see it? Oh, look, there's another one.'

She couldn't help thinking that she didn't want this day to end. How wonderful it would be to spend more time with Bernard and his son. She tried not to think too far ahead. This was a one-off day. A day to cherish and not to look into the future.

Bernard handed her a glass of Kir as they sat together in the conservatory, which was bathed in the evening sunlight. Philippe had gone to bed without protest, being completely exhausted by the activities of the day. But not too exhausted to listen to the bedtime story he'd requested from Julia.

She took a sip of her Kir before placing the glass on the small table beside her wicker chair. 'You know, Bernard, little Philippe fell asleep when I was only two minutes into the story. Doesn't say much for my reading, does it?'

'Oh, I don't know. He was almost asleep when I lifted him out of the bath. I gathered you'd be downstairs in the land of the grown-ups within half an hour. What took you so long?'

She raised an eyebrow. 'Need you ask? Marianne intercepted me to check I had everything I need in the guest room. You are all being so kind. I hadn't intended to stay but you both convinced me I had to.

'Then there was your son beseeching me to have breakfast with him and you telling me that you didn't want to drive back to the hospital and… I could have got a taxi, you know.'

'I know,' he said languidly. 'But I wanted you to stay and I got the casting vote.'

He moved his chair closer to hers. 'I wanted to have time to talk to you in an off-duty situation. I don't want to think about the hospital tonight. And…well, I just wanted to be with you. I like being with you.'

He leaned across and cupped her chin with his hands. Slowly, he lowered his head and kissed her on the lips, a long, lingering, deliciously wicked kiss.

As he drew back she reflected that she would have preferred the kiss to have lasted much longer, but that would do for now. It had whetted her appetite for more, more of…well, more of everything where that had come from. But she conceded it really was not part of the plan for a new start in life. Except men like Bernard wouldn't wait for ever while she achieved all her ambitions and then told him he was definitely the man for her.

'What are you thinking?' he breathed.

She looked up into his expressive hazel eyes. For a brief moment she longed to tell him. To ask him if he could possibly understand her yearning to start a relationship with him whilst having to cope with her sensible reluctance to change her ambitious plans. She couldn't have it both ways…or could she?

She hesitated before moving on from her impossibly romantic thoughts. 'I was thinking how peaceful it is out here. This afternoon you said you were glad Philippe loves this place. Are you planning he should spend more time here?'

He leaned back in his chair. 'The fact is, the situation has been rather thrust upon me. Gabrielle is going to marry Frederic, a rich, retired businessman much older than she is. He's got grown-up children and finds Philippe too much trouble when he's around their Paris house. Gabrielle has asked me to have Philippe to stay with me permanently.'

'But that would be good for you, wouldn't it?'

He gave a big, contemplative sigh. 'It is my dearest wish to have my son living with me. There are a few problems to be sorted before we can go ahead. Gabrielle, of course, is anxious to be able to get on with her wedding plans without having to think about what to do with Philippe.'

'But surely, as his mother… I mean I don't understand. Bernard, you've hinted that your marriage was a disaster but you haven't told me why. Is your ex-wife to blame for…?'

'I should never have married Gabrielle. She was totally wrong for me right from the start and for that I blame myself.'

He splashed some more iced water in his pastis and raised it to his lips, the ice clinking as he took a much-needed drink. If he was going to be seeing more of Julia in an off-duty situation then he owed it to her to fill her in on his background. She was watching him now with a wary expression on her face, as well she might if she suspected half of what he was going to tell her.

He trusted her implicitly. He didn't know why because he hadn't known her for very long. But it was long enough to know she was his kind of woman. Whereas Gabrielle certainly was not and never had been.

He leaned back against the cushions and stared up at the ceiling where a fan was whirling round above his chair, bringing welcome cool air to the warm evening.

'My only excuse for even talking to Gabrielle was that I was young and inexperienced. I met Gabrielle Sabatier in Montmartre. I'd gone with a crowd of fellow doctors to celebrate the fact that we'd all qualified in our final exams. Gabrielle was working as a waitress in the restaurant where we were having supper. She told me later that evening…' he paused as a sudden vivid recollection of that seedy flat in a narrow street forced itself upon him '…that she needed a wage to pay her rent while she was searching for employment as an actress, having just finished drama school.'

He got up and walked over to the window, looking out across the lovely garden so lovingly cared for by Marianne and Gaston, and beyond the garden wall the hills bathed in evening sunlight. He'd always loved beautiful things in his life. How could he have fallen victim to the tawdry life that Gabrielle had introduced him to?

Julia moved swiftly across the room and stood in front of Bernard, looking up at him, her eyes full of emotion as she recognised he was undergoing some sort of crisis.

'Bernard, you don't need to tell me about your past life if it distresses you. Come and sit down again.'

'If only…' He enfolded her in his arms, bending his head so that their cheeks were together.

She could feel the dampness of his cheek as he struggled to contain his emotions. She remained silent for a few seconds, feeling his heart beating against hers, experiencing a longing she'd never known before.

And then he kissed her with an urgency that thrilled her through her whole being. This was the man for her, with all his past problems, with all his future ahead of him to sort out which way he would turn. She longed to be a part of his life.

Gently he released her from his arms and stood looking down at her, the evening sunlight bathing the two of them as if blessing their emotional embrace.

'Julia, I want to tell you everything about my liaison with Gabrielle. Things I've never discussed with anyone before. I feel…I feel you will understand why I have such a lot of emotional baggage to contend with.'

He took hold of her hand and together they walked back to their seats. He settled her and moved his chair even closer. She took a sip from her glass and he reached for the bottle of crème de cassis to top her glass up.

'You see, I'd never met anyone like Gabrielle in my life. I thought I'd fallen in love with her even while she was serving on at the crowded table in Montmartre. My friends were joking, saying she fancied me. Well, I was overwhelmed by this vivacious, sexy creature, as were all my friends.'

Julia couldn't help jealous vibes disturbing her. Oh, dear, she was becoming more involved than she'd ever meant to be. Maybe she should insist he keep it all to himself? His past was something she didn't want to think about.

'Gabrielle asked me to wait until she'd finished work

and go back to her flat with her.' He paused and drew in his breath. 'I knew what would happen. I wanted it to happen. Yes, we became lovers that night and I was too enamoured to see what she was planning.'

'Which was?' As if she couldn't guess!

'She thought I was a good catch. A young doctor with a safe, well-paid career ahead of him. A meal ticket for life! Sorry, I don't want to sound bitter but…anyway, weeks later when she told me she was pregnant, like the idiot I was, I agreed to marry her.'

Julia felt a pang of sympathy for the young, inexperienced Bernard. She leaned across and squeezed his hand. 'It often happens to young men, even experienced men.'

He flashed her an endearing smile of gratitude. 'I hope Philippe has more sense when he starts growing up. Anyway, it transpired she'd been brought up in relative luxury in the sixteenth arrondissement of Paris, in between the Bois de Boulogne and the river Seine— in a very pricy house. Her father had been a successful businessman until he overextended himself, went bankrupt and took an overdose, after ensuring that his widow would keep the house, albeit living a frugal lifestyle with Gabrielle, her only child.'

'Did you ever think that Gabrielle had been traumatised by the death of her father?'

'Oh, I'm sure she was. Her response to the tragedy had been to turn herself into an even harder, more ruthless character. But I didn't know that when I agreed to marry her.'

He splashed more water into his glass as he tried to remember exactly how it had been. Julia was right in saying that Gabrielle must have been traumatised by the suicide of her father.

'Believe me, I've made so many allowances for her behaviour...but each time she disappointed me with her responses. Anyway, a few weeks after we were married Gabrielle told me she'd miscarried. I insisted on taking her into hospital where tests proved that she'd never been pregnant in the first place. She knew I'd seen through her plan. We became like strangers when we were together. She began to show her true colours, nagging me to rent a house in the prestigious area where she'd grown up and her mother still lived. I told her I couldn't afford it. I was at the very beginning of my medical career, working all hours I could, and I couldn't take on any more expense. I was exhausted most of the time.'

There was a sound of someone coming down the corridor. Bernard sat up his chair as Marianne appeared in the doorway.

'I'm going to prepare supper for Gaston now, Bernard. You're absolutely sure you don't want me to cook supper for you?'

Bernard smiled. 'We're not hungry yet, Marianne. I'm going to make an omelette and salad later on.'

'Well, if you're sure.' Marianne turned to Julia. 'I've put your jeans in the guest room. I do hope you have everything you need in there.'

'Thank you so much, Marianne, for everything.'

'You are most welcome. See you tomorrow.'

As the footsteps receded down the corridor Julia asked Bernard where Marianne lived.

'She and Gaston live in the old surgery at the end

of the house. After my father died we had it converted for them so they could be on site while I finished my schooling and moved to Paris to train as a doctor.'

They were both silent as Julia digested this information, thinking to herself that Bernard hadn't had an easy life. Perhaps that was one reason why he'd fallen in love so easily and so quickly with someone who'd appeared on the surface to be the girl of his dreams.

'So what happened after Gabrielle knew you'd seen through her machinations?'

'Oh, she started to make my life hell. There was I, trying to establish myself as a reliable junior doctor at the hospital and she just never stopped nagging while I was with her. I tell you, I was tempted to walk away from this disastrous marriage but I decided the honourable thing to do was to stick it out. In our family background marriage was a lifelong contract, not to be broken.'

'Didn't she work?'

'She got a small part in a TV soap and told me she'd got a long contract. But actually it was only for three months, to be reviewed. On the strength of that I gave in to her demands that I rent the house she wanted. We moved into the house. Two weeks later Gabrielle admitted her contract had been terminated. I phoned her director to enquire what had happened. He said she was temperamental and unreliable. Hah! What a wise man. If only I'd had the sense to see through her earlier.

'Anyway, I continued to work long hours and began to climb the career ladder. I was earning more and just able to scrape the rent together. Then one day when I returned home there was a note saying she'd left me.'

'How did you feel about that?'

He looked across and smiled. 'If I'm honest, I felt relieved. It was as if a burden had lifted from my shoulders. I assumed she'd met somebody…and I was right. But two months later she returned. She'd had an affair with a married man who'd promised to leave his wife but he'd gone back to her. She begged me to forgive her. I was too busy with my all-absorbing work at the hospital to contemplate divorce.' His voice dipped as he resumed a tone of resignation. 'I took her back.'

'Was she grateful?'

'She seemed to have changed. She even turned on the charm. I should have realised she was up to something. She began begging me to make love to her. I insisted she stay on the Pill. A baby at this stage of our fragile relationship would have been unthinkable.' He breathed out. 'And guess what?'

'She stopped taking the Pill and became pregnant?'

He gave her a wry grin of resignation. 'Why weren't you there to say that when I took her back! I saw right through her but it was too late. It was the last straw. Even though I'd always longed for a family, I knew I couldn't afford the added expense unless I earned more. I told her I was going to apply for a prestigious surgical appointment in St Martin sur Mer. If I was successful we would move there.'

'How did she feel about that?'

'She said she wouldn't leave Paris. I told her that if I was successful in getting this appointment I would support her and the baby, whether she came or not. When I told her I'd been successful she flounced out and went to live with her mother but not until after she'd demanded a large monthly sum to be paid into her bank account. The one good thing that came out of her move back to her mother was that there was a steadying influence in her life. Veronique Sabatier is a saint! How on earth she came to give birth to a daughter like Gabrielle I cannot imagine.'

'So Philippe has had a good grandmother to care for him?'

'Absolutely! What a relief. As soon as he was born I loved him with the all-consuming love that only a parent knows. And now…'

He spread his hands wide. 'I'm going to be able to have him with me always—well, until he's a grown man and leaves the family nest.'

She saw the loving expression in his eyes as he drew her to her feet, holding her close to him. 'Thank you for listening to me. I've never told anyone the full story of my disastrous marriage.'

And then he kissed her, this time more slowly, taking time to savour the joy of being with her. Neither of them was thinking beyond the next moment. The present was all that mattered.

He released her from his embrace, looking down at her with an expression of love on his face.

'Let's go and have supper together,' he said, his voice husky as he struggled to come to terms with the fact that all he wanted to do was lift her into his arms and carry her upstairs.

He put his arm around her as they walked towards the kitchen. She revelled in the connection that existed between them, wondering at how much their relationship had developed during the day. How much more could it develop before she found herself hopelessly in love and unable to sort out her conflicting emotions?

CHAPTER SIX

JULIA lay back against the goosedown pillows. She'd been able to tell it was goosedown as soon as she'd laid her head on the softness that had moulded itself around her head. Mmm. Everything about this room was luxurious, well appointed, but probably rarely used—she hoped! The idea of Bernard having a guest room like this made her think that he wanted to impress the girls he showed in here.

But then did he leave them here all by themselves to admire the room? Almost as soon as he'd shown her the superb bathroom, fluffy towels and expensive soap he had left!

But not before that goodnight kiss. Her legs began to feel weak again, even though she was now lying down. She'd been hanging on to her excited emotions, trying hard not to show her real feelings because she knew she simply couldn't have controlled her desire to make love with him.

When he'd taken her in his arms once more, just outside the door to her bedroom, she'd gathered her thoughts together in something of a panic. She'd wanted him physically, desperately, but her rational self had told her not to go there, not to upset the relative calm of their relationship, which worked with the current situation of professor and student. She'd made mistakes before when she'd allowed herself to give in to her passionate nature.

Yes, he'd kissed her gently at first and her wickedly fluid body had reacted with instinctive longing. Oh, yes, she wanted this man…oh, so desperately. But almost as soon as he'd started to kiss her with real urgency he'd pulled away and whispered, 'Goodnight, Julia,' in that deep, sexy voice. And before she'd known what had happened he had been striding away from her to his own room.

Shortly afterwards, in his room not too far away, Bernard, lying back against the pillows, was wondering why he hadn't stayed to make love with Julia, cursing himself for doing what he'd considered to be the right thing. He remembered how she'd felt in his arms. She'd given every indication that she'd wanted him to make love to her. He hadn't misread the signals. Would it really have complicated their relationship too much at this stage if he'd given in to his true feelings?

He rolled onto his side, waiting for the waves of desire to calm down. The cold shower he'd just taken hadn't helped as much as he'd hoped. He'd only known Julia a few weeks but he knew that he was falling in love. Being in love with a student—any student—wasn't an easy situation to be in.

Yes, they were both adults, so there was nothing untoward about the situation. Nothing that the hospital board of governors could possibly frown upon so long as they were discreet. It was more the problem of handling the emotion for the next few months before Julia finished the course and took the final exams.

For the final month he would find it easier. With the exams over he could relax. He would already have assessed her performance as a student during the course. A panel of external examiners would mark the exam papers and listen to her answers to their questions in the viva voce exam.

Thinking rationally, as he hoped he was doing now, helped to sort out his confusing thoughts. He realised she was the most talented student he'd ever had to deal with. He mustn't do anything to put her off track because she was obviously very ambitious and had a lot to live up to, coming from a prestigious family background like hers.

There was also the problem of her having been hurt by that dreadful ex-husband who seemed to have been hell bent on destroying her confidence. Since she'd arrived here, he'd been trying to build up her confidence again so she could realise her full potential.

Yes, he'd seen her blossoming into an excellent surgeon, relaxing with her fellow students and having an easygoing friendship with him. She already seemed to be more in control of her own life. He'd admired her when she'd first arrived but this increasingly self-confident woman was becoming more and more irresistible to him.

He turned on the bedside light again, knowing that it would be impossible to sleep, with Julia only a short distance away. The moon was shining through the open window onto his huge bed where he should have brought Julia if he'd given in to his true feelings. He gave an audible sigh as he wondered if she was lying awake staring at this same moon and if so, what was she thinking?

He'd been flirting with her all day so why did he have to rationalise himself out of going ahead with his natural instincts? He didn't even know how she would have felt if he'd suggested she sleep with him. As he'd held her in his arms on the pretence that he had simply been saying goodnight she'd been so wonderfully pliant. He'd felt every curve in that vibrant body reacting to his caresses. But he'd forced himself to leave her.

With the occasional dalliance making his off-duty time more interesting for a while he wouldn't usually have thought twice about making it obvious he wanted to sleep with her. If the woman was willing, they would go ahead. But it didn't mean anything. It was an experience that they both enjoyed as mature adults free of any committed relationship. He'd always checked that they weren't involved with a partner.

But Julia was special, the most wonderful woman he'd ever met. The only woman in his life who made him feel that he had to sacrifice his own feelings so that he wouldn't spoil her future potential. She was like a precious flower that he had to nurture.

The sun was shining in through the gaps in the chiffon drapes at her window. Julia stirred and cautiously opened her eyes, unsure of her surroundings. She'd lain awake half the night but the sleep that she'd just been enjoying had been very deep and she was reluctant to return to reality. Somewhere in a nearby room she could hear a child's voice singing.

So, she hadn't dreamed she was in Bernard's farmhouse. She hadn't imagined that wonderful day they'd spent together.

She sat up quickly as she heard gentle tapping on her door.

'Julia, can I come in?'

'Of course, Philippe!'

She pulled the robe from the bedside chair to cover her shoulders. Even as she did so she remembered how impressed she'd been when Bernard had produced the cream silk, extremely feminine robe last night. But then the inevitable moment of jealousy as to who'd worn it before her had threatened to invade her happy mood.

Philippe stood beside her bed, smiling. 'Marianne has sent me to tell you that breakfast is ready.'

The young boy described the delicious breakfast that Marianne had prepared and Julia listened, smiling at him. She raised her head as she became aware that Bernard was now standing in the doorway. He was wearing a dark blue towelling robe that covered most of him except for his athletic, muscular calves and bare feet. His dark, sleep-tousled hair was still damp from his shower and he was looking wonderfully handsome with the sunlight on his lightly tanned face.

'No need to hurry, Julia. I've brought you some coffee. Marianne is still making preparations downstairs so take your time.' Bernard placed a small tray with a cafetière and a delicate porcelain cup and saucer on her bedside table. 'Philippe insisted it was time to wake you.'

'Julia was awake when I knocked on the door, weren't you?'

'I was indeed, Philippe.'

Her eyes met Bernard's over the top of the small head and she felt her heart turn over. The warmth and love she'd felt yesterday had returned as she became wrapped up once again in this idyllic family situation.

Bernard retreated again to the doorway and held out his hand towards his son. 'Philippe, come with me while Julia gets herself ready.'

'Can't I stay and run her bath for her, like I do for you, Papa?'

'I think Julia will be happy to have a few quiet moments to gather her thoughts for the day ahead, so we'll see her when she comes downstairs.'

After they'd gone, she enjoyed a leisurely soak in the bath, balancing the delicate coffee cup in the small tiled alcove of the wall. It made a welcome change from the hurried shower she took most mornings in her tiny en suite.

When she got herself downstairs fully clothed in her workout gear from the previous day, the smell of freshly baked croissants drew her to the kitchen. Bernard was reawakening the dormant flames in the wood-burning stove. He closed the stove door and turned as he heard her coming in.

He put down the poker on the hearth and came across to pull out a chair for her at the table. Philippe ran inside from the kitchen garden and jumped up onto the chair beside her and began to eat enthusiastically. He urged Julia to join him and, smiling, she reached for a still warm croissant.

Julia was halfway through her croissant, spread liberally with the home-made apricot jam, when she saw Bernard answer his mobile.

'Bernard Cappelle.'

She saw him frowning. From the ensuing conversation she gathered it was an urgent call from the hospital.

'Of course. I'll be there as soon as I can.'

He looked across the table at her. 'That was Michel Devine from the emergency department. There's been a road traffic accident on the motorway, involving several vehicles. He's asked permission to call in as many of my students as possible to help with the patients who will be treated at the hospital. Are you willing to…?'

'Of course.' She was already pushing back her chair.

'Michel, I've just spoken to Dr Julia Montgomery and she says she's available.'

Minutes later they were driving down the hill towards St Martin sur Mer. Bernard had asked Marianne to take charge of Philippe, who would have to stay at the farm for another day. Philippe had been delighted at the prospect of a whole day with Marianne and Gaston on the farm and another night with his father.

Julia could see a couple of ambulances arriving outside the hospital as Bernard carefully negotiated his way through the traffic at the foot of the hill. The porter in charge of the hospital gateway directed several vehicles to the side so that Bernard could come through and park.

Inside, Michel was organising his staff. A triage system was being set up so that patients were assessed as soon as possible after their arrival.

A nurse was handing out white coats to the arriving medical staff. Julia pulled hers on and reported to Michel Devine for instructions. He asked her to check out the patient in the first cubicle.

'The paramedics have put a tourniquet round his bleeding leg to stem the flow but we need to do something more effective now we've got him here,' he told her tersely. 'There's a nurse in there who'll help you while you assess what needs to be done, Dr Montgomery. It's obviously a serious orthopaedic problem, which is in your field of expertise.'

She moved through the curtain to the cubicle and went in to take charge of the situation. The young man's eyes pleaded with her to help him as she took hold of his hand. He was lying on his back, his hands clenched over the bloodstained sheet that covered him.

She spoke to him in French, making her voice as soothing as she could. He was obviously in deep shock. Glancing down at the notes the nurse handed to her, she saw that his name was Pierre. She noted that sedation that had already been given at the scene of the traffic accident.

Gently peeling back the sheet that covered his injured right leg, she could see that this was a very serious problem. The right leg had been badly damaged and would require immediate surgery. She was already making a swift examination of the damaged tibia and surrounding tissues when she sensed that someone else had joined her in the cubicle.

Relief shot through her when she heard Bernard's voice behind her. He moved to her side and leaned across the patient so he could form his own opinion.

'I'll make arrangements for immediate surgery,' he told her.

She nodded in agreement. 'Are those Pierre's X-rays?'

Bernard was already flashing them up on the wall screen. She swallowed hard as she tried to make sense of the crushed pieces of bone. From the knee downwards, the leg seemed to resemble a jigsaw puzzle. Was it still viable? It was going to require some expert surgery and after-care if their patient was to be able to walk on it again. Maybe amputation followed by the fitting of a prosthesis might be the only option. A decision would have to be made during surgery.

She held Pierre's hand as Bernard made a swift call to the surgical wing.

'*Ma femme*, my wife,' the young man whispered. 'Monique. *Je veux...*' His faint voice trailed away as tears started trickling down his bloodstained face.

Even as Pierre was asking for his wife, the nurse, at the other side of the cubicle, was looking directly at Julia. 'The information is in the notes, Doctor.'

Glancing briefly down at the notes, Julia learned that his wife, who was seven months pregnant, had been unconscious since the accident. She'd been sitting beside Pierre in the passenger seat when the vehicle had crashed through. Their patient had cradled her in his arms until a doctor had arrived and taken her away in the first ambulance. She was already in the obstetric suite, undergoing an emergency Caesarean.

'Julia, I'd like you to assist me. Theatre Sister is making preparations for us.' Bernard went on to instruct the nurse about premedication for the patient. Julia was glad he was cool and calm because she knew that was how she must be—totally professional so that she could do her best for the patient.

Bernard came across to speak to Pierre, explaining the serious condition of his leg. Julia held her breath as the subject of possible amputation was broached. Pierre looked at her and then at Bernard.

'Is that a possibility? Can't you...?' His voice trailed away.

'Pierre, we'll do all we can to save the leg, but if it's too badly damaged it would make more sense to amputate. Prostheses these days are excellent and you would be taught to walk. I hope it won't come to that but the decision can't be made until we find the full extent of your injuries. Do you understand?' he added gently.

Their patient closed his eyes for a moment. Then in a clear voice he declared that he fully understood and would accept their decision, whatever it was.

Carefully, Julia withdrew her hand from the patient's grasp. 'I've got to leave you for a short time, Pierre. You'll soon be going to sleep but I'll be up there in Theatre with you and I'll see you when you come round from the anaesthetic.'

'*Merci*,' he whispered. 'Thank you, Doctor.'

She swallowed hard to force herself to be totally professional, aware of his sad eyes on her as she followed Bernard out of the cubicle.

There was no time for a break during the day. Julia assisted Bernard with Pierre's long operation and found herself scrubbing up for the next patient almost immediately. They were supported by a good team from the surgical orthopaedic department, each member adding their expertise to the operations that were performed.

In the early evening, when she and Bernard could finally take a break, he drew her to one side for a quiet debriefing. They were still both in theatre greens up in the recovery room, having just despatched their final patient to one of the orthopaedic wards.

As Bernard started to speak she sank down onto a plastic chair at the side of the water cooler and reached out to take a plastic cup.

'Here, let me do that for you.'

'Thank you.' She flashed him a grateful smile as she took the cold water from him.

Their hands touched and she felt a frisson of energy running through her at the contact. She drank deeply and didn't stop until she'd finished all of it.

'That's better! I feel almost human again.'

Bernard smiled. 'Michel just called to say the emergency department has dealt with all the accident patients that were assigned to this hospital. He's very grateful for our help and suggests we go off duty.'

'Well, if you're sure they can cope, I'd love to go off duty.'

'I'm absolutely sure. Besides, you look completely whacked, Julia.'

'Thanks very much! That's just what a girl needs, to be told she looks as exhausted as she feels. Still...' She sat upright, threw the plastic cup into the bin and stood up. 'There's nothing that a shower and a change of clothes can't put right.'

'How about supper? That would be reviving, wouldn't it?'

What exactly was he suggesting? She couldn't do anything to stop the anticipation running through her.

'Well, what do you say, Julia? Why don't you come back to the farm with me? I've got to return there as soon as possible because Philippe will be getting impatient. If you're with me, he'll be over the moon.'

He was waiting for her answer. She was very tempted at the prospect.

'Well?'

'Why not?' She didn't like the sound of her breathless voice, which completely gave away her confused emotions. She'd meant to sound so cool, as if this was just an invitation to a friend's tea party.

'Good! I'll call Marianne and tell her you're coming so she can get your room ready.'

'Oh, there's no need to—'

'Yes, there is! Because if you think I'm driving back to the hospital again, you're mistaken. And don't start talking about taxis. There aren't any out in the countryside. This isn't London or Paris, you know.'

She laughed and suddenly it was as if the sun had come out from behind the clouds. They'd been in a windowless theatre all day but she could almost breathe the vibrant country air that she would experience when they escaped together.

He put a hand in the small of her back. 'Can you be ready to leave in half an hour?'

'I'll try. I've got to spend a few minutes in Intensive Care with Pierre. I promised I would when he came round from the anaesthetic at the end of his operation.'

'I'll come with you to make sure you don't stay too long. The intensive care staff are experts, you know, and the orthopaedic staff are also checking on our patient.'

'Oh, I know he's in good hands but a promise to a patient is a promise.'

He bent down, cupping her face in his hands and kissing her gently on the cheek. 'You're not becoming emotionally involved with a patient, are you, Doctor?'

She felt a fluttering of desire running through her body. That was only a chaste kiss, for heaven's sake. She moved to one side as the swing door opened and a nurse walked in.

'We can continue this discussion as we go along to see our patient,' Bernard said gravely, leading the way out into the corridor.

Sister in Intensive Care gave them a brief update on Pierre's condition as soon as they arrived. He was on continual intravenous infusions of blood and breathing normally now after the initial difficulties following the general anaesthetic.

'It was a long operation,' Bernard said. 'Has he asked for details?'

'He's still very confused and the morphine keeps him semi-sedated. But he'll be pleased to see you so that you can explain what you actually did.'

Julia picked up the notes. 'Let's go and see him.'

Pierre's eyes were closed and he was lying on his back. His injured leg was up on pillows, covered by a cradle.

'Pierre,' Julia said gently.

Their patient opened his eyes and a slow smile spread across his face.

'Thank you,' he whispered. 'You did save my leg, didn't you?'

'Yes, we did,' Bernard said.

'And my wife, *ma femme*?'

Sister smiled broadly. 'I was just coming to tell you. I've had a call from Obstetrics. You have a beautiful little daughter, Pierre. She's very tiny because of being premature so she'll need to stay in hospital for a few weeks.'

'Et ma femme?'

'Monique is very weak so she'll be staying in hospital for a while until her strength returns.'

'You'll all be in hospital for a while,' Julia said. 'We'll arrange who can visit who as soon as possible.'

Pierre breathed a deep sigh of contentment. 'You've all been so good to us.'

As they walked back down the corridor and out through the front door, Julia looked up at Bernard. When they'd left Intensive Care he'd waited while Julia popped back to her room to change and pack some nightclothes. She met him at the hospital entrance.

'It's at times like this I remember that I love being a doctor,' she said quietly, lengthening her stride to keep pace with him.

He took hold of her hand as they continued walking towards the car park.

She glanced around to see if anyone was watching.

'Don't worry,' he said, as if reading her mind. 'We're off duty. We can do anything we like.'

'Anything?'

He grinned. 'Why not?'

CHAPTER SEVEN

As BERNARD drove up the narrow, winding road that led to the top of the hill above St Martin sur Mer, Julia could feel herself relaxing already. She leaned back, studying Bernard's firm hands turning the steering-wheel as he negotiated one of the bends. A white sports car was coming towards them, a young couple laughing together as they passed within inches of their car, driving much too fast on that potentially dangerous section of the road.

Bernard eased off the accelerator just in time as he realised the other car was going to encroach on their side of the road. The blaring music from the young couple's car became fainter as it disappeared down the hill.

He breathed a sigh of relief as he continued up to the top of the hill. 'They wouldn't drive with such abandon if they'd seen the damage that sort of driving can do.'

'I was thinking exactly the same. Michel told me the multiple crash we assisted with was caused by a van driver using a mobile phone as he was overtaking a car. He lost control of his van, ploughed through the central barrier and vehicles piled up around him.'

'Including our Pierre and his wife,' Bernard said

quietly. 'I'm so relieved it was possible to save them. The result of good teamwork throughout the day—paramedics, nurses, doctors, everybody.'

He took a deep breath as the enormity of the events finally hit him now that he'd left hospital and was able to assess the situation.

His voice wavered with emotion when he spoke again. 'Pierre and Monique had only been married a few months and that precious baby was a much-wanted child.'

Julia swallowed hard. 'All babies are precious.'

Bernard could hear the gentle, emotional tone in her voice as she said this.

'You love babies, don't you?'

'Yes, of course I do.' She hesitated. 'I'd love to have my own baby. But not until the right time,' she added quickly. 'I need to feel I'm in charge of my own life first.'

He eased the car over the brow of the hill. 'Since you arrived I've sensed you're becoming more and more in charge.' He changed gear as the road flattened out. 'But, Julia, you mustn't be too inflexible. Who was it that said life is what happens when you're making other plans?'

Julia thought for a few moments. 'I don't know who said it but it's very true.'

They were sailing down the other side of the hill now, into the green, spring-awakened valley. She could feel the connection between them growing stronger by the minute.

She clenched her hands as the truth of everything that had happened since she'd met Bernard hit her. This was the sort of man she wanted in her life. She drew in her breath. This was the actual man she wanted in her life. But even as the realisation came to her she reminded herself that the timing wasn't right.

She'd planned to make a fresh start. This was why she'd left the old life behind. She shouldn't be thinking of veering off course. She'd done that before and look where that had landed her!

But she needn't change direction if she was careful. There was no harm in enjoying the present without taking too much thought about the future. She needed the fun and enjoyment of being with Bernard. He lifted her spirits. So, all things considered, she could make her present situation work…couldn't she?

As they drove through the farmyard gates, she determined to enjoy the evening whatever happened. She was going to focus on the present and let the future take care of itself for now.

Bernard switched off the engine and reached a hand across to take hold of hers. 'You're very quiet all of a sudden. What are you thinking?'

'I was thinking about how much I'm looking forward to seeing Philippe.'

A little whirlwind dashed out through the kitchen door, tearing towards the car.

Bernard laughed. 'You've got your wish.'

'Papa! Julia! I was waiting for you to arrive. Marianne! They're here.'

Bernard suggested the three of them have an early supper together at the kitchen table. He explained to Marianne that both he and Julia hadn't had time for lunch and also they both wanted to spend as much quality time with Philippe as possible before he went to bed.

The supper was a riotous success with Philippe excited and happy to have the undivided attention of two doting adults.

'Would you like some more pie, Philippe?'

Bernard was already slicing through the pastry to the succulent guinea fowl underneath in anticipation of his son's answer. Marianne's pie was a family favourite.

Philippe grinned and held out his plate. 'Yes, please.'

'You must have had a busy day to give you a good appetite like this.' Bernard put a generous slice on Philippe's plate.

'It was brilliant!' Philippe recounted the day's happenings, including feeding the hens, collecting the eggs still warm from the nests, helping Gaston mend a wall and milking the cows.

'And you helped me with the pastry,' Marianne said as she came in with a platter of cheeses from the larder and placed it on the sideboard. 'I'll leave this here, Bernard, for when you're ready for your cheese course. I've also left some desserts in the fridge, if you wouldn't mind helping yourselves. I'm going over to see my sister in the village tonight.'

'Of course, I remember now. It's her birthday. You should have reminded me and gone earlier. Thank you for this excellent supper. Go off and have a great evening.'

Julia came down to the kitchen after putting Philippe to bed to find that Bernard had finished clearing up.

The dishwasher was whirring away in the background as he came towards her and handed her a glass of wine.

She gave him a wry grin as she took the glass from his hands. 'I try to stick to the rule that I don't drink after supper if tomorrow is a work day.'

'Ah, rules were made to be broken. This is only a *digestif.* Something to round off a delightful dinner.' He raised his glass to his lips. 'Here's to good food, excellent wine and congenial company.'

She took a sip of her wine, feeling suddenly shy now that they were alone.

'How was Philippe when you left him?' he asked.

'Trying hard not to fall asleep before you've been up to see him.'

He put his glass down on the sideboard. 'Don't go away. Take your wine into the conservatory and I'll be back shortly. And, Julia…?'

'Yes?'

'Don't fall asleep. I know you must be tired but…'

She laughed. 'I've no intention of falling asleep.'

As she settled herself on the comfortable, squashy-cushioned sofa she knew she hadn't felt this happy for a long time. Yes, she would go with the flow again tonight. She'd seen enough misery during the day. She was going to seize the moment and not think about tomorrow. If Bernard held her in his arms tonight as he'd done last night, she was going to make sure that this time she gave him the right message. She wasn't going to let him give her a goodnight kiss and leave her languishing in her lonely bed, thinking about what might have been.

* * *

'Philippe's asleep,' Bernard whispered as he sat down beside her on the sofa a few minutes later, putting his arm around her and drawing her against him.

She could feel the instantaneous awakening of her whole body. In the short time he'd been away from her she'd been fighting against weariness. But as soon as she felt his arm around her she was totally wide awake. She could feel every fibre of her body quivering with anticipation as he bent his head and kissed her, oh, so gently. She parted her lips to savour the moment. His kiss deepened.

This was the first time he'd kissed her with such glorious abandon. She responded in equal measure. She gave an ecstatic moan as his hands began to caress her breasts. Deep down inside her she felt herself melting, becoming entirely sensual, fluid, unwilling and unable to control the rising desires inside her.

Suddenly he broke off and leaned back against the sofa. His breathing was ragged as he looked questioningly into her eyes.

'Julia, I want to make love to you so much but we need to discuss what this will mean to our relationship. I'd love to settle into a serious long-term relationship with you but I don't think that either of us could make the commitment necessary. You've got your career to think of and eventually you will want a husband and a family of your own. I'm not sure after my last experience that I will ever be able to offer that to you, and I know that would be a great disappointment to you.'

She hesitated. 'Yes, it would. You have your son. I've always wanted children when I've established my career. My first marriage was a disaster but I adored my stepchildren. It was so hard to walk away and never see them again.'

Her eyes misted over. Bernard moved closer again, taking hold of her hand and kissing the palm very gently. 'I want you to have the experience of your own children because you have so much maternal instinct to draw on. Philippe already adores you.'

'I know. Getting close to Philippe worries me in many ways. Not only will I miss him terribly when the course finishes and I have to return to London, I'm also concerned about him getting used to me being with you. After what he's experienced with his own mother, I'd hate to cause him any more upset.'

'We could have a compromise relationship, don't you think? A short-term affair while you're here in France?'

He put his arms around her, drawing her closer, his eyes probing hers, willing her to agree.

She gave him a gentle smile. 'I think a short no-commitment affair would be fun. We should live one day at a time, enjoy being together and not think too far ahead.'

'Oh, my darling Julia...'

His lips claimed hers and the passion of his embrace deepened.

Briefly, he paused and looked into her eyes, silently questioning if she wanted him as much as he wanted her.

'Yes, oh, yes,' she whispered.

He smiled, the most wickedly sexy smile she'd ever hoped to see on his handsome face as he scooped her up into his arms.

* * *

Julia opened her eyes and for a brief moment she felt unsure of her surroundings as she struggled to leave the dream she'd just enjoyed. Moonlight was flooding through the open window and there was a scent of roses, damp with dew. This room looked out over the garden.

And then she remembered. It hadn't been a dream. The lovemaking had all been real. The gentle caresses that had become more and more irresistible to her. Her own hands had explored that wonderful athletic, muscular body, longing for Bernard to take her completely. And then when she'd felt him inside her she'd felt completely at one with this wonderful man who had been taking her towards the ultimate ecstasy. They had climaxed together in a heavenly experience when they'd clung to each other, feeling that they would never be separated.

'Are you awake?'

She heard his deep, sexy voice from the other side of her pillow. They'd slept together, very, very close. His bed was enormous and there was space all around them.

Gently he pulled a crumpled sheet around her. She realised they were both naked. The rose-scented breeze had probably wakened her.

He raised himself up on one elbow, looking down at her with a heart-melting expression in his eyes that made her feel she was absolutely special to him.

'Your skin feels chilly,' he murmured, his hands roaming over her in the most tantalisingly erotic way.

For a brief moment she thought he might leave her and go across the room to close the window. But, no, he'd had a better idea!

She moaned with desire as he covered her body with his own. This time their lovemaking took her to heights of ecstasy she'd never imagined existed.

As they lay back against the pillows, their arms still around each other, she could feel her body tingling with the excitement of a joyful consummation.

'Are you still cold?' he whispered.

She laughed. 'I think we should both run barefoot on the dewy grass outside to cool off.'

'You look wonderful when you're totally abandoned. You should stay like this all the time, no problems, no rules…'

'No tomorrow,' she whispered, as she realised they were both longing to make love again…

It was the early morning sun shining in through the still open window that woke her up this time. And this time she knew immediately where she was because she was still clasped loosely in his arms. Mmm, what a night! It had definitely not been a dream. In her wildest dreams she could never have imagined all that. Maybe she'd died and gone to heaven.

So, what now?

CHAPTER EIGHT

JULIA switched off her computer. In the past few weeks since that idyllic night she'd spent with Bernard her life had revolved around work. He seemed intent on working through the syllabus in great detail, with her and the rest of the students using practical sessions in Theatre and theoretical tutorials.

Her mobile was ringing.

'Julia, are you free this evening?'

Was she free? If she wasn't she would make sure she cancelled whatever it was that stood between her and an evening with Bernard. She'd seen precious little of him recently in an off-duty situation and was beginning to think he regretted suggesting a short-term affair. Or maybe he just didn't have the time.

'I'll just check.' She paused just long enough to flick to the right page in her diary. Totally devoid of any social engagement. 'What did you have in mind?'

'I need to talk something over with you. Actually, I feel I owe you an explanation as to why I've been a bit distant recently.'

He paused and cleared his throat.

She waited. Was he going to explain why he'd seemed somewhat distracted whenever they'd been together?

He sounded unusually nervous when he spoke again. 'It was a pity I had that phone call from Gabrielle so early in the morning when you were staying with me. Having to take Philippe back to Paris that day wasn't what I'd planned but my ex-wife can be very difficult if she doesn't get her own way.'

She waited again as he paused, not wanting to interrupt the flow. She remembered she'd crept out of his bed and gone to the guest room early in the morning before anyone else had woken up. So she'd been surprised when Bernard announced at breakfast he had to take his son back to Paris and had cleared his commitments at the hospital for a couple of days. Michel would be in charge of his students—who, of course, included her—and he would give them on-the-spot tuition in the emergency department.

'Frederic, Gabrielle's future husband, wanted to legally clarify the situation on custody of Philippe, to make sure that he wasn't going to be involved in any way and that I was going to take charge of my son. It's been hell sorting everything out for the past few weeks. I don't know who's worse to deal with, Gabrielle or Frederic. They deserve each other! Anyway, are you free to have dinner with me this evening?'

'Yes…I'd love to.'

No point in hiding her feelings. He sounded much more like the man she'd found so intriguingly irresistible when she'd first arrived.

'Are you in your room?'

'Yes, I've been working.'

'I'll reserve a table at the hotel restaurant for eight o'clock. Meet me in Reception about half past seven.'

* * *

He breathed a sigh of relief as he put the phone down. The past few weeks had been difficult for him. Besides coping with Gabrielle and Frederic's demands, going over to Paris every weekend, he'd also been trying to sort out his feelings for Julia. He'd had to make sure he remained dispassionate about her in his professional dealings. The fact that he'd convinced himself he could handle a short-term relationship before they'd made love that night didn't make it any easier. The practicalities of a relationship between professor and student took some careful handling.

Also she'd had a disastrous marriage. He couldn't be flippant about any relationship that grew between them. It had to be what they both wanted. Now there were other practical considerations. With Philippe's imminent arrival it was going to be difficult for them to see each other. Julia had spoken the truth before as well—if she became an item in his life Philippe would come to regard her as a mother figure. He suspected he already did but to what extent he couldn't be sure. So if she walked out of their lives—as well she might now that her confidence had returned and she was very much in demand—his son's heart could be broken as well as his own!

The fact remained that they ultimately wanted different things out of life. She deserved a husband devoted to her and children of her own. Was he the man to take that risk again? He'd vowed to himself while he was going through the hell that Gabrielle had created during Philippe's early childhood that he would never have another child. Even though he adored Philippe he still remembered the problems associated with having

a baby. Could any partnership remain a loving relationship while the parents coped with the problems that
babies posed, especially career-minded parents battling
with everyday work situations?

He sighed as he went into the shower to prepare for
this important date. He'd decided he would stay in the
medics' quarters tonight and had brought a casual suit
to change into.

He was relieved to see her welcoming smile when he
went into Reception. He'd almost forgotten how beautiful she was when she wasn't shrouded in a white coat or
a green theatre gown, or else frowning over a problem
that needed explaining in a tutorial. She was wearing
some kind of silky-looking cream dress and heels. That
made a change from the T-shirt, jeans and trainers that
seemed to be standard uniform among his students.

He felt a flicker of desire running through him as
he noticed how sexy she looked with the dress accen-
tuating her slim figure yet clinging to the curves of her
breasts and hips.

He took a deep breath to steady his emotions as she
began to move towards him. She seemed to glide in
those strappy high-heeled sandals that made her ankles
look so slim. The skirt skimmed her knees, hiding those
fabulous thighs, which he knew were oh, so tantalising.

'Julia, you look stunning!'

He rested his hand on the back of her slim waist to
guide her out through the door, aware that they were
being watched by various members of staff. He would
reserve his kiss of welcome till later.

He raised his hand. 'I think that should be our taxi.'

Checking with the driver, he helped her inside. They sat slightly apart on the back seat as the taxi drove off towards the seafront.

Julia could feel her excitement mounting. Glancing sideways, she saw her handsome escort was watching her. She smiled at him. He moved closer, took hold of her hand and kissed her briefly on the lips.

Her fingers tingled as his hand closed around hers. Mmm, they were on course again! She didn't know where they'd been but she knew, or rather she hoped she knew, where they were going.

The hotel was one of the older buildings at the far end of St Martin's seafront. She remembered reading about it in a good-food guide. It certainly looked like a very smart sort of place from the outside.

A uniformed man came to open the car door for her as Bernard was paying off the cab. Inside the ambience was relaxed and welcoming. They were shown into the dining room with a small discreet bar near the entrance. Their table by the window was ready. She sat down, her eyes catching a glimpse of the darkening sky over the sea. The sun had already dipped into the sea and the pink and blue twilight seemed so romantic.

She looked across the table at Bernard, her heart brimming with emotion, feeling so close to him again. He was ordering a bottle of champagne.

'What are we celebrating?'

He smiled. 'The end of an era.'

She gave him a questioning look.

'I'll tell you when the champagne arrives…ah, here we are.' He was glancing at the label. 'Fine. Yes, open it, please.'

The popping of the cork, the fizzing in her glass. She was intrigued, impatient for him to enlighten her.

'Here's to the future,' he said enigmatically, holding his glass towards hers. 'I've finally settled everything with Gabrielle and Frederic but it's been difficult dealing with them. They're going to be married next week and Philippe is safely tucked up in bed at the farm. Marianne is over the moon to have him finally living back home where he should be.'

'So, what was the problem?'

'Problems!' he corrected her. 'Where shall I start? Everything had to be legally sanctioned as regards Philippe. Gabrielle wanted him to be privately educated but I insisted I wanted him to have the same upbringing I'd had out here at the village school. I want him to enjoy the countryside. To bring his friends back to the farm whenever he wants to.'

'What did Gabrielle think of that idea?'

'Well, of course, neither she nor Frederic want to be involved in bringing him up themselves but they wanted him to be taken each day to a private school about twenty kilometres from the village where he would mix with "decent children," was how she described it to me. She pointed out that she wanted him to have the best education possible so he would be a success in life.'

Julia watched him take a drink from his glass, noticing the perspiration on his brow and the set of his jaw as he swallowed hard. It hadn't been an easy time for him, she surmised.

He put down his glass. 'I pointed out that Philippe had set his heart on being a surgeon like me and the village school had given me a good education, preparing me for eventual admission to the excellent lycée in Montreuil.'

'Did that satisfy her?'

'Well, Frederic and I had to convince her that the medical profession was well regarded. She pointed out that we'd had money problems when we were first married. I explained that the early days of a profession are always difficult financially but unless Philippe becomes hampered by a difficult marital relationship—as I was—he would be a success.'

'I bet you enjoyed saying that to her!'

'I certainly did. It also shut her up. She didn't want me to start making revelations to Frederic of how she'd made my life hell when we were first married. Oh, the poor man doesn't know what he's in for. I actually feel sorry for him. Still, it's not my problem any more!'

He smiled across the table at her. 'Anyway, let's order. What are you going to have, Julia?'

She picked up the menu that the waiter had left with her. She chose moules marinières as a starter, followed by a locally caught fish, with added prawns.

'This is pure nostalgia for me, Bernard. As a child I loved the fish dishes I ate when we were here on holiday—unlike my brothers, who always asked for steak frites.'

'Ah, yes, there used to be a small wooden café on the edge of the beach that served the most delicious steak and chips.'

'That's the one!'

They relaxed into their memories of St Martin sur

Mer, which they both agreed had been an idyllic place for children.

'It still is,' Bernard said. 'And the surrounding countryside is the healthiest environment to bring up a child. You've no idea what a relief it is for me to know that Philippe will breathe in clean air every day when he goes to school instead of fumes from traffic.'

'You're very lucky.'

'I am now,' he said, his voice husky.

He reached across the table and squeezed her hand. She felt desire rising up inside her. Did he mean what she hoped he meant?

Their meal was beautifully served. They took their time, caught up once more in their conversation, which flowed so easily.

Bernard told the waiter they would take coffee on the terrace. He took her hand as they went out of the dining room and relaxed in the cushioned wicker chairs by a small table overlooking the sea.

He was intensely aware that this was the first time they'd been alone since they'd made love on that idyllic night they'd spent together. It had been almost too perfect for him. She could be the woman of his dreams, but there were so many reasons why he had to be careful with her.

He took a sip of his coffee. 'You know, you've changed a great deal since you first arrived, Julia.'

'Have I?'

'You've become much more confident and your confidence seems to grow day by day.'

'I'm certainly enjoying the course...in an exhausting kind of way. So much work to get through and then the exams looming at the end of it all.'

'I don't think you need to worry. Hard work plus natural talent for your chosen profession will bring success.' He paused, trying to make his question sound as innocent as possible. 'What have you planned to do after the exams?'

The question, out of the blue, threw her completely. 'Well, I'd planned to go back to London. Don arranged for me to have a six-month sabbatical from the orthopaedic department. I enjoy my work there and it's a good springboard from which to climb higher up the ladder, either in my own hospital or wherever a promotion should arise. I've always been ambitious but...'

He waited, watching her struggle to find the right words. He sensed what she would say even before she spoke again.

'I can't help my longing to have a child, well, a whole family really. And fitting that in with the demanding career I've also set my heart on is confusing. I'm really beginning to appreciate my parents' dilemma. I wonder if I'll have time to fit in everything I want to do with my life.'

He watched her trying to deal with the conflicting thoughts running through her mind. Since telling Julia he wasn't sure about being able to marry again and have more children, he'd had time to think. Marriage and parenting with Julia would be a totally different experience from what he'd had with Gabrielle. If they split the responsibilities fifty-fifty, they could both continue their careers.

But such a situation would require total commitment

to each other as well as the child. Marriage really was the only way. But if he told her he'd changed his mind about children and asked her to marry him, would she agree simply to have him father a child? He had to be sure she loved him first and foremost before he thought so far ahead.

That was why he'd needed some space from her after falling so hopelessly in love during that night they'd spent together at the farm. The struggles he'd endured with his ex-wife and her new partner had given him time to think about his relationship with Julia.

She was watching his serious expression. 'You're very quiet. Is something troubling you?'

'No, definitely not. Except…' He took a deep breath, almost frightened to say what was on his mind. His feelings were intense and raw, he could even feel them manifesting themselves in every part of his vibrantly awakening body. Would she feel the same way?

'Will you excuse me for a moment?'

He was already walking back into the dining room. She sat very still. Through the open door she could see him talking to the head waiter and decided he was paying the bill.

Darkness had fallen. She looked out across the bright lights beside the seafront. There were palm trees planted at the edge of the beach, which looked wonderful in summer but took a beating sometimes during the winter.

She was so captivated by the view that she didn't notice him come back to the terrace. He took her hands and drew her to her feet. He was grinning in a boyish, mischievous way.

'I've got the option on the bridal suite for tonight. I thought it would be a perfect place to relax at the end of our busy day. You won't have to creep out before dawn so as to avoid being seen in my bed either. A discreet chambermaid will bring breakfast in bed too, if you'd like. What do you say?'

She giggled. 'I'd say you'd gone mad. Why the bridal suite?'

'Because that's the only room vacant tonight.'

'Oh, don't spoil it. I thought you wanted to lavish loads of money on me because I'm worth it.'

If she only knew! He wasn't going to tell her the real truth—that there actually were a couple of much cheaper rooms available.

'So, you're happy to stay here?'

'I'd love to check out the bridal suite. I've never slept in anything like a bridal suite in my life.'

He put his arm around her waist and led her to the door. 'Who said anything about sleeping?'

She really was confused this time when she awoke in the middle of the night. At first she thought she was in Bernard's bed at the farm. His head was certainly on the edge of her pillow. She put out her hand to touch the thick, dark hair. And then she remembered.

The first and last time they'd spent the night together had been fabulous but this time…! Her body was still tingling with the most consummately passionate experience…or was it experiences? They had been in each other's arms from the moment they'd stepped across the threshold of this sumptuously exotic room.

By the time she'd reached the top of the stairs with

his arm around her waist her legs had turned to jelly. Every fibre of her body had been crying out for his love-making, his wonderful, creative, heavenly lovemaking.

He opened his eyes and smiled his slow, sexy smile that told her the night was still young. They had hours and hours before daybreak and reality. When they would both try to come back to earth. But for the moment there was no tomorrow...

Julia said that, yes, she would love to have breakfast in their room when he asked her.

He picked up the bedside phone in one hand and reached for her with the other. 'Oh, no, you don't escape this time. Room service, please. We'd like to order two breakfasts please to room... Oh, great, thank you.'

He put down the phone. 'They knew we were in the bridal suite. We didn't make that much noise, did we?'

She laughed. 'I don't remember.'

'Oh, well, in that case, let me remind you...'

'Not now. What about the chambermaid?'

'Oh, never mind the chambermaid.'

'I'm going for a quick shower.'

'Spoilsport,' he said carefully in English.

She waved a towel at him from the door to the bathroom. 'Your English is definitely improving. You must have a good teacher.'

'And your surgical skills aren't too bad either since you found yourself a good teacher.'

'Sorry, what was that?'

'Not important.'

He settled back against the pillows to await her return, feeling blissfully happy with the way things had gone since his sudden daring idea to take a room here. If he could ever be sure that she really and truly loved him for himself and didn't just regard him as a baby maker, he would ask her to marry him. He'd been very careful to ensure she knew he believed in using a condom. An unplanned pregnancy wasn't what either of them needed.

But what about his dread of going through the early days of a new baby? Even the most loving relationship must be affected. His parents had survived and remained in love, but would he and Julia be able to replicate that when they were both ambitious and in difficult and demanding work situations?

For the moment Julia needed to concentrate on her work at the hospital and her exams. But a little light relief in her off-duty time would help to relax her and prevent too much tension, wouldn't it? He smiled to himself as he heard the taps had stopped flowing in the bathroom. She would soon be back in his bed and he would be able to check she wasn't becoming tense again.

There was a knock at the door. He'd have to wait.

Groaning with frustration, he rose to admit the waiter…

CHAPTER NINE

THE summer was moving along too quickly. As she switched off her computer Julia realised that they were more than halfway through the surgical syllabus that Bernard had set for them.

She got up from her chair and walked across her small room, which was now so familiar. It had become home to her and apart from the occasional night up at the farm this was where she'd lived all the time.

And there'd been that completely heavenly night in the bridal suite! She would never forget that. She was beginning to think it might have been a one-off but she hoped not.

She bent to straighten the sheet on her bed, which was exactly as she'd left it that morning before she'd gone down for a practical tutorial in Theatre. As she leaned across the bed to take hold of the sheet she decided to lie down and take a short break before the evening. It had been a long day, a hot day apart from her time in Theatre when Bernard had insisted the air-conditioning be turned up to full.

She stared up at the ceiling. He'd seemed sort of tetchy today. He often seemed a bit irritable when he was teaching and operating at the same time. She could understand it. She could well imagine how she would feel if she had to do the same. Maybe that would happen when she became a more qualified and experienced surgeon.

The life of a surgeon was a demanding one for sure. No wonder Bernard seemed like two people sometimes. There was the man who could relax when they were together. Ah, she loved him so much when they were alone! But she worried about him when he was working. Was that natural when she wasn't sure where this relationship was going? Worrying about her man with a kind of wifely instinct? Also worrying about his child, who was becoming more and more attached to her every time she saw him?

Her mobile was ringing. Maybe it was Bernard, cancelling their date for tomorrow. It had happened when he'd told her there was an emergency he had to deal with.

'Julia, are you free this evening?'

She sat up, alert and excited by this turn of events.

'Yes; just finished writing up this morning's op. Do you think you could explain that new way you demonstrated of closing up the patient? When I was writing it up just now I—'

'Of course I'll explain but not now. I've just finished so I'm driving home in ten minutes. I thought we could all make an early start together on our day off tomorrow. Can you make it?'

'Yes, but I'll need to pack a bag. Where are we going tomorrow?'

'Oh, let's decide this evening. See you in ten, OK?'

She leapt off the bed and started throwing things

into her overnight bag. Typical Bernard! He could be so impulsive at times—like booking them into the bridal suite.

She forced her mind not to think about that particular occasion because she wouldn't be ready in ten minutes if she did. She could think about that later when they were alone in his bed.

He smiled and came towards her as she arrived in Reception.

'Well done! I knew you could do it.'

'Why the rush?'

'No reason. Just impatient to leave my daytime self behind and put on my off-duty persona.'

He put a hand on her back as they walked out towards the staff parking area.

'Ah, so you admit you're a different person in hospital from the impulsive man you can be off duty?'

'Absolutely! Guilty as charged. And to think you noticed!'

'Difficult not to.' She got into the passenger seat.

Bernard closed her door and went round to the driver's side. He started the engine and then placed a hand over hers. 'Which of my personalities do you prefer?'

She smiled up at him, feeling the familiar stirrings of desire simply by being close to him.

'Definitely the off-duty man. The other one can be a bit of a temperamental tyrant when he's in Theatre.'

He bent his head and kissed her on the lips. Drawing away slightly he murmured, 'Ah, so you noticed? It's only an act I put on to keep the students on their toes.'

'Well, this student was certainly on her toes today.'

'I noticed. That's good!'

He put the car in gear and moved out towards the front gates. 'So the work's going well, is it?'

'Exceptionally well. If you could give me a few minutes' private tuition tonight on that point I mentioned when you phoned?'

'Oh, I can certainly give you my full attention later on when we're alone.' He changed gear as they began a steep ascent.

She felt her body reacting already to the thought of the night ahead and she sensed he was in a similar mood. His voice had been definitely sexy as he'd said 'when we're alone'. She couldn't wait for the personal tuition.

Sitting around the kitchen table with the excitable Philippe chattering to her, she relaxed completely.

Marianne had bought mussels from the fish merchant who delivered to the village on Fridays and she'd been delighted when Bernard had phoned to say that Julia was coming that evening. The housekeeper placed the steaming, aromatic dish of moules marinières in front of them now.

'Bernard, I think this is one of Julia's favourite dishes, am I right?'

'Marianne, you're amazing!' Julia said. 'You remembered!'

'Well, it's my favourite, also,' Philippe said. 'May I have that big one there, Papa?'

'Of course!'

Bernard beamed round the table, a feeling of total happiness descending upon him. This was how every working week should end. Sitting at the table with his son and his beautiful, talented...what was Julia to him exactly? Certainly he shouldn't take anything for granted. There was nothing permanent about the situation, even though he wished it could go on for ever.

He glanced across at her and saw she was watching him with those eyes that sometimes looked so questioning, as if she wasn't sure of something, as well she might be. She was the most wonderful woman he'd ever met but he still couldn't allow himself to think of her as being a permanent fixture in his life. He still felt unsure of the future. There were still so many problems to iron out before he could be sure she would always be there.

Bernard put the pencil down on his notepad. 'So, does that answer your question?'

'Yes it does, Professor. That's what I put in my notes but I had to be sure.'

He gave her a sexy grin. 'So may I forget my academic commitment to a demanding student and relax again, Dr Montgomery?'

She giggled as he put his arms around her and drew her into their first embrace of the evening. They were still downstairs in the conservatory but they were alone at last with the whole of the night ahead of them.

'Marianne has put your things in the guest room,' he said solemnly.

'Do you think she understands the situation?'

'Well, if she does understand what's going on, she's more clued up than I am,' he said enigmatically.

He took a deep breath. 'Of course she assumes we sleep together at the beginning of the night...well, not so much sleep but… Yes, of course she understands the situation. She also understands that you creep along to the guest room in the early hours before Philippe wakes up.' He hesitated. 'You don't have to do that, you know.'

'I just feel that…it's simpler this way. I don't want to confuse him.'

Bernard drew in his breath. He surmised she didn't want it to be taken for granted that she would always be there. She'd come out to France to make a new start, hadn't she? That had been her initial idea. Now that she'd found her confidence, she may well decide to spread her wings and fly away at the end of the course. She had the whole of her life in front of her. He must never take her for granted.

He drew her closer in his arms. 'Let's go to bed.'

Their lovemaking had been unbelievably tender. Afterwards he held her in his arms so tightly it had almost been as if he was going to keep her there, safe, in the place she loved to be. But there was something different tonight. She sensed a certain melancholy in the moment.

Bernard lay with his arms around her, trying not to dispel the mood. Their consummation had been heavenly as always but almost immediately afterwards reality had forced itself upon him. This relationship was all too good to be true so far. He wanted to make it go on for ever…but only if that was what she wanted. He couldn't burden her with the question of commitment to him when she was coming up to the difficult weeks before the exams and the end of the course.

And he could definitely not bring up the subject of

babies. If he told her he was beginning to think he'd love to father a baby with her, how could he be sure it would be him she wanted or a baby? She could be very loving, but so had Gabrielle been when she'd wanted her own way.

But the wounds of his suffering still hadn't healed properly. The thought of spoiling their idyllic relationship by commitment, pregnancy and a small baby to care for, along with dual careers in surgery, was a very daunting one. Julia had come over to France to make a fresh start on her own. Did he have the right to impose a different kind of life on her? He couldn't bear to spoil the brilliant future that lay ahead of someone so talented.

Julia woke in the early morning and stretched out her hand under the sheet. Bernard wasn't there. Of course he wasn't. She'd made an early departure from his bed last night. He'd seemed tired, less communicative after they'd made love, so she'd decided to come along here to the guest room to get a whole night's sleep before their day out.

He'd kissed her tenderly, lovingly when she'd explained, but he'd seemed somewhat distant, as if he was standing outside their relationship and being totally dispassionate. Maybe she should have asked him if he was worrying about something but she'd sensed he wouldn't have told her. He could be a very private person when he wanted to be. But she loved him, oh, how she loved every facet of his enigmatic character.

She sighed as she switched on the bedside light. Almost seven o'clock. The little whirlwind would come charging in soon.

Bernard had heard Philippe chattering to Julia in the guest room. He'd woken very early today, which was unusual. Last night had been wonderful, holding her in his arms, making love to her, knowing they would be together today. He wasn't going to worry about where their relationship was going. He would simply accept that they made each other happy and now wasn't the time to think too far ahead.

'So where are we going today, Papa?'

Philippe stretched his little arm across the table. Bernard reached forward and wiped away some of the jam and croissant crumbs that had collected on the palm of his son's hand with his napkin. Then he gave the still sticky hand a squeeze.

'Would you like to go out in the boat?'

'Yes, oh, yes, let's go in the boat, Papa! Out to the island?'

As Bernard steered his boat across the sea he could feel the cares of the past week disappearing. He could hear Philippe chattering happily to Julia, who was pointing out landmarks on the now distant shore. She too seemed happy to be out in the boat, reminiscing with his son about her childhood holidays in this area.

'Oh, we didn't have our own boat,' Julia was explaining to Philippe. 'We didn't live over here in France so my father used to hire one sometimes. My brothers always wanted to steer it and I was always the last to have a go…and then only under strict supervision.'

'What's supervision?'

'It's when a grown-up watches you the whole time you're holding onto the wheel and—'

'Papa, will you supervision me while I'm steering the boat? Or Julia could supervision me, couldn't she?'

Bernard turned, one hand still on the wheel. 'Pass me that wooden box. If you stand on that, I'll supervise you while you hold on to the wheel. At least we've got a clear route ahead of us. Nothing for you to bump into at the moment.'

Julia helped Philippe onto the box and stood at the other side of him while Bernard kept a light hand on the wheel.

'No need to turn the wheel, Philippe. We're going straight ahead towards that island.'

'That's our island, isn't it, Papa?'

'Technically, no, but…'

'What's technically?'

'We don't own it but we're allowed to go there.'

'But we've been there lots of times so we can pretend it's ours.'

Bernard stooped and planted a kiss on his son's head. 'We can pretend anything we like today.'

His eyes met Julia's as he raised his head. He could feel a lump rising in his throat as he saw the wistful expression in her eyes. Did she feel the same way as he did about the day ahead? Just the three of them, pretending to be a family?

As they neared the shore, Julia helped Philippe down off the box again so that Bernard had full control of the boat. As they reached the shallows she took over the wheel, as they'd discussed, so that Bernard could jump out and tie up the mooring rope.

'I always wanted to tie up,' she said to Philippe. 'But my brothers got there first. My father would be steering the boat and my mother holding tightly to my hand.'

'It's more fun being a boy, I think.'

'Well, I did used to think my older brothers had a lot of fun. But I always had fun too.' She was holding the young boy's hand as they stepped barefoot into the shallows, holding their sandals so they didn't get wet.

Bernard was holding out his hand to take their sandals as they reached the shore. They walked up the beach to settle themselves under the shade of the trees. Bernard started bringing their things from the boat.

Philippe was already stripped off and running into the sea. He'd insisted on wearing his swimming trunks from the moment he'd got dressed that morning.

'Come on!' he shouted happily.

'Is the sea warm?' Julia asked as she stripped to the bikini she was wearing under her shorts.

'Very hot, hot, hot. Come and try it.'

'OK, I will.'

Bernard took hold of her hand. 'It's going to be a scorcher today.'

She revelled in the touch of his fingers enclosing hers. 'Last time I was here it rained all day and we played under the trees, wearing our mackintoshes.'

He drew her closer, feeling a frisson of desire at the closeness of her bikini-clad figure. 'How old were you?'

'It was years ago! I don't remember. I...' She glanced

at the small boy in the sea. 'We'd better go and supervise Philippe.'

Bernard laughed. 'Supervise seems to be the word of the day. I'm glad there's nobody to supervise you and me today. I'm feeling positively reckless.'

She laughed as, still holding her hand tightly, he set off down the beach.

'If only the rest of your students could see you now, Professor!'

'Papa, there are some little fish nibbling at my toes. Look, look, they're everywhere in the water. Julia, come here, can you see them? What are they?'

'Well, my English father used to call them sticklebacks. My French mother simply called them little fish, like you do.' She wiggled her toes. 'They tickle, don't they?'

'Let's swim, Papa. I can swim, Julia. Watch me!'

One each side of him, he proudly swam out towards the deeper water. 'We won't go too far out,' Bernard said to Julia as they swam alongside. 'Philippe loves swimming but he'd go on swimming till he felt tired. He forgets he's got to go back.'

'Yes, but you always put me on your chest, Papa.'

'See what I mean?'

Bernard's arm brushed against hers. The water further out was colder than nearer the shore but even so she felt a warm glow stealing over her. Just being close to him in any situation was one of the joys of their relationship. Again she found herself wondering how long they could be together like this before decisions about the future had to be made. Well, there were no decisions to be made today. Enjoying the moment was her primary concern.

'Time to go back.' Bernard steered the other two around so that they were all swimming back towards the shore.

Bernard had brought everything they needed for a barbecue. He quickly built up the sides with the large stones they'd gathered and got the fire going underneath before placing the metal rack over it.

'I've never tasted such delicious chicken drumsticks,' Julia said, tearing at a piece with her teeth. She looked across at Bernard, who'd just put more chicken on to grill. 'Mmm, you must be a very experienced chef, sir.'

'Papa always cooks lunch when we come here. Why does lunch taste much better out in the open air than inside, Julia?'

She laughed. 'Good question! I've often wondered about it.'

Bernard dropped some more food on Philippe's plate. 'On this particular island it's because we've all been swimming, which is marvellous for inducing an appetite, and the sun is shining through the trees and we're all happy.'

'And we're going to stay here all night in Papa's tent and wake up in the morning to start swimming as soon as the sun comes up.'

'Oh, not this time, Philippe. I didn't bring the tent. Anyway, it wouldn't be big enough for three of us.'

'Yes, it would! Julia and I don't take up very much room, do we? Well, do we really need a tent? It's warm enough to sleep here under the trees.'

Philippe snuggled up to Julia, wiping his sticky hands on a nearby patch of grass. 'You'd like to stay here, wouldn't you, Julia? I bet you stayed here all night when you were here on holiday, didn't you?'

'No, I'm afraid we didn't. Why don't you just close your eyes now, pretend it's night-time and have a short sleep? You look sleepy to me.'

Philippe stared at her. 'How did you know I feel sleepy?'

'Because you got up very early and you've had a busy day that included a long swim. That's always exhausting.'

She was already tucking a dry towel around the small boy and lowering her voice. He snuggled closer into her side. 'You will wake me, won't you, Julia? I don't want to wake up and find it's all dark and I've missed the rest of the day. It's such a nice day. I don't want to miss anything. Don't leave me, Julia…'

His voice drifted away as his breathing steadied and his eyelids drooped.

Watching her, Bernard felt the urge to put his arms round his two favourite people and keep them here with him for ever. He could build a camp here under the trees and blot out the rest of the world and its problems. What a wonderful mother Julia would make when she had children of her own. But she was also born to be a talented surgeon. He forced himself away from the problem. Today they belonged together and the future was the future, something to think about tomorrow.

He sat down on the sandy, grassy slope and reached towards her, careful not to disturb his son sleeping nearby, visible to them through the long grassy fronds.

Lowering his head, he kissed her gently on the lips. His kiss deepened. She clung to him, aware of the poignancy of this tender moment. One day in a family situation with Bernard had made her sure of what she wanted in life—career and motherhood, hand in hand. If she could have both options with Bernard that would be perfect. But there were so many obstacles to clear before that could happen. Could she convince Bernard to take a chance on them?

He was pulling her to her feet, leading her to a shadier spot a short way into the trees.

'It's OK, we can see Philippe from here. He's exhausted so he'll sleep until we wake him up.'

She couldn't dispute that even if she'd wanted to, which she didn't! Her passion and desires were rising up inside her as his hands caressed her into a mounting frenzy of uninhibited lovemaking.

Only as she felt the onset of her climax did she attempt to stifle the moans that were rising in her throat. She mustn't cry out, mustn't wake the sleeping child...

'Julia, it's time to wake up.'

She opened her eyes to see Bernard kneeling beside her. The sun was slanting down in the sky. She glanced across at the still sleeping Philippe.

'How long have we been asleep?'

He gave her a sexy grin. 'Too long. There's a boat coming over. Look. I've started packing up. Would you wake Philippe?'

As she sat at supper much later that night in the kitchen, she knew she would remember this day for the rest of her life. Whatever happened in the future, the days, months and years of uncertainty stretching ahead of them, she would never forget what a blissful day she'd enjoyed before she had to go back to reality and deal with the problems that lay ahead.

CHAPTER TEN

THE end of the course was fast approaching and exams were looming. Concerned as she was about the state of her relationship with Bernard, Julia was just as worried about her performance in these tests. Succeeding at this course had been her reason for coming to France. Bernard had proved a delicious distraction.

As the warm water from the shower cascaded over her body she allowed herself to look back on those halcyon days of high summer when Bernard had taken her out in his boat to 'their' island. Mostly Philippe had been with them, which was always fun. On two occasions he'd been in Paris for the weekend, staying with his grandmother who was always asking for a visit. So they'd gone alone to the island, sleeping overnight in the small cabin on the boat.

She sighed as she patted herself dry with her towel. For the last couple of weeks it had been nose to the grindstone the whole time, revision for the written exams and preparation for practical theatre work. There wasn't much she could do about preparing for the viva voce where a panel of examiners would ask her questions. Either she would satisfy them with her answers or she wouldn't.

She glanced out of the window as she finished dressing. The branches of the tall oak tree at the side of the hospital garden were being buffeted around by a high wind. The leaves had turned an autumnal gold in the past week and some of them had been blown away already. Here in the hospital, where the air-conditioning had been switched to central heating, she would be warm.

After a quick coffee and croissant in the cafeteria, she made her way along the corridor to the orthopaedic ward to see the patient she was to operate on that morning. This was the part she really enjoyed; meeting with the patient, the human aspect of surgery. When he was anaesthetised on the table the situation would change. Especially this morning when there would be an examiner watching her every move.

'Good morning, Vincent. How are you?'

Her patient, a middle-aged man who looked younger than his age and had told her he still wished he could play football, smiled broadly as she arrived at his bedside.

'I'm good, thank you. But I will be happier when the surgery is over.'

She patted his hand in sympathy, secretly thinking exactly the same as he did. How happy she'd be when the operation was over!

'I just called in to check you're OK about everything. We really do appreciate you giving your consent to allow your operation to be assessed by an examiner and performed by someone who is currently qualified to do the surgery but aiming for a higher qualification.'

'Of course it's my pleasure! I'm happy to be of service to the hospital in any way I can. Professor Bernard explained to me about… Ah, but here he is.'

Julia glanced up and saw that Bernard had joined them. 'Hello, Vincent, hello, Julia. Yes, I've explained the exam situation to Vincent.'

Vincent pulled himself up against his pillows. 'Yes, I know I'm in capable hands. Dr Julia will do my knee replacement, with a more senior surgeon by her side, who I hope will be you, Professor.'

Bernard smiled. 'Yes, that's correct. Theoretically I could intervene and take over if I felt it necessary. But in this case I'm sure that won't happen. I've worked with Dr Julia many times and she is exceptionally experienced and talented.'

Vincent gave him a cheeky grin. 'And also very beautiful!'

The two men laughed together boyishly.

'Without doubt,' Bernard said, his eyes meeting with Julia's. 'Beauty isn't a prerequisite for a surgeon but I think it helps the patient to be cared for by someone beautiful on the morning of their operation.'

To her dismay she could feel a blush rising on her cheeks as her eyes met his. 'I was just about to check that the results of all our pre-op investigations will be made available to the examiner.'

'You're in charge,' Bernard said solemnly. 'I'll leave you to it.'

She was carrying copies of her patient's notes as she left the ward some time later. Everything was in order. The left knee had been prepared for surgery. The paperwork concluded. The results of Pierre's blood tests were to hand. No problems with his haemoglobin or electrolyte balance. He was a man in excellent health apart from the knee injury, which he'd told her had meant he couldn't play football any more, not even for the local team in his village.

As soon as she walked into Theatre a feeling of confidence and capability flooded through her. She was vaguely aware of a stranger at the back of the room who was obviously the examiner. But there was no reason for that to make any difference to her performance. She'd performed a total knee replacement before. No need to worry about the outcome.

The anaesthetist nodded. Everything was OK with the patient's breathing under the anaesthetic.

With a steady, sterile, gloved hand she took the scalpel she'd asked for from Bernard and made the first incision.

'How did it go?'

She looked up at Dominic, her fellow student, who was walking towards her in the corridor as she tried to slip away for a desperately needed coffee at the end of the operation.

She stopped to chat to him. He looked terribly worried and nervous.

'It went well. No need to worry. You'll be fine. I was introduced to the examiner at the end. He was absolutely charming but he gave nothing away.'

'Didn't you ask him how you'd done?'

'Of course I didn't! Bernard's talking to him now. I needed to get away. You're on this afternoon, aren't you?'

'Can't wait!' he said gloomily. 'Can't wait till it's all over.'

'Have you got a nice, co-operative patient?'

He smiled. 'Oh, she's very nice. Couldn't be more helpful. And I know I can do a good job. I'm just on my way to check on her. Thanks for the pep talk, Julia. Just one more question.'

'Yes?'

He hesitated. 'Will you be staying on in France or going back to England once this course is over?'

She drew in her breath. 'I'm still not sure. My consultant in England is waiting for me to let him know. He's still under the impression I'll be rejoining the orthopaedic firm.'

Dominic grinned. 'And your consultant in France is hoping you'll stay here?'

'No comment! Good luck!'

She turned and walked away. She had to make a decision soon about what she should do. But she was still not sure where Bernard stood on their future and she was afraid to ask. She knew she wanted to continue with her career but she also wanted to continue her affair with Bernard. If he would only put into words how he felt about her. Give her hope that their affair could become more permanent…possibly leading to marriage?

She walked on, head down so that she could think without having to break off and talk to someone. Marriage would be a step too far for Bernard. He didn't want children and she did. Could she persuade him to change his mind about that? But then he might think she only wanted him to father a child, wouldn't he?

She banished the thoughts from her head. If only Dominic hadn't opened up all her doubts and fears about where she and Bernard were heading. Perhaps she should phone Don in London and talk it over with him. And if Bernard was still keeping her guessing she'd book a seat on the train and go back to London. Couldn't do any harm. It might even make Bernard tell her how he really felt about her.

Her confidence about her career prospects continued to grow as the exam period continued. It had been a couple of weeks since she'd operated on Vincent and he'd made excellent post-operative progress. In fact, the orthopaedic consultant in charge of his outpatient care had told her earlier that day that he'd seen him in his clinic, walking extremely well with the aid of a stick in physiotherapy. The consultant had told her he wouldn't need the stick for much longer.

Yes, she was delighted with the news. And also relieved that the other operation she'd performed under examination, which had been the required emergency operation, had also gone very well.

She'd known that she was theoretically on call for the whole of the examination period except when she was actually doing a written exam, doing an exam operation or taking the viva voce. She'd been relieved that when the actual emergency call had come she'd been well rested after a good night's sleep in her room and ready to spring into action.

As soon as the call had come from Michel in *Urgences*, asking her to go immediately to Theatre where an emergency case and an examiner were waiting for her, she'd felt herself to be on top form. A teenage girl had been rescued from a burning car. Unable to move from the damaged passenger seat, she'd been pulled out by her friends through the side window. Her patient's ankle was badly shattered as part of the engine had smashed through the front of the car, crushing her foot.

Quickly assessing that she would have to pin the ankle to realign the shattered bone, she'd simply got on with the job, hardly aware until later that she'd been examined.

After that, the written exams hadn't caused her any problems. Everything in the syllabus had been covered by the questions, which meant there was a variety of choice.

Her phone was ringing. 'How did the viva voce go this morning?'

'Bernard, I thought you would know more than I do!'

'Well, if I did I wouldn't be asking, would I?'

'And if you did you wouldn't be telling either! Oh, the distinguished panel were very civil, very cool, didn't ask me anything I couldn't answer. All in all I actually enjoyed it.'

'Good! You haven't forgotten the party tonight, have you?'

'Of course not.' She sprang off the bed and dashed over to her wardrobe, flinging wide the door. 'I hadn't forgotten but I'm running late. What would you like me to wear?'

'How about that sexy nightdress you brought with you the last time you were here?'

'Oh, you mean that flimsy bit of silk I picked up in the boutique on the seafront? It's still in the bag it came in, as well you know. One day I'll wear it—when I'm allowed to take it out of the packaging!'

'I thought there wasn't much point when I was only going to take it off as soon as you got within reach.'

She heard him chuckling down the line. That was more like the Bernard she knew and loved. The last few weeks had been a tense time for both of them with little time for frivolous exchanges that had nothing to do with exams.

'I'll drive you over to the farm in about half an hour. OK?'

'Fine! How are my fellow students getting out?'

'I've paid for a minibus there and back. I don't want to have to worry about drunk driving amongst my students. I want everybody to enjoy themselves now that the exams are finished.'

Marianne had done them proud! As Julia surveyed the buffet supper the housekeeper had laid on for them she felt she had to quietly congratulate her.

'Oh, I enjoyed it, Julia,' Marianne said as they whispered together in the kitchen. 'And two of my friends from the village came out to help me.'

'They're the ladies who were serving drinks earlier, I presume? Honestly, Marianne, I would have been out to help you today but I didn't finish my last exam until this morning.'

'Julia, I didn't expect you to help when you've been so busy at the hospital. Bernard told me you were giving all your energy to the exam. That's why we haven't seen you out here for a while. Philippe was so excited when he knew you were coming. And I'm glad you read his bedtime story before he went to sleep. I'd hoped you'd give him some time.'

'I've missed him so much. I just love him to bits. He's…very special.'

Marianne gave her a searching look. 'He feels exactly the same about you, Julia.'

Julia swallowed hard. She knew the implication was that she shouldn't take that love lightly, that she shouldn't break a young boy's heart. Now that she'd finished her exams, all the emotional problems of her relationship with Bernard had begun crowding in on her again.

'Are there any more of those canapés, Marianne?'

It was Bernard, putting an arm round her waist as he rescued her just in time.

'Lots more in the oven ready to come out.' She raised her voice. 'Gaston, get the canapés out, please!'

'What were you two whispering about?' Bernard handed her another glass of wine as he steered her towards the window seat in the sitting room.

Julia smiled. 'I was congratulating Marianne on the marvellous buffet supper.'

'Oh, she loves having a party here. It doesn't happen as often as she would like. Thanks for putting Philippe to bed. He'd been waiting to see you all day, apparently, and I was too tied up with my guests to help you. I popped upstairs to his room just now and he's out for the count. I don't think we'll hear from him, in spite of the noise, until the morning.'

He wondered if she knew how nervous he'd been feeling when he'd said that. He'd decided, really decided, against all the odds that he was going to tell her how he really felt about their relationship tonight. He found himself holding back on the wine. He wanted to remember this night even if…no, he was going to be positive. He had to know the truth, whatever it turned out to be.

'I want to make a toast, everybody!' Dominic was standing in the middle of the room, raising his glass in the air. 'I think I know I speak for all of us on the course when I say that we've had the best professor guiding us every step of the way. I've learned a lot, rediscovered areas of surgical technique I'd forgotten and grappled with the new techniques Bernard has taught us. Whatever my exam results, I'll always be a better surgeon than I would have been and a much better all-round doctor. So, fellow students, please raise your glasses to Bernard, the finest surgical professor we could possibly have wished for!'

Glasses were raised high. The wine flowed. The conversation turned to what everybody was going to do now it was all over. Most of them were going back to the hospitals that were still holding their jobs open for them. The general consensus was that promotions were imminent if their exam results were good. Others were more pragmatic. They would pick up where they'd left off, happy that they'd had the experience to widen their knowledge of surgery.

'How about you, Julia?' Dominic asked. 'Have you made up your mind at last?'

She cleared her throat. She felt nervous with Bernard standing so close to her, listening to every word she was saying. They'd moved to be with the group in the centre of the room but his hand was still lightly on the small of her back.

'I'm keeping my options open for the moment,' she

said quietly. 'I'll have to return to London to discuss my future with my tutor, whatever I decide to do.'

'When will you go?' Dominique asked.

She hesitated. They were all looking at her, including Bernard whose expression was totally enigmatic. They hadn't discussed this and she now wished they had. She hadn't had time…or had she simply been avoiding this conversation?

'Well…I've reserved my seat on the Eurostar tomorrow. I'm going to London for a few days to talk things over with Don.'

Bernard swallowed hard, trying not to convey any emotion at the announcement. He should have known this would happen. This now confident young woman who'd come out here for a fresh start and made such an impression on all her colleagues. She was ready now to fly away and get on with her successful life. She was ready to combine career and motherhood whenever the time was right. And even if he'd told her he'd changed his mind about having a commited relationship again, it wouldn't have made any difference.

She didn't need him to be her husband and father her child. She was so charismatic, so utterly desirable, so talented, so sexy she could take her time in choosing the right partner for herself.

As he watched her fellow students crowding round her, wishing her well in the future, he knew that he'd lost her. She was going back to London tomorrow and she hadn't told him. Just for a few days, she'd said. But once she got back there she wouldn't return. Her colleagues over in London would gather around her, just as her French colleagues were doing now, and Don

Grainger would persuade her to return and climb the career ladder under his tutelage.

He had to let her go back to London. He mustn't try to dissuade her. It would be selfish of him to try. She was off the course now. Her reason for being here finished. Her exam results would reach her electronically, wherever she happened to be.

CHAPTER ELEVEN

JULIA breathed a sigh of relief as Dominic finally weaved his way across the farmyard to join his colleagues in the waiting minibus. She thought he'd never go so she could be alone with Bernard and explain why she hadn't told him she was leaving for London tomorrow.

She looked around the room but Bernard had disappeared while she'd been listening to Dominic's endless talking. Where was he?

'Ah, there you are, Bernard.'

He was coming through the door. She smiled and moved towards him but stopped in her tracks when she saw he was carrying her overnight bag.

His expression gave nothing away. 'I think it's best for you to go back to the hospital tonight. You've got an early start tomorrow. I've told the driver of the minibus you'll be going back to the hospital and will be with them as quickly as you can.'

'Bernard, I wanted to explain the situation to you tonight. I'm only going to London for a few days.'

'So you said. I'll wait to hear from you. Let me know your plans when you've discussed things with Don.'

He was moving closer, still holding her bag. 'I'll take you to the coach.'

He really meant it! She'd better go gracefully without trying to explain now. Maybe this was his way of ending their short-term relationship. Perhaps he was relieved to have an excuse to end it so easily.

She'd never thought it would end like this. But she'd never been any good at understanding men. She must have got it wrong again!

Her colleagues in the minibus had started to sing now.

Julia winced at the noise disturbing the peace and quiet of the valley but she needn't have worried. Everyone fell silent as she and Bernard reached them. Dominic made a space on the front seat for her and took her bag. For the sake of appearances she smiled at Bernard. He smiled back but it was a wintry smile that was there to pretend that all was well.

The driver was anxious to get going. Everyone started calling their thank-yous and goodbyes.

She doubted very much that Bernard could hear her saying goodbye to him. He gave a wave of his hand and walked back up the farmyard.

She woke in the early morning of a grey dawn. Even the clouds through the window added to her dark feelings. She stretched out her hand towards the other side of the bed. The sheet was cold. She knew he wasn't there. She'd come back to her room at the hospital. Correction! He'd sent her back to her room.

She propped herself up on her pillows and checked the time. She'd set her alarm when she'd got back last night. It would soon be time to get up and make final preparations for the journey.

She remembered the awful journey in the minibus last night. Her friends had become mercifully quiet after she'd joined them. They'd had the decency not to ask questions and they hadn't sung any more. But she'd been very relieved to get to her room and close the door on her own little sanctuary.

Her alarm was sounding. Time to get up. She threw back the duvet. She'd asked the hospital domestic staff to keep her room for a further week until she got back from London. But now she was unsure whether she would return. Her emotions were in turmoil and now wasn't the time to try and sort them out. She determined to go back to London to make her decision.

CHAPTER TWELVE

SHE stepped down from the Eurostar at St Pancras, marvelling at the speed with which she'd been transported from Calais–Frethun. Only an hour ago she was stepping on the Eurostar in France and now here she was making her way through the crowds, hearing English voices. She got a taxi after only a short wait and gave him the name of her hospital.

'Are you visiting a patient?' he asked her conversationally.

'No.' She climbed into the back seat.

Usually she enjoyed chatting with cab drivers as they struggled through the London traffic jams but today was different. She felt different, spaced out, unreal. Maybe when she was back amongst her colleagues in the orthopaedic department she would be able to make sense of her future. She'd gone away with such high, ambitious hopes. She hadn't been looking for an all-consuming relationship that had turned her world upside down and forced her to examine her dreams.

She wished she'd been able to say goodbye to Philippe. She forced herself to ignore her feelings of guilt about him. He'd come to regard her as a second mother figure and if she stayed in England he would feel she'd abandoned him. And she would miss him more than she dared think about just now. And as for Bernard... If their affair was over...

Her eyes misted over as she searched in her bag for a tissue to blow her nose.

One step at a time.

She felt a surge of apprehension as she paid the driver and looked up at the tall façade of the building that had been her home and workplace as a medical student and then a qualified doctor. It usually felt as if she was coming home again but this time was different.

'So, you'll get your exam results in a couple of weeks, I understand?' Don smiled across the desk at her. 'I was so relieved to get your email this week to say you were coming back to report on the course.'

'Thanks for your reply. I'm glad you were free to see me this morning.'

'I would have made time for you, Julia.' The consultant hesitated, running a hand through his steel-grey hair as he observed his star pupil. Something told him that she wasn't feeling her usual positive self.

'Would you like more coffee? You must be tired after your early start this morning.'

'No, thanks.'

She sat up straight against the back of her chair as she tried to brighten herself up. In the background she could hear the hum of the endless traffic outside on the forecourt of the hospital. An ambulance screeched to a halt and the siren stopped. It was weird. She should be feeling nostalgic by now.

'I've kept in touch with your progress over in France,' Don told her in a casual, friendly tone.

She managed a tight smile. 'I thought you might.'

'Oh, yes. I wasn't going to let you slip through my fingers. I've invested a lot in your training. Seen you grow up from student days. I'll be retiring soon, you know, well, in a couple of years.'

'No, I didn't know. You'll be missed here.'

'Oh, nobody is indispensable. Anyway, to go back to my progress reports from France, your professor, Bernard Cappelle, seems to think very highly of you. When I spoke to him a few days ago he told me you'd made excellent progress and he had high hopes for your exam results. From the way he spoke it seemed you might be staying on in France.'

Her heart gave a little leap of excitement but she remained silent, waiting for him to continue.

He carried on, wondering why she wasn't making any comment.

'That's why I'm so delighted to see you here in London today. There's the possibility of a promotion in the department, and then when I retire in two years my vacancy will be up for grabs. I've no doubt that, having excelled on the prestigious course at St Martin, you would be a strong candidate.'

He broke off. 'Julia, I think you should take a rest for a few hours to recover from the journey. I've asked Housekeeping to prepare your old room in the medics' quarters. My secretary has the keys. Let's meet up here in my office about four this afternoon.'

He stood and walked round the desk. She remembered how he'd been a father figure to her when she'd gone through the messy divorce days. He wasn't fooled by the brave face she was trying to effect. He held out his hand as she stood up, making a valiant effort to keep going.

She grasped his hand. 'Yes, you're quite right, a rest would be a good idea. I'll be back at four. Thanks, Don, for—'

'For treating you like one of my daughters.' He grinned. 'When you've got four girls at home you become an expert at sensing when something is not quite right.'

She smiled back, knowing she hadn't fooled him. She would have to sort out her problems, emotional and career-wise, before she came back.

She fell into a troubled sleep the moment her head hit the pillow. But the dreams that haunted her throughout were worse than being awake. She was dreaming that Philippe was seriously ill, that Bernard wasn't there with him, that he was on the island looking for her, calling her name, but she was calling out to him from the sea where she felt as if she was drowning. The water was over her head but her arms and legs weren't working properly... She managed to struggle up from the depths of her sleep. Relief flooded through her as she realised she was safe in her room. She was wide awake now and her mind had cleared. She knew she had to speak to Bernard as soon as possible.

He wasn't answering his phone. She tried several times. She'd get hold of Michel Devine in *Urgences*.

'Michel?'

'Michel Devine.'

His abrupt manner and the background noise told her he was on duty.

'It's Julia.'

'Ah, Julia. I thought you were in England. Bernard told me—'

'I'm trying to call him but he's not answering.'

'He's up in Paediatrics with Philippe—that's why he's not answering. I'll get a message to him if—'

'Is Philippe OK?'

'We're not sure. Bernard brought him in this morning. He's going through tests for meningitis.'

'Oh, no!'

'Don't worry, Julia. Philippe is in safe hands and Bernard is constantly with him at his bedside. What message shall I give Bernard?'

'Tell him…tell him I…tell him I'm coming back tonight. Thanks, Michel.'

She glanced at her watch as she zipped up her bag. Good thing she hadn't unpacked anything except her toothbrush. She went out into the corridor. She'd contacted Don, who'd agreed to see her earlier that afternoon.

He was waiting for her in his consulting room in Outpatients. A couple of patients were waiting outside as she went in and closed the door.

'Thanks for seeing me at such short notice. I'll make it brief because I know you've got patients waiting.'

'So why the change of plan, Julia?' He got up from his desk and moved over to the window where there were a couple of armchairs and a small table. 'Have you had any lunch?'

'I'll get something on the train.'

'The train?'

'I'm going back. Bernard Cappelle's son is ill with suspected meningitis. I have to be there with them. Sorry, Don, but it's put everything in perspective, coming back to England. I wasn't sure what it was I wanted but now I am.'

For a moment the consultant stared at her before he realised the reason behind her strange behaviour.

'Ah, I get the full picture now. I have to say I wondered if there was something going on between you and Bernard. So you're an item, to quote my daughters, are you?'

She hesitated. 'Yes, we've built up a relationship, a complicated relationship, and I don't know where it's going, but...' She stared across the small table at Don. 'I shouldn't be burdening you with all this.'

'Julia, you are talking to an expert in the affairs of the heart and in my opinion you've got it pretty bad. So I'm all agog to hear what you're going to do about it.'

She hesitated. 'I've got to think about it.'

'What's there to think about? You're obviously head over heels in love with the man. Call me an old romantic but you shouldn't turn your back on that sort of relationship.'

'But, Don, remember when I was going through that awful divorce and I told you I'd never trust my own judgement of character again? I was trying to be rational this time, taking my time to think through the problems of marrying Bernard and carrying on with my career.'

'You were too young when you married that obnoxious man. You'd had no experience of people like that.

Now you're an extremely intelligent and experienced woman. I'm sad to see you going back because I had great plans for your future here. But you've got to go back and stay there with Bernard. You obviously love both him and his young son. Let me know as soon as the boy has been through all his tests at the hospital.'

The journey seemed much longer on the way back. She was amazed to see Michel Devine waiting for her at St Martin station. She'd told him the time her train from Calais–Frethun would arrive.

'How's Philippe?'

'Still having tests.' He opened the car door for her. 'Bernard is with him the whole time but the paediatric department is firmly in charge.'

'I just hope it's not meningitis.'

'If it is, he's in the best hospital to deal with it. And he's got the best father to lavish attention on him.'

'Thanks for picking me up, Michel.'

'I thought you might be shattered after going there and back in the space of a few hours. I thought of sending a taxi for you but I'm going off duty now and I can get you back to the hospital myself.'

'Well, it's much appreciated.'

'I'm so glad you've come back. You definitely belong over here…with Bernard. As a widower of three years, I was pleased when I saw you and Bernard getting on so well. A good relationship like yours is worth sticking to. My wife and I were only married for three years before she lost her battle with cancer. While she was alive were the happiest days of my life.'

She swallowed hard as she heard the raw emotion in

his voice. They were drawing into the forecourt of the hospital.

'Thanks, Michel. I'll go straight up to Paediatrics.'

He switched off the engine and came round to help her out. 'I'll put your bag in Reception till you need it, then I'll go off duty.'

'Thanks for the advice.'

He gave her a sad smile. 'What advice?'

'Not in so many words but you nudged me in the right direction.'

'I hope so.'

CHAPTER THIRTEEN

JULIA pushed open the swing doors that led into the paediatric ward. It was late in the evening now and most of
the children had been settled down for sleep. The lights
had been dimmed in the main ward. She could see the
ward sister walking towards her now.

'Ah, Caroline!'

She was glad they'd met socially during the summer.
She also knew that she was one of the most experienced
and well-qualified sisters in the hospital.

She began to relax. 'How is Philippe?'

Caroline frowned. 'I'm afraid the tests are still in-
conclusive. Bernard is with him. He's been here all day.
I thought you were in England, Julia.'

'I made a brief visit to see the boss of my department. I'm back now. Change of plan. Where is...?'

'Let me take you to his room.'

Caroline took her to a room near the nurses' station.
The door was slightly ajar. She pushed it open.

'A visitor for you, Bernard.'

He was sitting by Philippe's bed, hunched over his
son, his head resting in his hands, his elbows on the
sheet. He turned his head and for an instant she saw a

flash of welcoming light in his eyes before the mask of total dejection returned.

'I thought you were in England.'

Sister went out and closed the door behind her as Julia approached the sick child's bed. Bernard stood up, running a hand through his dishevelled hair. She could see that he hadn't shaved that day. The dark stubble she'd noticed he always had in the mornings was now much more prominent—positively designer stubble, she couldn't help thinking. She longed to draw him against her and hold him there but sensed the cold aura surrounding him.

'I came back,' she said lamely. 'I was worried about Philippe.'

She leaned across the small patient now, automatically reaching for his pulse. It was racing along too fast, almost impossible to count the beats. His skin was dangerously hot.

'What's the latest?'

Bernard handed her the notes. She was still scanning the test results as one of the doctors on the paediatric firm came in.

'What's the latest news from Pathology, Thibault?' Bernard asked, his calm voice belying the obvious anxiety that cloaked the rest of him.

'A glimmer of hope, Bernard. The latest blood sample gave negative results for meningitis. I'm going to take another sample now.'

She stood beside Bernard as the blood sample was taken.

'It could be septicaemia, couldn't it?' he said to the

young doctor as he prepared to return to the pathology laboratory.

'Or it could be the antibiotics beginning to kick in,' Julia said quietly, thinking out loud.

The three of them pooled their ideas, each anxious that the dreaded diagnosis of suspected meningitis should be proved to be wrong.

'We'll just have to hope, Bernard,' Dr. Thibault said gently. 'Tonight is the crucial time. As you know, if we don't have an improvement in your son's condition by tomorrow morning there is a chance that—'

'Yes, yes,' Bernard said, his voice wavering now. He didn't want to contemplate that his son's illness could be fatal. 'We can beat it! This is the twenty-first century and we'll pool our skills to save Philippe.'

'If I might suggest, Bernard,' the young doctor said, carefully, 'you've been here all day and you must be tired. I think I could arrange for you to take a break if you would approve of that?'

'I can't leave Philippe at this stage.'

'I'll call the path lab and ask them to collect this blood immediately. I can stay here with your son for the next hour.'

Julia looked across the small table at Bernard. The canteen had been deserted when they'd arrived but she had phoned the kitchen and the staff cook on night duty had turned up to prepare some food.

Chicken and vegetable soup had been placed in front of them, along with a crusty baguette heated up in the oven and a basket of fresh fruit—apples, oranges and bananas.

It wasn't until they'd started to eat the soup that they both realised how hungry they were.

'Did you have lunch over in England?'

She put down her spoon, having polished off her first helping. 'There wasn't time. I meant to get a sandwich on the train but I wasn't hungry. I'm hungry now.'

'There's more soup in this casserole,' Bernard said, dipping in with the soup ladle the waitress had left on the table.

It was only when she'd finished the last piece of her apple that her brain seemed to function again.

'Dr Thibault was quite right to send you off for a break. You looked terrible when I first got here.'

'Thanks! You weren't looking your usual self either.' His eyes seemed to be boring into her. 'Care to tell me why you're here?'

'I told you; I was worried about Philippe.'

'And?'

'Bernard, I don't think we should talk about this until we've got through tonight.'

'We? You don't have to stay, Julia.'

'Oh, but I do. I can't rest until I know that…that he's out of danger.'

Bernard stood up. 'Neither can I.'

She must have dozed off in the high-backed armchair beside Philippe's bed. Bernard, at the other side, was wide awake, she could see, sponging his son's chest with cold water.

As he dabbed it dry he looked across at her. 'The rash isn't so pronounced. It's disappearing in places. I'm beginning to hope it's septicaemia.'

'Still dangerous,' Julia said quietly. 'But easier to treat than meningitis.'

Bernard nodded. 'He's opening his eyes… Julia!'

She jumped up from the chair and went round the bed. 'Philippe?'

'Where am I?'

Julia could feel tears of joy pricking her eyes as she heard the weak little voice. A tear trickled down her cheek as she leaned over Philippe, taking hold of his tiny hand. She'd been right to come back here. This was where she belonged.

Philippe was propped up against the pillows, eating a small carton of yoghurt. It was what he'd asked for as soon as he'd begun to feel stronger. Since the amazing recovery in the early morning he'd gradually gathered strength. The diagnosis was confirmed, septicaemia. His treatment and medication had been adjusted accordingly and there was every chance now that he was going to have a full recovery within days.

'Papa, can we go home? I want to see the cows. Gaston will need some help with the milking today.'

'We'll need to stay here for another night at least.'

'But you'll both stay with me, won't you? Julia, you can stay, can't you? You won't leave me, will you?'

She looked at the anxious eyes of this young boy who meant so much to her and across the bed to his father whom she loved more than she'd ever imagined possible.

What would she do if he didn't want her any more?

CHAPTER FOURTEEN

SHE'D spent the night in the guest room. On Bernard's instructions Gaston had moved another bed into Philippe's room before they'd all arrived back from the hospital yesterday. Bernard had insisted she get a good night's sleep.

'You've spent the last three nights in an armchair so you must get a proper rest tonight,' he'd told her.

She'd argued that so had he. They could take turns at caring for Philippe during the night.

But Bernard had been adamant that he wanted to do the night watch. As she pulled the curtains fully back and fixed the ties, she raised her face to the morning sun. There was little heat now in the late autumnal rays but it was soothing to her nerves. Bernard had been right. She did need a good rest. Her nerves had been totally frazzled over the last few days since Philippe had become ill.

And the journey to London and back had tired her more than usual. Well, the discussion with Don Grainger had set her thinking.

She sighed as she looked out over the garden. The fallen leaves on the lawn. The roses drooping and waiting to be dead-headed. She'd pushed the emotional problems that still existed between Bernard and herself to the back of her mind until they were absolutely sure Philippe was out of danger. And she didn't want a discussion while Philippe was the main priority in Bernard's life.

Maybe she should simply go back to her room in the medics' quarters at St Martin? Marianne and Gaston were taking care of all the practicalities of the situation. Was she really needed here?

'Julia, I've brought you some coffee.'

She raced to the door at the welcome sound of Bernard's voice.

He was standing outside in the corridor, carrying a small tray, the expression on his face totally unreadable.

'How's Philippe?'

'He had a good night. In fact, so did I. I slept until Marianne brought the coffee tray just now. She's taken over to give me a break. I feel that now Philippe is out of danger and you're back from London we should talk. My place or yours?'

For the first time for days he looked relaxed again. There was a half-smile on his face but still that awkward coolness that had to be resolved if she was to convince him that she'd made a mistake in returning to London without discussing it with him first.

She'd had time to think and she knew that she wanted Bernard on any terms. She could be happy with him without them marrying or having a child of their own. Philippe felt like her own child already and if Bernard didn't want more children, neither did she. But did he want her? Had the short-term affair been enough for him to decide to go back to his independent lifestyle?

She moved towards him. 'Which room would you prefer?'

'I'd like to install myself back in my bedroom so let's go there. I need to shave and everything is in my bathroom. We can talk while I'm in there before I arrange my schedule at the hospital for today. I plan to go in for a couple of hours this morning. I've arranged for a nurse to come out from the hospital to be with Philippe, and Marianne and Gaston will be in charge here.'

She followed behind him. This wasn't how she'd planned to discuss her change of heart—in a bathroom!

He held the tray in one hand and pushed open his door with the other, walking swiftly over to the small round table by the window. She sank down into one of the armchairs and watched as he poured the coffee into the cups. He took a sip and swallowed. 'Mmm, that first coffee taste of the morning. Nothing like it!'

She watched, mesmerised, as he began to walk towards the bathroom, the cup firmly clenched in his fingers.

'Bernard! You're not really going to shave while we have the most important discussion of our lives!'

He turned, a half-smile again on his face. 'Ah, so you do have something to tell me? Don said you might have.'

He moved swiftly back to the table and stretched his long legs out in the armchair across from her.

'Don?'

'Who else knows you almost as well as I do? Well, professionally anyway. He phoned me last night to check how Philippe was but also to fill me in about your discussions. He said he thought you would be staying in France and conceded that his loss was my gain. He'd hoped to guide you up the career ladder in London until his retirement and he was sad to lose you.'

'So you were simply talking professionally?'

'What else?'

She was beginning to feel alarmed. The two men who'd been most influential in her career had been discussing her.

'He didn't touch on anything...er...well, personal?'

He feigned surprise at her question. 'Such as?'

'Oh, Bernard, you can be so infuriating at times!'

She leapt out of her seat and went across so she would have the advantage of looking down at him. 'Such as whether our relationship was over or not?'

'Ah, that.' He half rose from his seat and pulled her down onto his lap. 'Well, he might have mentioned it.'

She turned her head and looked up at him. He had the advantage now and she'd really wanted a discussion. She needed to convince him that she'd come to the right decision at last.

'I've had time to think over the last few days,' she said quietly. 'I know you don't want another child but I've realised that I can live as a surgeon so long as I have you...and Philippe, of course...in my life. I don't need a baby any more.'

'But I do,' he replied gently, drawing her so close that she could feel his heart beating. 'I've known for some time now that, contrary to how I used to feel, I would love to have a baby...but only with you. I've watched you caring for Philippe and I realised that you would be the most wonderful mother to our baby.'

'So why didn't you tell me you'd had a change of heart?'

'I wanted to be sure you wouldn't choose to have a baby with me just because I could fulfil one of your dearest wishes. I had to be sure that you loved me as much as I love you.'

'But I thought that was obvious!' She put her hands against his cheeks and drew his lips against hers.

She felt his response deepening, his hands gently caressing her body. Gently, he lifted her up into his arms and carried her over to the bed.

'Can I make my love any more obvious?' she whispered as they both lay back, exhausted by their lovemaking and panting for breath.

She turned her head on the pillow to look at him as she curled her toes against his, one of the positions she loved to adopt after they'd made love.

He smiled. 'I think you've convinced me… But, then again, I just might be having doubts.'

He rested on his elbow, looking down into her eyes. 'I'll need convincing often if we're going to stay together for the rest of our lives.'

She gazed up into his face. 'And are we going to stay together for the rest of our lives?'

Before she realised what he was doing he was on his knees beside the bed, looking up at her with those devastatingly sexy eyes that were expressing the love he felt for her.

'Julia, will you marry me?'

His voice was husky, full of emotion as he asked her the question she'd thought he might never ask. She'd had her doubts before but now that they'd sorted out the problems that had been holding them back she was free to commit herself.

She leaned forward and put her hands over his. 'Of course I will.'

He was in bed beside her, drawing her into his arms. 'Oh, Julia, my love…'

'Bernard, the nurse is here to look after Philippe.'

Julia struggled up through the tangle of sheets as she heard Marianne's voice outside in the corridor. She swung her legs over the side of the bed.

Bernard put out a restraining hand. 'I'll go,' he whispered. 'Stay here and rest. There's no hurry. Take your time before you come downstairs.'

He was smiling fondly down at her. 'As soon as Marianne hears our news, you'll need all your energy to cope with her. She'll be thinking ahead to the wedding and all the plans that will be needed.'

'Please don't tell her till I come downstairs.'

His smile broadened. 'I won't need to. That woman is psychic, I'm sure. She's been expecting an announcement ever since you stayed that first night here.'

It was only as she climbed out of the bath and reached for a towel a little later that she realised the enormity of the tasks ahead of her. There were phone calls to make to her parents—that must be a priority. How would her mother take it? Last time she'd announced she was going to be married her mother had been very unsure. She'd gone ahead with it defiantly and had lived to regret it. But this time she was absolutely sure of her man.

But the practicalities had to be dealt with. Where would they have the wedding? France? England? There'd have to be a long list of guests. How much easier if would be if they could just sneak away, the three of them.

As she thought of the three of them making a real family unit at last she felt a great longing to see her soon-to-be stepchild as soon as possible.

Hurrying along to his room, she slowed down to check that she was presentable. It was still early but so much had happened, so much had been resolved and so much needed to be sorted out. As her mother would say, she should gather her wits about her.

Yes, there would be a nurse from the hospital taking care of Philippe and she didn't want to look as if she'd been rolling about in Bernard's bed all night. It had only been this morning when she'd given herself completely to the joy of being finally sure that their future was well and truly together.

She smiled as she recognised one of the nurses from Paediatrics. 'Hello, Florence.'

'Julia!' Philippe's voice was croaky and weak but his happiness at seeing her again was expressed in the way he held out his thin little arms towards her.

She leaned down and clasped him against her. 'Oh, Philippe, it's good to see you looking so much better.'

'Can I come down and have breakfast with you and Papa? I'm feeling hungry now.'

'You said you didn't want to eat anything,' Florence said gently. 'Let me bring something up from the kitchen for you. I don't think you're strong enough to go downstairs yet.'

As if on cue, Bernard chose that moment to come in. 'What's this about breakfast, Philippe?'

He reached down and picked up his small son in his arms. Julia grabbed a blanket from the end of the bed and wrapped it round him. He snuggled happily against his father.

'Take a break, Florence,' Bernard said. 'Come down and have some breakfast with us. The more the merrier around the table today!'

Marianne was waiting for them in the kitchen, cafetière in her hand. The delicious smell of coffee had wafted up the stairs as Julia had walked behind Bernard, followed by Florence. Julia sat down beside Bernard, as close as she could to Philippe so that she could make sure he was comfortable in Bernard's arms. She doubted he would eat much, if anything, after the ordeal he'd been through, but it was the experience of being once more part of the family that he needed.

Their family! Her heart seemed to turn over at the implications of what was happening.

What a momentous occasion. Was Bernard going to make an announcement here at the breakfast table? With Florence here the news would spread like wildfire at the hospital. Was that what he wanted?

She glanced up at him as he cleared his throat. He was looking oh, so pleased with himself, happiness oozing from every fibre of his muscular, athletic, tantalisingly sexy body. His happiness was infectious. There was a feeling of total unreality about the situation but she'd never felt as happy as she did at that moment. Yes, she wanted to tell the whole world that she was soon to be married to the most wonderful man on the planet.

'Come and sit down, Marianne,' Bernard said. 'I want everybody here because I've got an announcement to make. Where's Gaston?'

'He's just finished the milking. He's going to take a shower as soon as—'

'Ask him to come in here, Marianne, if he's still out there, taking off his boots.'

Gaston glanced around the table as he walked in, treading carefully across the room in his socks to sit next to his wife.

'I haven't even washed my hands,' he complained to his wife before looking across at Bernard. 'What's this all about? I need to clean up.'

'Julia has just consented to become my wife. I want you all to share in our happiness.'

'And about time too,' Gaston said, now grinning from ear to ear. 'Creeping around in the middle of the night when the two of you—'

'Gaston!' his wife hissed at him. 'Be quiet.'

'No, I won't be quiet. This is the best news we've had in this house since I came to work here and told you that Marianne had set a date for our wedding.'

'And that was a long time ago, wasn't it, Gaston? I was much younger but I remember it well because my father opened one of his special bottles of champagne so we could drink a toast. I haven't been down to the cellar recently. Do you know if there's still a bottle of that vintage?'

Gaston struggled to his feet. 'I checked a few weeks ago because I was hoping you'd get a move on, Bernard. Shall I put a bottle on ice?'

'Bring a couple. We'll have a glass now and drink

some more this evening when we can all relax at the end of the day.'

'Julia, are you going to be my new mother?' Philippe asked shyly.

She swallowed hard. 'I'm going to be Papa's wife. You can carry on calling me Julia because I'll never replace your real mother, will I?'

'I suppose not. Well, you can be my second mother, then, but I'd like to still call you Julia.'

Gaston arrived with the champagne. 'It's freezing cold down there in the cellar. I've brought the ice bucket but we don't really need it. And it needs polishing. Hasn't been used for years. I cleared away the cobwebs but...'

He glanced across at his wife, who was already holding a duster.

Julia gathered Philippe into her arms as Bernard stood to do the honours. The cork was expertly removed with barely a hiss, the champagne was poured, the glasses raised.

Marianne was in tears now that she'd got the situation she'd hoped for. It was almost too much for her as she raised her glass to the happy pair.

'Congratulations!' she said, through her tears.

Florence was overwhelmed at being the first to acknowledge that there was some truth in the rumours that had been circulating in the hospital. Just wait until she got back there at the end of the week!

'Well, that all went very well today,' Bernard said, as he climbed into bed. 'Do you think you could put that list down and give me some attention? There can't be that much to do when you're organising a wedding, can there?'

'You must be joking! Not for the groom perhaps. So long as you write a good speech and...'

'Oh, do I have to give a speech? I'd better start now, then. Just lend me that notepad you're still scribbling in.'

He reached across and grabbed it from her, glancing down as he did so. 'Oh, how did your mother take the news?'

'Very well, actually. I gathered that you'd phoned Don this morning and he'd phoned Mum to prepare her for the news. They're old friends from way back at medical school. He'd also given you a very good character reference, I believe, because she said she was looking forward to meeting you.'

'And did you agree on where the wedding should take place?'

'The church where my grandmother and my mother were married in Montreuil sur Mer. I was baptised there because my mother insisted on keeping our French family connection going.'

'So, a very interesting family choice.'

'And do you approve?'

'Absolutely!' He drew her into his arms. 'Is that all the business for the day completed? The night nurse has taken over from Florence in Philippe's room so we're free to go to sleep or...'

As she gave herself up to the delights of their lovemaking she knew she was going to be the happiest bride ever.

EPILOGUE

THE day of the wedding dawned with a flurry of snow-flakes drifting outside the window. Julia had spent the night in a hotel in the village with her parents in line with the tradition of not seeing her groom before the wedding. It had been hard to be separated from Bernard but as he'd reminded her when he kissed her goodnight it was only one night apart and then they would be to-gether for the rest of their lives.

After Julia had eaten breakfast in bed, her mother arrived with Claudine, the dressmaker, and Monique, a hairdresser who was going to shampoo and arrange her long blonde hair so that it would fall over her shoulders underneath the delicate lace veil.

Claudine was going to dress her and make sure that the stunning silk dress they'd designed between them was shown off to perfection. The dressmaker held out the stiff petticoat and Julia stepped into it, one hand on Claudine's shoulder to steady herself. It looked gor-geous!

The ladies in the room asked for her to give them a twirl. She obliged. It didn't feel at all stiff and starchy as she'd thought it might.

Finally, she stood in front of the mirror fully dressed

in the superbly beautiful dress while her mother, Claudine and Monique stood around to admire her. Behind her reflection she could see her mother wiping away a tear. She turned and hugged her.

Her mother hugged her back, but gently. 'Careful of your dress, darling. I'm so happy for you. This time you're going to be very happy.'

And as she walked into the church on her father's arm she knew she really was going to be happy for the rest of her life. She'd chosen and been chosen by the most wonderful man in the world.

Walking down the aisle, she felt like a fairy-tale princess on her way to marry her prince. He was there in front of the altar, her own Prince Charming. He turned as she was nearing him, his eyes shining with love and admiration at this vision of perfection, his soon-to-be wife.

As she reached his side she realised there was someone else with her in front of the altar. Glancing down, she saw Philippe smiling up at her. He'd left his place in the procession of bridesmaids behind her and come to join her and his father. He looked adorable in his tailor-made suit.

'Let him stay with us,' she whispered to Bernard, who smiled and nodded in agreement.

The organist stopped playing. The congregation fell silent. The marriage service began.

There was another flurry of snowflakes as they came out of the church and stood on the steps for the photographs. Julia and Bernard smiled for the cameras. Her parents joined them with her brothers and their families. Philippe joined them and then agreed to leave the bridal pair to join Julia's parents, who were going to take him back to the farm. The photo shoot would have gone on longer but the descending snow put an end to that.

'The kiss!' everyone was calling out.

Bernard took her in his arms and they kissed to loud shouts of approval.

'Encore! Another kiss!'

'Just one more,' Bernard whispered. 'I want you all to myself now.'

As soon as they could get away into the car, they did so.

'See you back at the farm,' Bernard called out to everybody as he drove away. He'd insisted on going against tradition by driving his own car over to the church so that they could be really alone on the way back home.

'I wanted you to myself for the first few minutes of our marriage,' he said, pulling the car in behind a tractor on the narrow country lane. 'I'm taking a short cut, which should be quicker than the main road so we'll be back at the farm before our guests arrive, I hope. We'll have to be sociable for the rest of the day.'

She smiled. 'It's been such a whirlwind of organisation for the last few weeks. I'll be so glad to have some normal married life.'

'Do you think we'll ever have a normal married life, whatever that is?'

'I know we're both continuing with our careers but as we both understand what the other's going through we can pull together, help each other…until we have a baby, when it might get a bit harder.'

She glanced across at him. His eyes were on the narrow road ahead. The tractor had turned into a gate and left the road clear at last. The snowflakes had stopped now and the pale wintry sun was peeping out from behind a cloud.

He changed gear as they went down into the valley where he could see smoke spiralling from the farm chimneys. 'I wonder when that will be?'

'Well, it could be sooner than we expected. I promised I would tell you if…well, don't get too excited but I'm seven days late.'

'My darling! Why didn't you tell me?'

'I'm telling you now! But it could just be the excitement of the wedding and all the preparations. Don't, for heaven's sake, start getting your hopes up.'

He pulled into the farmyard and switched the engine off.

'Come here, you gorgeous girl, my wonderful bride.'

He kissed her gently on the lips. As his kiss deepened she moved in his arms.

'Later, darling. Our guests are arriving.'

'Keep me informed, won't you?' he whispered as a car pulled in behind them.

'Of course.' She smiled happily as Gaston opened a door for her to climb out. A long strip of red carpet had been laid in front of her leading to the kitchen door. Bernard was already there for her holding out his hand to guide her indoors.

Bernard's speech was hilarious. Everybody was still laughing as they raised their glasses for another toast. They were all crowded into the dining room, the food spread out as a buffet.

'There's more food in the kitchen, Julia,' Marianne said quietly. 'Shall I bring the desserts yet?'

'I'll tell everybody the desserts are in the kitchen when they would like to help themselves. Nobody's standing on ceremony here. Everybody seems to be getting on well.'

'I should think so,' Gaston said, topping up her wine glass. 'Good thing we've got plenty of bottles in the cellar.'

She moved through the guests, trying to have a word with everybody. They all complimented her on her dress, especially her cousin Chantal. They'd been great friends as children and nothing ever changed when they met up again.

'Your dress is absolutely gorgeous, Julia! It fits you perfectly.'

'I had it made in Montreuil by the daughter of the dressmaker who made the wedding dresses of our grandmother and my mother, who's over there looking very happy to be the mother of the bride, don't you think?'

'She's also happy to be chatting to my mother. You can tell they're twins. They're so alike, aren't they? And they don't see enough of each other nowadays so they never stop talking when they do meet!'

'Just like we do!'

They both laughed.

Chantal turned back to admire Julia again. 'You're so slim. That dress fits you like a glove.'

'I suppose I am…at the moment.' Now, why had she said that? Was it because Chantal had always been more like a sister when they'd been small? The antidote to all those brothers bossing her around?

Chantal moved nearer and put a hand on her arm, guiding her through the throng of guests to a small window seat where they could whisper together. 'You're not…? Are you?'

Julia smiled. 'Maybe. Too early to say but I hope so.'

'So do I! Please remember me when you're choosing godparents.'

'Chantal, you would be my first choice! I'm so glad we're going to see more of each other now that I'm going to be living in France. It's easy for you to come over from Paris by train, isn't it?'

'I may be coming back to this area sooner than you think. I've split up with Jacques.'

'No! But I thought you two had the most perfect relationship.'

'So did I. He's gone back to his wife. He'd managed to fool me completely for a whole year. I didn't realise I was his mistress. I felt such a fool when he told me.'

'So are you thinking of leaving the hospital?'

'I've left! Couldn't stand working alongside him when all the time—'

Chantal broke off as Bernard arrived.

'Not interrupting anything, am I?'

'No! Well, actually Chantal was just telling me she's leaving Paris and moving back to this area.'

'I'll be looking for a job, Bernard. Any vacancies for a well-qualified and experienced doctor?'

'Send me your CV and I'll see what I can do, Chantal.'

'I'll do that!'

Philippe came running across the room to join them. 'Papa, I've got an idea. You see my friend Jules over there with his parents? Well, he got a little brother during the summer. Now that Julia and you are married, does that mean I can have a baby brother or sister? Maybe as a Christmas present?'

He was looking up beseechingly now at Julia.

She looked across at Bernard, who was smiling happily. 'We'll have to see what happens, won't we?' he told his son. 'These things take time.'

Philippe looked pleased. Papa hadn't ruled the idea out. He ran back to his friend Jules to say he might get a baby brother or sister but probably not for Christmas.

'These things take time,' he told Jules airily.

'I didn't think they would stay so late,' Julia said as she slipped into bed beside Bernard.

'Sign of a good party! I'd say it was a huge success.'

'It was wonderful to see my parents and all three of my brothers again but I'm glad they're staying at the hotel in the village, otherwise we'd still be downstairs, having supper.'

'Today has been a wonderful day!' he said, drawing her against him.

'It's been the happiest day of my life. Wasn't Philippe sweet when he asked for a baby brother? I don't know about Christmas but he might get one for his birthday!'

'Wonder woman!'

She laughed.

Bernard drew her closer. 'Just one request.'

'Yes?'

'You're not going to leave me in the early morning and go to the guest room, are you?'

'Not now that you've made an honest woman of me.'

'Any regrets?'

She sighed as she felt his arms drawing her even closer.

'Only that we didn't get together like this sooner.'

'You mean like this…or like this…or like this…?'

She laughed. 'You know what I mean.'

'I certainly do…'

* * * * *

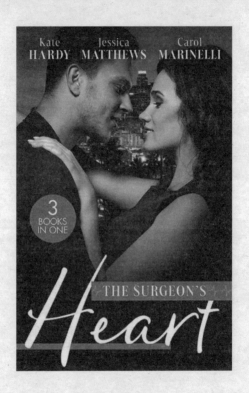

OUT NOW!

Available at
millsandboon.co.uk

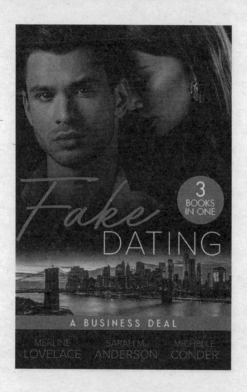

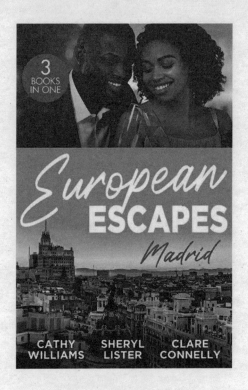